## Praise for Sean Kane's *Raccoon: A*

How can we live without Sean Kane's inspired madness? His loopy intelligence, and the amplitude of his heart, provide necessary medicine for all creatures working for a collective swerve away from ecological catastrophe and finding themselves wounded by the battle. Kane's cure-all goes by the name of laughter.
— **David Abram**, Senior Visiting Scholar in Philosophy and Social Ecology, Harvard University. Author of *The Spell of the Sensuous* and *Becoming Animal*

Prepare to be transported. Sean Kane's *Raccoon*, like the animals at the heart of his story, is curious, mischievous, lovable, and fierce. A tale that uses the foundations of a children's fable but builds upon it a fiction for all ages, and decidedly for our time.
— **Andrew Pyper**, bestselling author of *The Residence* and *The Demonologist*

*Raccoon* feels real and has bite. It has Sean Kane's—but how does he do it?—grasp of where the imaginative and real meet. Everything in his story sparkles with that and because of that.
— **Gordon Teskey**, Francis Lee Higginson Professor of English Literature, Harvard University

Wonderful in the full sense of the word, *Raccoon* is an extraordinary work of fiction. Alive with incident, madcap excitement, quirky humour, and many poetic turns of phrase, it is at once a satire, a wondertale, and a thoughtful work of ecological commentary.
— **Don LePan**, Founder and CEO of Broadview Press and author of three novels, most recently *Lucy and Bonbon*

This account of a quest for an ideal Commonwealth is in the tradition of some of the finest animal adventure stories ever written. Sean Kane's clear-eyed, beautifully written tale offers a critique of society as it is and a model of what it could be.
— **Stan Dragland**, C.M., novelist, poet, critic, founding editor of Brick Books, and Emeritus Professor of Canadian and Children's Literature at Western University

*Raccoon* will be recognized as a classic of its genre. It joins all those currents of thought that see the creative imagination as the ultimate force that can reshape and somehow, some way, redeem the planet.
— **Eugene Benson**, novelist, literary historian, and playwright. As Professor of English at the University of Guelph, he co-edited the *Encyclopedia of Post-Colonial Literatures in English*

# Raccoon
*A Wondertale*

Afterword by
MARGARET ATWOOD

ESSENTIAL PROSE SERIES 223

Canadä

Guernica Editions Inc. acknowledges the support of
the Canada Council for the Arts and the Ontario Arts Council.
The Ontario Arts Council is an agency of the Government of Ontario.
We acknowledge the financial support of the Government of Canada

Sean Kane

# Raccoon
## *A Wondertale*

Afterword by
MARGARET ATWOOD

GUERNICA
EDITIONS

TORONTO • CHICAGO • BUFFALO • LANCASTER (U.K.)
2023

Guernica Founder: Antonio D'Alfonso

Connie McParland, Michael Mirolla, series editors
Gary Clairman, editor
Cover design and interior design: Rafael Chimicatti

Guernica Editions Inc.
287 Templemead Drive, Hamilton, ON L8W 2W4
2250 Military Road, Tonawanda, N.Y. 14150-6000 U.S.A.
www.guernicaeditions.com

Distributors:
Independent Publishers Group (IPG)
600 North Pulaski Road, Chicago (IL) U.S.A. 60624
University of Toronto Press Distribution (UTP)
5201 Dufferin Street, Toronto (ON), Canada M3H 5T8

First edition.
Printed in Canada.

Legal Deposit—First Quarter
Library of Congress Catalog Card Number: 2023930327
Library and Archives Canada Cataloguing in Publication
Title: Raccoon : a wondertale / Sean Kane ;
afterword by Margaret Atwood.
Names: Kane, Sean, 1943- author.
Atwood, Margaret, 1939- writer of afterword.
Identifiers: Canadiana (print) 20230140092 | Canadiana (ebook)
20230140149 | ISBN 9781771837828 (softcover)
ISBN 9781771837835 (EPUB)
Classification: LCC PS8571.A433 R33 2023 | DDC C813/.54—dc23

*For Graeme*

# ACT I

## *Home Schooling*

*Slypaws*, a patient mother and single parent
*Clutch*, her senior son, a traditionalist
*Bandit*, her junior son, an aspiring alpha male
*Touchwit*, her precocious daughter, an artist

*Uncle Wily* (deceased), brother of Slypaws and Pawsense

*Aunt Pawsense*, Slypaws's socially superior sister
*Goodpaws*, her head daughter and bossypants
*Sensibella*, second daughter, a romantic heroine
*Friskywits*, younger daughter and a clever subversive
*Nimbletoes*, the junior daughter and family messenger

*Smartwhisker*, father of the four sisters and Pawsense's mate
*Meatbreath*, father of Slypaws's three cubs, a deadbeat dad

# I

THE CREATURES LIVING behind the wall of my study are in a quandary. As I sit at this desk, they are three feet away, at ear level, in a disused chimney. At the suggestion of milder weather, the whole family of them wakes up, and breaks immediately into hissing and snarls. Only one kind of animal is so full of anxiety and quarrel.

I put the stethoscope to the wall. The instrument is left over from my partner's professional life. For no reason I can explain, it gives me the power to understand the speech of raccoons.

"Eeeuuw!"

"Ssh. Mustn't wake up."

"Eeeyowp!"

*"Alright, what's the problem?"*

"It's Clutch. He's having another nightmare."

*"Clutch, honey. Remember what I said. Just tell it to Scat."*

"SCAT! SCAT!"

"Shove over. Your tail is in my face. I need to scratch."

"It's no good, Mom. It won't go away. It's about Uncle Wily. He's staring up at me from the road."

*"Just think of something nice instead. Clams with honey sauce."*

"Uncle Wily went *splat* instead of *scat*."

*"That's not very helpful, Touchwit. Your Uncle Wily died a noble death. Now go back to sleep. If you wake up, you'll be hungry. And then what? The river's frozen and it's not garbage night."*

"I'm hungry."

"We can eat Bandit. He's full of Delissio pizza."

"Sssh! The Idiot behind the wall is listening. I can hear him breathing."

Silence.

Thus intimations of spring come to the Eastern Woodlands – in chance breaks in the Arctic cold, hapless stirrings and false awakenings.

# 2

As far as I can tell, the raccoons haven't left the chimney. The snow has stayed, and now it is raining – bad weather for animals with heavy fur coats. But I can hear a rapid thumping: someone is scratching fleas. They're awake and must be hungry after a long hibernation. I press my stethoscope against the wall and overhear them chittering ...

"Mother, why can't we go out and pop organic waste bin lids?"

"We require a clear sky and a warm Spring night" is the answer.

"When are we going to get a clear sky and a warm Spring night? The rain has been pattering on the roof forever."

"You will get a clear Spring night when the Great Raccoon Ancestor has left his den and is high above the southern horizon."

"He is aloft now, yet we see him not on account of the excess of clouds."

That was the older brother speaking. At the mention of the Great Spirit he had spoken in the High Tongue.

"Time is truly askew if the Ancestor beckons his clan out of their burrows, yet the clouds contradict him."

That was Touchwit. I'm coming to tell them apart now. The elder brother seems to be the one called Clutch. The younger brother is Bandit. Then the sister is Touchwit. Their mother is called Slypaws. They don't talk about their father.

"The Great Raccoon Spirit withholds himself from our gaze," Clutch said solemnly, "so as to keep us sheltered and warm, thereby sparing us the grumes, running gleet, the mumbles, and suchlike afflictions."

"I'm not really up to theology first thing in the evening," Mother Slypaws said.

"Theology isn't the issue," Touchwit said, returning to the vernacular. "The issue is that we are in a new time on Earth, and theology is as useless as plastic wrap."

"Watch your speech, Touchwit. It is foolhardy to be heedless of the One in the Sky who eternally holds us in his paws." That was Clutch. As elder brother he was surrogate family head.

"He's not in the sky, is he? He's not anywhere. Like Dad," Touchwit said.

"Perhaps he reveals himself not because of the Abuses we have heaped upon his shoulders."

"The Great Raccoon isn't going to get us out of this mess. Have you smelled the scent of crab apple blossoms lately? No. That's because they withhold themselves from gaze and reveal themselves not." I can imagine Touchwit glaring savagely at her big brother.

"Touch is right, Mom. We're living proof that time is broken. We were born out of season," Bandit pointed out.

"That is true, children. You were born at the wrong time of year, when the leaves fall. I had little opportunity to street-proof you. So I stuffed you with Delissio pizza crusts for the hibernation and hid you in this chimney."

"Street-proof us now, Mom. If the Ancestor can't be bothered to guide us, then we'll have to survive by our fingertips."

The mother raccoon sighed. It was so like Touchwit to think she could face the world armed only with cunning and hand-eye coordination.

"Why *were* we born out of the love-season?" Bandit asked suddenly. Tense silence.

Elder brother deflects the question: "We should ask, rather, where do Raccoons come from in the first place?"

Noise of shuffling. Mistress Slypaws is straightening her back and folding her paws in her lap. The cubs tuck their tails around their feet, arranging themselves for a story.

"It was the time of beginnings, and the Great Raccoon lay dreaming," she said. "And he lay dreaming in his hollow. So vast is his hollow that it fills the southern sky, and its entrance is marked by the path of the Moon. And all that time it was winter, and rain fell upon the Earth."

The cubs huddled closer together. Their chimney didn't feel so small now, nor their time in it so long.

"And feeling lonely, the Great Raccoon Spirit said: 'I think I'll find a companion to warm my side.' And he dreamed he was foraging in a stream, they say, and a clam was glowing furiously in the moonlight. The clam caught his eye. So he took it in his hands and he scraped the mud of the stream bottom and the tiny snails off the shell. Ever since that first night, Raccoons are careful to rub off the matter adhering to their food, though they appear to be washing their hands."

At the mention of the Hand Acknowledgment, the three cubs automatically made washing motions with their hands.

"Then he blew upon the Radiant Clam, and cast it upon the stream. And it bounced once, and it bounced twice, and it opened and out of its shell stepped the first Woman. A Woman Raccoon! The Great Raccoon Spirit wondered at her. Now, all Raccoons are fluent and tactile, but of all the Raccoons in the land, none was more elegant of speech nor dexterous of paw than she."

"Did he jump her, Ma?" Bandit said, breaking in.

"Oh, really, I don't know where you get these vulgar thoughts," Slypaws said.

"We get them from the Idiot behind the wall," Touchwit said, giggling.

"I shall resume the story: Then they did … mingle, and lo! The first litter was born. Three smart cubs." At this, Slypaws glanced lovingly at Clutch, her first born. There wasn't a green bin lid in the neighbourhood he couldn't pop. So wondrous a son who can so astonish a mother!

"This story is dumb," Bandit said. "We happen to know Raccoons are born because the mom lets herself get jumped."

Mother Slypaws sounded flustered. Not even the width of my study wall could muffle her embarrassment. "One has to recount the High Stories in their accustomed order before studying their practical applications."

"I think Mom got jumped around Midsummer," Bandit said.

Mistress Slypaws examined her tail. It was a bushy tail once. Now, after a winter in this soot-lined hole, it hung limp and bedraggled. "If you must know, he took advantage of the fact that the love season is askew in the general rhythms of things. He caught me at the end of a limb and made me great with cub. It was either that or a thirty foot drop into the rhododendrons." Slypaws looked up grimly. "And you can bet the rings on your tails I'll never get caught on a limb again ... Ever."

"Way to go, Mom!"

"Instead, I shall go to the fabled city under the southern sky that is called Raccoonopolis, where the Idiots have invented a green bin that can be popped in nine seconds."

"Let's all go."

Touchwit had been quiet. She was going to say something crucial.

"That's why you don't want us to go out tonight," she said. "You're afraid of getting jumped."

"I'm not thinking only of myself, dear."

"I can look after myself."

"Good luck!"

Again, the elder brother filled the silence with earnestness. "Who is our father then, if he isn't the Great Raccoon Ancestor?"

"You will meet him in good time. When you're big enough to hold your place at the end of a tree limb against a distempered, hormonal mass of raging stupidity. Until that night, you shall remain scarce in our chimney."

"But, what's his name?" Clutch insisted. "At least, tell us his name."

"It doesn't matter what his name is. He's a jerk."

"Mom, we need to know his name. He's our *father*."

"Your father's name is ... Meatbreath."

"Our Dad's name is Meatbreath. No way!"

At this, I tactfully withdrew my stethoscope from the wall. One hot Spring night, there was going to be a terrific confrontation, and it was hard to guess which of the cubs was going to be the one who would reckon with their father.

# 3

THE FIRST WARM NIGHT OF SPRING. I expect the raccoons behind my office wall will venture out. Sure enough, a discreet scratching ascends the interior of the disused chimney. Probably the mother going up to check the weather. After a while, the scratching noise descends. I press my stethoscope to the wall so I can hear her report:

"A light breeze is blowing from where the Sun went into his burrow. The Ancestor is high in the southern sky. His light will allow us to see the silent vehicles before they come upon us. Once, they used to be noisy, which gave us a warning."

"*Eeeuuw!*"

The cubs were remembering the late Uncle Wily. An amiable, harmless bachelor, he used to entertain them by recounting with glee all the threats he had outwitted. Then one wet winter night he was flattened by an electric car. It caught him while he was telling a yarn to the cubs by the roadside. One minute, he was a garrulous ball of fur; the next, he was staring at them from the pavement, both eyes on one side of his face like a flatfish and his teeth still grinning in mid-story.

"Since then," Mother Slypaws said, "we have found that going around the neighbourhood from house to house and unplugging the vehicles diminishes the threat."

"We shall continue to unplug vehicles in remembrance of Uncle Wily," the elder brother declared.

Mistress Slypaws shook off the proposal. Sometimes the solemnity of her eldest son could be irritating. "Threats: Brief Review," she announced. "After vehicles, what's the number one threat?"

"Our Dad," Bandit said.

"Get real. He's hanging with the Dudes," sister Touchwit said. "They've formed a men's club. To protect their common territory, which means us, from other males."

"We shall speak of him last," Slypaws said, "since he is connected with the subject of latrines. Other threats. Think of something else that is silent."

"Owls. The ones that have horns like the young moon. They see and hear great distances, and glide silently to their prey."

"Very good, Bandit. You must stay close to me at all times. That way we shall present an indistinct mass to an attacker. What else?"

"Droolers," Touchwit said.

"And what do we know about Droolers?"

Clutch put his hand up to answer: "They are of two kinds. First, there are the ones that are walked by the Primates, who restrain them by means of leashes. Second, there are the ones who run free and don't know quite who they are, being part dog, part wolf."

"And by what sound do we know they are approaching?" Mother Slypaws's street-proofing lessons had the quality of a catechism.

"We will hear them panting. Whereupon we scurry to the nearest tree."

"Very good!"

Clutch had a further point to make about Droolers: "They don't think for themselves like us. They think as a pack. That's what makes them act superior."

"They have a saying," Bandit said: "*Families that prey together, stay together.*"

"Yes, well we have a better saying," Slypaws said: "*Families that scrounge together, lounge together.*"

This seemed to put the threat of coyotes into perspective. "They are venturing into the city more and more," Slypaws told her children, "but when they do they keep to the paths which have been made for walking and riding vehicles with two wheels. Foxes, which you haven't mentioned, also use these paths, but you are now so big you needn't fear them. Any other threats you can think of?" Slypaws offered a hint. "It is near the River."

Bandit knew the answer: "Fishers, otherwise known as Weasels. They eat everything in sight and they attack from behind. They are said to carry off raccoon cubs."

"Good! Though Fishers live north in the great forests. You are more likely to see their smaller cousins which are called Mink and are harmless to ones your size. But you have neglected the largest threat of all. I shall put it in a riddle:

*What is largest of all because it is smallest of all,*
*and something that every Raccoon overlooks?*

"A nose. A Raccoon overlooks his nose," Clutch said.

"No," Bandit said. "It is a flea."

"I know," Touchwit said. "It is a virus."

Of course, they knew that! They knew that there is a disease that makes raccoons foam at the mouth; another that makes them drool. Distemper. Rabies.

"Therefore, we shall keep our distance from animals whose behaviour is erratic. On which note, we come to the subject of your father. So far, he has been unable to smell our whereabouts. That is because I chose this chimney to hide in. It confines our scent and whatever scent it releases is dispersed high in the air, and so cannot be traced to its source."

"What do we do if we meet him?" Bandit asked.

"Fathers have been known to destroy cubs sired by another father. They do not harm their own children. But now Spring is here and it is constantly on their minds to make more cubs, if you know what I mean."

"I'll deal with the slimeball," Touchwit said.

"It is a brave daughter who goes nose-to-nose with her own father. But if he doesn't mate with you, he'll force you off the limb so that you go splat and end up resembling a pizza like Uncle Wily." Slypaws didn't know whether to be proud of her daughter or afraid of her. "Anyway, we'll only be out for a short time. Just long enough to find out where the community latrine is."

This was interesting. Raccoons are private animals, and they establish a latrine for the immediate family. It is usually hidden so that it doesn't give away their location. But they may sometimes use a neighbourhood latrine, which is more distant from their dens. This is where the various mothers of the community meet to exchange news while their cubs tussle. But why was the father of these chimney cubs connected with a latrine?

"Your father will check the latrine periodically," Slypaws said, as if reading my mind. "He wants to determine how his families are faring. How many cubs he's sired. What food they're eating, and whether they have worms in their tummies. Other fathers in his club will do the same for their families. We shall find out from my sister where these various fathers are, and if there are any other threats."

It seemed the father was more a threat to his children's peace of mind than to their bodies, though the precocious daughter soon coming into her maturity had something to fear. It was significant that the cubs never mentioned their father's name.

Behind their wall in my omniscience, I silently mouthed the forbidden name as the raccoons ventured out to discover the facts about their world. The chief fact was *Meatbreath*.

# 4

Bustling behind my wall – the sound of three excited kids getting ready for a family outing. It is a soft Spring night, and a breeze from the south brings news of a distant sea.

To exit their den, the raccoons will need to climb the interior of the chimney to where it projects four feet above the roof. Then they have to clamber down the exterior brickwork of the chimney to the roof, then down a steep slope to the eavestrough. The slope is so steep that roofers shake their heads grimly and smoke a cigarette before they set up their ladders. But the raccoons scramble along the roof easily.

You may be asking: how did the raccoons get into the chimney in the first place? Chimneys have a chimney pot, usually made of aluminum nowadays. Its purpose is to protect against rain, but the roofers told me the covering also deters birds from dropping things into the hole. Apparently, a cavity in a high place invites the idea of a nest, and birds will instinctively deposit twigs and leaves into the empty space. But did the chimney pot deter the raccoons? Not at all. They simply extracted its four screws and hurled the object 36 feet down into the garden.

What route will these clever animals take tonight? They can either leave the roof by means of the thicket of cedars beside my front door, or they can descend down the one slender cedar that I've let grow just outside my bedroom window at the back so I can watch birds close up. Descent at the front is easy because what was once a nicely trimmed cedar hedge now towers over the house. The cubs can take this easy way down, except that doing so makes them visible to humans and dogs, and gives away their hiding place. Tonight, Slypaws will likely take them to the back of the roof where they will use the single slender cedar, which offers privacy but requires skill. This is what they have to do:

When they come to the eavestrough, they have to reach out with one arm for the top of the cedar while holding onto the eavestrough with the other. This isn't easy, and they paw at the tree several times, almost tipping off the roof, before they get it in one hand. Then they must pull the top of the tree to their body, then leap and grab at once. It is undesirable to be suspended in midair, holding onto the cedar and the eavestrough simultaneously. Returning from their outing, the raccoons have to accomplish the reverse. That is, they ascend to the top of the cedar, then use their weight to bend the tree top close to the eavestrough, then let go and drop. I have seen the cubs do this expertly in total darkness.

But there is a human factor in this situation.

I'm not sure what the raccoons make of me. Probably, I'm just another example of the species they call Idiots. Yet I am respected by the local squirrels, who regard me as a source of play. This is because a door off my bedroom allows me to go out on a second-floor balcony forming the southwest corner of my house. Here I am likely to appear at any moment without warning, holding a deadly weapon. It is my son's Super Soaker.

A Super Soaker is a plastic, pump-action submachine gun holding about a litre of water. Every squirrel around knows it's capable of shooting a stream that is accurate to twenty feet. In fact, it's become a neighbourhood sport for squirrels to test their reflexes against the Primate who squirts water. All the squirrels take up the game, not just the happily married couple who have eaten a hole in the roof peak of my house. The squirrels bring their family to watch. They invite their relatives. They squat in rows exactly twenty-one feet away and make bets on who will escape undrenched. All know that at worst a victim of my weapon will be soaked from head to tail. This fate isn't unpleasant so much as embarrassing because it demonstrates to the spectators that the reflexes of the loser leave something to be desired. But enough of squirrels.

It is after midnight, and the raccoons are whimpering at the edge of the roof above my bedroom window. They are torn between bravado and timidity concerning descent by means of the slender cedar tree. But no – it turns out that they have a larger dilemma. Clutch, the elder brother, is having a crisis. I press my partner's stethoscope against the bedroom windowpane.

Mother Slypaws: "Whatever is the matter with you, Clutch? The gap between the roof and the tree is no greater than it was last Autumn. In fact, the space is less because the tree has grown and so have you."

Clutch: "*Can't move.*"

Slypaws: "Is it the Idiot who squirts water?"

Clutch: "*No.*"

Slypaws: "Is it the slope of the roof?"

The mother was thinking back to when the cubs had emerged last year just after the first autumn frost. One by one, they skidded off the icy roof and shot straight into the cedar tree. Clutch as senior cub had spun off the roof first, ending upside-down in the branches, much to his shame. It was her fault they slid off the roof. Raccoons have a flexible joint which allows them to splay their hind legs so they can come down a tree nose first. She had forgotten to teach them to use their hind feet as brakes for the descent. That first night, over my bedroom window, the chorus of complaining cubs and an apologetic, guilt-ridden mother raccoon was epic. Tonight, they were repeating the original descent.

Touchwit looked at Clutch clinging with one arm to the top of the cedar tree which was bending downward with his weight. Her aptly named brother was paralyzed, holding onto the tree desperately while unable to let go of the eavestrough, suspended between the two.

"It's something existential, isn't it?" Touchwit said.

Clutch nodded his head.

"Perhaps if you say it in High Words, it will be easier." Touchwit knew that raccoons switch to this ancient, formal language whenever they need to consult First Principles. And as first-born cub, Clutch was fervently drawn to First Principles, conditioned to grasp a firm bough then reason his way out to the end of the limb.

"Okay, I'll try," he said. "It is ... er, appropriate that I ... ah ... commence by expounding on the theme of the State of the World as it was originally fashioned by the Great Raccoon Ancestor ..."

Bandit interrupted in the High Tongue. "Brother, I beg you spare us this discourse which however worthy is not timely. You are swaying betwixt a house and a tree, kicking the Void."

"Bandit," Touchwit said wearily. "Be helpful, or shut up."

"Put the analysis aside and go one way or the other. Then you can philosophize to your heart's content." Slypaws turned to Touchwit. "Whatever is wrong with him?"

"He's having a Big Nothing Attack."

"I am," Clutch said. "There is something wrong with the state of the world. I smell the fumes of burning trees in the wind, and yet the selfsame breeze tells of constant rain, and sheets of ice are floating down our River, and the lawn between it and our dwelling is a small lagoon. The rhythms are a tangled ball of worms. The Geese People were supposed to fly over our house before the last full moon. They haven't come. I dread the world and am afraid to venture out in it."

Touchwit considered the situation of poor Clutch. Her high-minded brother, the one who relied on standards to live up to, was at a loss. There were no standards to live up to. The standards had refused to join the Spring migration.

Mother Slypaws sat and listened. I saw her soot-streaked tail hanging over the eavestrough. She'd know what to do.

"If you descend the tree, loving son, and let the rest of us proceed, we will go and see Aunt Pawsense and her bumptious daughters. We'll grab some worms to eat on the way; maybe an egg that's dropped out of a nest. You can share your Big Nothingburger with her. Then we'll come home and turn it over in our hands. Is that alright?"

This seemed agreeable to Clutch, because he let go of the eaves-trough and sprung into the cedar. He descended the swaying tree tentatively, facing upward. His brother and sister followed, then the mother, all nose first, unaware of my presence behind the windowpane.

# 5

THE RACCOONS MUST HAVE BEEN exhausted by the experience of meeting their aunt and cousins because it wasn't until late the following night that I again heard them talking. They were still excited about the event. Living in isolation from all their kind except a strange uncle, now deceased, they suddenly discovered they were members of a clan.

"Aunt Pawsense smells like crayfish and crab apples."

"And our cousins are such athletes!"

"They've taken climbing classes, and tree lore, and tussling lessons, and swimming instruction."

"They talk funny. They sound really well-mannered."

Mother Slypaws intervened. "Yes, well that's called *polite discourse*. I didn't have time to teach it to you, and it's not like we've had a whirl of social engagements. Remember, they're older than you lot by a half a summer. But our winter in a chimney wasn't wasted. You were home schooled."

"I know, Mom, but we could still use some Outdoor Ed. You never told us about crayfish."

"It's fun to pick them apart. First throw away the head and tail."

"And the corn! Did you see the way they ate it? They turn the ear of corn between their paws and nibble from one end to the other."

"That's old corn. My sister got it from a feed bin for animals. Wait till I give you Sweet Corn."

"And the hamburger scraps!"

"We'll have to have a lesson in Food Groups."

"Not now, Mom. We've got too much to discuss."

"Not to mention *my* problem."

That was Clutch. Apparently, the night with his relatives had scarcely begun to resolve his crisis. I considered it brilliant of Slypaws to immerse her son in fresh perspective. Horizons would widen; attitudes would blur. The crisis would look after itself. And now the little family that had spent the first half year of its existence in a dark hole was about to indulge in a debriefing.

"Okay. What did you like about them the most? Yes, you go first, Clutch."

"I liked how they're so full of themselves. The world is totally confused, and they don't care one bit. It doesn't seem to bother them that something really intense could happen."

"What about you, Bandit?"

"The girl energy! I didn't know what a girl was until last night."

"I've got girl energy," Touchwit said.

"You're not a girl – you're my sister."

"You should know what a girl is now. You wrestled with four of them at once," Clutch said.

"I just wrestled with Sensibella. The other three kept trying to barge in."

"What did you like about them, Touch?" her mother asked.

Touchwit thought for a moment. "I like how they're so exotic. Their father isn't from around here, is he?"

"No," Slypaws said. "He's from the Greater Raccoonopolitan Area. Before that, I don't know. Somewhere east where the sun awakens. Near an ocean where the air is moist and the winter is moderate."

"They have such high cheekbones and golden fur," Clutch said. "I suppose I could get used to them. After all, they're my first cousins."

"They brush out their huge glossy tails so you can see every ring. They must spend all evening on their tails," Touchwit said.

Clutch seemed ambiguous about his relatives. Touchwit was analytical. In contrast, Bandit was over the moon. "I'm going to mate with them," he declared.

"All four?" Clutch asked.

"Trust Pawsense to have a big family," Slypaws said. "But her instincts are out-of-sync. There's going to be too many raccoons soon."

"What's wrong with too many?" Bandit asked.

"I couldn't find many Crayfish last Autumn," Slypaws explained. "And there's something amiss with the Frogs."

"Do you think other raccoons are eating them up?" Touchwit asked.

"No. Something is changing the River. I think it may be the Wolf-fish. They're grazing on the riverbed. They're eating up everything. Fish eggs, Crayfish, Snails, Turtles, Water Insects ... We didn't have so many Wolf-fish before."

I quickly looked up Wolf-fish. It's another name for Catfish, the bottom-feeders with whiskers. I didn't know their bodies have taste buds. People around here call them Suckers. People from the Greater Metropolitan Area come up and fish for them, regarding them as a species of Carp.

"Is that why there aren't any Frogs?" Touchwit asked.

"I don't know. The Frogs may be scarce for the same reason the Wolf-fish are plentiful: the warmth of the water. This is supposed to be a cold, wild River."

"Why don't we go and live with Aunt Pawsense on her pond?" Bandit asked.

"It's up to her to invite us. You see, it's the mothers who decide how many raccoons will share a hunting ground. They look at how much food the territory offers, and then have large or small litters accordingly. There's minnows galore, not to mention a corn field up your Aunt's way, so she has four fat cubs and lots of space for them to inherit. Still, I doubt if she wants us in her neighbourhood. She's rather snooty."

"I thought raccoon fathers decided on the size of territories."

"No, they only defend them. The mothers produce the population, so they determine the territory."

"Including the number of fathers in a territory?"

"The number of available fathers depends on the number of available mothers," Slypaws replied. I heard the laughter in her voice. "Which makes you rather special."

"*I don't want to be special, I don't want to determine a territory, most of all I don't want to have cubs and have to hide in a chimney ...*"

Touchwit's hissing was audible through the wall without the stethoscope.

"What happens to the leftover raccoons who aren't needed to balance the population?" Clutch asked.

"They migrate. Some become bachelors like Uncle Wily."

"If feeding and breeding processes balance out, I don't see that I'm needed," Touchwit said. "I shall become a Random."

"It's not balancing out in Raccoonopolis: too many clan families in one territory. They're coming up here to get away from each other. They want fresh air and a rich hunting ground for their children, like what your Aunt has."

"How can the rhythms of the species not balance out?" Bandit asked.

"They do ... eventually. But in the in-between times you get conflict. Too many mouths and too little food means the fathers start brawls. You can't scavenge in peace without two males lashing their tails and screaming blue murder at each other. What's the matter, Clutch? You're silent."

"I'm confused. The holy rhythms of our species are so tangled up and there's nothing us raccoons can do about it. All we can do is live by our instincts, which means fight or flee – fight for a place in a territory or flee to another territory. Living like that brings out the worst in a raccoon. We are a noble species, endowed by our creator with virtue."

"I consider it a virtue to jump a fat Lady Raccoon, and thereby serve the holy rhythms of our species," Bandit said.

"You're so sick," Touchwit said. "The Primates have pretend mating relationships, isn't that right, Mom?"

"Yes. They choose their mates somehow. I can't imagine how it's done. And they don't produce cubs until they're good and ready to."

"Why don't we do that as well?"

"Hormones. We come into season and it's let's make cubs at first sight."

"Not me!" Touchwit declared.

"Then you're going to have to talk to your body and the seasons about delaying the hots."

Silence. Slypaws must have smiled at the successful conclusion to her teaching moment, because I heard no more conversation that night. Just sighs of weariness as bodies nestled together.

"Such a long journey!"

"And yet we hardly got to see the City."

"It felt like a dream."

"Good night gang!"

"Dream no small dreams."

# 6

THERE WAS LITTLE ACTIVITY behind my wall for the longest time. Occasionally, someone shifted position and disturbed the others, and once Touchwit sang in her sleep. The rainy season would have to pass before the next event in the family saga.

Instead, I amused myself by feeding seeds to the alpha male chickadee with two wives. One morning, feeling full of himself, he broke into the chickadee mating call which sounds like *Hi sweetie* and shooed his wives away from my outstretched hand.

He saw my partner's red hair through the bedroom window and called:

*Hi Sweetie!*

Where had she found a stethoscope that translated animal speech? The instrument, which came with her job, was quite ordinary. A smartphone with a universal translation app proved to be useless and the diagnostic smartphone app reported only four hearts beating slowly in the manner of hibernants. This act of lurking made me feel uneasy. What right did I have to overhear and retell a family's private conversations? Yet the raccoons seemed to enjoy my presence so long as I stayed on my side of the wall. They had referred to me casually during the Fall, even at times addressing me deliberately.

Still, ethical concerns linger as happens with technology. How much of what the stethoscope translates is authentic raccoon speech and how much is a human equivalent meant to help me imagine what the creatures are saying? Raccoons don't say "Delissio pizza." But the popular brand-name stands for all the common pizza crusts that end up in waste containers in my city and get raccoons through the winter, along with birdseed fallen from backyard feeders and kibble left on porches for stray cats. You see, it isn't the name but the context that does the naming. Context does most of the work in animal communication which isn't made up of words but gestures, displays, mood signs, pawprints, scents, and movements. The raccoons wouldn't have said "glutton" or "voracious," but simply turned with one mind towards the pizza-stuffed Bandit, sniffed with one nose the body scent of this indiscriminate omnivore, and come to the same comical conclusion.

My partner's stethoscope is also sensitive to that animal awareness of context, which is called etiquette. For instance, it translates them speaking in an ancient, formal "High Tongue" when addressing the subject of gods, ancestors, and first principles. I would go on to learn from the stethoscope that raccoons have a cultivated polite idiom which they reserve for exchanges with a social equal who is unfamiliar. This is what you'd expect of a mammal raised in a snug family hierarchy and unsure of others until they demonstrate their place in an ordered system. Another example: over three-fifths of the sense-making area in the brain of *Procyon lotor*, the Common or Northern Raccoon, is directed to touch, not to sight or sound or smell. They have four to five times more sensory cells in their hands than humans. Their brains are in their paws. It is easy to imagine them washing their paws so as to stimulate the touch centre in their cortex in a ritual of self-affirmation. The very name *raccoon* as heard by colonists in Jamestown from the Pawahtan people indigenous to Virginia is *aroughcun* (pronounced a-raw-coon), meaning "one who scratches, rubs, scrubs with its hands."

Eventually, I consulted the literature of the shamans, the original human experts on animal behaviour, who taught through storytelling. Their narratives show a wary, affectionate respect for most animal people. That respect might be summed up as *courtesy* – a reticence to presume to know things about someone who is mysterious and strange. And this courtesy is shown by a playfulness in the storytelling, a spirit of mischievous fun in exaggerating details and coincidences. "Don't be solemn. This is only a story – we don't know for sure how the animal people really think. We just know that they can reason and feel as well as you and me. Enjoy the story for the fun of it, and if you pick up some wisdom along the way, that's good."

I read shamanic tales on and off until Spring came and my brilliant house-mates woke up.

## 7

ANOTHER RAINY NIGHT in a Spring that is happening in a series of stop-action frames instead of a uniform surge. Raccoons can handle the cold, but if they don't have to leave their dens to eat they can put a wet night to use by being clever. The familiar chittering behind my wall suggests that Mistress Slypaws has resumed her home schooling.

"Sex Ed. Or for aspiring alpha males present, *Relate, then Mate*," was how my partner's stethoscope translated it.

Clutch: "Snore!"

Slypaws: "We shall tiptoe around any discomfort raccoons may be feeling by talking about Trees. Trees are hot. Soon they'll be drenching us in their love-talk and making Touchwit sneeze."

Clutch: "Like I said, boring."

Slypaws: "Raccoons need to know their Trees – which ones to sleep in, which ones to climb. Trees 'R Us."

Slypaws has the clarity of an army boot camp instructor. She often begins with "Listen carefully: what I'm going to say will save your life," then proceeds to "There are three basic facts you need to know … Fact One." But tonight she puts method teaching aside.

"Snap Quiz: Name the Tree People surrounding our den. Touchwit."

"Cedar families, front and back. The folk along the roadway on the winter sun side are Silver Maples. They have hard bark, slim trunks, few branches, and zero escape options except straight up. Do not climb."

Touchwit is being diplomatic about my barricade of trees. They grew together in a row all at once, causing them to trade off spread for height in their race for sunlight. Their tops wave in the breeze like poplars, and they leave a carpet of pale yellow seeds on the service road that runs along the south side of my property. In the Fall, they cover the road with yellow leaves. My neighbours are grateful for the opportunity this gives them to sweep the leaves up. They lean on their rakes and exchange good-natured gossip about neighbours and their attitude towards trees. When they're feeling really devoted to cleaning up after the trees, they use a power blower. You don't know what it's like to enjoy a Fall Saturday morning if you haven't heard the sound of a power blower through a two-pane insulated window with the drapes drawn and a pillow over your head.

"I like the Silvers," Touchwit says. "They'll throw a shadow over our dwelling and keep it cool so we don't pant in the Summer."

Dear Touchwit! She's taking my side in a neighbourhood dispute about what to do about these messy trees that might be my responsibility or the City's, depending on where the property line runs. For some reason, no one has cared to find out exactly where that is. It disappears on its way to meet the river into an impenetrable thicket of buckthorn and grapevines, and that is the end of the question. Besides acting as twelve air conditioners, the silver maples keep me in relative obscurity from the parade of people who use the service road to cross a footbridge over to the city. There are mothers pulling their toddlers in grocery-laden carts, men returning from the store with cases of beer on their shoulders, elders driving their electric rickshaws, groups of joggers wearing lime-green vests and lights on their foreheads, families strolling, individuals bicycling, groups walking for a charity, and people walking their dogs, especially an athletic woman with a greyhound.

Touchwit says: "Turning to the sunset side of our den, there is the mighty Sugar Maple halfway down the lawn – she's a matriarch. And on the riverbank is her elder daughter."

The grandmother sugar maple that Touchwit mentions appears in a city photograph of around 150 years ago and is now over a hundred feet tall and so old her branches are drooping.

"And in the Buckthorn thicket there is a Red Maple. Everything about him is red: twigs, buds, flowers, and leaves – but only when they appear and when they fall."

"Excellent," Slypaws says. "But you forgot the brawny Maple who has muscled his way in among the Silvers. Treat him with respect. He's a survivor, like us raccoons. His kind grow in the back lanes of cities, wherever they can grab a toehold. Maybe you passed over him because you don't know his name."

I know its name. It's the Manitoba Maple that leans dangerously over my house, trying to reach a patch of sunlight in the unanimity of shade thrown by the Silver Maples – an opportunistic individualist sticking out brashly in a sedate arboreal community.

"It's a good climbing tree for raccoons," Bandit says.

"We call it the Maple That Wants To Be Different because its leaves are like those of the Ash in their design, and because it separates its sexualities."

"Mom! You said *separates its sexualities?*"

Bandit, of course. Just like him to be intrigued by the phrase. I'm intrigued too. Mom's explanation is going to be fascinating:

"By *sexualities*, I mean what a tree shows in its flowers when it blossoms. The flowers contain its reproductive organs. The Maple That Wants To Be Different keeps its sexualities a distance apart from each other by separating their reproductive organs so that male and female are not in the same flower. There are girl Raccoon bodies and boy Raccoon bodies. So, in the same way, there are girl Maple bodies and boy Maple bodies of this kind of tree."

Silence follows. Presumably, Bandit is pondering this news. His sister and brother are considering it in their different ways. Who will speak next? I guess it will be Touchwit because she has an impulse to leap ahead of discussions with her insight. Or will it be Clutch, drawn out of his innerness by the fact that in the tree world individual male and individual female bodies are the exception, not the rule? But it is Bandit who breaks the silence.

"Do the male trees jump the females?"

"Bandit is uneducable," Touchwit points out.

"Trees mate without tussling with each other," Slypaws says. "Take the Sugar Maples. Soon you'll see them wearing their mating gowns of pale green. The garments are composed of clusters of flowers with long stalks. Their sexual organs dangle from the ends of the stalks. The boy flowers are longer than your finger and they're hairy. The girl flowers are shorter than the boys' and they have two long tubes with widened tops that are sticky. Sugar Maples are tricksters. They can make their boy and girl sexualities appear on separate trees, or on separate branches of the same tree, or even on the same branch of a tree. Boy flowers are mostly low on the tree; girl flowers are mostly high up."

Touchwit asks: "Don't we also keep our two sexualities in the same body?"

"It can't be that perfect," Clutch says. "Otherwise, we'd mate with ourselves."

"Clutch is right," Slypaws says. "Maybe what you're asking is: does a Boy Raccoon have two sexual energies in his one body? Of course, he does. The girl energy holds back while the boy energy goes looking for a Girl Raccoon. Similarly, a Girl Raccoon has two energies in her one body, but the boy in her is smart enough to keep his mouth shut while the girl is courting." Slypaws is looking hard at Touchwit.

"Trees 'R Us," Clutch repeats knowingly. "So we should normally expect to see boy and girl features in the same flower."

"Oh, I see," Touchwit says. "Our bodies are girl-boy, but at any time we are a little more girl than boy, other times a little more boy than girl."

"When you were tussling with cousin Sensibel," Clutch tells Bandit, "there were – count them – *four* sexualities at play all at once."

"But the Tree That Wants To Be Different is unique," Bandit insists. The remark is a statement, not a question.

"Let's just say it separates its sexualities obviously. So do Willows, Poplars, Aspens, and Hollies. Girl flowers on girl trees; boy flowers on boy trees."

"I get that. But can we go back to the subtle: that is sexualities joined in one tree?" Clutch asks. He is uneasy about the shapeshifting Sugar Maple. But Slypaws has a further surprise:

"The Red Maple holding sway over the thicket. That's a very subtle Tree. It can keep its sexualities together in one body or apart in two bodies. In extreme situations, she-he-they can switch from boy to boy-girl, and from boy-girl to girl."

"!"

"Are there raccoons that want to be They?" Clutch asks suddenly.

"Uncle Wily, maybe. But each of us is *they*, aren't we?"

A thoughtful pause …

34

"It's interesting," Clutch says, "that most of the Trees escape from the fight-or-flee contest by concentrating their differing sexual energies in the same body."

Touchwit comes back into the conversation. "Would that we could simply cast our seeds to the wind like Trees and not have to worry about territories and child-raising."

"You'd be a non-stop sneezing station," Bandit says.

"I'm sure Trees worry about territories and child-raising too," Slypaws says. "I've often felt that they sort everything out underneath the ground where their roots mingle. The Lilacs: are they a one tree or a family? And how do the Silver Maples plan it so that they each one gets their share of sunlight without obstructing another's branches?"

Bandit has an idea: "Maybe a reason trees are so sexually inventive is because they have to stay in one place. They can't just pick up their roots and migrate to a new location. But us Raccoons tiptoe around on our roots, so our sexualities need to be portable. Sexualities need to be portable to compute the size of our families in relation to the size of available food resources."

The silence of unanimity.

But no, Touchwit sees things differently: "Tree People migrate on the back of the wind. Then where they find a place to settle, they burrow in headfirst. Trees are upside-down people. Their minds are in their roots. Their legs kick the air."

"So what are their minds thinking about all the time?" Clutch says, cutting in.

"That is all for tonight," Slypaws says. "Let's do some dreaming."

I wondered what she meant by *do some dreaming*. Do raccoons dream their own separate dreams like us, or do they all dream the same dream? The way the raccoon mother invited her cubs to dream suggested their dreaming was like watching the same home movie together.

## 8

"HERE'S THE PLAN. Clutch and Touchwit – you'll lollop up the street and pop lids. Bandit and I will follow and tip over the containers. We won't start eating until you double back. Our job will be to watch for droolers. Bandit can see best of all of us. He's got his father's dark mask. It cuts down glare from the street lights."

Mother Slypaws is organizing a raid on the Green Bins. In the morning, the organic waste truck will lurch along the street, picking up what it can from a battlefield of coffee grounds, tea bags, egg shells, rice, pasta, apple cores, squeezed oranges, uneaten salad, potato peels, pasta, samosas, nachos, sushi, bacon fat, hot dogs, and peanut butter and jam sandwich crusts.

But my bin will remain untouched. I like to think the raccoons make a courteous exception in my case in exchange for free rent for my chimney, but the truth may be that they don't molest bins in the vicinity of their den so as not to give away its location.

"Precisely what are we sniffing for?" Touchwit asked.

"Turkey, red meat, tuna fish, the usual delicacies."

"Anything but pizza crusts," Clutch said.

"Okay, what are we *not* sniffing for?"

"You just asked a good question." The raccoon mother pauses to let a teaching moment gather. "In the old days, there was good raccoon food in every bin. So we just tipped the first one over and gorged, then moved on to the second, then the third until our tummies were full and we staggered home. And in those days, the lids were simple snap-offs so we didn't waste time analysing how to open the bins."

I thought I heard Ma Slypaws sigh at the memory of the old days.

"But today we can't find what we like to eat in every bin, and we lose precious seconds trying to outwit the cunning new locks. It has become a colossal fluster."

"The Primates aren't eating our kind of food anymore?" Like many of Clutch's interjections, the remark hung between an observation and a query.

"No, they've altered their diet. Only a few diehards are eating normal city raccoon food. That's why there's a problem."

"What are they eating, then?"

"Most of them aren't eating meat."

"Great Raccoon Spirit preserve us!" Clutch exclaimed.

The family waited for Clutch's piety to ascend the chimney and join the constellation that inspired it.

"They've become vegetarians or vegans – especially in Raccoo-nopolis to the south. Does that tell you something?"

"It tells me why a city raccoon wanted to come up here and marry Aunt Pawsense," Bandit explained.

"Precisely. He migrated here because his people had nothing to eat in the city but veggie burgers."

"Now he gets to eat fresh Clams and Crayfish with Cranberry sauce, surrounded by his fat daughters," Bandit said wistfully.

"We shall have to return to the Old Ways of living off the land," Clutch said.

"The Old Ways require a lot of effort now because you can't just enjoy them; you have to protect them. You have to defend your hunting ground against intruders who want to eat the nourishing food. Your Aunt can afford to live the Old Ways because her partner assists with the defense."

"His scent empties the forest."

"Clutch, dear. Don't you think that's a little uncivil?"

"Uncivil? Aunt Pawsense married him so she can build a dynasty. She'll marry off her daughters to his relatives, and they'll all move up here and protect her territory. Suddenly you have an Empire. It'll be called *New Raccoonopolis*. Not exactly living close to Nature in the Old Ways!"

"Do consider what you mean by *the Old Ways*? They're not as wild and pure as you think. Raccoons have lived beside Primates for as long as anyone can remember."

"Actually, I think Uncle Smartwhisker is cool," Bandit said. "He cares about his family, even though he can't remember their names."

"As for us, we have our River," Slypaws said. "There's always some-thing juicy in a river. My sister only has a pond. If she tries to steal an egg, she gets swarmed by Red-winged Blackbirds. We have acorns and nuts and grapes in our little forest, and chestnuts to dig out of the ground where the Squirrels bury them, and peanuts and black oil sunflower seeds which the Idiot gives to the Chickadees, who jam them in the tree bark for storage."

I thought that Mother Slypaws might be feeling inferior to her older sister in the eyes of her cubs. Hadn't she chosen a safe habitat for her little family?

"That's how you got us through the winter! Nuts and seeds. Food for Squirrels and Birds," Clutch said. "You've turned us into vegans."

"Plus pizza," Bandit said.

"I wonder what the neighbourhood Primates have been eating this week?" Touchwit bringing the discussion back into focus. There is the sound of noses sniffing.

"You'll find out when you tip the bins."

Slypaws was ensuring that her cubs used their initiative. After the Summer Solstice, they'd have to survive on their own instead of relying on her. In these parts, the Summer Solstice is when mothers take their cubs out to survey future dens.

"Give us a clue."

"Alright. The Primate two houses away eats food delivered in boxes. That's where I got the pizza for you during the Winter. Further up the street there's a vegan whose bin isn't worth the effort. You won't find fish or flesh or fowl in her bin. Not even eggs. Vegans are becoming numerous."

"What's wrong with eating meat and fish and birds?" Clutch asked.

"They're living creatures. Some humans think that it's wrong to kill a living creature just so that you can eat its body."

"Plants are living creatures. We kill them and eat their bodies," Bandit said.

"True," Slypaws said. "When you eat a crabapple, you're eating one of the tree's ovaries."

"I see why vegans won't eat certain things," Touchwit said. "But I don't understand why they won't eat creatures who aren't going to live a long time anyway. Like Crayfish or Clams."

Slypaws's reply was delicate: "I don't know. Maybe some eat Clams, but never Crayfish. Worms, but never Frogs."

"I get it!" Clutch exclaimed. "Vegans won't eat creatures who have faces."

"Or anything belonging to a creature with a face. Bees have faces, so vegans won't eat honey. And vegans won't even use the skin or fur of a living creature. They consider it theft."

"What if vegetables had faces?" Touchwit mused.

"So, what's left for us to eat when we pop a lid?" Bandit asked, trying to clear his head of his sister's whimsy.

"These days, we have to be selective about our food choices. *As Primates evolve, so Raccoons evolve*," Slypaws said, quoting a proverb.

"That means we have to sniff out the choice bits and pull them out of the bags like Skunks," Touchwit said. She didn't make this comparison with scorn. Skunks, in spite of their ability to send an attacker reeling with their spray, are very hygienic animals.

"We don't have time for that," Clutch said. "After we pop a lid, we strew the contents of the container all over the garden and especially the front path. All the better to eat selectively in our own spaces without getting on top of each other. Also, it leaves a statement."

"That's our mob!" Bandit said.

"But how will we know what's good for us to eat today?" Touchwit asked.

"Experiment. Whatever doesn't make you retch will make you stronger. And don't guzzle the dregs of spirit juice from the empty bottles in the open bins. It's not good for raccoons."

At that remark, they began their sortie. For creatures who are secretive, the mess they were about to make would be a flagrant manifesto, a vivid claim that they owned the neighbourhood. I stayed up late. I usually do. I'm a writer and my profession is nocturnal. That's why I feel I have a special bond with the *Procyon* species and am able to understand them. I would guard the fort until they returned.

Return? Absolutely! They came home like they were returning from a party, and one of them missed his footing and dropped straight down the chimney well to the bottom and passed out. Untranslatable growling up and down the chimney. But at the open top, singing. One of them was singing. It was Touchwit singing a moist lullaby to the stars.

I don't understand raccoons at all.

## 9

ANOTHER OUTBURST IN THE CHIMNEY! Brimstone pits and hell! These snarling explosions of petulance are becoming more frequent now that the sun is hitting the chimney top.

"Mom, tell Witless to stop pulling hairs out of my tail."

"I need them for my Making."

"Get them from your own tail."

"That wouldn't be right. The material has to come from something other than the maker."

"Your material is taking up all the space in the den. Especially the grapevines."

"Your Makings are very beautiful, darling – but Bandy has a point. Do you really need all these vines for your objects? I like the grass ones better. I don't get caught in them."

"The whole idea is to get caught in them."

"Is that why you're weaving my tail hair into the vines? I'm supposed to get caught in it?"

"A little bit of you. Yes."

"What, pray tell, does *my* body hair have to do with your Making?"

"Your hair makes it more authentic. Like I said, the Making can't be all me; it has to be a little bit me and a little bit something that's not-me. That's what gives it meaning."

"What does this one mean?"

"I don't know. I have to find out by making it."

"It means *I need more space*," Clutch says.

"What are you finding out from this one?" Bandit asks.

"I'm not sure. Something about a balance of the materials of the Making. If there's balance in the composure of the materials, there's probably a balance in the environment where the materials came from. What do you think?"

"I think that I find out about a balance by tiptoeing along one of those thick wires that hums under your feet."

"You would! I find out about balance by fashioning Makings. It's less scary."

"But it's more … authen – whatever you call it?"

"New word, Clutch. *Auth-en-tic*. It means being your whole true self."

"I am my whole true self."

"No, you're not. Parts of you are out there in the River and the Forest. Or in the Sky with your Great Raccoon Ancestor. Or in Dad – wherever he is. You're scattered all over the place."

"I shall venture forth and find my missing pieces."

"It's not enough just to find them. You have to coax them to cohere in just the right way. I know what – I'll create a Making for your quest. It might guide you."

"What am I supposed to do? Wear it around my neck? I'll trip over the stupid thing."

"You just have to think of it." Touchwit sounds hurt.

"I don't think you should call Touchwit's Makings 'stupid'," Slypaws says.

"At least, it gives her something to do with her hands. They are always fidgeting," Clutch says.

"Think that she's adding something to the world," Slypaws says.

"She's adding clutter to the world."

"Clutch, until you find yourself, all your bits and pieces are going to be cluttering up the world. Your name is synonymous with clutter."

"Touchwit has a glitch in her hand-eye coordination. She has a virus."

"Maybe she's got the mumbles."

Time for Slypaws to intervene. This is getting personal.

"Clutch, love. You too, Bandit. Your sister might be bringing something entirely new to your eyes. Something that wasn't there before. Isn't that it, Touch?"

"That's right. But it isn't clutter like Clutch thinks. It isn't useful or useless. It just is."

No one spoke further. They were content to leave the issue there. However, a larger issue was finding its voice in Touchwit's makings. The world was very big and the chimney was getting smaller by the hour. It could no longer accommodate the three cubs and their energies.

I DIDN'T HEAR MY COLLEAGUES behind the wall for some time. They came and went discreetly at odd hours like boarders. Outside my study window, moss began to grow on the limbs of the Manitoba Maple because of the rain. My neighbour's Forsythia held its yellow blossoms under grey skies and the robins sang for a sun that rarely shined. About mid-May, the weather changed and in the first full day of sunlight the mosquitoes and flies hatched, warblers appeared out of nowhere, the ferns unfolded, and the crabapple tree exploded into crimson blossoms like a firework. Soon the blackbirds would be plucking mayflies off the lilac blossoms. Then Spring would be here in its fullness, not begrudgingly but triumphantly. But what were the Raccoons up to?

I guessed they were exploring their world and discovering the nourishment that is available to them in the wild: tadpoles, clams, crayfish, minnows, water spiders, pinheads, rock perch, sunfish, chub, and every other creature called up from the riverbed. In the trees, robins' eggs and spiders. On the river bank, frogs and turtles and snails.

But just when I began to feel they had left the chimney to start a new life on their own, there was the familiar chittering at ear level behind my wall. I reached for the stethoscope:

"Well, we're certainly not going to go *there* again!"

The voice of a stressed mother, relieved that her family was safe at home.

"What shall we do if we can't use the community latrine?" That was Clutch, tentatively asserting his status as elder brother through a question. It seemed that Clutch possessed all the qualities of leadership as an intellectual notion, without the desire to engage in a single one of them. His whole existence was a question mark.

"We'll start our own latrine," Mother Slypaws announced. "Any ideas?"

"The upper verandah where the Idiot sprays water at the squirrels."

Thanks, Touchwit. That's all I need – to wake up in the morning and go out on the balcony to greet the day. The first thing I see is a pile of raccoon scat. The fact that it is exquisitely tidy only adds to the offense.

"That's a good place, except Dad might see us," Clutch said.

"Do you think he recognized our scents?" Bandit asked.

Slypaws replied. "I don't know. There's no clue in our scents to separate us from the other raccoons in the clan. Now that it's Spring, we're eating the same food as the others. And I doubt if the Creep will be interested in checking out this house. He's too heavy for the cedars anyway, and if he does make it onto the roof I'll hold my ground at the top of the chimney."

"We'll need to be quiet though," Bandit said. "Which means no more drinking the leftovers in the Blue Boxes."

The remark was directed at Clutch and Touchwit. I hoped they didn't hear me laughing. It appeared they had discovered alcohol that night Touchwit had come home singing and Clutch had fallen through the chimney. Raccoons love anything that has sugar in it. Sugar is a fatal weakness.

Touchwit seemed uncharacteristically silent. She wouldn't be embarrassed at drinking wine and beer for the first time – she was bursting to be a grown-up.

"Your father is only the face of the problem. The problem itself is political economy." Slypaws's voice diminished to a whisper. I had to press the disc of the stethoscope hard against the wall to hear her elaboration. "Look, kids. We've learned some things from our reconnaissance. Precarious things. There are pressures on the River. More raccoons want to settle here. The Clan Fathers can't protect their territories individually against all the newcomers. They can't look after the scattered hunting grounds of their respective families. They are considering that they need to unite and serve under a Supreme Male in order to protect the whole clan territory. Meatbreath is promoting himself as the overall leader."

"Our Dad!" I heard awe in Clutch's voice.

"Help! It's every Cub for himself!" Bandit said.

I'm not sure from these sentiments if the young family understood politics, but I do. First of all, there is no universal model for the social organization of raccoons. They organize themselves variously depending on the landscape and the species. But in the Eastern Woodlands, a common model is a network of clan families dominated by the senior males. These family heads hang out together like oligarchs, boasting about the number of cubs they've sired and gossiping about the competing raccoons in the adjacent territories. As males sharing a common clan responsibility, they are relaxed most of the year about crossing into each other's family hunting grounds. Two or more families can co-habit the same hunting ground, with the one father visiting his various wives and children. There are other kinds of social organization, but this versatile model prevailed on the River. Now in the face of migrating raccoons, the breeding males, the Clan Fathers, were yielding up their paternal roles in exchange for the security offered by the strongest male, Meatbreath. And this centralizing of power was occurring at the height of the mating season, which made the autocracy all the more intense.

"This is going to mess up all the balances in the hunting grounds. They depend on local knowledge and nearby fathers. What are we going to do?" Touchwit put the question to her whole family.

"Hey, here's an idea. Why don't we stop getting drunk and instead stand up for ourselves? The only thing an alpha male understands is brute force."

"Go right ahead, Bandit. Me? – I'm going to consult our Customs. They will tell us what to do."

"Clutch, what's the time-honoured Custom for negotiating with a power nozzle?" Bandit asked. The sarcasm was beginning to mount.

"I don't know, but there's a Custom for every situation so there must be one for dealing with a raccoon who's become a bully. I'm sure the problem has happened before."

Silence. The children are turning to their mother for an answer. But Slypaws is saying nothing.

"If we can't fight, we have to turn tail and flee. That's the best Custom I know," Bandit said eventually.

"That's because it's the only one you know," Touchwit said.

"Where are we going to flee to?" Clutch asked.

"We can go to Aunt Pawsense's pond."

"Sure, that's going to work. Four more mouths for her to feed. And she's already got plans for inviting *grown-up* raccoons to defend her pond. All they have to do in return is marry her daughters."

Pause. Again no reply from the mother. Is she holding something back from the debate or is she really out of options? Touchwit broke the silence: "Clutch, it seems there is no Custom to meet this particular dilemma."

"There must be. Nothing can happen without a Custom directing it."

"Bandy, it seems you can't fight or flee."

"I can too!"

"You'll meet a loathsome, grotesque end."

"Perhaps our superior sister has the solution in her paws. If it's not Custom, what is it? Has she invented a new Custom?"

"A person can't invent a Custom. Customs invent themselves."

"Meatbreath has."

"This is getting nowhere."

Finally, the voice of Slypaws: hesitant, thoughtful, calm: "What raccoons usually do at this time of year is go out and discover their future dens."

This suggestion provoked three busy silences. The children were considering the implications of starting a new life on their own. They hadn't thought of this eventuality and they were shocked. Finally, they all spoke at once.

"Mom, are you abdicating and retiring to the city?"

"Do you want us to scatter?"

"Will we ever see each other again?"

"No, dear ones. I don't mean that we should split up as an emergency measure. Meatbreath can track us down one-by-one anytime he feels like it. I'm only saying that if you require a Custom in order to know what to do, the Custom at this time of the year is for cubs to determine where they are going to forage and maybe start families of their own. I should have given you a lesson on dens and showed you some examples. But alas, I am a neglectful Mom. Unlike my sister Pawsense."

"You're a wonderful Mom," her first son replied. "Why can't we stay here forever with you in this chimney?"

"Because your friends will hang out at all hours and party on the roof top."

Bandit had a question: "Do you intend that we should discover our future dens now, for habitation later?"

"That's what Custom dictates."

"I don't see how our dispersal according to Custom solves the issue of Dad hogging the River to himself." That was Touchwit.

"It might. Then, it might not."

"I don't see how it might," Clutch said.

"You can't find out what's inside a container unless you pop the lid."

"Mom, stop being ineffable."

"*Que será, será!*"

"How does Custom dictate that we should go about seeking our futures?" Bandit asked.

"Isn't the future something that is not yet accustomed?" Touchwit asked.

"What have cubs done in years past?" Clutch asked.

"Go far, and farther than far. Each of you go in your own direction and at your own fair speed."

Clutch caught the spirit of adventure in the lyrical High Words spoken by his mother. "I shall discover where Dawn rises from her bed to paint the clouds each morning," he said.

"And I – I shall go to the back of the North Wind," Bandit said.

"And you, Touchwit?"

"I shall find out where the Sun goes when you can't see it anymore," the daughter said. "What about you, Mom? What are you going to do?"

"I don't know. Maybe redecorate the chimney. Start a school for lost cubs. Learn how to create Makings. I'll be here when you return with your stories. A can of tuna with a pop-off lid to the one who brings back the best tale."

From this I learned that it wouldn't be until the late summer that I'd hear their stories – if all the cubs returned from their quests.

NIGHT AFTER NIGHT I waited for a conversation to begin. I fondled the stethoscope draped over the arm of my study chair, listening for the rough, affectionate chittering which had become so familiar. But there was only a hollow silence. I felt like a parent whose kids had gone away to college. If at least the mother had stayed, I could have shared my sympathy with her through the wall. But Slypaws went too. With her children out in the world, there was no need to inhabit the chimney.

There's a tree beside my house that I haven't told you about. I never mentioned it because it didn't figure in Slypaws's lesson on gender. The tree will be gone soon – it is quite dead and would have been cut down two years ago except that the City Parks department appreciates how a tree that is dead can enjoy a second life as an ecosystem, and besides this tree remains beautiful in death.

She is a Catalpa tree, so stooped and withered in her old age that her lower branches touch the ground. Even in her prime, she seemed unable to revive with the Spring and her branches were still dormant in early June, well after the surrounding trees were in leaf. Inspecting her brittle branches, neighbours walking by my house would pronounce her dead in a voice loud enough for me to hear. Then she'd proudly put out her leaves and blossoms – immense, heart-shaped leaves and huge white wedding bells with a violet and gold interior that smelled pungent and covered the street like snow when they fell. The Catalpa was remembering the season of a distant climate in which her kind flourished, even though she has shaded an intersection here since the days of horses and carriages. She died from having lived.

Now her body is the hub of a community, a tenement for nesting birds and squirrels, and a cafeteria for woodpeckers. A chipmunk has dug a burrow between her roots.

It was 4 in the morning. Robins were singing all across the city like the rollicking lilt of church bells. First I checked the state of the river under a half moon, then looked out a second-floor window at the intersection. The Catalpa was backlit by the glare of an L.E.D. streetlight, making the spectral tree seem like an old photographic negative, its limbs outlined by a silver glow from the moisture left by the last rain. She had become a spirit tree.

Then a darkened shape moved on one of her branches.

It was the mother raccoon etched in cold starlight that radiated from her fur and danced around her ears. She stood up on the limb where she'd been lying, arched her back, and leaned forward into a satisfying stretch. Then she sat on the branch and licked her paws. She washed one paw, toe by toe, then the other paw, toe by toe. After, she began to work on her tail. I watched her at ease and caring for herself after a winter of motherwork.

She must have sensed me, because she stopped washing and looked straight at my window. My face must have looked ghostly in the streetlight. She casually took me in as a familiar feature of her environment. It was good to think that she was done with the chimney. That she no longer needed a secret shelter for her family. She could live outdoors, waiting for the first of her cubs to return with a story.

## 12

VOICES BEHIND MY WALL. In daylight. But they seem faraway. Where is the stethoscope? *I can't find the stethoscope!* Then it occurs to me that the voices sound faraway because they are echoing down the chimney from the chimney top. Of course, it is a warm spring day, and Slypaws has woken up and decided to bask in the sunlight. But who is she talking with? Has one of her cubs returned home prematurely, broken and defeated?

I tiptoe out to the second-floor balcony. The voices are clear and elegant.

"Oh, but this is a most commodious burrow! However did you find it?"

"You are kind to say so. But no – it is not at all roomy and it is open to the sky. In addition to the wet weather, one has to endure a rain of twigs and straw deposited by earnest birds who fancy the concavity to be the foundation for a nest. Yet this hole suits the uses of privacy."

"I smell cubs. Three small ones. Congratulations. May one ask where they are?"

"They're out making their first solos."

"And you are not worried about them? In these tense times, my body thought it prudent to produce only two children. But they are brave cubs. They are so brave they left home and never came back."

This remark was followed by laughter. I heard Slypaws chuckling too. It must be a pleasure for her to participate in polite discourse again, after listening to months of bratspeak. The visitor seemed free-spirited and prone to irreverent mirth. Two mothers on holiday.

"You are a fellow Clanswoman from Creek Town, if I'm not mistaken. What brings you upriver?"

"Yes, you are right. I am of the Creek Town community. But, alas, that is no more. We are scattered to the four winds on account of the impulses of the Overlord. Do you know whom I speak of?"

"Up this way, he is called *Meatbreath*."

Giggling.

"Meatbreath. He has many names. Dissatisfied with the thought that he might be ordinary, *il ponderoso* changes his names daily. He does so in order to confuse us. Yet he tricks no one because every name he chooses is more grandiose than the last."

"What's the Creep up to now?"

"He is obsessed with migrants. He claims to be shielding us from the hordes who are spilling over from the south, but all he is doing is transfixing us in a tiresome and enervating melodrama. Politics is raccoons too close together."

"Or too far apart. What of the Clan Fathers? Can't they restrain him?"

"They are scared witless of him. He threatens to assume the headship of their families, including their wives."

"This is monstrous! He is trying to live above the Customs. He will singlehandedly erase the boundaries of family hunting grounds." Slypaws hesitated. "Forgive me, but may I ask you a personal question?"

"You may ask."

"Has Meatbreath violated your person?"

A pause. I heard the wind whistling in the chimney top.

"He has violated many. Wrath and venery prowl together and are his companions. He longs to replicate himself in countless children whom he calls his High Guard, watching over them with satisfaction just as the Raccoon Ancestor watches over those whom he has created in his image. But to answer your question (which I do not find the least importunate), no, he has not molested me. I escaped him by a whisker. He tracked me to where I was hiding in a tree by the lake – it is where the Primates bring their cubs to play – and I jumped into the lake and swam for my life. I've been swimming upriver since, in small stretches so as not to leave a trail."

This information gave me my first knowledge of the geopolitics of the clan families. The lake is Little Lake, a widening of the river made by a dam at its southern end. The tree is in Beavermead Park along its eastern shoreline where there is a creek. With barbecue leftovers from the campsites, and organic vegetables from the ecology park, and clams in its public beach, this is prime raccoon territory. Or was, before Meatbreath took it over.

"You may stay here for a time, if you like. I am in need of company. But whither are you bound, if I may ask?"

"That is gracious of you. I would like to stay and rest. Then, I think I will try my luck in the City."

The City. She didn't mean the Greater Metropolitan Area to the south. She meant the central part of my city across the river, with its stores and restaurants and old neighbourhoods. Of course, it would be densely populated by raccoons, but their lifestyle would be quite different from that of Creek Town.

"The Raccoon with a Hundred Names won't extend his dominion there. It's too complicated. And besides, it's on the far side of the River. Apparently, the Jerk doesn't like to swim. He says it messes up his hair."

"The times are perilous enough without having to watch one's back for a rogue alpha male with a headful of politics. But you speak of him intimately. May I dare to ask if ..."

"Yes, it is true. He has had three cubs by me, out-of-season and against my wishes. But I love them. Clutch, Bandit, and Touchwit. I love them all the more because in order to grow up and be themselves they are going to have to use the strengths they have inherited from their father without being devoured by his weaknesses. It is going to be a risky coming of age for each of them."

"It will be breathtaking watching them succeed."

"We shall have to learn to live differently, but we're good at that! We're Raccoons! We can adapt to any condition. Since we are to be fellow survivors, may I ask your name? I am Slypaws of the River Clan Family at the Islands."

It is apparently a point of courtesy among raccoons to exchanges names last. The exchange puts a seal on the introduction, which is done through telling stories. The stories convey the personality and circumstances of the stranger. Names are just a label.

"I am Twitchwhisker. Erstwhile of the River Clan Family at Creek Town, now a widow with no hierarchy or kin."

"Then you shall live with me for a spell and *I* shall be your kin. Let us go down and scrounge up a repast for you to eat."

Giggles. Then the scratching of claws on the brickwork of the chimney.

I heard no more of Slypaws and her new friend for the rest of the Spring. I guess they hunted together until the refugee was strong enough to swim across to the city. They probably spent much of their time hunting on the Islands that Slypaws takes her clan-family name from. These islands are just off my back lawn, muffling the noise of the Quaker Oats factory, but not the scent on certain days of oats, honey, and raisins. The islands – there are two close by, separated by a narrow channel, and a small one west of them halfway across the river – were formed in the nineteenth century by wood chips from the lumber mills, which gathered on natural shoals, then were held in place by the roots of trees. Later on, decorative plants took root from cuttings thrown into the river by gardeners. Now that the Spring flooding has receded, the channel separating the two near islands is an underwater sushi bar for raccoons. The nearby river willows and tamaracks provide safety from roving males.

Before the clan mothers descended, I managed to get out onto the street and take a photograph of them, head to tail, licking each other's fur and talking. This was the first time Slypaws made eye contact with me. At the instant she took her own mental photograph, I realized that I had left the stethoscope on my desk. I had understood her speech directly, without it.

# ACT II

## *To Seek a Fortune*

*Clutch*, travelling east
An impertinent Mouse
*Sleekfoot* and *Lightfinger*, brother and sister refugees from Creek Town
A mighty Drooler
A wise Fox

*Bandit*, travelling north
His Aunt *Pawsense* of the Marsh Pond
*Goodpaws*, her bossy senior daughter
*Sensibella*, the second sister, a romantic beauty
*Friskywits*, a clever younger sister
*Nimbletoes*, junior sister and family messenger
*Smartwhisker*, their father, an urban gentleman
Lord *Padmind*, a suitor for Sensibel

*Touchwit*, travelling west
A solitary *Stranger* who leaves behind a Making
An angry Beaver

# 13

CLUTCH WAITED for the night he wanted – a clear sky with a south-easterly breeze bringing scents of dangers ahead. He already knew some things from analysing the wind from the top of the chimney on previous nights. And his mother, though she had never been very far east, told him what she'd heard from gossip at the community latrine. This is what Clutch knew:

His biggest obstacle would be a Primate thoroughfare. Full of traffic at any hour, it was a treacherous crossing. The road marked the eastern boundary of the inner city. Beyond it lay a neighbourhood of newly built houses without a mature tree to climb or porch to hide under in a crisis. And some houses had fenced yards containing Droolers and every Drooler that was imprisoned outdoors had to be considered vicious. The neighbourhood was no place for raccoons. Yet it would provide sanctuary if he had to escape from the powerful raccoons who made up the Clan Fathers. They wouldn't risk going into the suburb.

He also knew that if he could find a creek amid the new housing, he could follow it northeast into the countryside. The creek was an ancient pathway for animals travelling into the city from afar, bringing them to where it drained into the Lake. Here the prosperous raccoon settlement called Creek Town had flourished since antiquity, but he intended to travel upstream, away from raccoon society to seek his fortune.

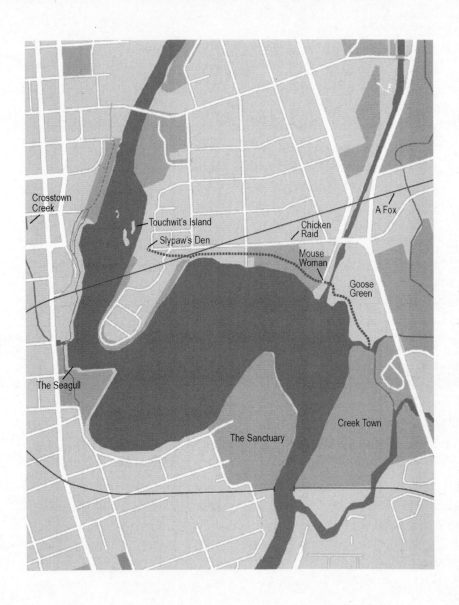

Clutch was the first of the cubs to go. He touched noses with his brother and sister, committing their scents to memory – he might never see them again. Then he gave his mother the hug that a first-born son gives when he is about to start his journey to become a man.

Clutch left the roof by the front-door cedar and travelled with the Great Raccoon Ancestor high in the southeast sky pointing the way.

"*I wasn't sure then,*" Clutch subsequently recalled, "*what it was I was seeking. I just felt it had something to do with the Great Spirit and with my Father. I felt that to become my own self, I had to find my relationship with my celestial and earthly forebearers. Was it a service to one of them I was meant to perform? Was it a problem between them that I was supposed to fix? I didn't know. But I set out with a high heart, knowing I'd find the answer.*"

He must have gone east along the arterial street that runs across the top of the lake. I know this because he recounted coming to the spot where Uncle Wily was killed by an electric car. He sniffed his death-place, but no trace of his spirit lingered on the road, only oil and rubber on the worn asphalt. Yet the moment with his uncle was powerful, and as Clutch honoured the only relative he had known as an infant he hoped that some of the old raccoon's wisdom passed into him. Then he picked his way parallel to the street through the back gardens of houses on the lake until he came to his first obstacle.

A canal extends up the east side of the city from Little Lake. It was constructed a long time ago to take people up to the lumber mills and summer resort hotels, getting around the rapids and power dams on the river. Today, the canal carries yachts and touring boats. Clutch had to cross the canal before he faced the next obstacle – the hazard presented by the adjacent highway. The best way across the canal, which his mother mentioned without enthusiasm, was to sneak south down a canal service lane. A row of poplar trees flanked the lane, offering a series of evenly spaced escapes. Just before the canal met the lake, he would find a walkway along the top of a canal lock. He'd have to cross it in the dark with water plunging twenty feet down from a sluice. It led through some pines to a park extending around the northeast corner of the lake directly to the creek, and if he went upstream, away from Creek Town, he would find a culvert that would get him under the highway. If he ran into trouble, he could find refuge in the ancient raccoon colony.

From his account, it seems Clutch reached the canal without incident. He cleared his mind of a distracting scent of chickens kept in the backyard of a nearby house, and analysed his rejected options. Yes, the swing bridge in front of him was just as his mother had described it – a lifeless, metal monster daring him to dart across between vehicles. He noted the railway bridge to the north. A way for animals to cross the canal, it might be handy in a crisis. But the service lane to the south was right where his mom said it would be, and he scampered under the swish of poplar leaves in the breeze, south to the lock. And crossing the narrow wooden walkway wasn't as dreadful as he feared. The experience was over in an eye blink. He crouched in the pines waiting for his heart to stop racing and then took a pathway through the park around the shoreline of Little Lake in the direction of Beavermead Creek. Strange that there were no fresh raccoon scents. Creek Town was a major raccoon community at the juncture of creek, lake, parkland, and forest. He ought to have been challenged by a sentry before now. Instead he was challenged by a serious danger.

*Geese!* And many of them, and they had goslings! This meant they wouldn't be relying on their usual half-hearted hissing to warn off a territorial nuisance: they'd be ferociously aggressive. A warning hiss, and the males would charge straight at his face, striking his head with powerful shoulder bones, biting and kicking, driving him away. He couldn't detour around the flock through the pines to his left because the geese would think he was stalking their goslings; for the same reason, he couldn't take to the water where the geese had an advantage. Time for diplomacy. Were geese open to reason?

Clutch looked up to the sky for guidance. There, outlined by stars, the brilliant form of his Ancestor said "*No!*"

"What should I do then?"

"*Use your clever Raccoon mind.*"

Clutch consulted his clever raccoon mind. There was a puzzle here. What was it? The geese were sleeping except for the periodic honk of *all's well* by the designated watchgoose. They hadn't sensed him downwind. But why were the geese here at all, so close to the top of a raccoon town? Geese wouldn't be parenting goslings near raccoons, and from the scent of the goose scat the geese had been here for awhile. Where was the huge Creek Town clan family?

Only one way to solve this puzzle. Ask the geese.

Clutch approached slowly. He perched on his hind legs at intervals to make himself conspicuous in the gloom. A series of urgent honks. The geese rose with effort to their feet and began bobbing their heads, spreading alarm. He stood still and looked away from the flock so as not to appear to be an intent predator. No effect. The mothers were leading their goslings towards the water while the fathers covered their escape. One enormous Gander stood his ground, the rearguard for the flock.

"*Pisssss off! This is our pasture. We have children.*"

Standing still and looking away was completely useless. The Gander advanced, loosening its wings and arching its neck.

"I do not intend harm. I am only a solitary Raccoon of no consequence looking for my Clan."

"*You're a Carnivore, and your very existence is an insult to Grazers. Also, you're full of tricks.*"

"I assure you I will not interfere with your parenting."

"*Go home and mind your own business, which is eating garbage.*"

"I beg passage through your grazing place to the Beavers' creek, where I hope only to be reunited with my own kind."

"*Forget it! There are none of your kind there. They have taken flight, which you ought to do too before I peck out your eyes.*"

Witnessing the standoff, the other male geese turned and began advancing behind a barrage of hisses. Clutch counted six family heads, full of attitude. Geese had the impulse of many flocking creatures to excite each other into a state of frenzied purpose. If they attacked him, he wouldn't be able to run away. He conceded ground in slow, deliberate movements, always facing his attackers. He tried to appear relaxed, though he felt tense as a closed clam. Also, his feelings were hurt. He was a peace-loving raccoon. True, he had a predator's impulses, but they were well under control.

Clutch walked away alone, not daring to look back at the self-satisfied ganders.

It wasn't until he was back on the west side of the lock that he felt himself unstiffen. All through the confrontation his hackles had been raised, contradicting his peaceful intent. So much for diplomacy.

Clutch lay under a poplar tree and licked his paws, recovering his dignity and his options. Why did he let a self-superior goose stop him? He could have charged right at the bird, grabbed him by the throat, flipped him over wings still beating, and bit into his neck, sucking his blood. Only the certainty that the other geese would have swarmed him had prevented him from asserting himself.

But then when he'd settled down more and his heart had stopped pounding under his ribs, he began to recover his reasonableness. No, he'd never go head-to-head with a pumped-up goose. Or anybody, for that matter. The impulse was silly. It was against his principles. Ever since he was a cub, he had committed himself to the refined reasoning of diplomatic persuasion instead of the coarse logic of fight or flee. He took after Uncle Wily who avoided bloodthirsty aggression.

But where had diplomacy got him? He was back on his home side of the canal. His Ancestor was splendid in the sky, on the distant side of the canal. And he was feeling hungry. Aggression gave a person the munchies.

Clutch picked himself up and went north on the service road to the lockmaster's house. Here, where boaters came ashore to use the washrooms and tourists gathered to watch the lock in operation, there were recycling bins. But first, he scented sandwich crumbs beneath a park bench against the wall of the house. And what was that tiny scuffling noise around the corner? Someone else was looking for crumbs. Someone succulent to feed a hungry raccoon.

Clutch waited in the dark until the mouse crept around the corner. One pounce and he had it between his paws. A quick, merciful decapitation, then he'd chew its body with leisure. But the object in his hands began to speak:

*"Oh, please don't eat me, Sir. I am but a tiny mouseling with no flesh on my bones and scarcely worth the swallow."*

Clutch instantly regretted that he hadn't devoured the mouse on the spot, for now his supper was reasoning with him. "Why shouldn't I eat you? You're a Rodent," he replied. He picked up his prey by the tail and carried it in his mouth around the corner of the gatehouse, dropping it under his paw below the light from an outdoor lamp. Grey, with a white belly. A Field Mouse. Too young to be a mother.

"*Reasons why you shouldn't eat me. Number One: everyone is moving away from meat to plant-based substitutes. Two: you're not really all that hungry anyway. You're feeling out of sorts, and people shouldn't try to get out of their depressions by eating comfort food. Three: ...*"

"If you had as much muscle as you have reasons, I'd have eaten you before you opened your mouth." Clutch tried not to sound piqued. Prey had no right to argue with their predators. That wasn't how the system worked.

"*Indeed, I was stupid enough to make myself vulnerable, and you caught me fairly,*" the mouse went on. It certainly was a chatterbox. "*However, people nowadays like to be responsible for their actions. They like to know* why *they are doing what they are doing, the context of their decision as well as its consequences. Especially when it involves a member of a minority.*"

"Since when did mice become a minority? They are underfoot everywhere, and they multiply like fleas."

"*I am a minority in the sense that I am the victim of an imbalance in a relationship of power, for instance between a responsible Raccoon and an errant Mouse.*"

Clutch closed his eyes and prayed to his gods until the rage provoked by this display of impudence passed. First he prayed to the Great Raccoon Ancestor who gave Raccoons their cleverness. Then he prayed to the First Mother, consort of the Spirit Ancestor, she who is called Hapticia, who bestowed her hand-eye coordination on all Raccoons. Meanwhile, the animacy was watching him keenly with its bright eyes. He felt its little heart beating in his paws.

"Since when did you corner the market on victimhood?" he asked it.

"*I didn't. We are all victims. The world is a mean place, and it's getting meaner by the minute.*"

"I'm not a victim," Clutch said.

"*You're not? Where is the River Clan Family?*"

"You tell me, if you know so much."

"*Its people are cowering under porches and in tree hollows from here to the horizon. Like mice.*"

"Who is preying on them, to make them as cowardly as mice?"

"*That is for you to find out. But don't let your mission distract from my main point. My point is that most of us are victims in this unbalanced world. We are all minorities.*"

Clutch grew tired of this argument. It sounded like one of those path's of reasoning that led to an entanglement, and it was only delaying the inevitable. He cleared his throat for a gulp. This victim was going down the chute. Conversations about bully versus victim power imbalances were going down with it. What next? Were vegetables going to start arguing with their eaters?

"*Besides,*" the mouse said casually. "*You shouldn't eat me because I can tell your fortune.*"

Clutch hesitated again. It was bad enough to be bested by a Goose. But now a Rodent full of a pesky pertinency. Yet in all fairness, he should hear it out. Mice don't know much, but what they know is close to the ground.

"What do you know about my fortune?"

"*I know that you are going to squeeze through a tight space into your future. And that you will become a responsible Raccoon.*"

"You could be less vague."

"*You have kinfolk hiding nearby in a boathouse on the lake. They haven't eaten in nights and they are hungry.*"

"I am hungry too, but you've taken away my appetite," Clutch said, releasing the mouse. "Now I don't want to eat anymore."

"*Neither do I.*"

"You've made me pointless, moody, and malnourished."

"*But you're a better Raccoon.*"

"Anytime you want to have a disquisition on moral philosophy before lunch, let me know," Clutch said gruffly.

"*I will. Cheers.*"

The mouse curled her tail above her ears and watched the raccoon turn sharply away and walk stiff-legged back down the service road in the direction of the lake.

# 14

"NO FACE OR FIGURE is more pleasing than his – so regular his features, so open his countenance! Oh, what a blush of health is upon him, and such an agreeable height and size, a firm and upright 'Coon! There is health in his air, yea, even in his glance." Fanning herself with a willow branch, Sensibella let out a sigh.

"Lá! What a crush!" Frisk said.

A little breeze from nowhere stirred the tops of the bulrushes. A yellow powder, pollen from a nearby ridge of conifers, covered the open water. It was the quiet part of the day. The only sound was the *kek-eree* of a Red-winged Blackbird on the far side of the pond.

"But do you not find him somewhat lacking in means? A remarkably fine specimen with dexterity and wit – I'll give you that. But hardly a gentleman of property. He has nothing but himself to commend him."

This was Goodpaws, who had the bossy kindness of a senior sister, even though she couldn't have been born more than five minutes before the others. Frisk and Nimble made up the rest of the sisterhood that was enjoying the shade of a River Willow.

"He has his intricate Makings to commend him, for he is an *artiste*," Sensibel declared.

"One who presents to the eyes things that never wert in Nature, like raccoons with wings, clams that talk, and suchlike drolleries," Goodpaws said. "I beg you reconsider Squire Hairball, who is of our parish and offers the virtue of familiar Customs, not to mention a handsome territory."

"Phoo! Phoo! He has a projecting tooth and a clumsy wrist."

"Yet he possesses an acute mind and assiduously pleasing manners," Goodpaws said.

"I am quite determined to refuse him."

"Ahem!" Aunt Pawsense clearing her throat, marking an intervention. Plump on turtles' eggs and fresh spring clams, she moderated the conversation by means of an amiable corpulence and the application of moral axioms: "There is hardly any personal defect which an agreeable manner might not gradually reconcile one to."

"I think very differently," Frisk said. "An agreeable manner may set off handsome features, but can never alter plain ones."

Bandit silently applauded the forthright Friskywits. She made up for an impoverished allure with high animal spirits and a spontaneous cogency. At the end of the bough overhanging the pond, Bandit felt like he was held at paw's length, permitted to overhear the girl talk for the singular reason that he was decidedly not part of its subject matter, which was a suitable mate for Sensibella. Besides, he had picked up every disagreeable smell in the world during his quest up the Cross Town Creek to see her.

"Bandy, dear. Pray what is your opinion on the matter?" Sensibel asked.

Bandit choked while his opinion on the matter was driven inward. It was driven so far inward that it lodged at the base of his tail. His opinion was not suited to polite society. It involved a suicidal gesture of embrace that would carry the flighty Sensibel clear off the tree limb and into the bulrushes, her fan still fluttering.

"I think," he said eventually, "that a lady's heart alone must determine the choice, even if it leads to heartbreak."

"Oh, nobly said! But do you intend me to break my heart?"

"It will make you wiser."

"Then I shall break my heart constantly."

"Yes," Frisk said. "Again and again."

"Ahem! *Le coeur a ses raisons, que la raison ne connaît point.* A wise lady makes room also for the reasons of the reason. Found together in the right Proportion in a lady, the reasons of the heart and the reasons of the reason draw forth an inward grace that does the choosing. It naturally chooses the suitable mate. Yet it is Custom that guards the sense of right Proportion."

The young ladies plainly didn't know how to take their mother's declarations. Her pronouncements fell with a triumphant thump, evoking the silence of assent.

"I would not call him *mate* but rather *sleeping partner* since he is with his beloved scarce long enough to serve the function of marriage, then farewell, he is gone," Frisk pointed out.

"Nay, he lingers in the environs as protector of his family's hunting ground and he is present in the moral beauty of his children," Pawsense replied. "That is why when thinking of a *mate* there are considerations."

Sensibella held her peace, regretting with a deep blush that she had implied so much as a vagrant affection. It was Cousin Bandit's fault: he had voiced the forbidden topic of *l'amour libre*. At the moment, he seemed to have been invisibly pushed further out on the limb by Mother's frown. He was going to be pushed right into the pond. Mother didn't correct opinions; instead, she subtly adjusted the boundaries of what could be said and what was better left unsaid. Stay silent then. Here come the Considerations.

"I must take leave to observe that, provided it is selectively controlled, the intended migration to our parish of Raccoonopolitans speaking diverse tongues is much in our favour," Pawsense began. "They will all be wanting homes. It could not be a better time for making a choice of tenants, very responsible tenants. They have liberal notions, and are as likely to make desirable tenants as any set of people one should meet with. And among them will be fine young men, with a great deal of intelligence, spirit, and brilliancy which they will apply to maintaining our hunting woods and marshes."

Pawsense's mood dropped on her daughters like a shroud. Bandit surveyed his cousins. Goodpaws nodded her head sagely at the sagacity of her mother. Frisk, squinting against the bright June sun, watched a solitary ripple make its way under the pollen dust covering the pond. Nimble lost herself in an examination of her tail. And Sensibel – poor Sensibel – had the vacant eyes of a lady whose dream has abruptly ended without the opportunity for her to return to reality. The sisters he had tumbled about with in the early Spring now formed a still-life painting of arrested beauty. They were midsummer lilies on the edge of wilting. Their spirits flourished in the game of imagining a future husband, a pastime that balanced fancy with equal measures of good sense. It now seemed to Bandit that his opinion about educating the heart through heartbreak was immature. Instead it was through this idle conversation between sisters that the heart was educated. He wondered if his own heart was being educated along with theirs. But the education had been crudely brought to earth. Choice of a mate was reduced to a single-minded concern: marriage to a Raccoon of Property or existence as an Old Maid. An Old Maid like Goodpaws, who appeared to be set in this disposition as if by some law of Nature. Bandit decided that her real name was Dullzilla.

"Heigh-ho! We must away and gather Clams. Your Father is visiting at dusk, and I would be quite surprised if he did not bring with him a most intriguing young man."

This attempt to rouse the curiosity of the daughters evoked no fluster of excitement. Instead, the girls silently rose as one out of their languor and began descending the tree.

"Coming, Bandit?"

"No. I'll just sit here a little longer, if that's okay."

"As you wish."

Bandit closed his eyes and felt the midsummer sun on his fur. What a contrast this spacious open vista made with the chimney! And there was a contented ease to this place, unlike the anxiety of the wet night streets where he had been a cub. He could thrive in this paradise. A stream trickled down through the pine trees on the ridge into the bulrushes beneath him, feeding a huge, shallow pond that stretched away surrounded by a mixed hardwood forest on one side and parkland on the other. A tiny island with two cedar trees seemed to be placed in the water for no other reason than to be beautiful. Away at the distant end, the pond drained through another stream into the creek which was the main raccoon pathway across the city. There at the end of the pond, over the stream, was a footbridge, and over the footbridge was something fanciful – an ornate, painted roof that sloped with a pronounced curve and held a line of little gabled window dwellings for birds to fly in and out of. A wonder! A house without walls set over a stream, something he could not give a name to.

But I can. Bandit was gazing at a piece of late nineteenth-century Garden Architecture influenced by the East Asian style which was a fascination for artists at the time. It is called the Pagoda Covered Bridge or alternatively the Gazebo Bridge, and was the apt place for Sensibella and her golden-furred sisters to greet their father, who was himself a pagoda-like figure in his community on the Heights.

Inhaling the fragrances of this setting, Bandit idly considered what he would need to do to become a gentleman of means and mate with one of his cousins. Which one most suited his nature? Goodpaws was out of the question. Entombed in the role of Dutiful Daughter, she inherited her mother's propriety with none of her cunning to the extent that even her sisters found her terrifying. Yet beneath her stolid exterior lay a dormant strength of mind. It would take an intelligent mate to awaken that power to think for herself, perhaps the nearby Squire whom she had generously offered to Sensibel. Thank heaven for Friskywits! Yet Frisk reminded him of Touchwit – the same disruptive prescience – making her too familiar to be desirable. Nimbletoes, on the other hand, was one of the two sisters who was patently exotic. Obviously, she took after her father. Her fingers and toes, like her muzzle, were delicate and slender, and she entertained the family with her singing. But she seemed ephemeral beside the other exotic sister.

What magical spell drew him to Sensibella? Was it her proud, romantic nature? Her elegance of spirit? Her companionable affection? It seemed sister, mother, friend, and playmate cohabited her honest body. And from her proud cheek bones to the tip of her bushy tail her fur had a honey-coloured sheen that spoke of her mixed ancestry. And she was the most huggable wrestler. The scent of her anal glands still remained in his nostrils from the early Spring. Really, he didn't know why he was so drawn to her, but he concluded sadly that Sensibel was destined for a highborn mate while he, Bandit, would be lucky if she let him lick her toes.

"Bandit, love? Are you awake?"

Sensibel! She had returned to the tree. Why ...?

"Press in closer and talk to me."

Bandit opened his eyes and saw his cousin stretched out on her tummy at the beginning of his tree limb. Now that her mother had gone, she was relaxed. Perhaps she wanted to share her relief. He tiptoed toward her along the branch and sat. Not so close as to be a sibling, not so far as to be a suitor. Just a cousin. Since his arrival last night, that relationship had permitted an easy sharing of feelings.

"Mother's not so commanding as she seems. She just wants the best for her children."

"I understand." It was nice not to have to speak polite speech. "But she's a total change from my Mom. She never got in our heads. She just taught us some skills, then kicked us out into the world."

"But that must be so frightening!"

"It's not frightening here."

"I don't think that is so. Our sunny place is subject to the odious pressure of politics. They have turned Mother into an indomitable matchmaker. Tell me, does Aunt Slypaws care about whom you marry?"

"My mother? She doesn't give a flying clam about marriage."

Sensibel giggled. "I thought that being sisters your mother and mine would embrace the selfsame view. How are you going to find a mate?"

"I am going to find a mate by a process of elimination."

"Oh, you are a dangerous one!"

"I don't know why I said that. Really, I have no idea how I am going to find a mate. I have no property or sense of proportion. Would you want *me* as your mate?"

"If you weren't my cousin, you mean?"

"Yes, okay – if I weren't your cousin."

She didn't reply at once. She was thinking the prospect over. Obviously, the idea of being mated to him had never occurred to her.

"You are not without companionable features," she said guardedly. "Good company requires only birth, education, and manners, and with regard to education is not picky. A little learning is by no means a troublesome quality in good company. But birth and good manners are essential."

"Do you really believe that?"

"..."

"You don't believe in good breeding, do you? That's just your Mother speaking. She stuck me at the end of this tree branch because I was born in a chimney."

Sensibel tossed her willow branch into the pond. "Bandit, dear. She put you there because you have fleas."

Bandit hung his ears, head, and tail. It was one thing to be tolerated because he was innocuous; it was another thing entirely to be a physical discomfort. He would never have a place in Sensibel's family tree. He would be merely her decorative admirer, midway between a plaything and a problem.

"But I do adore you. I have thought of you ever since we tussled together ..."

His ears almost jumped off his head. And how his heart leaped!

"Let us be companions in mind. We shall be the most enduring of speech-friends and we will keep each other's secrets forever."

## 15

HALFWAY ACROSS TO THE ISLANDS, she started to belong to the river. She'd never swum any distance before and never alone – just splashed around the shoreline when she was a cub, sifting for crayfish. The water felt fluid then, it slipped away through her fingers; now, it filled her paws with its heft.

When she joined with the river, its people came alive all around her. Water spiders flicked out of reach. A shape drifting by in the night held her in its infrared eye. A solitary Duck. No danger. She paddled on with her nose just breaking the surface. The scents of oats and sugar from the factory on the far side of the river. The Raccoonopolitans her Aunt Pawsense had married into had settled on the Heights to the north, attracted by the honeyed raisin cereal they pillaged from vehicles that belonged to a factory. She had it in her mind introduce herself to her new relatives – but first the islands. They had beckoned her ever since she'd seen them in the autumn drought sitting above the level of the water, with the roots of their trees exposed, and then again in the spring when they were submerged by the flooding. She took her clan-family name from these islands.

Touchwit looked up to check her direction. Hapticia the Moon was floating on a clam shell across the sky, watched by her partner, the Great Raccoon Ancestor. She repeated a rhyme her mother had taught her:

> O Lady Moon, your horns point to the east.
> Wax, be increased.
> O Lady Moon, your horns point to the west.
> Wane, be at rest.

A waxing Moon pointing out her journey. What would befall her? It was exciting to interpret the voices of her senses instead of having their news bundled into sayings by her mother.

Nervous honking. The Geese downriver at the toe of the south island were agitated. What made them alarmed? It couldn't be her. She wasn't in their scent vector and they couldn't see her flattened against the water. The weather then. Geese react to a whisper of change in the weather.

A flap against the water. A fish jumping. Not a danger. The ones that are dangerous are silent and strike from below. Cold-water carnivores with protruding lower jaws that make them look insolent. They eat ducklings. Sometimes they will pull down a full-grown duck. The bird will be bobbing along happily; then, it will cease to exist. Touchwit trembled, and swam faster. The river was warm and she could swim forever, this paddling motion so natural to her, but she felt insecure without a tree close at hand. And the Geese were right. The weather was going to change. She needed to get to the island quickly.

Touchwit chose a Swamp Oak to dry off on because it sent a branch out over the river. Lying on it, she could be in three worlds, the earth and air and water. She settled into the music of her senses.

After touch, which is intimately connected with their thinking, smell is the sense that raccoons trust most. The ears give information about current happenings and bring the other senses to attention. The eyes indicate a creature's attitude and motion. But the nose provides news of settled truths – who has made a home here, who has passed through, and how long ago. Raccoons can construct a mental map of a place by nose alone. Yet with the breeze carrying scents off the island faster than she could analyse them, she began to feel apprehensive. Her adventure, which had started out proudly, was dissolving in mystery. This Island, with its indistinguishable mass of new spring growth and old rotting trees, its tangle of ground vines and variety of berry trees, and its rustlings, scurryings, and scratchings, held a deep meaning. *Withheld* was a better word, because the Island seemed unwilling to offer its meaning to her senses. It felt as if it belonged to some forgotten god who visited rarely. Her hands reached for a shoot of long-stemmed acorns to fashion into a circle.

A branch of Alder leaves was going upriver. How could a branch travel against the current? It looked like it was in a hurry.

Then, an explosive assertion nearby. She knew what *that* was. It was an Owl, a Horned Owl. The call of an owl means someone is going to die. Maybe she should climb higher in this tree. She felt exposed so close to the water – the tree branch going upriver had unnerved her. The island with its distinctions blown away by the wind had become an unknown. It was a concentrated nothingness, a zone where life begins and ends. But raccoons are nightsiders, and darkness gave her an advantage.

It's hard to tell from her story where Touchwit went because she recounted her movements according to the scent map she'd composed from a few certainties. The smell of water lilies tells us that she reached a narrow channel of still water separating the northern from the southern island. This channel, I mentioned earlier, is where the food is. It is an underwater larder for raccoons and other creatures like great blue herons and mink who use the islands as a seasonal fishing camp. But she ate only some elderberries to sharpen her senses. Touchwit was too intent to be hungry. For, out of the density of growth and decay in this mysterious nothingness, one scent stood out. It was the smell of a Raccoon, a senior male, who travelled alone and covered up his tracks with care.

## 16

CLUTCH WAS GLAD to see the boathouse the silly Mouse had pointed him to. He needed the company of his own kind. What had the Mouse said? *You are going to squeeze through a tight space into your future. You have kinsfolk hiding in a boathouse and they haven't eaten for nights and they are hungry. You will become a responsible Raccoon.* The prophesy sounded heavy with fate but he discarded it. The Mouse was trying to sound significant so it could escape its own fate. Of course he was going to meet some kinsfolk! He was in the proximity of the largest raccoon colony in the city. By telling him about the hideaways in the boathouse, the rodent had made the prediction come true, since no self-respecting elder brother and acting family head hearing this information would fail to help clan members in distress. If not for the mention of kin in a boathouse, he wouldn't be here, wondering how to break in without alarming its occupants.

Clutch stood on the boards of a dock still warm from the afternoon sun. He understood the building and its function, though he'd never seen one before. It was exactly what the Mouse had said: a boathouse, a den for boats.

The slap and gurgle of waves under the dock echoed inside the boathouse. There was water inside for the boat to float on. But how to get in? The door had a lock that required a key. The fly screen covered a closed glass window. He sniffed the sides of the structure for the scent of raccoons to determine how they entered and exited. Nothing. Not even a strand of fur.

He'd been tricked! The Mouse had contrived a situation that didn't exist just to obtain its freedom.

Clutch sat in the lee of the wind in a temper, listening to lakewater splash against a closed boathouse door. The south-easterly breeze had shifted around to a stiff west wind making the lake raise its hackles. Water hitting the door the boathouse! Yes! Why not go in the same way the water got in?

Clutch dug his foreclaws into the wood door, swung over, and slowly descended tail first into the lake. This was scary. It was like the time he was suspended between the eavestrough and the cedar tree, kicking at nothing and having a panic attack. In its fear, his body had forgotten how to breathe. Well, he was going to have to forget how to breathe now while he scrambled underwater around the bottom of the door.

He took a deep breath, reached underwater with his foreleg, grasped the bottom of the door, swung himself around under it, and popped up beside a boat. There! That was easy. No existential crisis. On the contrary, he was quite proud of his ingenuity. He clambered onto an inside dock and sniffed the darkness. Fresh pine-wood. Varnish. An empty container for fish. Canvas. Gasoline.

*"If you're an Otter or a Weasel, we'll rip your ears off!"*

The voice came from overhead. Two arched shapes. They were hiding in the rafters.

"I am not an otter nor a weasel. I am Elder Brother of the Island Family of the River Clan, and I have come to help you."

*"Go away. Find your own hiding place, which is the Custom."*

Scents of a young male, a season older than himself, with a female, not fertile, probably his sister. They were hiding just as the Mouse had said. Who were they hiding from? The Creek Town raccoons had all fled and were taking refuge in holes everywhere. The Gander was right – but why? There could only be one threat they were hiding from. His father.

"I am a Raccoon who is unwilling to fight on principle. That should assure you that I can do you no harm."

*"You can do us no good either. If you're unwilling to fight, you're unable to help us."*

Well, that was logical. He was negotiating with reasonable raccoons. If he could only persuade them to relax.

"This is a clever hiding place. None of your scent reaches the outside, and if you go outside to forage, none of your scent returns with you, since it is lost when you put your body in the water."

The female broke her silence. *"That is most true. And moreover we are protected by a barricade of geese. The raccoons that have gone rogue dare not meddle with them, and if they do, we'll hear of it and have sufficient time to be out of here."*

Clutch noted the modest pride in her choice of the sanctuary.

The brother added: *"Nevertheless, we have been unwilling to venture out of this shelter. And we haven't eaten."*

*"For nights,"* his sister said.

*"And now we are too weak to go out or even dive down and sift the lake bottom beneath this housing."*

It was a dire situation when a male raccoon confessed his weakness to a stranger. "I pray you, come down and show yourselves so we can talk about food," Clutch said.

First the brother, then the sister, left the rafters. They were covered in cobwebs, but they squatted proudly on the dock and made their introductions.

"I am Lightfinger of the Clan Family at Creek Town, and you ought to tell us the purpose of your travelling before we think of giving you refuge here."

"I am Sleekfoot, her brother, of the selfsame family. What happened to yours?"

"We have left home to seek our own dens."

"And have you found one?"

The question approached rudeness. No raccoon asks another about their den. Still, these were perilous times, and Clutch considered that the question was innocent. In nights to come, the Clan might have to bend etiquette and talk about sharing accommodations. "I have not begun to look," he said.

"You won't find a den if you run for three nights," Lightfinger said. "There is a scarcity of homes in which to raise a family. They are all taken by fleeing raccoons. Who knows what's left for us to live in? We may even have to live in a chimney."

"How can there not be dens? There are cavities in trees, openings beneath porches, holes in attics, hollow logs in the forest. Not to mention the city across the River."

"The rogue males track us down and nullify our hiding places one by one. That is why there is a shortage of homes."

"And most of the places in the city are possessed by newcomers," Sleekfoot said.

Clutch listened carefully because he felt some responsibility to the situation. It was a pitiful state of affairs. It meant that all the raccoons on the River would have to become migrants themselves. They'd have to travel for three nights or longer, then claw out a hunting ground from a foreign tribe. This was easy for people like his aunt's in-laws to do. Raccoonopolitans had tight kinship bonds and were closely organized. The raccoons of Creek Town were uprooted and scattered. And what of his sister Touchwit? And Bandit, his brother? Where would they find homes? They might have to run beyond the horizon to find a home, and never come back. "Who are these rogue males?" he asked.

It was for Sleekfoot to explain the situation: "They are the alpha males from the once mighty Creek Town families. The Clan Fathers. They have put their trust in the Raccoon Without a Name. He gives them license to plunder while they guard the boundaries of his expanding territory. Normally, they would be restrained from this impulse by the bonds of kinship. But kinship is gone. So they behave like unleashed Droolers, roaming around in packs with one mind only, and that mind is without the power to reason."

"Except to declare that everything is open for plunder," Lightfinger said. "And plunder goes to the strongest. The weak and ordinary folk must scramble for a den, a hunting ground, and a future."

"They will be lucky if they even find a companion," Sleekfoot said.

"A hunting ground," Clutch said. "Let us address this issue first. You are hungry, and there are chickens in the backyard of a house upwind from here."

"We're not going out there," Sleekfoot said.

"The Lake is throwing itself at the door," Lightfinger said.

"Consider," Clutch said. "The street is nearby; it runs across the top of the lake, from the canal west to the River. The geese will guard our east flank. The weather may be our friend too, because it is changing. It feels like it may swing around to the north. That means we can't be threatened from that direction and not know of it. Not even a rogue alpha male is fool enough to run down the wind.

As for the west, that is my family's territory and it is free of other raccoon traffic."

"Have you ever done this before? Killed a chicken?"

"No."

"Neither have we. We are fish-eaters from Creek Town."

"I expect catching a chicken is not something one raccoon can do very well," Clutch said. "I am told to be wary of the Rooster, if there is one present. He will die to protect his wives. Lucky, there are three of us. One can contain the Rooster."

"What if there's a Drooler to guard them?"

"Well, then, that is a different problem. We'll have to improvise. We're good at that. We're Raccoons."

"I don't know ..." Sleekfoot said.

"You figured out how to get under a closed door that sticks down underwater. You can do anything."

That persuaded them. They resolved to carry out the raid the following night when the weather changed.

## 17

NIMBLE BURST THROUGH the raccoon-shaped hole in the fly screen, trembling with excitement.

"Did you see them? Are they coming?" Goodpaws asked.

Nimble nodded her head, smiling shyly. Too much to say. It would tumble out of her all disorganized.

Sensibella, reclining on the middle of the floorboards, showed no interest whatsoever. Aunt Pawsense was brushing out her daughter's tail for the occasion. To Bandit, the labour had the endlessness of ritual. In fact, each and every detail of the morning had been fussed over and commented on as if the day was made up of Significant Moments within a frame titled *The Courtship: Their First Meeting*. Was his cousin's tail not already fluffed out to its utmost? It seemed to fill the room, as it would doubtless fill the eyes of her approaching suitor. But perhaps even this attention to a feature of his cousin's beauty wasn't directly related to her wooing. It was just another manufactured memory: *The Preparation of the Tail*.

"Well?" Pawsense said.

"The tail is beautiful, Mama."

"No, Nimbletoes. I mean, what have you got to report?"

"He is to die for! So silent and composed, like our Father's people. And he ambles most correctly yet casually one half body length behind Papa, so deferent and inured to Custom is he!"

"Immense!"

It was impossible to tell if cousin Frisk's punctuations were genuine, perfunctory, or deeply ironic. Frisk sure was a puzzle. He was starting to like her.

"Where are they now? We have scarcely time to make Bel's tail luxuriant."

"They have come up from the road for Primate vehicles, and are processing in stately measure toward the pretty decorated roof set over the stream."

"We shall proceed thence ourselves," Pawsense said. "You, Nimbletoes, shall walk first as befits an emissary. Then Goodpaws – Goodpaws, where are you?"

"I am here, Mama."

"You will walk next, as Senior Sister. Then I shall come behind you with Sensibella. Frisk and Bandit shall bring up the rear. Friskywits?"

"Yes."

"Try not to say anything. If you must speak and you can't think of anything appropriate to say, you may mention the weather."

"I shall do just that, Mama."

Pawsense sniffed the air. "I fear the weather is going to do something crude."

The daughters trooped outdoors to take their places in the procession. Bandit stood behind Sensibella's great tail. He wondered if he was supposed to walk upright and carry it above the fallen bulrushes so that it wouldn't become soiled. He felt a suppressed fit of giggling starting up in Frisk. The whole affair was ridiculous. Sensibel wasn't feigning indifference in order to provoke a more earnest courtship. She didn't want to be courted at all.

"They have reached the stream-house without walls."

This was where the courtier would set eyes and nose on the courted one. Then, after greetings and light talk, they would come around to the wilderness side of the pond, to a derelict doll's house of a cottage by the water, where Pawsense's family lived. Its large windows had fly screens instead of glass because it was built by the original owners for the nights when the main cottage on the ridge above it became too hot – there's nothing hotter than a summer cottage during a heatwave – and they could sleep close to the breezes off the pond. Sometimes the parents told their children that they needed to be near the pond even on a cool night. The original cottage up on the ridge had been torn down and replaced by a modern weatherproofed building, half cottage, half suburban mansion. Its present family members must have kept the doll's house to honour their progenitors.

"*Festina lente*. Make haste slowly," Pawsense announced. "The better for Sensibel to be admired from afar."

Bandit sensed a slow-motion disaster in progress. *The Arrival of the Intended Bride*. For the Intended Bride had no desire to assume the role that had been assigned to her at birth. Her heart was fixed on a romantic stranger whose virtues she had extolled to her sisters in the tree. But Bandit knew even this romantic infatuation was unreal. It had the quality of desperate whimsy. It served no other purpose than to help Sensibel imagine the idea of an existence beyond the control of her mother. In the meantime, whimsy gave her an excuse to dally with the Raccoonopolitan lord. She would dally with him so assiduously that his ardour would flame out and he would lose interest. Deep down, he knew, Sensibella's feelings were not for aristocrats or tall dark strangers, whether sighted from afar or presented to her gift-wrapped. Her heart was set on him, Bandit, and was all the more romantic because her heart's affections could never come true. The joining of cousins was forbidden.

* * *

Nimble hadn't said that a whole retinue of dancers had come with the party, complete with bodyguards. They weren't important to her imagination, so she left them out of her report which was already breathless. Yet the matter of appropriate theatre for the occasion was clearly a concern to Smartwhisker, husband of Aunt Pawsense, who conveyed the marriage proposal visibly in the form of a Raccoonopolis lord. Who could refuse this shyly grinning young man? Who could turn tail on this portrait of physical and social prowess?

Sensibel could.

Bandit noticed that her tail began to droop at the sight of her intended fiancé. Her gait became unsure. She looked desperately over her shoulder for him. Her eyes met his just long enough to transmit a message. *Get me out of here.* His eyes answered: *Play the game. An opportunity will present itself.* Frisk, walking beside him, licked his ear mischievously. She understood.

In contrast, Nimble at the front of the procession seemed ready to fling herself on the Intended. Even the stolid and ungainly Goodpaws, caught up in the spirit of the joining, appeared to float along the path through the bulrushes. And Aunt Pawsense had acquired a further rotundity, as if inflated by the pear-shaped utterances she was about to deliver.

Bandit watched with the bemusement of one placed on the sidelines. As first cousin, he ought to have been accorded the role of close family relative, but even this status was denied him. He had fleas and his family wasn't respectable. He lacked good breeding and property. Bandit considered that his want of a background that would propel him into a secure future might actually be the reason Sensibel was attracted to him. He was the romantic opposite of the perfect hereafter that was now being staged for her.

Staged? Absolutely. The delegation had formed into a half circle on the path at the pagoda. The dancing girls shifted their weight from one side to the other and exchanged knowing glances. Across from them stood the bodyguard – a line of sleek-coated family sons, presumably brothers and cousins of the Intended. There was no way this urban family – no, this clan, was going to be forced off its new hunting ground. At the middle of the semi-circle, the young lord acted his role according to the script. He was one of those ideal people who always know the right thing to do, not because they are especially moral but because they can't imagine an alternative to the obvious and proper. Yet his importance was overshadowed by the personality of Smartwhisker. Hearty and expansive, the tribal father filled the space with benevolence. The sight of his four daughters made him even more benevolent. And the sight of his wife brought his benevolence to a boil. She was the most sensible of Raccoons, with her unquestionable pedigree: Pawsense of the River Clan Family at the Pond Marsh, said to be related in some obscure way to the Raccoon with No Name who was lord of Creek Town and the Lower River. That was why her pedigree was irreproachable.

What would become of Sensibella in this hypocrisy? Would her husband grow up to be a version of Smartwhisker, possessing the social ease of a Raccoon of Property? Would she turn into a portly matriarch like her mother, arranging opportune marriages for her multiple children? Sensibel, who had tussled with him all afternoon in the new Spring bulrushes, free as a girl can be in the daylight, completely without inhibition. He affectionately touched the place where she had playfully bitten him on the flank.

The daughters of Pawsense formed a line. Bandit stood at one end, where it met the teenage dancers. They automatically began throwing poses at him. He looked away. Sensibel had been like them once. Now, she had the frozen mask of a sacrificial victim. What was she thinking? This marriage arrangement marked the end of her girlhood, unless she found a way out of it. But what if for some reason she found the Twit attractive? What if she decided to lose one freedom, the freedom to be young and undecided, for another, the freedom to be secure? Bandit was beginning to understand that freedom is relative to the situation you are in.

*The Greeting of the Bridal Party.* Goodpaws, as first-born daughter, was presented first to her father.

"Goody. I hear you have your bonnet set for Squire Hairball. Decent man. Nothing wrong with him 'cept his name. Marry him at once, I say."

Goodpaws blushed and finished her curtsey.

"Ah, dear Sensibella. You're not just beautiful, you're a work of art. Marry you myself, if I could. I'd marry you just for your tail. Heh! Heh! And here's Friskywits. What have you got to say for yourself?"

"I fear the weather is going to do something crude."

"Why, so it is! So it is! Weather is always changing. Yes, that's what weather does. Now you – please forgive me. I have quite forgot your name." Smartwhisker tapped his skull to dislodge the missing name from where it had become stuck.

"I am Nimbletoes, Papa."

"Nimbletoes. Never heard of you! No matter. The more the merrier. Everybody, I introduce Lord Padmind, first in line to succeed to the headship of the families on the Heights."

Four curtseys exactly synchronized.

Bandit watched the colours of the sunset passing over the fur of his cousins. The hazy yellow evening had produced a memorable sunset, and the sisters reflected its changing hues of orange, and pink, and purple. The same hues provided a dramatic backdrop to the personage of Smartwhisker. It seemed he had brought the sunset with him. A blue dragonfly alighted on Sensibel's tail. The high-toned voice of Aunt Pawsense penetrated his reverie:

"*I would rather have young people settle down on a small property at once, and have to struggle with a few difficulties together, than be involved in a long engagement ...*"

"Begad!" Smartwhisker said, interrupting her speech. "A long engagement is regrettable. It is all very well for young people to be engaged, if there is a certainty of their being able to marry within a season. In any case, there will be no difficulties for these two to struggle with, I assure you."

"*A woman of good fortune is always respectable,*" Pawsense said. "*A very narrow income has a tendency to contract the mind and sour the temper. Those who live perforce in a very small, and generally very inferior society, may well be illiberal and cross.*"

Funny, Bandit thought. Smartwhisker and Pawsense were braying like tribal heads facing each other formally, even while they were husband and wife standing close enough to each other to be intimate. He guessed their speeches were meant to be overheard by the young.

"*An uncertain engagement,*" Pawsense said, "*an engagement that may be too long. Imagine! To begin without knowing that at such a time there will be the means of marrying. I hold such an arrangement to be very unsafe and unwise, and something, I think, all parents should prevent as far as they can.*"

The sunset looked like it wanted to break into pieces at the hypocrisy! It was as if witnessing this absurd union of two raccoons, it couldn't stand it anymore and was about to fold itself up and go somewhere else to grace another betrothal. Its colours twisted and darkened. Bandit felt a change in air pressure. The dancing girls looked apprehensively at the sky. And then, the earth lifted and dropped. Abruptly, the wind shifted to the north, whipping the tops of the bulrushes. Behind it would come a pelting rain. The marriage party huddled together seeking a new script for the circumstance. Smartwhisker pulled his wife to his chest and frowned in all directions. Goodpaws began taking charge of her sisters, persuading them to bunch together, heads down, in a measured retreat to the house when the sky relieved itself like an angry bladder and the surface of the pond shot upwards in fountains.

Bandit, standing alone in the downpour, was considering what to do when another raccoon blew into him. The raccoon held him tight, buried her face in his mane, and whispered. *"Now's our chance! Run with me!"*

# 18

THE STRANGER HAD SWUM in a determined way from the other side of the channel and then continued up her northern island. His scent trail wound through chance openings in the thicket, not following a communal path, the choices made by a solitary individual who wasn't leaving his fur on branches. Yet he was a long, tall Raccoon. It was a wonder he had got through here at all. The centre of the island was a maze of trees and bushes and saplings and vines and mosses and grass, whose seeds had floated downriver or been deposited in the feces of birds. A compost heap which had taken on a life of its own, based on random contradictions that had settled over time into collaborations.

Here the traveller had been careless and left a strand of his top fur on the spike of a hawthorn. Touchwit tried to discover what she could. She held it to her nose, then rolled it around in her fingers to feel its texture. Not River Clan – there were no molluscs in this one's diet. And not the newly arrived Raccoonopolitans her aunt had married into either, who liked spicy Primate food. A stranger coming over to fish, having arrived on the Islands randomly like the trees and bushes? A loner. Whoever he was, he was the only raccoon on the island besides herself. His scent was as fresh as this morning.

Touchwit nosed north through a puzzle of bushes. Here he had left some scat. No, not "left." He had scraped away the loamy soil to make a hole, used the latrine, then replaced the soil, patting it down with his paws. What raccoon buries his scat? And why? This one wanted to go unnoticed. Was he an outlaw?

Touchwit sniffed his trail northward. One creature the island certainly was a home for was mice. Their paths crisscrossed openly with a disregard for predators, most of which couldn't reach the island over water. The mice fed on tall-bush cranberries, and black hawthorn berries, and grain that had floated down from the factory, creating patches of long prairie grass.

She came out of the thicket suddenly at the water's edge at the top of the island. He had lingered here to scratch off some burrs that were caught in his fur. He had relaxed for a moment. His trail now led to the right along the shoreline until it came to a heap of branches and mud partly submerged in the water. An organized pile. Somebody had built a home. The stranger's trail led to the top of the immense covered nest and paused at a hole where he had sniffed. She did the same. Scents of alder, birch, and aspen. And a dark, pungent body oil that made her sneeze.

"*You there! Get off my roof!*"

Her sneeze had wakened the occupant. "My apologies." Mom hadn't told her about this animal in her Outdoor Ed class – probably because he was of no account. Imagine! A vegetarian who eats trees! She tugged gently at the end of a stick jutting out of the lodge, so she could understand the inhabitant. Giant incisors had made those cut marks. This island was a sanctuary for Rodents big and small.

"*Replace that element exactly where it was.*"

"Sorry!"

"*This is my Making. Every stick holds up every other stick in the Work – though I don't expect you to understand this principle. It is called Beauty.*"

"But I *do* understand. I, too, am a Maker. I did not see your den was a Making. I thought it was just a dwelling."

"*All Makings are Dwellings, if they are well-made. They are things to dwell in. Now go off and make your own dwelling place.*"

"Thank you for your wisdom."

She picked up the stranger's scent on the other side of the stick house. He had looped diplomatically around the Beaver's home and returned on his own scent trail to the northerly point, then gone down the shoreline facing west. This one was clever! She found the western shoreline easier to traverse than the interior thicket, but she had to climb over a tree that had tipped over in a storm, leaving its naked roots facing the west winds. Her loner seemed as purpose-bound as earlier, but she could not glean what that purpose was. She knew only that he was far away from his clan, that he was compelled by some inner necessity, and that he was at peace with himself.

And then she lost his scent. It was as if her realization about him had made his track vanish. She pushed further along the riverbank in the direction he had been headed, then made a circle through the forest back to where his scent ended. He hadn't veered into the interior of the island: it was low-lying ground intersected by inlets of water, intriguing for its food possibilities but unpleasant to traverse. She stood in a bracken of ferns wondering where he had disappeared to. Dawn would be coming soon. She could gain some perspective in the morning light. But first she should find a shelter to spend the day and wash the mud from her paws.

Touchwit looked around for a big tree where she could curl up out of the wind. This would do. A Tamarack that had rooted deep in the soil and survived countless storms. She climbed up to the lap of the tree where the great lower branches divided. Humans, using the word "climb," think of guided, decisive movements with pauses inbetween. Raccoons simply walk up a tree evenly. Touchwit walked up, then froze. Someone was already in her chosen shelter!

She sniffed. Nothing. She listened for the sound of its breathing. None. The person, whoever it was, wasn't breathing. She edged closer. The shape had a nose, it had eyes, and those protuberances at the top were ears. But there was nothing in between. Nothing. The wind blew through empty spaces where the skin and flesh of the head should be. Should she get closer?

What decided her was the smell of him on the nearby bark. The Stranger had climbed this tree earlier. She immediately checked its upper branches for him. No, not there. But examining the bark she saw evidence of his claws, his large claws. So he had gone up this tree recently, and if he had tolerated that non-breathing head, then it would be safe for her to examine it.

When she got closer, the spirit thing revealed its shape to her. It was the head of a raccoon. And when she touched the places where saplings had been woven together to form a jaw, with tiny snails shells sunk into the wood in a row so as to resemble teeth, she felt the Stranger's hands all over it. And how cunning his hands were, to tie these strands of birch bark into knots. She created pretty makings out of vines she intertwisted, but the Loner made intricate knots – knots of three different kinds, depending on the required force exerted on the joins.

But what was this Raccoon Head for? If it was a Making to dwell in, its dweller was the spirit of a raccoon with a very firm mission. It stared west toward the city. She wouldn't know until the full morning light what alerted it, what caused its ears to stand up, and its powerful eyes, represented by two silver clamshells, to see so far.

Was the effigy meant to be a Watcher? Did it stand guard over the island, scaring away other raccoons who wanted to settle here? Did it assert the Stranger's ownership of his hunting ground? If he owned this insular compost heap, he was hardly a gentleman who cared to have property. But then it occurred to her that the representation wasn't a deed of title. Like all the little forms she wove with her restless hands and left on the ground, this watchful Somebody was made just for the delight of making it. Getting the space just right between the rounded ears represented by fungi, burnishing the nose, which was a tree root with the soil meticulously rubbed off it. All the right Proportions. The Head was a Making composed out of the life of the island. It was as if the spirit of the place had risen from the twigs and soil and vines where it slept, and thought itself into a Raccoon. *I exist*, it said. And by fashioning this raccoon form, the maker of the form could also say *I exist*. Even though he covered all traces of himself, all identifying markers that could say anything further about him than just *I exist*.

With that perception, it became clear to her that she had lost his scent at the place where he had left the island and swum west. The Head gazed forlornly in his direction. She sat in the lap of the tree, looking into the night where her Stranger had gone.

# 19

THREE RACCOONS analysed the problem presented by a chicken coop. Having approached it cautiously from downwind, they lay under a hedge ringing the backyard, listening to the wind gusting through the poplars beside the canal. There was no drooler tied up outdoors, but a scent indicated one was in the house, which meant they would have to take a chicken and get out quickly. The wind held no news of threats.

"We've been told that lights may suddenly come on outside a house during a raid," Sleekfoot said. "Then a Primate will charge out with a bat."

"Not to mention a drooler," Lightfinger said.

"We could circle and attack from the north," Clutch said.

"Our scent would announce us."

"But we would be less visible and wouldn't provoke the lights."

"Perhaps the lights won't notice us if we attack from here," Lightfinger said.

Clutch didn't pursue the question. Really, he wasn't all that good at tactics. Better at strategy. "Why don't we think through the attack backwards? Which of us does what in the action? What is our escape route? Wouldn't those questions help decide our approach?"

"Worth a try," Sleekfoot said. "The main problem is that we face a hot-tempered rooster who can make one of us lose an eye. He'll jump up, whip his legs forward, and rip outwards with his spurs." The older male raccoon was assuming command of the raid.

"That does present a certain complexity," Clutch said.

Brother and sister waited for the elaboration promised by this knowing remark. There was no elaboration. Clutch had no idea how to decommission a rooster.

"Two of us have to distract the rooster. The third one grabs a chicken," Lightfinger said, barging through Clutch's indecisiveness.

"Then what?" he asked.

"Drag the hen into the woods."

Clutch felt a weakening in his knees. Perhaps the other raccoons were being unnecessarily grotesque. Carnivore though he was, he had never killed a creature bigger than a clam. Instead, he had eaten Delissio pizza. Why couldn't it be organic waste pick-up tonight?

"Can't we just scarf an egg?" he said.

"We've come all this way dripping wet just to split an egg?" Clutch heard the note of impatience in Lightfoot's reproach. He hung his muzzle on the verge of the grass lawn. How was he going to back out of this situation? It was his idea, which he had proposed with some bravado, to raid the chicken coop. The three of them would each need to accomplish their precise task in the killing, otherwise the plan wouldn't work. Plan? What plan? They'd been lying here for a dangerously long interval figuring out what to do. And it was his indecisiveness, his anxious need to ponder all the angles beforehand, that was delaying the action.

"You and Light can get in the hutch and corner a hen," Sleekfoot said. "The trick is to get your fangs well into her neck until she submits. I'll take the rooster." Sleekfoot sounded like he was prepared to lose an eye.

Silence from Lightfinger. She was waiting for Clutch to agree. He felt like a useless third party. "Agreed," he said weakly. In fact, every cell in his body disagreed.

"Agreed," said Lightfinger, brightly.

"It'll be easy," Sleekfoot declared confidently. "The hens will be inside the hutch on roosts. Roosts are like tree branches. Some may be hunched up in nesting boxes. They'll all be sleeping. They'll be useless when they wake up. They can't see in the dark."

The raiding party left the safety of the hedge and moved like spirits: Lightfinger – she was good at locks; then Sleekfoot – he would distract the rooster; then Clutch. The coop was a small yard of scratched-up dirt enclosed by chicken wire. Inside stood the hutch, elevated above the ground on stilts, where the hens were locked up for the night so they could sleep in safety. Through the gate into the coop now. It smelled like there were lots of chickens, and it would be easy in the contained space of the hutch to catch one.

The rooster was wide-awake and ready to die when Lightfinger slipped the latch. Clutch saw it leap in the air and come down on

Sleekfoot's head with its legs clawing and wings beating before it forced him out into the backyard.

"This way," Lightfinger said. "Don't worry about Sleek – he'll be okay."

They forgot to close the door after they went in.

Chaos inside the warm, pungent darkness of the hutch. Hens shrieking, and he and Lightfinger got their signals crossed among the darting targets, and they chose separate prey. Clutch's left behind a mouthful of feathers before it shot out the door. Lightfinger boxed her target into a corner. But Clutch wasn't there beside her to cut off its escape, and the hen leapt over her and outside into the coop. He was funneled outside in a swarm of frantic hens.

Then the wind banked suddenly and brought a downpour.

Back out in the yard, hens raced in circles in the rain. Too many targets, all in motion. Clutch felt paralyzed by indecision. All around him was a panic attack made visible. Sleek had the rooster by the throat but he had lost his belly fur and couldn't keep his body behind the twisting bird. Should he go and help Sleekfoot? He'd have to force himself on the rooster and take damage.

Now, Lightfinger had trapped a hen in a corner. Help her finish. Clutch ran across the mud. He realized he was limping. A hen had done something to his leg in the whirlwind stampede out of the coop. Check Sleek first? He was in a death-struggle with the rooster. Leave him to sort it out. He had to work with Lightfinger; that was his role in the plan. The lights in the yard came on. And a burglar alarm.

The rooster got him just before he reached Lightfinger. It landed on top of him and began raking his spine. Sleek couldn't reach him: he had lost part of his mask. He was bleeding from an eye socket and seemed dazed. Clutch rolled onto his back like he did when he wrestled with his brother and sister. Now he had four lethal paws extended. This rooster wanted to die!

Behind him, he heard the war cry of the River Clan. Lightfinger had taken her first chicken. Then two new shapes slipped through the brightly lit rain, and everything changed.

\* \* \*

Clutch, halfway up the closest poplar tree, licking his wounds to stop his heart from racing, tried to put it all together afterwards. Two Clan Fathers from Creek Town. They'd been crouched all this time out of the wind at the eastern edge of the back lot, preparing their attack. When they saw three juvenile raccoons go in first, they held back until everyone was engaged. Then they came in low to the ground and picked up the pieces. First, they dispatched the rooster. Clutch was astonished at how efficiently they killed – they operated so indifferently that they barely gave him a glance afterwards as he lay in the mud. After that, they took the exhausted hen from Lightfinger. They took the bird in their mouths and fled just as the back door of the house opened.

The last thing he saw before the dog got him was Lightfinger leading her brother away, his face covered with blood. They wouldn't get far before the alpha males finished their meal and came back for them.

Clutch had no training in fighting dogs. His instincts were to raise his hackles, pull his haunches in, and go through the ritual preparatory to a fight, which was mostly issuing well-known taunts, curses, and dares that went back to antiquity. But droolers didn't fight by the rules: they were like roosters; they simply charged at their adversary without thinking, and before he knew it the dog's jaws had closed on his hind leg, his left leg, around the moveable joint. The growling mass was shaking him, trying to overpower him with might and terror. But Clutch fought back. For the first time in his life, he fought and he knew as he buried his jaw in the drooler's throat that he would have many more fights in his life but no fight would be as glorious as this one. His blood raced. For once, his mind became clear and simple. It held only one idea – Triumph. Then the drooler released his leg to get a better advantage, and Clutch gave him none. Its growls turned to frightened yelps – the cries of the defeated. The door of the house opened. Clutch spat the blood out of his mouth and limped away in the rain, dragging his leg behind him.

## 20

" **F**OLLOW MY TAIL," Sensibella said.

She was leading him up the tiny stream, quickly becoming a torrent in the downpour. The water would carry away their scents. His cousin had suddenly changed from a sacrificial victim to a determined survivor. He had to hand it to her. She really knew how to disappear.

The terrain ascended suddenly and he was in a cool, dark forest with cold stream water racing around his legs. He felt the exhilaration of escape, and he was alone for the first time with Sensibel, and they were having an adventure. What could this lead to? Never mind. It was fun just being around her with her elegant hind feet kicking spray in his eyes. The night was creepy, the weather had gone crazy, and they were the only raccoons at the party who were having fun. Behind them, the Betrothal Ceremony lay in ruins.

They emerged from the woods onto an open lawn. The stream now became an ornamental feature in a setting for a large modern house and a garage with three doors. Bandit paused to analyse the scents. Fresh-cut grass, a pebbled driveway, a sandbox for children, fresh baked bread, a big family of Primates. It occurred to him that this property was the counterpart to the security Aunt Pawsense wanted, and it was fitting that she'd made her home nearby. There were no obvious dangers. "No pets, no threats" – to quote one of his mother's sayings. The rain stung his ears. Where was Sensibel taking him? Please, somewhere warm and dry.

"We are going to our sisters' hideout where we gossip and tell silly stories," she said, as if reading his mind.

A secret den kept by cubs! He'd never heard of such a thing. "Won't they tell your Ma we're there?"

"Goody Two Paws won't, because she hasn't a clue where it is and doesn't want to know. Nim won't, if she values her ears and her tail. I'm not sure about Frisk. No one is ever sure about Frisk. She'll probably find us – she loves intrigues."

Intrigues, she calls it. This isn't an intrigue. It's a family mutiny. What's the punishment for disobeying one's parents? For surely they would be caught once the bodyguard was organized into hunting parties. The searchers would pick up their trails where they left the stream.

Overhead, a half Moon broke through scudding clouds. The lawn danced with half-crazed shadows.

But they weren't leaving the stream. Sensibel was tiptoeing through the water to where the stream widened near the house to form a decorative pool. She lifted her nose in the air, looked left and right, then lolloped across a stone patio that formed the outside of the pool. She headed towards an eavestrough downspout gurgling on the side of the house. Brilliant! The downpour would wash away their scents.

Bandit began to regard his first cousin with awe.

Up the spout then. And onto the roof. Was she really going to leap into that chestnut tree? She glanced back, grinned wickedly, and flung herself into space. The tree caught her, and she disappeared at once into its foliage.

That looks easy. But his cousins were such athletes. He'd never made a jump like this before.

Bandit felt the leafy branch rock under him as he landed with his eyes closed. Soon he was curled up beside Bella in a hole in the tree. Outside, the sky was preparing another squall; inside, it was snug. He'd never been this close to her, not since they'd wrestled together as cubs.

"We'll rest here until dawn," Sensibel said. "Then we'll run forever."

"Where?"

"As far away from this boring existence as my tiny feet can carry me."

"I don't know, Bel ..."

"What don't you know? Please take your nose off my tail."

"I don't know that it's a good idea."

Bandit heard the beginning of a growl.

"Let me explain," he said. "You've been living in a nice, soft place. Good hunting ground. All the clams you can eat and a cornfield nearby. Security provided by your Dad. I don't think you know what it's really like out there."

"What's it really like out there?"

"It's like … I don't know, it's like climbing a tree and every second branch is designed to break under your paw. Like eating food that doesn't taste what it smells like. Like meeting a friend and they suddenly bite you for no reason. As soon as you go out the door of your den, you're in a world of trickery and deceit."

"I love trickery and deceit."

Should he go on and describe the world in more detail to her? Describing it felt good – like he was a street-smart protector. She had nowhere to go, no safe place in the world to sleep. He would provide her with security. But he had no idea where to look for it. In fact, he wasn't able to think outside of the comfort of a den himself. He never intended to go to the Back of the North Wind; he planned to come straight to Sensibel in her paradise of bulrushes. Talk about deceit in the world! Without even venturing into that distrustful realm, he had deceived himself.

"We could swim downriver and seek out a life in the city," he said.

"Let's snuggle, then talk about it later." Saying this, Sensibel immediately fell asleep.

Unable to sleep, Bandit listened for a quaver in the flow of the outside news that would justify alarming her. Only the north wind whistling through the chestnut leaves. He began to feel dozy.

A crash! Someone had fallen out of the sky! Sensibel shot to her feet. Scrambling, then …

"I knew you'd be here!" Frisk squeezed in through the hole and touched noses with her sister. "Isn't this exciting? They're searching for you in the bulrushes and even down where the pond drains into the Crosstown Stream. And all the time you're up here in our hideout – with your First Cousin, no less. Hi, Bandit! I knew you two were planning to elope."

"We are not planning to elope. I intend to go out and make a world for myself."

Frisk checked Bandit's face for affirmation of this bizarre desire. No expression behind his implacable mask.

"I think you should go to the city," Frisk said. "It's a free community and you meet people easily. You can live alone and not be regarded as an Old Maid and you don't have to mate. People respect you as an individual, or so I'm told."

"Come with me, Frisk. We can live together and go out on dates and talk about them afterward."

Bandit felt his heart sink. Being with Sensibel certainly was an experience. It was like walking along one of those heavy wires that buzz under your feet. Such a high! Any second, you'd miss your footing, and you'd be traversing the wire upside down, all your weight pulling at your shoulder muscles.

"I can't go to the city," Frisk said. "Not right away. Maybe I can join you later. If Mama loses *two* of her children, she'll turn the world upside-down and shake it till we tumble out. One lost child is okay because she can think of someone else to blame for it besides herself."

"She has no one to blame but herself," Sensibel said.

Bandit had no trouble identifying who the blameworthy party was in Aunt Pawsense's mind. It was him. He wondered if he felt guilty about abducting her daughter. No – she had abducted herself. "I think it might be a good idea to go back to your mother in the morning and explain your feelings to her. You might appear at least to be an unreliable bride. That would get the burden of marrying the Tosh off your back."

Sensibella was examining him in the dark. He felt her withering contempt.

"Because, if you go to the city," he said quickly, "your Mother will decide that you have left her family for good. You'll be the most desolate thing in the world. A raccoon without a clan."

"You don't seem all that desolate," she said.

He looked to Frisk for support. The energy had drained away in Sensibella before his eyes. He had called her dream into doubt and substituted tactical deceit in its place. The romance adventure was over. He had just ended it by being realistic. He was only trying to be practical for her sake, but he had questioned her outlook, her romantic dream of escape. Her dream was gone. Maybe not gone, but retracted into her interior. And with her sense of enchantment in doubt, she had no means of imagining her own freedom. Bandit felt a sourness in his mouth. It was in his gut. It was coming out on his breath. He had betrayed Sensibel. Betrayed the wild hope to which all her beauty was tied.

"I shall sleep on it," Sensibel mumbled.

Frisk touched noses with her sister, then squeezed out the hole without speaking. Everyone understood the situation. He tried to put it in its best light. He had done some good. He had saved Sensibel from headlong flight. Maybe a crisis had been averted, or at least postponed. It had been a long day. They could discuss things in the morning.

Bandit listened in his sleep to the pattering of rain on the chestnut leaves.

Dawn brought a clear, purposeful day. He stretched out, feeling for Sensibel's body beside him. Nothing. He felt suddenly, starkly alone.

Sensibel had gone.

## 21

D URING A RESTLESS NIGHT, Touchwit wove a mental map of the island from the sounds that came to her in her sleep. When she awakened fully, she knew the location of every significant person. She discarded the background noise of the city – the subdued roar of vehicles, the rhythmic clanging of the factory, the train that rumbled over the bridge and on into the countryside, making lonely calls to other trains that went unanswered. These sounds had been the constants of her childhood. In contrast to that busy world, the island was a place of repose, its few sounds clear and distinct. The splash beside the riverbank during the night. A Muskrat. The Owl flying out and back to a tree on this side of the channel dividing the north and south islands. The nightlong scurrying of Mice. On the toe of the southern island, the Geese maintained their nervous vigil. At dawn, the Beaver at the top of the north island started to gather branches and float them up to his house. The important thing was that no one had arrived on the island during the night. Not even the Stranger. That meant he'd be hungry and would come back to the island this evening.

Touchwit left the safety of her tree. A long day to fill. After exploring a little, she would fill it with her missed sleep.

New to her since the day before were the scents of vegetation. Strange exotic plants had taken root here during the various spring floods. She knew them as the ornamental flowering shrubs and ground-covering vines that the Primates cultivated on their front gardens. As she nosed among them, she found out-of-place surprises: this huge, many-petalled pink flower that burst out of its pod because of the ministration of ants. What was it doing here? And the dark-green crawling vines with tiny blue flowers whose sharpness went to the inner eye. These and other curiosities must have grown from cuttings which lazy gardeners had thrown into the river. And look! Here were mushrooms. She tried them too.

Better save some room for her main meal. She knew what that would be from the Stranger's scat. He visited the island to eat fish which he caught in the shallow channel. A good idea. She would do that. Slide into the water and wade until a juicy fish swam into her paws.

But first, she took some long, soft marsh grass, and some high, flaxen grass. And she found some grapevines and some of the dark-green vines with the pretty flowers that ran along the ground. She braided the grasses deftly and tied them with the vines. A Making. The Stranger who visited from the west would be here tonight. Because it was rude to track someone who guarded their privacy, she'd leave a message for him. She left it at the base of the tree where he came ashore. *I exist too!*

Now, have breakfast and explore the southern island before he arrived.

Touchwit picked her way around bushes and over rotting logs down the city side of the island. The shoreline was higher in the water than the eastern side, forced up by the roots of trees. That made the growth denser. A family of sleek-headed ducks swimming low in the water scurried out of reach. The ducklings tumbled over each other, trying to remain a family. Relax, Ducks. I'm not going to bother you. Dragonflies and Damselflies skimmed the surface of the river – especially the many iridescent light blue ones. Won't eat you either. That excited high-pitched calling that hurt her ears was a group of fly catching birds with tiny crests and black raccoon masks. Sociable, joyful, masked, as if at a costume party: she'd call them the Raccoon Birds. It felt clean and pure to make these identifications, as if she had awakened on the first morning of the world.

The channel turned out to be an idyllic place of its own, with the stillness of a pond. White water lilies crowded the water. Turtles basked on a floating log in the sun. She left them in peace – it didn't feel right to violate them. After all, they were at home in their own burrows, which they carried outside their bodies, ready to withdraw into them if they were threatened. The Turtles displayed in yet an-other form the spirit of individual existence which typified this island. She caught a Rock Perch that swam into her paws like a gift, and ate it on the far bank. Then she found an ideal privacy to pass scat, and thinking it was the right thing to do here, she buried it well. It seemed to be the custom not to leave a mark that suggested one owned these magic islands. The Stranger's Making faced the city, indicating that he could be nothing more than a visitor. The Islands were their own Making, emerging out of the river every year, washed free of the history of scents by the spring flood, a new creation.

The south island differed from the north because its trees were long established. But when she approached the far end, its landscape changed completely. The shallow terminal spit of an original shoal, it gathered fewer seeds and therefore less diversity of vegetation, and of the few trees that grew on it several had blown over in wind storms. Bulrushes and marsh grass had taken over the open space, with clumps of purple loosestrife, elderberries and milkweed. Ducks nested in the reeds. And the Geese also favoured this southern tip because it tapered off into shallows that extended for a distance, with water weeds that were easy to reach, if you liked eating upside down. And she guessed that the shallows were a place where the fish that had whiskers like Uncle Wily grazed on the riverbed and laid their eggs. This wasn't a good place for raccoons – too few trees to climb and too much exposed space. But it dwelt in its own busy harmonies and the eel grass beckoned her fingers.

Within minutes, Touchwit created a second Making. The Stranger, when he ventured down this way, would appreciate that she had constructed it out of the materials of its place. It spoke of the balances of life at the tip of the South Island. Maybe, if it was really well-made, it spoke of the imbalances too.

Going north up the low-lying, mucky shoreline facing her house, she felt herself returning to her comfort zone. The South Island was expansive, the way it opened out to the sky, but it offered its freedom to creatures that fly like ducks and geese, not to raccoons. Freedom was having lots of options, including escape routes if necessary. She realized she hadn't been relaxed on the tip facing the train bridge. Some vague threat lurked in the weeds. Perhaps it was just an imagining, an expression of the discomfort of her body out in the open during daylight. She should get back in a tree and nap.

Touchwit swam back across the small channel and up the western shoreline. She was soon inconspicuous in the leaves of the Stranger's tree, with his Making close by for company.

* * *

The River came to life at dusk in the tiny, discreet ways of nightsiders. First the mosquitoes. Then the rustling of mice. She let herself stay half asleep so she would take these happenings into herself as a continued reverie. She learned more about their relationships that way when they were out of reach of her busy fingers and able to compose themselves freely into patterns. The Geese off the southern tip were going on about something. With daylight gone, they became fearful about threats they couldn't see. That roundness disturbing the surface of the water. The Beaver. Nothing for him to take alarm in – he could simply vanish into his second world with a slap of his tail. A fish jumped in the channel between the islands. That's a good idea. She should get some food in her before the other personality of the island revealed itself to her – its night side which she hadn't yet explored in its particulars.

It was dark and complex at the channel, with the water lilies closed up for the night. She decided this was her favourite part of the island, in spite of the nearby Owl with its superstitious omens. She began washing her hands. Hunters need to be clean even if all they are going to catch is a minnow. A fish can smell the scent of a predator.

Touchwit was washing her paws when a darkness moved up the channel from her. She froze and watched. It transformed into a shape. The shape turned into an animacy, a large creature. It moved silently to the channel's edge. Stopped. It was checking its surroundings. Upwind. It couldn't smell her. It moved again. The animacy began washing its paws. Another raccoon. The Loner.

She knew it was him because of his style of discretion. He didn't transition between a sociable world and the solitary world of the hunter. He left no scent.

The Other slipped into the water without making a ripple. And this was interesting: he didn't wade with his hands in the water ready to grasp a fish. He had put his whole head underwater, leaving only his long arched back breaking the surface. Like a turtle, she thought whimsically.

His head shot out of the water, then his whole body leapt for the shoreline, water cascading off his fur. Something twisting and splashing in his mouth. A fish. He had caught a fish. With his mouth! Not one of those shoreline fish with spiky spines that weren't worth the effort, but a gleaming yellowish monster. He dragged it into the forest. Soon there was the sharp smell of flesh.

She practically tasted the fish, but it wasn't right to crash another hunter's catch if he wasn't kin, and besides he'd be offended at being watched while he was hunting, which is an even worse mistake in etiquette. Hunting was when things transform, when in this case a Fish is turning into Raccoon. In fact, it turned so swiftly she anticipated he'd leave no leftovers for her to eat. Then again, he'd likely bury what he didn't consume. That was his way. But she was in no way prepared for what he did next. The Stranger emerged from the ferns holding the skeleton of the fish in its mouth. Then, instead of washing his hands after the meal he washed the bones of the fish. He did it with the care for every detail that goes with ritual. And then, holding the cleansed skeleton in his paws, he slipped it affectionately nose first into the water as if setting it free.

Only then, he washed his paws.

Touchwit had a lot to learn. There were going to be meaningful nights ahead. So long as the boy energy in her kept his mouth shut. Not all at once, but in little bits. Like ritual. Getting to know him would be a ritual. Like washing the paws before eating.

He swam soundlessly across the channel and disappeared into the bracken of the South Island. Perhaps he'd see her Making and smell the scent of her hands on it, its Maker.

# 22

DAWN PAINTED HER CLOUDS with brilliant pinks and oranges. She painted them so well that she painted out the Great Raccoon Ancestor, producing in his place the idea of a Sun. Clutch left the poplar tree to take advantage of the early morning light. He needed to find his companions. He didn't know what had happened to them after the senior males returned – he'd been too involved with the dog to witness the aftermath of the raid. He only knew he had betrayed his new kin. He had run away when the door of the house flew open, revealing a Primate holding a club.

Clutch found Sleekfoot's trail easily. Not very sleek of foot now because the boy raccoon was limping and dripping blood. A second trail showed that he was supported by Lightfinger, his sister. She appeared to have come out of the brawl unharmed. But two other scent trails beside the first two belonged to striding male raccoons. Powerful Creek Town Fathers who had recently eaten, because one of them had shed a chicken feather. At least they hadn't killed his comrades in arms. But what use did they have for a wounded boy and a maiden not ready to breed?

The mixed scents led to the canal, then to Clutch's surprise turned north in the direction of the railway bridge. That explained their vector of attack. The two males had skirted the geese by moving through brush to the railway tracks and then crossed the canal by means of the train bridge. That was why they were able to avoid the geese and ambush the chicken coop from the east.

Clutch knew what tell-tale clues he was leaving in his own scent. They would show a loser in a fight, with a left leg whose muscles were frozen, a slashed, stiff back, and possibly a gash on his face. A stubborn loser, dragging his defeated body behind him. But more than the weight of defeat, he was dragging a burden of guilt, cowardice, and betrayal. He had failed his kin. He hoped his scent would now show determination. He, Clutch, senior male of the Island Family of the River Clan, was going to stand or fall beside Sleekfoot and Lightfinger.

Now, the railway bridge. Awkward to walk and smelly with the tar in the wooden cross ties and the metallic tang of iron. He pushed on a few yards further and crossed a highway free of traffic at this hour. Now, the safety of railway tracks providing a view in front and behind, with the wind on his left flank, so he couldn't be surprised from that quarter. But on either side of the tracks there was only scrub forest to retreat into, nothing to climb out of reach of a fast-moving predator.

Clutch licked some condensation off the rails – an excuse to rest. He had to stop. His left flank was seizing up. He reached around to lick it – licking a wound subdues the pain – but this wound went deep into his thigh. He looked ahead: an empty track disappearing into oblivion. Behind: home, but he couldn't go back a failure, and he wasn't sure he could even reach home anyway. He was in a vulnerable spot. If attacked, he couldn't fight or flee.

Well, Clutch thought. I've tried, and I've done my best. Nobody will think less of me if I curl up here beside the tracks and go join Uncle Wily.

He cast his eyes up to the southeastern sky where the Ancestor had disappeared into his den to escape the brightness of the day. What would he advise?

"*Unswerving loyalty along the crooked path of cunning.*"

That was a contradictory formula. How am I going to go straight ahead along a crooked path? Thanks a lot, Ancestor.

Pondering this dilemma, Clutch realized he was being watched. Every sinew in his body sprang to attention; he flexed his back in pain. To be tracked by a silent hunter even while you are moving like a hunter! He checked behind to see who was following his scent. All clear. His downwind side. Nobody. Then, where?

A boulder sat balanced on the track. About four bounds away. He must have missed it while he was lost in his thoughts. Typical of him. The boulder seemed to be grinning at his plight. No matter, all of nature could take amusement in his plight as far as he cared. But this boulder had big woodland ears. One of them drooped. Prominent ears and bushy tail. Could this be a Fox? Not to be regarded as a threat, merely a nuisance, and like raccoons (and unlike weasels, skunks, and mink) hunters who didn't leave the remains of their kills for all to see.

"Stay away. You have Rabies," it said.

"I don't have Rabies."

"You're a mess. Who knows what's bitten you?"

"Well, I'll tell you what's bitten me: a Rooster and a Drooler. Do I sound like someone with rabies?"

The Fox considered this information. "My condolences," it said. "Did you get a chicken?"

"No."

"Tough luck."

"You should see the Drooler. He looks like roadkill. And the Rooster is toast!"

"I'm sure you put up a brave defense," the Fox said.

I wish it would stop grinning, Clutch thought. It was grinning with its tongue hanging out, like a drooler. He couldn't get over the fact that the Fox was, technically, a canine.

"I'm sorry I interrupted your prayer," it said, changing the subject. "You appeared to be praying to a fading group of stars. This seemed unnatural to me, since a group of stars can't do anything to help a person. That is why I thought you were rabid."

The Fox seemed to be inviting him to explain his source of inspiration. A discourtesy. All people, most of all a Fox, know that hunters never give away their spirit helpers. It was time he took charge of this discussion: "What's a Fox doing tiptoeing along a railway track? Looks sketchy to me. Perhaps you're getting old and need to practice your balance."

"The metal of the track doesn't take a scent," the Fox said.

"Coming home from hunting, are you? Empty-handed by the looks of it."

"I'm guessing you're not looking for another argument. You're looking for two wounded raccoon youngsters who came this way."

"Tell me where they are, and I'll think better of foxes."

"I can do that. But first, you should do something for your wounds so you can get to where you're going. Follow me." With this, the Fox wheeled around deftly and began trotting down the rail. No problem with that one's balance.

Clutch hobbled along until he came to where the Fox was standing, overlooking one of the tributaries that made up Beaver Creek. Now, up close, he appeared to be an elderly Fox. The flop of his left ear indicated his age.

"What's that tree?" Fox asked.

"It's a Pine."

"Let's go and see what a Pine has for you."

"Alright."

Clutch stood beside the Fox at the base of the pine. The stranger was letting him get close. What was important about the pine?

"That's Pine Sap," the Fox said, pointing with his muzzle. "Rub a little of it on your wound, and you'll be able to walk without pain."

Clutch did as he was told. After all, the Fox was an elder, and he knew some things. Most foxes don't get to grow old. The sap was sticky and he'd never be able to get it off his paws, but when he patted it on his left flank, it numbed the pain.

Foxes and Raccoons ought to be colleagues, Clutch thought. They have a lot in common. The independence and privacy of being hunters kept the two species apart.

"You can wash your paws in the creek, then follow it south and then west through the culvert. You'll come out on the parkland surrounding the lake. Things won't be what they seem. You're in a tricky place, so you must use some trickery."

"What kind of trickery?"

The Fox seemed to be consulting a circle of vulpine elders deep in his interior. "You smell like Creek Town aristocracy."

"I do?"

"Something to remember. It will give you a cover. We'll go our ways now. It was good meeting you."

"Thank you. And thanks for the idea."

The Fox blinked, and turned to go up the tracks. He called over his shoulder.

"*Tally-ho!*"

## 23

THE EXCITEMENT OF THE CITY overwhelmed Bandit, making his fear just another element in a continual intense high. Most stimulating of all was the spontaneous kinship of fully urbanized raccoons. People greeted him like a friend without asking where he was from or where he belonged in society. No one had a past here. There were no clan territories, no inhibitions about trespass. At night, the whole downtown with its laneways and back alleys became a communal feeding ground, with cubs underfoot everywhere and mothers foraging in small groups until dawn before sorting out their children and taking them home to sleep. There were raccoons of every age and hue. Among the mix, Bandit noticed newcomers from Raccoonopolis, the great city over the horizon. They too joined this panorama of individualists who gave the night streets the atmosphere of a carnival.

What permitted this urban commonwealth to flourish was the abundance of food. The first place Bandit went to after he left the river was the district where Primates enjoyed their nightlife, which involved a great deal of eating and drinking. Restaurants meant edible waste, and edible waste meant continual nightly provender. In the downtown core, waste pick-up was twice a week, giving raccoons two nights in which to pillage green bins lined up on the streets and blue bins outside of bars. On the non-partying nights, the organic waste in the smelly back alleys was picked clean by roving, high-spirited bands of raccoons. And the quality of the garbage was mouth-watering: on his first night, Bandit tasted food he never knew existed, food from far-off places around the world. And the kinds of alcohol left in bottles – glad he wasn't a drinker. As well as the easy food there was an abundance of accommodation to support the growing raccoon population, though most of the lodgings were precarious dens high up in the vines that draped some of the downtown buildings or in the roof pastures which the Primates had fashioned. "As Primates evolve, so evolve Raccoons," Bandit thought, remembering the saying of his mother's.

The second biggest stimulation offered by the city, he soon discovered, was the sheer volume of communication. The scent-trails left by raccoons zigzagged everywhere, intersected, dispersed, concentrated again at major sites. And these trails were deposited in layers of time over the course of a night, composing an up-to-date, four-dimensional space-time map of city life. Bandit noticed that this map was checked regularly, in some cases compulsively, by the city dwellers. Who had gone to the outdoor Farmers Market. Who was just returning from sifting the river bottom. Who was on their way to visit their folks by means of the creek which traversed the city and was a thoroughfare for raccoon traffic. Another saying: "The nose is before your ears, so trust it first!"

This scent-map was accompanied by an oral map, offering a matching volume of detail and a great deal more meaning, though much of it was untrustworthy. Bandit listened keenly to the news from talkative fellow raccoons he kept bumping into. They conveyed anecdotes, gossip, urban myths, transient enthusiasms, trivial sightings, ghost stories, affectionate accounts of cats, aids to meeting other raccoons for the purposes of mating, and irrational outbursts of rage. The common theme of the oral map, if it had one, was the state of the world. Its common tone was that of an upbeat fellowship of survivors enduring Short-Sighted Stupidity in High Places. Tonight the news was about Migrants Pressing on the Borders, the Serious Den Shortage, Is There a Future for Cubs? Dangerous Drugs in the Food, and Raccoons Killed by Cars. Everywhere in this mix of scarcely reliable and flagrantly false information, one personage figured repeatedly. It was the One with No Name.

Accompanied by his High Guard, he had fought a distant Battle on the Southern Frontier thought to be at the lower tributary of Beaver Creek behind Creek Town. Whether this was a Heroic Victory over Criminal Invaders or a Crushing Defeat inflicted on No Name and his Maggots depended on which version of the news one heard. In any case, it was agreed that the migrants must have been starving to attempt a passage up the creek in broad daylight. But no sooner had this newsflash rippled through the population than it was replaced by notice of another event. No Name was Coming! Following his Mighty Victory, he had decided to deal with the Diseased Migrants already in the city, hiding out in the general population. In fact, he was coming to the city to Study the Problem Himself. Indeed, he might have already arrived and was holding High-Level Consultations with the City Elders. Bandit discarded this false news. How could No Name be in two places at once? More to the point, there was no problem of illegal immigration to study, and the legendary leader had no jurisdiction on the West Bank of the River, least of all in the Commonwealth City. Yet Bandit felt an obscure pride in the fact that the subject of so much of the news was his father.

Nowhere in the spoken exchanges did he hear news of Sensibella.

She'd like it in this place where people dreamed out loud, sharing their innermost feelings with strangers who listened sympathetically, waiting for their turn to do the same. But beneath the open-spirited greetings and exchanges lay a margin for trickery. And Sensibel, while she enjoyed trickery as much as the next raccoon, wasn't street-proofed against a casual urban deceit which required, Bandit came to realize, an equally open-spirited skepticism. He realized this when without introducing himself a male raccoon promptly invited him home to his den. (Bandit declined.)

How could Sensibel survive this seductive deceit? And she barely had any experience with motor vehicles. She would be terrified.

He'd arrived in the downtown a whole night later than her because he had awakened at the break of day when it was dangerous to travel. And he'd done what she'd likely done on arrival: use the night to find a place to sleep, then spend the following day in privacy to de-stress. He had to reach her before Smartwhisker and her prospective in-laws found her.

But where to begin?

Bandit went back to where he'd spent his first night in the city, under the bridge carrying traffic across the river beside the factory of sugary tastes, and looked at the reflection of the moon on the water. Because no one had seen her using the Crosstown stream, she must have gone east, skirted the Heights where her father's people lived, then entered the River and let the current carry her down to the city. Brilliant! Where was the likeliest place for her to come ashore?

The question became useless as soon as he asked it. There were too many possibilities and it would take the rest of the night to sniff each of them out. Even then, it wasn't certain if he could pick up her trail at the riverbank. Ask a different question. Where were the unlikely places for her to come out?

This question worked immediately. It eliminated the whole shoreline from the bridge he was sitting under to another bridge at the Heights to the north. So he'd start his search a short distance downstream where the current slackened as the river broadened.

Bandit worked his way along a steep shoreline parallel to a railway track that ran out of the factory. Suddenly he broke out into forested parkland. This was a surprise. It seemed to be designed by the Primates so they could stroll through specially planted settings of trees and flowers. He came to a pond contained by shale rock just as if it was a piece of wilderness. He stopped to drink, watched by the statue of Primate child, then continued south. At night, the park was a fragrant silence amidst the smell and noise of the city. He came to a grass lawn wide enough to hold all the raccoons in the city. At its far end were tables and chairs: an outdoor restaurant. Check for threats. None. He scurried across the lawn, ignored the waste collection bins outside the kitchen, and found himself on a wooden plank floor overhung by tree branches. It smelled of dropped salad bits, bread crumbs, ice cream, and of creatures who had come to clean it up: sparrows, mink, ants. Here was a water bowl for droolers. Down below where the shoreline curved in to make a cove was a dock for boats. Every instinct in his body advised that this was where Sensibel had made landfall. It was sheltered, close to the downtown, and free of raccoons.

Wait! That shape on the dock. It was clearly a raccoon. It held something long and thin that glittered in the moonlight. Why would a raccoon expose themselves at the end of a dock? Ah, the sugary scent of alcohol. It must be that one's habit to drink alone here. That meant it saw things which normally passed unnoticed, for instance, the arrival of Sensibel.

Bandit left the porch and shuffled awkwardly down wooden steps to the dock. That other one must be senseless not to be aware of him. As he got closer the smell of liquor stung his eyes.

"Grrr!" Bandit said.

The raccoon didn't leap and spin around. It seemed to be labouring to come out of a drunken daze. "Join me," he said eventually. Without turning his head, he offered the bottle to Bandit.

"Thanks. Not now," Bandit said. "Nice night."

"Not so bad," the other said. Then took a long, gurgling drink.

"Good place to sit and watch the River go by," Bandit said. "Come here often?"

"S'okay. Lots to see."

Bandit paused, trying to think of a more direct path into his question, one that didn't seem intrusive. This was the other person's special place to be alone. It must be special because it had only one escape route – straight into the water.

"Do many raccoons come ashore here?" he asked.

"Naw. Too open a swim from the Islands." The raccoon gestured with his bottle at the islands at the back of Bandit's house. "And nobody goes to the Islands, anyways. Those Islands are sacred."

The raccoon looked long and knowingly into Bandit's eyes, verifying a solemn truth.

"Didn't know that about them," Bandit replied.

"Yeah, they're sacred, alright. Folks say they're haunted."

"Sure," Bandit said agreeably. He sensed the prelude to a story. He really hoped the raccoon wouldn't ...

"Time ago, they say, the Great Raccoon Ancestor" – the story-teller immediately made the Hand Acknowledgement – "came down that there tree that goes through the Island ..."

"Which tree?"

The raccoon paused to have another glug of spirit-sugar.

"... You'se can't see the Tree. It's invisible, like. But it's there. The tree pins the Island to the riverbed so's it won't float away. And it holds up the sky, and on its branches hang the stars. Including the Great Raccoon, when he's at home in his tree ..."

"This is interesting, but ..."

"Folks say he's gonna come down his tree one day and save the world."

"I have a question."

The storyteller swept his interruption aside with a wave of his bottle.

"Questions 'r fer later. Right now is the story. Where was I?"

"You were saying nobody swims over from the Islands. Do Raccoons float downriver, then?"

"Yeah. Sure do. There was this lady just last night. You should'a seen the tail on her. Looked great when it was wet!"

"Good looking?"

"Great tail," the storyteller repeated and leered at Bandit. "Pretty smart too. She didn't use the dock. Too obvious. Leave her scent on the planks. So she came out downwind there." The storyteller pointed to a rock at the far side of the cove.

"It's not every night a person sees a beautiful lady float by," Bandit said. "Anyone know who she is? Where she went?"

"Don't know nothing about 'er. If you want to know, go ask Lockjaw."

"Who's Lockjaw?"

The other raccoon seemed to chew on the question as if it were a hard nut. "Lockjaw looks after people who come to the city and don't know nobody," he said eventually. "He gives them lodgings and jobs to do."

A job? The idea was ludicrous. Sensibel wasn't the sort of person who did menial work. It didn't smell right. Menial work in exchange for a lodging. And the temporary lodgings in this city were squalid and had fleas. "I need a job. Where do I find Lockjaw?"

The informant continued gazing at the moon that had fallen into the river between the island and the cove. He'd lost interest in answering questions. Change the topic.

"Do you know where I could find a raccoon who's an artist? A male, said to be handsome."

"The lady swam to the City to be with her boyfriend? What happened? Did he steal your girl? Sorry mate. Here, have a drink."

"Yeah, it's something like that." Bandit, against his principles, took the bottle anyway and drank. Whiskey – he'd tasted it before. He felt an instant bond with the drinker and all his sorrows. The other raccoon felt the bond too because he began to be helpful.

"Don't know the Maker in question. You might look for him up in the Heights. The Makers are said to hang out there. They're a secret society, you know." The raccoon hung his head guiltily as if he'd mentioned something forbidden. Bandit returned his bottle.

"Where's Lockjaw?"

"I don't know where he is. Drooplip. It's her you'se 'r after. She looks after the ladies."

"Where?"

The other gestured downriver with the bottle. "I don't know. I didn't see him take her. I didn't see nothing …"

"I get it. You didn't see anything happen, right? Your place in the world is to sit here and see nothing."

"Tha's right."

"Where would they have gone?" Bandit got to his feet and took the bottle from the informant's paws.

The other raccoon looked up desperately as Bandit hovered over him. Pleading watery eyes. That one didn't have many options. His only option was to be left alone and not get into any trouble.

Bandit waited for the answer to his question with the understanding that it would be the last thing he'd take from this used-up Raccoon.

"I dunno. But I reckon they took her up the Crosstown Creek …"

"Which is where from here …?"

"Down there. Just after the tracks. Where the River turns into the Lake. There's a boardwalk sorta like this dock. Stretches along the river at the back of the hotel to Crosstown Creek."

Bandit already knew this route to the Creek. It was the one his mother had used when they went to visit Aunt Pawsense. But he had to hear the Drinker say it to be sure Sensibel had gone that way and that she had been *taken*.

\* \* \*

The creek was covered where it discharged into the harbour. Higher upstream it broke into the open, resembling the original forest stream it had been before it served a second use as a stormwater drain. Access at the open stretches allowed raccoons a thoroughfare to avoid the traffic of vehicles on streets. But where did Sensibel's captors leave the stream? It turned out that people didn't want to talk about Lockjaw or the abduction of newcomers. One of the things Bandit was coming to learn was that the free and open discourse of the city was punctuated by diplomatic silences.

But he didn't count on Sensibella's cunning. He found the first bit of her tail hair on the muddy bank. And another where the stream, having come out into the open air, disappeared into the next extended culvert. And this was the pattern, continued through muck, and bats, and plastic bottles, and dead rodents, and syringes, and shopping carts, and masses of indistinguishable raccoon scents until the creek broke out into a long open stretch through a mini-ravine that ran beside a patio bar.

Here, she left a part of her tail on the bush and another part up the slope at the edge of the patio. It didn't take long to find a third sign – a wisp of golden hair at the base of a tree that grew beside the brick wall of a building overlooking the patio. The rest would be easy. He could ascend her scent-trail up to the roof.

But what was driving her to sacrifice her tail? Despair, or a cunning attempt to make herself unbeautiful? Or was it trust in the stubborn persistent loyalty of her rescuer?

# 24

WAKING TO HER SECOND NIGHT on the river, Touchwit decided it was time to assert herself. The most direct and courteous way of meeting the Stranger was to swim across to the small island halfway between here and the far shore of the River, where he must have gone to sleep out the day, because he wouldn't have found any privacy in the city. She'd simply come ashore and introduce herself. Then, with the mystery of him and his Makings cleared up, she could get on with her quest to the West Bank. It might happen that the Stranger would be part of that adventure because he was a Maker like her. Yet it might turn out that he preferred his own company to another's. *Que será, será.*

But first, she needed to check if he had come back over to this island while she was sleeping. Besides, she'd be leaving her island for good. She ought to say goodbye to the place. She'd better not make it a lingering farewell because the westerly breeze felt uncertain. The weather was faltering; it wanted to shift around and bring a storm.

Touchwit left her tamarack tree with the Making on its branches and sniffed around the northern point to the Beaver's house. The giant rodent was already out and about. His work began at dusk and continued through the night. Must be an effort to chew down a tree and guide the trunk with its branches over here. And he had no family to help him. He was a Bank Beaver, not a Lodge Beaver. Uncle Wily once explained the difference. Bank Beavers were solitary, and for that reason couldn't invest the effort that a family of beavers brought to damming up a stream. The Beavers down at Beaver Creek on the Lake were Lodge Beavers. Maybe the solitary ones, those who preferred to live alone, left the community and became Bank Beavers.

The Stranger was a Bank Raccoon, if there was such a thing. He hadn't come to the northerly tip of the island, so she began a search of its western shoreline down to the channel. She snacked on clams, then swam the channel and continued down the shoreline of the South Island to where it sloped into the river and became a cattail swamp. Why not say goodbye to her Making? The curious thing about these hand-made objects was that they seemed like people with minds of their own. The Stranger had created the face of a person in his Making. Hers was just a ring that could be worn around the neck, acquiring its personality through contact with its wearer. Perhaps her ring was waiting for a wearer.

But what's this? An object standing at the place where she had positioned her Making? Where had it come from? She felt her hackles rise. Whatever you don't know is not to be trusted. She didn't feel comfortable on the South Island in the first place.

Touchwit approached the Something warily. It smelled of forest pickings – grapevines and bulrushes, so it couldn't be a threat. It was plainly an Animacy.

Then, as she approached closer, it showed the ears of a Raccoon – yes, it was a Raccoon facing south, towards the lake. A Making. The Stranger had fashioned a second Making. Beside hers.

And it was wearing her wreath around its neck!

How? When? He must have fashioned it the previous night after eating his fish, when he left the channel to go down to the South Island. He'd discovered her wreath and constructed a second Raccoon to wear it.

The message went deep into her heart. For the first time in her life, she felt confusion. That confusion was a fluster of feelings trying to speak all at once. She resisted the impulse to force them into unison. Had he been tracking her all this while? How much did he know about her? Why did he care about her at all? – he was a loner. He'd have known from the scent of her paws on her Making that she wasn't in the mood to mate. Yet he'd told of a kinship with her by fashioning this likeness beside her wreath and linking the two Makings so that together they created a new being.

Touchwit came around to the front of the Object and examined it with her nose. No distinguishable scent. How could that be? Still, the Making was patently his. The same silver clam shells for eyes, giving it a special, far-seeing power of vision. Those familiar high, alert ears on a skull so broad that she wanted to pet it. The Making must be an image of its Maker.

*"Do you like it?"*

Touchwit peered around the statue toward the speaker. Her nostrils dilated, her ears flattened, her back arched. Nobody. There was no one to see or smell.

*"It's okay to relax yourself. I'm not a threat."*

The voice seemed to come from a crabapple tree at the verge of the forest. Four or five pounces away. Though she couldn't see him, she'd grabbed enough of his speech to analyse. Calm, reasonable speech. Youthful in its straightforwardness. Not earnest, like Clutch. Not ironic, like Bandit. But deep-down male. She hadn't met a grown-up male except for Uncle Wily and he was an oddity. She sensed a power in this one's voice that came from his toes. Why didn't he show himself? The breeze blew his scent off him and carried it away from her.

"I appreciate that you don't want to be seen," Touchwit said to the tree. "I'm a visitor here too, and I walk lightly. But we should really figure out some way we can greet each other."

Laughter from the tree. It seemed the whole tree was shaking.

*"Sorry,"* the tree said. *"I'm not good with people."*

He was shy. Touchwit understood. Shy and vulnerable. He probably didn't have roughhouse brothers to play with when he grew up. He might have been an orphan cub. She'd heard of orphans left to grow up on their own in the world, their parents trapped in a cage and taken away by Primates. She'd have to assume the lead in this conversation. What should she say? Touchwit looked in the direction of her house. What would her mother say?

"I like your Making. It does your speaking for you. However did you learn to fashion such a cunning resemblance?" She listened for his reply. It was growing darker quickly. He could come out in the open and not be easily seen. Maybe he was embarrassed about his smell. He didn't leave his scent lying around.

*"There is a school where Raccoons learn to Make things – don't you know? I attended the school."*

A school for Makers? What's that? Her school had been a chimney. Aunt Pawsense's daughters had gone to all kinds of schools, and the education they received made them superior. The Stranger didn't sound superior. Yet he had attended a school and learned to make a well-proportioned Making. "I have not been schooled in Making," she said. "I trust my little wreath is well-proportioned and meets a standard."

"*It is a good Making. Especially if it is spontaneous and untaught, as yours is.*"

Now she'd got him talking.

"*But its power is only in its Form. It fails to convey a Meaning.*"

Why does a Making have to convey a meaning? She thought. She felt an impulse to be argumentative. How exciting to talk about Makings, whether meaningful or not! As far as her brothers were concerned, her need to fashion Makings was a curse that oughtn't to be discussed outside the family.

"*Most of us don't appreciate Makings,*" the Stranger said. "*Imagine that! No creature is so gifted with its hands, yet Raccoons don't like the idea of a Making. Termites care more about Makings than we do. And Honeybees. We think our hands are just for climbing branches. For opening bins. For washing food. We'll tolerate a Making so long as it doesn't mean anything. So long as it's just a pretty form.*"

That stung! He'd called her Making a *pretty form*. Actually, a form *had* meaning, though what it meant was anybody's guess. A form helped you find meanings.

Touchwit told the boy in her to shut up. The boy energy was pushing her to start an all-out argument, and that wouldn't help her find out more about Making, Meaning, and this reticent Maker. This was the most important discussion she'd ever had. She held her peace. At least, she'd got the Stranger to reveal something about himself. He wanted to talk and he suddenly had a lot to say. Maybe he'd come out of his tree.

"Isn't the world big enough for all kinds of Making?" she asked. "The ones that say what they mean and the ones that don't say anything."

"*If Raccoons took Making seriously, they could remake the world.*"

"They could *what*?"

"*They could fix what's wrong in the world. I can take you to the School, if you want. It's a place for reasoning about kinds of Makings. You'll see Makings you never knew existed …*"

"Do they all have meanings?"

He didn't answer. She was left staring at a tree. Why didn't he answer – he'd been so chatty.

*"It's better for you to see them with your own eyes than for me to describe them."*

Okay, that made sense. "Where is this School?"

*"It's in the city."*

"Can you take me there?"

Pause.

*"Easier to meet me there."*

I get it. He has a disability. A limp maybe. Or a torn ear.

"Tell me where to be." This was exhilarating. She was going to the City. To a guild of Makers. It felt easy to come to the City and already have a place to settle and someone to introduce you to people. Her kind of people.

*"Swim to the Halfway Island. Then across the water from it you'll see a cove with a dock. There's a Primate restaurant. I'll be there."*

"When?"

*"Right away, if you like. Before this storm hits. Just give me some time to get started."*

"Okay, I'll be there. Before the wind shifts." At last, a turning in her quest. She would find a life in the City. A society of Makers. And someone who understood what Making was.

# ACT III

*Freedoms and Responsibilities*

*Slypaws*, a tourist in the City
*Twitchwhisker*, her friend

*Clutch*, leader of the defense of Creek Town
*Sleekfoot* and *Lightfinger*, his field commanders
*Lickfoot* and *Silverheels*, two Town Mothers
*Clawface*, a scout for *Meatbreath*

*Bandit*, a spy in the City Honour Guard
*Friskywits*, Bandit's cousin and sidekick
*Lockjaw*, a panderer, and *Drooplip*, a bawd, procurers
The *Judge*, a City Father
*Sensibella*, a secret agent masquerading as a courtesan
*The Directory of Security*, a city official

The Guild of Artists (Makers)
*Mindwalker*, a wilderness artist and leader of the Resistance
*Touchwit*, his fellow artist and strategist
A Herring Gull, her colleague, messenger, and scout

## 25

BEAVERMEAD IS A CITY PARK stretching along the east side of Little Lake. Generations of kids, including my partner, have walked there in groups in their flip-flops, wearing bathing suits and carrying towels and pocket money for snacks, to swim at its supervised beach. Older kids, including our son, have played city youth league soccer on its playing fields. Families come from as far away as the Greater Metropolitan Area to spend their summer holiday on its campground. Today, outdoor education classes for school children are held at its Ecology Park, while their parents come to pick up information about the use of native plants in gardening and to buy those shrubs and trees. At the north end of the park is the Canoe Museum, for this city is where the canoe was first manufactured in quantity using designs based on Indigenous models.

For as long as raccoons can remember, Beavermead has been the site of the original settlement of the River Clan. Several historic clan families live here at Creek Town, staying in touch with their relatives who have started colonies to the east along the meandering strips of wetland meadows or "meads" from which the park takes its name. What makes raccoon civilization possible here is the coming together of streams, a lake, a forest, and a picnic area.

The complex watercourse system needs to be described because it is central to Creek Town geopolitics. First, a stream named South Meade Creek on the map flows into the park from the east, then divides into one branch seeking its way to Little Lake by going north, the other seeking the lake by going south. The diverging waterways encircle Beavermead Park and act as its boundary. For canoers, they offer an idyllic tunnel overhung by tree boughs to paddle through. Green Herons are common here. I have seen Kingfishers, but not recently. If you look over the side into the deep, slow water, you might see a Beaver keeping pace with your canoe.

Then, a separate stream system flows into Beavermead from the northeast, also seeking the lake. This is North Meade Creek. It has the same idea as its southern sister about joining the delta to enter the lake, and where it joins it makes a beautiful lagoon. *Lagoon* is just the right word for what you'll find here, because it comes from the Latin *lacuna* meaning a "cavity" or "hollow," and then, by extension, a "pond" or "pool" that is made by a *lacus* or "lake." The lagoon beside the Canoe Museum is a cavity in the shore of Little Lake. It is on one of these tributary creeks that Clutch found an elegant stone bridge over dark water with lily pads, overhung by trees. Here in this quiet reflective place, he climbed a river willow, relaxed into his habitual thoughtfulness, and fell asleep.

He was awakened by the voices of raccoon ladies.

"Oh, but this is thankless labour for the Clan Fathers, gathering food for their community bins!"

"They intend such work to be for women and those feeble and infirm of wit. It is meant to keep us busy so that we don't conceive Idle Notions."

"While they lie on their backs in the shade, reciting epic poems and guarding their precious bins," the first woman replied.

"Those bins are all that feeds us now. No personal hunting or scrounging is permitted. What they control in bins is portioned out equally by Fathers."

"Thereby making us equally grateful."

"And denying sources of nourishment to Migrants, who would otherwise flock here in numbers."

The second speaker sounded a note of weary resignation. In contrast, the mood of the first speaker seemed to Clutch to be one of resigned weariness. The difference between tonalities of oppression is subtle. The second woman had come to accept the condition. The first hadn't.

"Nevertheless," came the first voice, "I have conceived an Idle Notion."

"Pray, share it."

"Tip the contents of the effing bins into the lake bottom and run like your tail's on fire."

Muffled laughter.

"*Sssh!* There's a male hereabouts. I can smell him."

Silence.

"Look! He's up there. Asleep on that branch over the water."

"Is he one of *them?*"

"He must be. There are no full-grown males in the Town except Clan Fathers whenever they drop by."

"But they run in twos. He's alone."

Clutch, without lifting his muzzle from the branch, opened one eye.

"Hapticia save us! Now we're for it. He'll report us for Idle and Inappropriate Notions."

"We'll be nailed by our tongues to a goalpost."

Clutch stretched and yawned, partly because he needed to, partly to convey an attitude of unconcern to the ladies. They were waiting for him to react.

"Good morning, gentlewomen. I am a visitor to your community." Did he need to make the Hand Acknowledgment gesture? No, it was useless in the state of tyranny which the women described. In fact, it was useless in all circumstances. "I am seeking someone."

"It is our duty to report you," the second woman said.

"Hear me out first. Then decide if you should report me." The women were surreptitiously sniffing him from below, trying to determine who he was. He could hear their whispering.

"*We might as well find out what he wants. It wouldn't do any harm.*"

"*Consider: he could very well report us.*"

"Go ahead, *monsieur*. Tell us whom you are seeking."

"I am seeking a brother and a sister, Sleekfoot and Lightfinger by name."

"They are escapees, *monsieur*. They were captured and returned here by a pair of Fathers."

"What will happen to them?"

"Sleekfoot will be trained to serve in a war band, as soon as his wounds heal. Lightfinger will be groomed to be someone's mate for when she comes into season. Until such time, they must perform the most lowly of tasks: licking the collective food bins clean and monitoring the communal latrines so as to prevent an outbreak of seditious gossip. And ..." – the lady raccoon broke into a moist lament – "it is a cruel misfortune because they are my cousin's cubs, and she died of sorrow when they fled the colony, so she did, and they do not yet know she died."

The other raccoon caught the mood of her companion. "Their misfortune is all the more poignant, considering that they were rescued from death themselves by a hero who stepped out of a brilliant light and vanquished a mighty Drooler. He destroyed the monster just with his hands, they say, whereupon the hero vanished back into the blazing light." The speaker paused to let the immensity of the deed be appreciated.

"Only to have two slimeballs from the Clan Fathers take Sleek and Light away."

"Hush! Don't speak that way, sister."

Clutch spent some effort applying this heroic perspective to himself. The Idle Notion could only have been originated by Sleek and Light. The pathos of their capture and the courage of their rescuer would have caused the account to be exaggerated at every retelling. In the process of its transmission, the story had acquired a warning: if the Clan Fathers didn't treat Sleekfoot and Lightfinger well, this Mighty Hero would step out of his light again and bring justice to all.

"What is the name of this hero?" Clutch decided to ask.

"It is unknown. Sleekfoot and Lightfinger will not reveal it. They are being starved of nourishment, allowed to eat only grass until they do, yet still they won't reveal the name of their champion."

Interesting, thought Clutch. But his next thought was for his kin. "If they are starving, we must get food to them."

The two ladies looked at him as if he was crazy.

"I am coming down from this tree. Pray do not be alarmed." Clutch tried not to show the stiffness in his thigh as he descended the willow. It wouldn't help Sleekfoot and Lightfinger at all if the two ladies identified him as the mysterious hero. At least, not immediately. This was the circumstance the Fox had predicted. It called for *unswerving loyalty along the crooked path of cunning*. Helpful that he didn't look like a mighty hero. He didn't look like anything. He was an unknown. The women's noses were twitching. They were sniffing him.

"Blessed Lady Hap preserve us! He's a spy!" The two ladies leapt backward in alarm. They were ready to flee.

"He's a spy. A personal spy. For the One Who Can't be Named."

Now what was he going to do? Being a spy was even more threatening than being a Clan Father. Of course, it was. He was Meatbreath's son.

The two ladies huddled in fear. He had to find a way to persuade them he was friendly, to show that he could be trusted.

"Let me gather food with you. Then you'll have more to take back. By the way, how *do* you carry it back?"

The ladies nodded silently. They were in no position to refuse his offer. He smelled River Clan elite. Funny to think he was superior – he who'd been born in a chimney and raised by a single parent. Yet the Fox's second prediction was coming true: *You smell like Beaver Creek aristocracy.* How do aristocrats behave? He had an idea that they swaggered and drawled their vowels. Whatever they did, he had to imitate their manner. Use it as a cover. The wisdom of a Fox.

"We drag the gleanings home across the grass by means of a cunning invention of the Primates. It is called a bag."

"We find them in the waste bins. Some we unearth from the lake bottom." The second lady was trying desperately to be helpful.

"Alright, then – let's gather food." Clutch looked down into the water. There was Star Duckweed in the lagoon, a favourite of the Mallards. And Water Celery, and the aptly named floating plant called Coontail which everyone ate: fish, ducks, geese, and muskrats. "I'll throw it up to you from the pond and you can put it in your bag."

"But *monsieur*, you're wounded. And I smell infection. You must be treated immediately."

"I shall dive down and find some Crowfoot. It stops the bacteria," the first woman said. She turned to her companion. "You get the bag."

"*Monsieur*, I must go and fetch the bag from where I've hidden it."

"Yes, let us do that and I will get started in the pond." He hoped this display of kindred effort would help the ladies relax. Relaxed enough to be trusted with his secret. While the second lady was away, he'd talk to the first lady. She still had some defiance in her.

He waited on the shore for her to surface with a mouthful of tiny white buttercups.

"Tell me something about yourself," Clutch asked while she rubbed the antiseptic plants into his torn back.

"I shall tell you my name only – otherwise I will cry. My name is Silverheels. I am of the Firefly Family of the River Clan at Creek Town."

"*Ouch!*"

"A little tender there. In the thigh. Whatever have you been doing?"

"Is No Name at Creek Town?"

"Sir, he has gone across the lake to the city. I don't wish to speak of him further. We are not permitted to."

The tyrant is away, Clutch thought. That made it easier for him to continue on his eastward quest. But first he had to rescue his two friends, Sleekfoot and Lightfinger. And stay in Creek Town long enough for his wounds to heal.

# 26

F ROM BENEATH A TABLE on the patio of the bar, Bandit heard a
rustling at the top of the vine where Sensibel had been taken. Two
descending shapes making no effort to be discreet. Raccoons in this
town owned the night, and it showed in their heedless, carefree spirit.
The city was a place to be young in, and these two dandies sounded
flagrantly young.

"I wouldn't take that Barbi-coon out on a date if Lockjaw gave
me a bottle of beer for every hair in her tail."

"She sure fills the eyes though."

"For that eyeful, you have to pay by the word. Did you listen to
her go on? Total word-dump! Where does Lockjaw get his ladies?"

"That one floated down from the Heights by the look of her."

"But she's half River Clan, or my nose is off track."

"The corn-fed wench wouldn't even let me smell her glands. Said
it was rude. Then she asked what hole I came out of."

"But you're Creek Town elite!"

"And then – get this! – she says I need to go to school and acquire
manners before I dare court a lady."

"She thinks Lockjaw brought her here to be courted."

The abbreviated exchanges of urban raccoons, like messages on
the web. No threat here. Bandit shuffled out from beneath his table.

"You waiting for a tussle? Good luck, mate."

"Don't go up there unless you want a lesson from Miss Manners."

"It's not worth it. You'll lose your wits."

"Better girls at The Pit."

The two youths went off into the night, leaving Bandit at the base
of the vine. Sensibel was up there alright. She could turn a man into
a puddle of want with just one of her sighs.

Scuffling in the leaves on the stream bank, a corpulent raccoon
hauled himself panting and wheezing up onto the patio.

"You there! Stand before me so I can see you."

A male of the highest rank: middle-aged, successful, accustomed to being obeyed. The two youths hadn't outgrown their juvenile years and probably never would. This one carried his many years evenly like rings on his tail. Bandit began counting the rings …

"Issue forth, I say. Nothing to fear. I'm off duty. Out on the town."

Bandit shuffled into the open to be sniffed.

"Oh, sorry old chap! Thought you were the doorman. What's the action up there?"

"I don't know, sir. I haven't been up yet."

"Well, I hear Lockjaw's got a real pistol."

"I believe so, sir. Yes. She's a pistol."

"I'll go up and give her a shot."

"Good luck, sir." No hindering this male. Anyway, he wasn't Sensibel's type, and she could look after herself.

It wasn't until the personage had disappeared, puffing and groaning over the lip of the roof, that Bandit noticed another raccoon watching him. "Who are you?"

"Bodyguard to His Worship."

The bodyguards at Sensibella's betrothal ceremony were just decoration compared to this dude. He was the real thing. Instead of counting rings, Bandit counted scars.

"Nice soft night, sir!"

"Yes – yes, it is." Bandit was flustered. The bodyguard had called him "sir." In the frequent exchanges he'd had in the city, no one had been interested in his social rank. He had no social rank. But the off-duty judge whom the bodyguard referred to as "His Worship" had treated him as if he was of high social standing.

"Tell me, what does His Worship do in the city besides administer the Customs?"

"You mean the Judge that you didn't see just now going up the vine for a roll?"

"I didn't see anybody."

"Why, he's a City Father. I'm surprised you don't know that, sir, if I may say so."

"Never saw him before."

"Quite right, sir."

"I'd like to speak with him again briefly. Do you think it's alright if I go up?"

"So long as you don't barge in on his transaction. His Honour needs to feel what it was like when he was young and went a-courting – if you know what I mean." The bodyguard winked.

Bandit knew. He'd heard lots of advertisement for escorts on the net. For a price, they'd go out on a date with you, make you feel like a total alpha. For a further price they'd play-tussle. Nothing consequential. Most of the women in the City were set in their non-fertile phase because of the pressure of population. Sensibel had been put on the market as a party girl and didn't know it.

"Forget you saw him."

"I already have." Bandit walked across the flagstone patio and began climbing the vine. He found himself on rooftop pasture still damp from the rain. Tall meadow grass with buttercups and daisies on their long stems swinging in the moist, warm breeze vented by a fan. Shiny black panels cooled in the night air. It was Sensibella's kind of place – a paradise gone to seed. Voices came from a glass house at the far end of the roof. He tiptoed through the meadow to listen. The glass house had once been used for nurturing plants, but now only a vine pushed its way to freedom through a pane that remained open. He crouched beside the window, making sure his ears didn't show.

"Is she not worth a whole brewery, Your Worship? I promise you, you won't find a more promising girl in any of my houses of transaction."

"That is certainly the case," the Judge's voice boomed, "since your ladies have more fleas than a donkey's armpit. In fact, the chief transaction of your houses is the transmission of mites together with the diseases they carry, the abatement of which cost the City's physicians in time and effort. It is a surprise you don't sell Distemper by the bottle! Doubtless, you'll recompense the City Public Health Department by actually paying your taxes for once this summer. Otherwise, I'll close you down for good."

"Oh, mustn't do that, milord. Once you have sampled the lady, you'll want to keep my service open forever."

"That remains to be seen. Your name, fair one?"

"*Name? What gentleman is so wanting in manners as to demand a name without the other first introducing herself through story? If name be needed, name me Nullia, because my freedom of the City is null and void, having been stolen from me by this poxy bawd.*"

"Shut your muzzle, dearie. Else I'll have ye on worms for a week."

"*Worms! Indeed you know aplenty about worms, since your habituation to wigglies has made your lips go numb. And your man's refusal thereof has caused his jaws to clamp shut. He's afraid to open them lest you pop another worm in his mouth, to join the Infusion already in his swollen belly.*"

"I beg yer ladyship's pardon, I'm sure."

That must be Drooplip, Bandit thought.

His Worship's voice, gentle now: "I shall not tax you for a name, my dear. You are quite within Custom. A story of your recent doings by which one may picture you and perhaps a glimpse of your ancestry will suffice. Then we may exchange names. Once known, then named, as we say in Law."

"*A story about myself? Then I'll begin.*"

Great Raccoon Ancestor help us! thought Bandit.

"I told you. You should've given 'er to the pair of toffs and have done with 'er."

"They didn't have enough bottles to acquire her."

"Then you should've acquired her yourself and taught her how to please a lord."

"The Judge will make that determination himself. I fancy he'll judge the product well. He's listened to many a tale of woe in his time."

Sensibella's sing-song voice wended out the open window.

"*Mine is a tale of passion and tragedy, of a love-lorn heart tossed upon a sea of sorrow. I shall begin thus. Once upon a time …*"

Lockjaw was making retching noises.

"You two, get out," the Judge said.

"With pleasure, Your Worship."

Bandit edged around to the wind-free side of the greenhouse so he could hear their conversation when they came out.

"Friggin' relief to be out here! I pity His Worship. He must endure her tale ere he gets her tail."

Sensibella, fainter now because he was distant from the window, was telling her life story to the judge. Yet in her spinning haze of impassioned notions and supercharged images, she wasn't revealing a single item of information about herself. In fact, Sensibel had no life story at all, other than back-to-back classes in deportment followed by field hockey.

"I beg you, *Mademoiselle*, abbreviate your intellectual biography. Much as it teases the imagination, I find it completely without substance."

*"Then it shall gain in elegance as it gains in simplicity. Where was I? Oh, yes. I was saying that a lady's heart sits ever in a court of judgment. As it does likewise, I presume, in a gentleman of consequence such as Your Worship, though I have not yet met a man whose heart is true ..."*

She hasn't met a single man in her life, Bandit thought. Except possibly the tall romantic stranger she had extolled in the willow tree. The *artiste*.

*"But a lady's heart is true, simple and pure, and having this disposition it will for its own benefit spontaneously obey someone whose judgments are just and lawful."*

"To be sure," the Judge said.

*"Yet assisting the force of instinct is the power of natural reason. For reason draws significance from this disposition of the heart in that one animal who best perceives the order and seemliness in things. I speak of course of the noble Raccoon. The rational Raccoon perceives the beauty, constancy, and the congruence of all the parts of the object that she senses. Natural reason transfers this sensation from the heart to the mind, thinking that beauty, constancy and order should be preserved – and much more so – in a Raccoon's deeds and decisions. Doubtless in your offices as a magistrate, Your Honour has likewise made judgments based only on a sense of Proportion in the accused's actions and character when factual evidence is lacking."*

"I have indeed," the Judge said, taken in by Sensibella's flattery. It was clear he possessed the rare quality of harmony in his emotions necessary to a magistrate who has to make determinations on the fly.

*"Then in likewise manner, Your Worship will allow that my heart dances with the play of your Proportions upon it, and my heart tells*

me: 'Here is a worthy Gentleman and an upright governor withal. If he would but resist the fetish of viewing every relationship between Raccoons as a transaction'."

"Wow!" Bandit whispered. He had come back to the open window to hear the discourse better.

"Alas, the habit is a commonplace of our pinched and mercenary times," the Judge replied. "I wouldst have a relationship with you that cannot be bought or sold."

"*Then you must woo me.*" Her sigh came clearly through the open windowpane.

"Ancestor in heaven – where do I begin?"

"*Begin with the Beauty of the disposition of parts of your Paramour as they meet your Senses. Sight, hearing, taste, smell, and, lastly and most urgent of all, touch. Each sense must be accorded its due measure. Whence, dilate on these Sensations as they find their order in your heart's affections, paying heed to the inner Beauty, Constancy, and Orderliness of your beloved. Thence, extol your desire in a pleasing sonnet in the fashion of a Poet.*"

Sounds easy, Bandit thought. He was being ironic. In reality, he found that articulating his feelings for Sensibella was impossible. He'd just open and close his mouth like a wolf-fish. And she wanted her paramour's feelings arranged in a sonnet, whatever that was. Maybe he could find one on the web. Why couldn't poets come right out and say what they felt?

"*Of course, when you praise a lady, your words must show a moderation and restraint. For just as the eye, aroused by the beauty of her body, arranges her limbs and tail with delight that all her parts are in graceful harmony, your words must ...*"

A crash inside the greenhouse. Should he take a chance and look? No, someone was rushing out. It was His Worship with a look of horror on his face. He was clutching his throat, stumbling to the edge of the roof to throw up. Clearly, he wasn't a poet. It gave Bandit some comfort that he shared this disability with the judge.

Instead of vomiting, the Judge stood swaying at the edge of the roof. A concerned Lockjaw and Drooplip rose on their hind legs above the meadow grass.

"Prepare her by daybreak or else I'll close the place."

"If Your Worship would be patient, I'll prepare another escort."

"No, this one will do. She looks good on the arm. But a single word out of her mouth is enough to dampen the ardour of any suitor. She simply must keep her muzzle shut."

"I'll make sure she doesn't speak."

"She is intended for a very important Visitor to the city who's making his appearance tomorrow."

"Understood, Your Honour."

"Oh, and her tail is wet and bedraggled. Looks like it's been around the block. Get her a false tail. The fluffiest one you can find."

# 27

THE STORM HER BROTHERS had weathered caught Touchwit halfway across the river. A wind funneling out of the north plucked the tops off the waves and hurled them downriver in a blinding spray. Then the sky dropped, pinning her to the surface. Halfway Island shot by in the rain. The far shore vanished. She tried to swim at a right angle to the current, but it outwrestled her and spun her towards the concrete supports of the railway bridge. She closed her eyes and braced for the blow of the pylon. But at the last second the current chose to take her around it. When she opened her eyes, the bridge was in the past. The river was getting tired of her and considered throwing her into a wooden walkway lining the shore at the back of a hotel. But a second current joined the contest and decided otherwise. Cascading out of the Crosstown Creek spillway, it muscled her right back to the middle of the river. And now to get through a narrowing between the two shorelines, all the currents of the river were squeezing together and moving faster. They wanted to carry her through the narrows to the Lake and leave her there, too exhausted to paddle to shore. Wait! What was this? A harbour for boats. If she caught a back eddy and used up the last of her effort, she might just escape the hold of the currents.

Touchwit bounced along the side of a yacht rolling violently in the wind. Behind it was a small pocket of water. She bobbed with the weeds and flotsam, wondering how to climb the rusted metal siding of the dock.

She had no idea how she did it because she lost consciousness once she reached the top. She rolled up in a fetal ball under the rain and forgot everything. The great sea that flows across the sky had descended and joined one of the rivers of Earth. There was only a narrow strip of existence between them. That is where she lay until dawn.

\* \* \*

An eye gazing down at her. A yellow eye holding the knowledge of the atmospheric sea and its earthly child, this river. A strong bill hooked at the end for prying out soft tissue like the flesh inside a clamshell. The storm had left behind one of its wind spirits in the likeness of a Gull.

"I'm alive," Touchwit hissed. "Don't think about plucking out my eye or I'll make you wish you were back inside your egg."

The bird pulled in its wings which it had outstretched when she hissed at him. Was that a chuckle? She wasn't sure. It could have been a cough. Grey wings. A Herring Gull then. A male. Hard to tell.

"I have seen some things wash up in my time, but never a raccoon dumb enough to swim across a river in a storm. Where were you headed?"

"That's my business. Yours is to go to a garbage dump and lick Primate baby diapers."

"Good one!" the Gull said.

Touchwit felt her hackles collapsing, and anyway the bird wasn't a threat. He was one of those retired Seniors who had a lot of leftover attitude and nothing to do.

"I have three homes," the Gull said in his wizened voice. "And none of them is a chimney."

He knew where her den was!

"A chimney," he repeated. "You know, having only one home gives a person mundane ideas about territory. You River people think your place on the river is ancestral. Now you want to take over the West Bank. You think all the other creatures who have lived there longer than you lot can shove off."

"If you have several homes, you don't have any home," Touchwit responded.

The Gull waved her interruption aside and went on with his comment. "Then, the next thing you do is start to brawl among yourselves for territory."

"Gulls fight over a single French fry in a parking lot."

"We are free individuals. Differences of opinion about who has first right to a French fry is an exercise of our freedom."

"Where are your homes?"

"My homes are in the elegy of winds and weather and turning of the year. They are not in space. My homes are in time."

Okay, there's something to be learned from this bleached, weather-wise piece of driftwood. But not now. What stuck out wasn't his attitude but the fact that he knew where she lived. No one should know where she lived. Yet it seemed reasonable that a seagull would know. He spent part of the day soaring in circles over the city. And he had an eye for detail. He must be a flying encyclopedia. Time to be deferential. But she wasn't going to lose her edge.

"I understand your wider picture. But I won't be able to appreciate it fully until you lend me your wings."

"Flying Raccoons! Good one!"

Again that series of choking rasps, as if a spiky sunfish had gone down his throat sideways. He was laughing. No. Something was wrong with his bill. And he kept turning his bill away so she couldn't see the defect.

"Maybe I can fix that," she said. "Raccoons don't have wings except in old tales, but they have really clever hands."

The Gull considered her offer. Then he bravely turned his head to reveal the other side of his bill. A metal fish hook. It was firmly embedded where the bill met his cheek which was scarred and featherless from his futile scratching.

"I got it going fishing."

"It's preventing your bill from fully opening. It must be hard for you to swallow fish now."

"I would be glad to swallow a whole fish again."

"Try not to squawk until I'm finished. This is going to hurt."

"I'd also be glad to have a good head-in-the-air squawk again. I haven't squawked in ages."

Getting the hook out was a matter of going in the direction of the barb, not against it. She estimated the angle correctly and slid the object out in one easy motion. The Gull didn't even blink.

"Thank you," the Gull said. "Now, I must persuade breakfast to come to the surface." With that, the bird hopped into the wind, glided to a flower bed close by, and began stamping his feet, first one then the other.

"What in heaven's name are you doing?" Touchwit asked.

"I'm getting a worm to come up."

"You eat worms?"

"No, of course not. Raccoons eat worms. I eat seafood. Worms are for bait."

"I see. But what's the point of the ritual dance? Is it supposed to compel a worm to rise by magic?"

"Exactly. I'm pretending to sound like rain hitting the soil. That will get a worm to come up. Like magic." The seagull gazed at the ground severely. "Ah-ha!" He tugged the worm out and walked back to the dock with it twisting in his mouth. The bird dropped the worm into the lake and waited. Suddenly in a flash, he opened its wings and alighted on the water below. He quickly ducked his head under and returned with a fish in his bill. Holding it against the dock with one leg, he bit off its tail, tilted his head back, and swallowed it in a series of spasms. "Part for you," he indicated.

Touchwit ate the rest of the fish gratefully. "If I had wings, I could find someone in the city. I swam across the River because of him."

"Describe whom you're seeking."

"He's a loner. I was supposed to meet him on a dock below an outdoor restaurant."

"More facts please."

Oh, *visual* facts. "He's a male. Long and tall for a raccoon. He doesn't have a family, or at least not one he spends much time with. He conceals his tracks." Saying this, Touchwit considered that the Stranger didn't have a home.

"Fascinating. A Raccoon without a territory," the Gull said. "But I am not aware of the fellow. He must be a consummate Nightsider."

The more accurate the Gull's identifications, the more frustrated she felt. The Seagull couldn't help her.

"But I'll go ask my colleagues."

New word: *colleagues*. She liked the sound of it.

"They're riding out the storm on a field. The canvas cover on that sailboat is loose." The Gull pointed with his pointed wing.

She looked in the direction he indicated – a cave to get out of the rain. She felt awe and gratitude for this laconic bird. Like him, she survived by scavenging, she in space, he in time. She thought of a silly saying: Colleagues who scavenge together, manage together.

* * *

A thump above her head. The rain had stopped drumming on the canvas. She pushed open the flap and poked her nose out to see a pair of naked, pink legs. How long had he been away? It was daylight now.

"Good morning. A high ceiling with a light westerly. It should clear in the late morning. Come out and see the cloud pattern. Did you sleep well?"

"Yes, thank you." Why is it people who are wide awake and voluble don't realize others need to wake up in stages? Daysiders are insufferably cheerful in the morning.

"Much happening in the world of Groundlings today," the bird went on. "There are meetings beginning all over the city, going on into the day. Something big is going to happen. Creek Town Raccoon males have been slipping into the city for the last two days while your folk are asleep."

*Get to the point.*

"Your loner is on the move."

"Where's he going?"

"A hilltop in view of the traffic bridge. He goes there sometimes."

"Can you guide me there?"

"I can, but it will take you full on morning to get there. By then, he will have left. He goes there to join with other Raccoons."

Why is meeting someone so complicated? Meeting in space does not intersect with meeting in time. Would that she had wings.

"Will you carry a message to him?"

"Herring Gulls don't talk to Groundlings. I broke Custom to talk to you."

"I'll give you something to carry in your bill."

"Describe it."

"Better than that, I'll make it." Touchwit began pulling hair out of her tail.

142

"Why are you destroying your tail feathers? For us, they're crucial for flight. We can't do stall turns without them." To demonstrate, the Gull spread his neat, squared-off tailfeathers.

"I'm sending a scent-message," Touchwit explained. She wove the first swathe of her fur into the beginning of a ring. "Our tails are crucial too. Our personal scent glands are located just under them."

"I wish I had your busy fingers. I wouldn't have to drop a clam thirty feet onto a rock to open it, then have to pounce on it before other Colleagues get it."

The ring was complete. She tied it with the three knots the Loner used on his Making.

She placed it in the seagull's bill. "Pretend it's a French fry."

## 28

"Look! That's him. That's the one."
"He looks badly hurt."
"But the Champion wears his wounds proudly. Imagine! Vanquishing a Drooler."
"No Raccoon has ever killed a Canine that big."
"That wasn't just any Drooler – it was the monster Droolzilla."
"Actually, the Drooler was part Wolf. I heard it from Slickfur who heard it from Fleatail who got it directly from Sleek."
"He sacrificed himself for the Twins. Sleekfoot and Lightfinger wouldn't be with us if it weren't for him."

Clutch looked down at his feet. He hoped the gesture would be mistaken for modesty. In fact, it wasn't modesty he felt – it was confusion about his sudden change of fortune. Even the senior male above fighting age who was portioning out the clams and water plants for the line of waiting raccoons regarded him with awe. Fortunately, the two warriors who had intervened in the chicken raid weren't here to provide their account. But what would happen when they returned to Creek Town? He needed to act fast. "Tell me, mate. Where is the One Who Can't be Named?"

"Better use his preferred name for the day," the elder male advised. "He is using the name: *The Protector*. Be sure to say *the*. We think he's in the city."

"*The* Protector," Clutch repeated.

A raccoon in the line-up was limping. Sleekfoot. And Lightfinger supporting him. Clutch walked over to greet them. As he approached, the whispering in the line rose to a chatter.

"The Great One's Son!"
"I want to touch my nose to his."
"Don't do that. You're not permitted to touch him."
"Who says so?"
"Custom says so."
"He's speaking to someone – I think it's Sleekfoot."

"Hello, Sleek. Lightfinger, dear. I'm glad you're free."

"This," Lightfinger whispered, "is not free."

"I know. But at least they're not starving you to get you to talk."

"Talk? You can be sure I talked," Sleekfoot said grinning. "I trust you're enjoying the result."

"I never thought Raccoons were so given to rumour."

"We aren't," Lightfinger said. "But if we are forced to sleep in clumps and work in shifts, we have nothing to do but pass on news."

"They say rumour is even more rife in the city."

"*Next.*"

They had reached the front of the food line. Clutch stepped back to let his new kinsfolk take their food – he would eat last. The custom was to swallow the clam on the spot, then carry away the water vegetables in their mouths to eat in the trees. Everywhere there were raccoons in twos and threes eating together. Mostly mothers and daughters, Clutch noted, as he watched the empty food bins being tipped over on their side in the lake. They would be submerged and invisible until the next communal feeding. They were small recycling bins filched from the Primates. It was dawn, before the Park filled with early morning joggers, cyclists, and droolers on leashes. The Creek Towners slept for the rest of the day, then resumed food-gathering after the last of the swimming children and soccer players went home.

Later, hidden in an ancient weeping willow that hung over the beach, Clutch, Light and Sleek resumed their collusion.

"The fighting-age males are away in the High Guard securing the Southern Frontier," Sleek explained, answering Clutch's puzzlement about the absence of young males.

"Though some went over in the City to plan No Name's arrival," Light said.

"Is it safe to talk here?" Clutch asked.

"Yes, but we'd better plan quickly," Sleek said. "Because when the news of your esteem reaches the Great Nothing's ears, he's going to come back here and sort you out."

"He's busy in the City," Light said. "Gossip has it that he's arranged an occasion. He's going to name himself The Protector of the

City. But Sleek's right. No Name would postpone his coronation just to make sure he doesn't have a challenger."

"To him, a powerful son is a threat."

"He prefers dumb sons."

"But that's not how it works," Clutch said. "Custom says that sons and daughters inherit a territory through their mother's lineage."

"Nameshifter has forgotten Custom. He has no sense of it."

"What do you plan to do?"

"I don't know," Clutch answered. "All I can think of is dump the bins in the lake and run like our tails are on fire."

"You have the respect of everyone here. Even the senior males. You're equivalent to a Clan Father."

"I'm not a natural leader."

"There's no such thing as a natural leader. Leaders are created by circumstance," Sleek said. "Look at you. You became a leader when you hurled yourself at a Drooler."

"That circumstance happened because I didn't have time to think."

"You don't have time to think now."

"I know. But I need to be alone and gather circumstances into myself. Maybe I'll figure something out."

A raccoon at the bottom of the tree was gesturing vigorously. It was Silverheels. What was the matter? Clutch waved her up to climb the tree.

"My companion, Lickfoot – she fled."

"That's good news, isn't it?"

"No," Silverheels cried. "She's run to the city to tell the Almighty Anon that you're starting an Insurrection."

## 29

CLUTCH WAS SURPRISED by how quickly the people of Creek Town transferred their loyalty to him. Having no clan families to belong to anymore, the population had become like algae in a lagoon, a suspension of particles swayed this way and that by currents of gossip and attracted to the only social structure available – one man rule. No Name had created an autocracy by dissolving the boundaries of the hunting grounds on which the traditional families depended, then substituting himself as the central authority assisted by a group of alpha males with the rank of clan family head but no actual family. This system was kept intact by creating a state of fear, with daily campaigns of disorienting gossip mainly about Invasions of Migrants Bringing Disease.

Clutch, without intending to, took over the headship of this power structure. The act was a temporary measure only, to get Creek Town through the coming struggle. After victory had been won, he would restore the Clan Mothers to their family hunting grounds while he went off to do what he enjoyed best, which was being alone with his own thoughts. He recalled a quotation of Uncle Wily's from raccoon oral sayings: *In solitude, be to thyself a throng.* Perhaps he would contribute a saying to raccoon literature himself one day.

But he couldn't be certain he would bring about a victory for his present throng who were looking up to him for direction. Sharing his uncertainty with Sleekfoot and Lightfinger, he was dismayed by their quixotic enthusiasm.

They were lying at No Name's headquarters in the part of Creek Town that Primates had left in a wilderness state. Here, in the fork of a massive elm that had somehow escaped disease, the Nameless One would pronounce new Customs at nightfall, then enforce them by punishments the following dawn.

A cool morning breeze blew a promise of autumn across the river from the city. But it carried no information out of the ordinary. They would have to rely on scraps of gossip.

"One of Nobody's scouts came in last night," Sleek said. "His loyalty did a back twist when he saw we were running the show. I told him we were enforcing No Name's punishment for treason. That made him talk."

"What's a scout?"

"Someone who does special missions. A spy. A secret agent. An assassin. He said Nameless assigned him to slip into the city and spread disinformation in the gossip network about an attack by Migrants. Then, when Nameless installs himself as *Protector of the City*, he's going to say that the City Fathers asked him to protect the city from the invasion."

"I see."

"After the Great Nothing is installed, this scout's mission will be to sniff out traitors to the new regime hiding in the city population. And Migrants."

"What else did the turncoat tell you?"

Lightfinger took over the report. The twins had the habit of speaking alternately, finishing each other's sentences.

"The Big Tail is going to host a feast. It's timed to coincide with some outdoor celebration planned by the Primates. There will be heaps of meat and spirit sugar. When he's gathered them all together, he's going to give it out and announce to the hungry, frightened masses that he's their Protector."

"Against himself," Clutch said. No Name had a unique ability to create a problem and then offer himself as the solution. The problem in this case was too many migrants. The solution … what was the solution? It was probably to increase the population of raccoons in the city by extending its territory to include the East Bank. The bonus for Creek Town would be free movement across the river and the acquiring of primate food. For the City dwellers, access to crayfish and clams.

He didn't know much about the city and its folkways. It had always been a mystery to him – not a beckoning wonder as it was to Bandit and Touchwit. He needed to know more about the Occasion.

"I must talk to the scout. What's his name?"

"Clawface. I'll go get him."

"When is the Occasion happening?" he asked the scout, once he was produced.

The warrior was a fighting raccoon with a wound mark down the side of his face. But his eyes were unimpaired and keen.

"Judging by the arrival of food trucks, it will begin tomorrow night. We can smell raw meat, potatoes, and corn in the trucks, and we've figured out how to break into them. The Primate feast is a two-day event. After they depart the first evening, we will pillage the organic waste bins and then break into the trucks."

It was an old raccoon trick, but on a grand scale – to take a primate picnic and graft a raccoon feast on top of it. He had to admire the Nameless One's cunning.

"What does he want Creek Towners to do here?"

"Just stay put and keep the Invaders at bay."

That piece of information was significant. No Name didn't have enough fighting raccoons to subdue the city and hold the frontier against Southerners at the same time. He had divided his forces on two fronts. Remember that, Clutch.

"Is there likely to be trouble on the frontier?" Light asked.

The spy looked to Clutch for permission. Should he answer a question from a subordinate?

"Go ahead."

"No, sir," Clawface said. "The Invaders never begin the battles. We're the ones who start them. Whenever we need to stir up trouble."

Clutch could tell by Clawface's reticence that this was a state secret. "Thank you," he said, not knowing how he would use it. There was another piece of information hidden in this secret. What was it?

"How do you get to the city?" he asked.

"Our usual route. Down to the highway bridge just south of us. Then across to the park where Primates bury their bodies. Then up the lakefront into the downtown."

"Why don't you just swim across from here to the burying place?"

"Some of us do. But not No Name. He doesn't like it when his tail looks wet and limp. He wants it fluffed out. Same with his ruff."

"Can he swim at all?"

"When he has to."

Remember that too, Clutch. The powerful leader with the buoyant ruff and tail may surprise you by swimming.

## 30

"A GENTLEMAN CALLER for your ladyship," Drooplip announced. Lockjaw turned to Sensibella: "Give him everything he wants. He says he's the emissary for the Great Leader who is visiting the City tomorrow. The agent is named *Il Signore Incognito* and he is masked. And keep your muzzle shut."

"How intriguing. Have him enter."

*Il Signore* filled the greenhouse with mystery and danger. "I venture to present myself, milady," he said from behind his mask. "Yet following Custom, I will reveal my name indirectly through a display of Wit."

"*Mmft!*"

"I have ventured to compose a poem on the subject of your Ladyship's elegance and beauty."

"*Mmmh?*"

"Regrettably, she is unable to speak. She has a disability involving her tongue," Lockjaw explained.

"*Mmmm.*"

"It begins thus, milady:

> *To put in words my love's Proportions*
> *Is my vain task. Who dares elaborate*
> *The beauty of her thighs, her tail, the torsions*
> *Of her sinews whilst tussling as her mate?*

"*Mmmpf, mmph!*"

"There's more ..."

"She says your poem is not entirely without merit," Lockjaw said.

"Oi think it sucketh, if yer wants my opinion."

"Though my poem be unworthy of My Lady's excellence, I trust that it gains in sincerity for what it lacks in technique. I shall go on ..."

"*PHOO! PHOO!*"

"I'm sorry. I'm not very articulate. I can't help it. I am a suitor of few words. But it doesn't mean I don't appreciate your beauty as much as any stout gentleman. And by beauty, I don't just mean your eyes which are so wide-set and full of adventure. Or your paws – how so intelligently you ply your fingers. Your …"

"What about her tail?"

"I'm getting to her tail. I have to work my way down. That's what poets do."

"Not just poets, oi fancy."

"Not that My Lady's tail is the summit of her allure. Only that Poetic Custom requires that the poet treat every detail of the beauty of his beloved. After he has extolled her physical beauty, he may then proceed to contemplate her spiritual assets." *Signor Incognito* paused to clear his head. What he had just said had made him dizzy. Where was this stuff coming from? Then he blurted: "You have an Inner Beauty you don't even know about."

"*Mm mmmh!?*"

"Believe me, you do!"

"*Mmmmmnah!!!*"

Lockjaw leaned close to Sensibel to hear her whisper. "She says, if *Signor Incognito* but remove his mask, she will regain the power of speech by magic."

"She can speak?" *Incognito* asked.

"Yes. Provided she is modest in her verbosity."

"*Signor Incognito*, what a delight to meet you." Sensibella curtseyed.

Bandit untied his mask made from a wild grapevine and bowed deeply. "The pleasure is mine, my lady."

Even starved, bedraggled and in hideous company, Sensibella looked like the spirited girl he knew. That high, proud heart. That energy of affection flowing from her body. She was trying to conceal her tail.

"The *Signore* pleases me. I would like to speak with him alone."

"We can go outside. Can't we, Droops?"

"Suits me fine. Don't want to be no wet blanket on milady's pleasure."

"You could go down to the courtyard and wait there," Sensibel said. "I shan't be long."

Bandit followed them to the greenhouse door to be certain they left the roof.

"Bandy, darling. How kind of you to rescue me from this vulgar couple."

"Did you like my poem? I only recited the opening lines. It's a sonnet."

"Your poem was ... it was, well ... Oh, Bandit, it was terrible." Bandit hung his tail.

"But it touched my heart. And the things you said about me afterward – no poet could have said those."

"Thank you."

"Look, you've got to get me out of here. Take me, where ere the heart wanders! Do you believe it? The panderer and his bawd are going to rent me to some Potentate who's visiting the city? I'm supposed to appear on His Potency's arm and look beautiful."

"Don't let him near your tail. Did they say what his name is?"

"He doesn't have one. But he's dreadfully important. Names don't adhere to him because he creates stories about himself faster then children. I'm supposed to give him the delight of my company and keep my mouth shut."

"I know who he is."

"Who is he?"

"He's all over the networks. He's taken over the management of Creek Town from the Clan Mothers. He wants to extend his regime here."

"I'm not very interested in politics."

"Not if it involves your family?"

"Bandit, what does my family have to do with it?"

"He is ... my father."

"My uncle!"

Sensibel had turned white. Bandit felt storm clouds gather over her brow. There was going to be an explo ...

"*To think I am to be a public mating toy for my uncle! Shameful!* Lock and Droop, together with Judge Ponderous who is orchestrating this pitiful scheme, are strictly lower drawer. They have no class at all. No sense of the propriety of family lineage."

"That is true, but I have to explain ..."

"Raccoon nature may be great in times of trial, yet it is weakness that appears in this stressful time. Impotence and impatience, not fortitude and endurance, rule the world. Oh, there is so little one can trust."

"Didn't I tell you that at your hiding tree?"

"Indeed, you did, Bandy. But I wanted to make a world for myself. And now I have discovered the world I am given to work with is full of trickery and deceit."

"You said you loved trickery and deceit."

"Yes, My own, not other people's."

Bandit was having an idea. He could feel it trying to get out of his fingers. He felt his mind reaching down to coax the sensation upward and welcome it into his brain.

"What is it, Bandit? Are you alright?"

"Do you think you could hold your tree limb against No Name, if you had to?"

"I could hold my own against any man, except my one true love."

"Would you like to give yourself to the people instead of to your insane uncle? You could bring free love to the City. Freedom to love whomever one chooses. There are so many raccoons on the web seeking *l'amour libre*. So many going un-mated."

"What would you have me do?"

"My idea is that you dally along with His Nothingness. Just play the game. But don't get onto a limb you can't back off of."

"I always wanted to be a courtesan. But what are you getting me into?"

"No Name is taking over the city. I want to know his plan. Then maybe we can stop him. If we can't, he'll turn every raccoon relationship into a transaction. An item that can be bought and sold."

"You were listening. Shame on you!" Sensibel laughed. "What shall I do? You want me to practice trickery and deceit, don't you?"

"Just for one night, while you're nose candy for No Name. You can find out about this Occasion he's hosting for himself. Where it's happening and when. There are people on the networks who want to wreck it once they know where it is. They call themselves Makers."

"Ah! *Artistes*." Sensibel paused. "Where will you be hiding? Among them …?"

"No, I don't know where they are. But I'll be hiding in plain sight. Your uncle's secret agents think I'm one of them already."

"Do you know? It occurs to me that I require a personal protector. He can be concealed among the City Honour Guard. I shall demand of His Worship that *Il Signor Incognito* serve me in that capacity. He must wear his mask. It makes him look mysterious and romantic. He can perform special missions for me, such as find out where the Makers are. What is a courtesan without mystery and romance?"

"Sensibel …"

"Yes. What is it, Bandit?

"It's a thrill working with you."

"*Mmmmpft!*"

# 31

T HE ROAR OF A CITY coming to life in the morning overwhelmed her senses, and she was fidgety by the time she left the harbour to cross a short footbridge over a spillway. This was where the Cross-town Creek exited, pushing her away from the shore the previous night. The stream wasn't a threat now; it was once again the allure it had been when Mother took her family through it to visit Aunt Pawsense – a thoroughfare for animals under the City.

She rested on a grassy lawn of a hotel beside the lakefront and looked for her next seagull. Always there was a seagull to guide her. Looking north, she saw one standing on a lamp post. She couldn't be sure if it was her friend or one of his colleagues leading her in this lap of the relay. Funny how one gull will perch on a vantage point, then a second seagull will come along and the first will dutifully yield its place to the newcomer according to a tacit time-sharing agreement. Respect for each other's spaces comes easily to creatures without a territory. Born sentinels, they survey a frontier in time, not space.

The gull led her to the northern end of the hotel where the railway bridge crossed the river. Her den was on the other side, just up from the tracks. How often she'd stayed awake while her brothers slept, listening to the train clanging through. But it was forbidden to cross this bridge without supervision – her mom had made that clear. It was long, and she could be caught out in the open by a primate cart or a bicycle. She felt nervous, just crossing the tracks.

Now, a reward for her effort – a long pathway overhung by trees extending north beside the river. The elegant tunnel of greenery meant a park. No threats here except a primate jogger. Where did they run to? She could never understand where they went with such determination. Yet it was easeful here. The bushes in the park had been arranged by Primates so as to recall the kinds of growth found in the wild. This was intriguing too – that they fashioned an experi-ence of wilderness for themselves in this park.

A restaurant overlooking the river. No cooking smells. Must be too early in the day for Primates to have breakfast. But Mallard Ducks already busy in the water. The next gull wanted her to follow a single rusty railway track that ran north behind scrub bushes alongside the park, dividing it from the city. Safer here because she could avoid an open lawn behind the restaurant, evidently a meeting place for primates. Then the park again – and what was this? She crouched; her hackles shot up. But it was only the semblance of a human child beside a beautiful forest pool. A Making! Here was a natural resting place, and she let her fear subside to the comforting chirping of birds flying in and out of a wall of foliage overlooking the park. It stretched to the sky. The Primates had covered an entire building with vines and shrubs!

Just beyond the living building the park ended, and she was left on the railway track. It led towards a noisy traffic bridge in front of the factory of sugary scents. Her mouth immediately started to water. Stop it! – you're too smart to be a lush. Concentrate. Under the bridge and up the bank – old trodden dirt and garbage. Where's the next gull?

The next guide stood on a fire hydrant at the top of a short, steep hill beyond the traffic bridge. Why don't seagulls perch in trees like normal birds? Because trees don't grow on lakes and oceans. The hill turned out to have a large stone building at the top overlooking a park with ancient trees, flanked by old brick residences. The guide gave a goodbye squawk and flew across the river. Now she was alone in broad daylight in unknown terrain. This was scary. From now on, she was going to be a dedicated Nightsider, like the gentleman she was seeking.

A polite call. A new gull stood stiffly beside the door to a cellar of one of the houses. Could it be? Yes, it was her friend.

"The one you're seeking is in there. There are colleagues with him. Don't be afraid. The Raccoons in this city are discovering something from Seagulls. They are learning to flock together."

She sniffed the cellar door curiously. Old musty, soil smells. Root vegetables. A gust of warm raccoon scents. And another ... what was it? A Groundhog. It was probably his root cellar. She looked questioningly at the gull.

"The one you want sniffed your Making when I dropped it at his feet. He examined the knots. You certainly made him puzzled."

Puzzled? Why would he be puzzled? Was she being too pushy introducing herself through her Making? Makings aren't aggressive. Not if they are good Makings.

"He carried it into the meeting."

"Thank you, dear colleague. I owe you a gift."

"You owe a colleague nothing, except respect. However if you were to snatch a bag of French fries someday, I wouldn't turn my beak at it." The seagull lifted into the air and soon became a speck of freedom.

Inside, an excitement of attentive bodies. Blessed relief of darkness – warm, dry darkness. No one noticed her come in. Take this place at the back in this old cellar. Listen to who is speaking. A senior male artist who speaks with the wisdom of Procyonides.

"We are creatures of the Wild, and we carry Wilderness in our bodies. But we are at the end of a slim branch because there is so little Wilderness left to nourish our Wildness. We are forced to survive under porches and in chimneys, scrounging the garbage of Primates and losing our nobility. So is it any surprise that we find ourselves at the feet of a so-called *Protector*, who is about to extend his Wildness-hating impulses to this already barren habitat?"

A rustle of approval. Clutch would approve too, if he were here. He puts his trust in the Wild and its natural customs. But the approval comes from the front of the cellar only; the younger raccoons at the back are restless. They must like cities. The speaker clearly doesn't.

"And forced to be refugees surviving in cities, the best thing, the *only* thing, we can do as Makers is memorialize our ancient Customs in our Artifacts so that the few survivors who come after us will know what Wildness is, and will seek it out, and be nurtured by it. Our task is to show them our grace as a species. And the grounding of that grace, which is Wilderness."

Audible stirrings. This is a call to die nobly in the face of a catastrophe. But where's the catastrophe? She doesn't see any catastrophe. Only the world changing. It's something a world does.

"Then our descendants will take note that we faced extinction with a high heart and noses to the wind. You ask: what are our Customs? Remember Procyonides, the great Raccoon sage. First, Inventiveness, the mark of a true raccoon given to each of us by the Raccoon Ancestor, to hold an object in our eye, separate it from its surrounding objects, and understand its essence – what is proper to it and nothing else. Second: Beauty, the sense of Proportion in an object and in its relationships with other objects. Hapticia herself bestowed this virtue on us at the beginning of time when she put her mind in our fingers. We handle the balances of life, know them, respect them, and relinquish them ..."

An easing of rapt bodies, expressed as a sigh. Raccoons are being called to remember the old ways. The ways of antiquity. But her body isn't relaxing. She's taut with questions. What's troubling these lovely Makers? It's not extinction. If raccoons were really about to go extinct, she'd be having a Big Nothing Attack. Like Clutch.

A reticent clearing of a throat near the door where she came in. It's the Groundhog who owns this cellar. A male. He wants to speak, but like all of his kind he's shy and doesn't enjoy attention. Crowded bodies shuffle to fasten their noses on him. Ears rise. What is the wisdom of a Groundhog?

"Earth gives us every breath we take. Earth takes back every breath we give. And that is true in every habitat we live in, whether it has Primates or not. Take it from one who lives in the margins, on the edges of paths and roads. There is no pure, wild nature – there never was: it is always already parceled up into territories and regulated by all the species who created and inhabit it. Wilderness teems with civility; cities are pregnant with wilderness ..."

This is interesting, but if he keeps talking in his gentle way he's going to stop anyone from having a point of view whatsoever. Is having a viewpoint aggressive? A Spider who has descended from the ceiling to listen strolls back up her thread. There are woman raccoons in this room. Why aren't they speaking? They're Makers too. Are females not allowed to speak as Makers? The wilderness gentleman is in this room somewhere. Probably in a corner where he can't be noticed.

A raccoon at the front of the room comes to the rescue of the reluctant host whose den this is. He seems to be the leader of this Guild of Makers. His front paws are clutched together as if he's taking the pulse of the universe in his wrists.

"Dear people, our distinguished colleagues have called on us as Makers to honour our history as a species." (*Colleague* – she likes this word more and more.) "Their Makings show how Earth lives its life to the full in us. However, we might be living in the early years of a better civilization. And to make our way to that future we must confront a threat – a figure who dares to be unnameable, as if he were the very incarnation of Being. I ask my fellow Makers to consider how to take the measure of his empire and prevent him from forcing it on our City."

Agitation. Everyone wants to speak. She does too, though she's not sure what she's going to say. The cellar has a lot more raccoons than she thought. All these Makers!

"*Imagine being told what we can Make and not Make ...*"

"*And eating the food he provides ...*"

"*And not being allowed to choose mates ...*"

"*We need some facts. Something we can grasp.*"

A body that has been lying without movement or expression, a long, slender body, unfurls like a banner. Could it be ...? Yes! Her Stranger! He has the mark of a leader. And leadership starts to pour out of him with a boyish enthusiasm.

"This is what we know as of daybreak. The scent-net shows signs of Creekers sneaking into the city. We guess they're High Guard because they're travelling in pairs. They smell like young adult males of the same father. The word is that they are advance agents of this self-made leader of the River Clan Families at Creek Town. He's coming this way. There is messaging that he's going to do something dramatic, and because this news is repeated like drumming on a hollow log, we think it's planted on the net by his agents. Maybe somebody has hard information ..."

What commanding relevance! A young male beside her speaks: "I have something."

"Go ahead."

So many eyes and ears turn in her direction, it feels like the room itself turns.

"Thank you. We've learned that he is renting a female companion for an Occasion, said to be a grand, open-air event. She's said to be mate-worthy. This is supposed to make him look virile and potent. He is obsessed with becoming a father to many."

Wry murmurs. Even a chuckle. She is shocked. This isn't funny. The leader they're discussing can only be one person. Her father. And he has a name. Meatbreath.

*"His seeking a companion suggests the Occasion is imminent."*

*"I heard it was tomorrow night."*

*"The only reason to have an Occasion is to announce something."*

*"Regime change."*

*"What can we do? We aren't organized."*

*"We need more time."*

*"Can't we delay the Announcement?"*

*"How?"*

Her body is humming. Humming with ideas. But she can't choose one idea over another because they're all wound up around each other like grapevines. The Maker in her is in control – it is thinking *Relations*, not *Things*. Hard to do if your paws are designed to grasp objects. Objects are isolated. They can be moved around and put in another place. They can be eaten. They can be buried. But she's not a handler of Things – she's a perceiver of Relations, and Relations can't be tossed away. They can't be disposed of – they are living things. The Stranger replaced a fish he had eaten. The object turned into a relation again, and the relation swam away ... Well, actually, raccoons need to have *both* skills – perceiving relationships *and* manipulating things – and they need to braid the two skills together beautifully if they are to be superior Makers. Maybe this is *our grace as a species*. Grasp this: Meatbreath can't see beyond his paws. He only sees Things he can grab. He's a compulsive Grasper. He grasps so blindly that he grabs Relationships and treats them as if they're

Things. Disposable objects. She needs to speak. *My body needs to speak.* Don't do it, Touchwit, or you'll sound like you're vomiting a stream of poisoned clams.

"I want to speak. May I say something?" That was herself she heard, asking to speak.

"Please go ahead."

"Thank you." She took a deep breath. Five points. One for each finger. Need to put what she's thinking into a pattern for these pattern-thinking Makers. Ready? "Five points. Point one …" Just like her Mother. (*What I'm going to tell you will help you survive someday.*) She began again:

"Point One: we do not have time to fashion examples of grace for posterity. What has posterity done for us? We need to survive right now ourselves. Point Two: we can't do anything about the changes in our habitat – that's a Primate thing – but we *can* choose leaders who will make wise choices. Point Three: we must absolutely oppose the Protector in every way we can. And we need to muster the Citizen Raccoons of the city to do the same. Point Four: we are Makers. The natural way for us to oppose is to create Makings that subject Old No-name-daddy to ridicule. To cause his followers to see him as what he really is and desert him. And to ridicule him, we need to expose his technique for manipulating others. What is his technique? Simple. It is to duplicate himself. He duplicates himself in names, in rumours, in cubs, in wives, in territories. This one single raccoon simply outnumbers us. But we can mock this endless duplication. One thing we can do is we can make hoards of identical No Name Daddies and place them all over the city. We can do this tonight. Raccoons will get the point really fast."

She paused. Oh, she shouldn't have paused because now she can see her colleagues trying to figure out what on earth that last bit was all about. Some are shaking their muzzles as if trying to remove cobwebs. Some are nodding and frowning politely. Point Five. Crumbs! She doesn't have a point five …

"Point Five," the Stranger said. "This mindless duplication of sameness: we can counter it by flooding it with diversity. Makings of each and every kind." A glance across the cellar at her. Whoa! Did time just stand still? "For this diversity we learn from the Makings of other raccoon peoples who have migrated here." He's taking her thinking and extending it out into the world. Hap in Heaven! He's as cosmopolitan as a Seagull. The Stranger's voice drops. "I guess everybody knows I study Makings from all the Islands of Earth. You wouldn't believe how far raccoons have spread. We're in cities that haven't known wilderness for aeons. And we're thriving in places where there is wildness with little habitation. Do you know, there are Desert raccoons to the south on our own Island, beyond where the Ancestor goes to his den for the winter? I think what my colleague is saying" (another shy glance in her direction) "is that in each and every locale the Makings of raccoons show a style of surviving that is proper to the habitat and climate in that place. That's why we should welcome migrating Raccoons. They bring all these different styles of surviving."

"Style." The convener at the front of the cellar repeats the word reverentially. "Style is the intuition of Being – not a boast of cleverness as it is a way of saying glory to the Ancestor for enabling a creature to display such dexterity."

Glory be to Hapticia, she thinks. The Stranger is imagining a treeful of different Customs for Raccoons to choose from, instead of duplicating one Custom endlessly. Oh, it's going to be fun for smart Raccoons to make the best choices among all these styles of surviving. Say it! She spoke calmly and evenly from the back of the room.

"My colleague" (respectful pause) "has said that to let all these differing styles flourish, we cannot be dictated to. No one, least of all a pop-up Protector, should tell a Raccoon how they're supposed to think and feel. And Make. Our Makings tell us how to choose a future. They teach us style which is another name for survival. The coordination of paw and eye, the sign of a body alert in its habitat. Nobodaddy" (laughter) "is trying to rip apart that sacred bond between eye and paw. But that's how we survive. We're specialists at eye-paw coordination. Raccoons will show the world how to survive."

That brought the rough scraping together of palms. Applause. She had said enough. She was emptied. Raccoons began nudging their way across the dirt cellar floor to talk to her. She had to wave them away with a regretful smile. She needed air.

Outside, the cool morning had mellowed into a golden, hazy stillness that stretched across the horizon. Autumn was coming. A Seagull stood on top of a steeple guarding her.

*"Thanks for thinking with me."*

She turned. The wilderness gentleman held her Making in his paw.

"We don't have time to present ourselves appropriately through stories. My name is Touchwit."

"I'm Mindwalker."

Exactly like his scent-track. He thinks by walking, leaving his mind in each paw print.

"You didn't need to introduce yourself. Your Making speaks for you. But why did you send it to me?"

*Why? Because you're interesting, that's why. Because you seemed unapproachable any other way. Because you are totally wrapped up in your Makings.* "So you'd recognize me from the Making I put on your statue," she said.

"You were on the Island?"

She is confused. Only one island? "I don't mean on your statue on the *north* island."

"Oh, the Watcher. He's guarding the island. To let the Great Anonymity know the Makers have their eye on him."

"I put my wreath on your Watcher on the *south* island."

"I didn't put a Watcher on the south island."

She felt a sickening chasm open just beneath her heart. Who? Why?

"Someone must have copied my Making," he said.

This is bad. This is terribly bad. Take a breath, then say it. "He was stalking me. My own Father. I almost took his lure."

# ACT IV

## *Setback and Betrayal*

*Slypaws* and *Twitchwhisker*, ex-mothers and tourists in the City
*Clutch*, Governor of Creek Town and its war bands
*Bandit*, agent of the Secret Police and double agent for the Resistance
*Touchwit*, artist and strategist for *Mindwalker's* Resistance

A Seagull, her colleague and message-bearer

*Sensibella* of Pawsense Manor, Bandit's first cousin and love interest,
lady escort of *Meatbreath* the would-be Protector of the City

The Director of Security, a City bureaucrat with a personal militia
*Drooplip* and *Lockjaw*, procurers to the City

Clutch's bodyguard *Silverheels*, a Creek Town lady
*Frisk*, junior sister of Sensibel and Bandit's sidekick
*Lightfinger* and *Sleekfoot*, field commanders of the Creek Town army

The Voice of the Great Raccoon Ancestor

# 32

COME WITH ME TO THE PARK along the west bank of the river because this is where the destinies of the cubs will meet their destination. Here Bandit found an outdoor café overlooking a cove near where Sensibella came ashore. Touchwit made her way through the park, guided by seagulls. This is Millennium Park. The outdoor café is called The Silver Bean.

I come here often in the summer to sit and write. From my house on the east bank, I walk downriver along a public path to the railway bridge. There's only one track, an extension from the metropolis to the southwest. This was a busy line in the early twentieth century: five passenger trains and several freight trains used to come through here daily. Now the railway is used only to bring grain to the Quaker Oats factory, and crushed rock, a kind of feldspar, to the metropolis where it is used to make glass, ceramics and polymers.

The public pathway continues along the north edge of the railway bridge, giving a view of the river. There's usually something special to see, even if it's only the Kingbird who has overseen the bridge walk for several years. Once, in March, I saw a pair of Trumpeter Swans swimming along the shore ice. And I will never forget the autumn evening when line after line of Canada Geese set down at dusk. There were several hundred of them – they filled the river basin with excitement. Then at an invisible signal, the whole river rose from its riverbed in exultation. This early summer, I saw a Loon. She kept her body submerged, only showing her head and neck. Every spring, a migrating Loon will put down here. You're asleep at dawn, and your unconscious is naked to the world. A Loon splits the dawn with her soulful, gothic call. And you wake up in tears.

On the city side of the bridge, a path leads upriver under tree branches that meet over your head. You come to a freshly cut young tree lying on the grass. Pieces of it are scattered all over the lawn, and bark is missing from its branches. This is a city of seventy thousand people, and a Beaver is cutting down a tree in its showpiece park!

It's a short walk to the café under the trees. On this busy city side of the river, there are groups of cyclists, public school field trips, service club picnics, seniors from the retirement residence, and mothers passing time with their children.

The café patio overlooks a little harbour circled by a rocky point. This morning, a Cormorant is standing on the tip of the point holding his bill aloof at a proud angle. A female Mallard Duck facing him dozes in the early morning sun. A pair of Seagulls stand on the base of the point where they can keep an eye on the café diners. It is the still interval near the end of summer when nature rests. The work of parenting is done.

If you look east across the river, you'll see the little halfway island where Touchwit was caught in the storm and carried downriver. The north and south islands are visible, but not the house with its chimney which is behind them. Today, there is an Osprey at the top of a high dead tree on the north island.

I want to say something about Ospreys. Though they don't come into the cubs' stories, they show a contradiction the cubs are facing. This is a contradiction between the needs of the river and the needs of humans.

Once Ospreys nested on this part of the river. A pair built their home on a disused electricity pole below the southern island. For the residents along the east bank and everyone who took the path across the railway bridge, the birds presented a daily domestic drama of child raising. Like eagles, they swoop down and grab a fish with their talons and take it back to the chicks who are clamouring in the nest. All morning long, then again in the evening, the river rings with the demanding cries of the chicks and the excited hunting call of their parents. Everything about these confident raptors is obvious: their nest, their young, their loud clear whistles, their splashdown on the water surface. The family drama reaches a crisis when the chicks become fledglings urgent to command the sky like their big, bold parents. For now it's time to fly, and the children don't know how to do it. They crowd to the edge of their platform of sticks. They look down with dismay at the water fifty feet below. They look out at their parents sweeping toward the nest, then veering away, hoping that in a sheer spilling over of emotions their children will sponta-neously cast themselves into flight. The panicky screaming reaches an unbearable breaking point of fear, protest, excitement, opportunity. What will happen if they throw caution to the winds and shut their eyes and launch themselves into thin air? *It's alright*, their parents call back. *Do it! Join us!*

Then, all at once, the screaming changes and there is one, no two, no all four children in the sky, and they are wheeling, diving, ascending as high as they dare, doing stall turns, and the morning is full of ecstasy. The joy of creatures becoming themselves.

Wilderness flows through the heart of a city. In that instant when children launch themselves into the future and turn magically into grown-ups, humans rediscover a fact of life. The meaning of wildness is ourselves.

Do we feel that joy in our own lives today? Once, on the river-bank below the wooden porch of the café, I saw a baby squirrel in the throes of ecstasy. It cavorted, it somersaulted, it scampered, it wheeled, it rolled – it tried to do all these actions at once, each free-dom overtaking the last. A newborn soul surprised by its body. These are the kinds of things the river teaches.

But today, its people are dozing in the sun in that downtime be-tween responsibilities at the pause between seasons. Mink are scam-pering in the bushes below me. Maybe the giant Toad will emerge and make a series of delayed hops across the patio. It may come over to your table to stare at you. Those huge, unblinking eyes. What is it thinking?

The Sparrows are thinking I might buy them a muffin. They alight at the edge of my table and cock their heads politely.

I look back to the rock at the end of the archipelago. The Cormo-rant has flown away. Then a Mesozoic *gronk!* A Great Blue Heron glides in, scaring the others off the point and occupying the place relinquished by the Cormorant. The two outraged Gulls dive-bomb it, then fly away stoically. The scene recomposes itself into an oriental stillness. The Heron gazes at her reflection in the water.

The café begins to fill up with people with pocket phones and briefcases – workers from the government Office of the Environment building that rises above the north end of the park. Built of local quarry stone and covered all the way to the top with foliage, it seems like an upthrust of the wilderness.

There are still river people, and there are fish in the river. But I miss the family of Ospreys. What made this part of the river uninhabitable for them? It might have been the adjustment of the water level to control flooding. The installation of LED lighting on the railway bridge. The percussion of fireworks on a spring night. Or a wild individual on a jet ski trying to achieve through the control of raw power his own shrunken ecstasy. This is what I mean by a contradiction. The natural world and the human world are at cross-purposes.

Every summer, this contradiction becomes acute for two days and nights. That is when local rock bands play on a podium facing a grass lawn behind the café. The lawn is filled with tables and chairs for people buying their food from a group of catering trucks and enjoying a massive outdoor picnic. The smell of cooking fat, pork, beer, buttered corn, and throat-searing sauces is conveyed across the river by the pulse of bar-room rock. The amplified pounding shakes the mud-and-stick home of the Bank Beaver. It penetrates the shoreline burrow of the Muskrat. It resounds inside the tree hole of the Owl. It translates a wilderness river into a stage for the celebration of the triumphant species, *Homo carnivorus*. This is the annual Ribfest and Corn Roast.

Besides the Seagulls, only one other creature took interest in this Primate self-indulgence. The Raccoons of the city.

# 33

"I COMMEND YOU on your sidestroke. You are a tireless swimmer."
"Thank you. It is because I grew up on the Lake. Creekers are born to the water."

"Swimming is a good skill to have."

"It helped me evade Name-Shifter, I can say that. I still smell his rotten breath. But you may be tired. Would you care to rest on Halfway Island?"

"No, I can make it across if we go slowly." Slypaws rolled onto her back and looked at the stars. It was a clear sky of the sort one gets in autumn. The heavens gazed down on her fondly. "You know, it's really quite liberating to be out here in the open yet not have to worry about Droolers and Cars. Where are we going to stay in the city?"

"I found us a place in an old tree. It's totally pocked with burrows, and we'll have young neighbours all around us. It's said to be a party tree, but there are no fleas. I checked. I know you don't like fleas."

"I don't."

"The advantage of the tree is its location. It's just off the downtown strip."

"Yearling boys and girls roving around in bands. All-night cooing and hissing spats. I'm too old for roistering." Slypaws resumed her front paddle. It was like walking, except that she was underwater but for her muzzle.

"Look at you! You're an alpha female in your prime. Just because you've had cubs doesn't mean your life has to go saggy."

"No, I suppose not," Slypaws said hesitantly.

"We're two ex-moms out on a spree. Sly and Twitch. They have a name for Coonettes like us."

"I don't want to hear it."

"The unmated bucks are a nuisance. One simply swats them away."

Slypaws was afraid she was going to share with her new friend what she might do with a young alpha male out for a roll. Regrettably, because of the adventure of being in the world her hormone levels were rising. She changed the topic. "I'm glad the rhythmic pounding has stopped."

"In fact, the pounding hasn't really begun yet," Twitchwhisker replied. "What you were hearing was just the Primates practicing for tomorrow night's feast."

"Merciful Hapticia, Healer of the Hundred Sorrows of Womanhood, preserve us!" Slypaws looked up to see if she could find Hapticia among the stars. The goddess had taken her clamshell and gone.

"The noise persists for two more days and nights," Twitchwhisker said.

"You know, I'm prepared to live with most everything that Primates do, but I can't for the life of me appreciate the pleasure they obtain from deafening themselves with rhythmic pulsations. It provides no survival advantage whatsoever, except the elimination of noisemakers from the species."

"Most true. If a group of Raccoons banged garbage can lids in unison against the pavement, the act would have the same deleterious effect. I refer to those old shiny lids that were made of a light metal. Do you remember them?"

"I do. The ones that were always bent. They popped off at a touch."

"Ah, those were the days!"

At this sentiment, the two women paddled together in silence. They skirted the dark shape of Halfway Island at its northern end so they could let the strong current along the west bank of the river carry them to the boat dock.

"Bless you for coming back across the river and getting me," Slypaws said. "You know how moms worry about their cubs."

"No, I don't."

"Well, I still do. It's quite irrational. You feel something's building up, and you're sure your children are going to end up in the middle of it."

"You're worried about the one who went west. Touchwit, wasn't it?"

"No, I'm not worried about her at all. She'd rewrite reality in order to survive. And I'm not concerned about Bandit. He survives by being normal."

Slypaws recited a saying:

> The one who keeps a nose to the ground
> Follows another's scent around.
> The one who lifts a nose to the wind
> Ventures far, but travels blind.

"It's Clutch I worry about."

## 34

A LL NIGHT LONG, raccoons arrived under the stars. First to come were the scattered families nesting nearby along the South Creek system all the way to the Southern Frontier. Once proud families of the River Clan, they recovered their tribal organization as soon as they reunited on the land they'd fled. Around midnight, the isolated Creekers living along the North Creek tributary came, bringing with them some of their new friends from an undiscovered clan living on Primate farms in the countryside. Then came separate families no one had ever heard of. They too had suffered at the hands of No Name's marauders and were keen to ensure his reign of terror ended. Finally, towards dawn, disparate raccoons trickled in from far-off places, including a group of dark-furred Southern people who had slipped past the High Guard units holding the frontier. All had heard that a mighty hero had assumed the leadership at Creek Town. Some said he was the favourite son of the One Who Cannot be Named. Others told that he was the terrestrial son of the Great Raccoon Ancestor himself. Still others couldn't be sure which, but it didn't matter. What mattered was that No Name had created a vacuum by going to the city, and another protector had filled it. The upstart was worth coming to have a look at. Raccoons could tell their descendants that they had witnessed a moment in Clan history.

Clutch, watching this historical moment take form, was beginning to think it would lead to a short-lived, sputtering glory. Even with the Clan families conjoining through the magical sap of Custom, he didn't have time to organize a defense of the Town against Meat-breath's veteran warriors. At best he had the remaining part of the day to prepare the defenses. But at dawn, Sleekfoot returned with a captured spy, a second one sent by No Name to find out what had happened to the first. The second spy, after a little reasoning, saw where the future lay, and told Clutch that Nameless intended to declare himself Protector of the City, then send part of his High Guard back to the Creek.

"High Guard? What High Guard?" Clutch asked the spy. "They're defending the Southern Approaches against migrants."

"True," the spy said. He was a tough but honest veteran, once a territorial family head but not one of the Clan Fathers. It was significant that Meatbreath couldn't trust his privileged families to undertake independent missions, but instead chose soldiers whom he could count on to be trustworthy. This one was rubbing his jaw where Sleekfoot had bit him, helping him become even more trustworthy. "But the Nameless One has some of the High Guard with him. They infiltrated into the City in ones and twos over the last several nights."

Clutch turned to Sleekfoot: "How large is this High Guard?"

"Nobody knows for sure," Sleek said. "They are a specially trained unit of alpha males sworn to fight to the death to protect No Name."

"They are comprised mostly of his sons." The spy added. He stopped and waited for Sleekfoot to elaborate. It was a touchy subject. Seeing Sleekfoot look away, he explained the formation himself. "They are sons that No Name has sired in this last season. Separated from their various mothers, they are given special privileges in return for swearing to defend their All-Father."

I am one of his sons, Clutch thought. But he kept the thought to himself. "Nameless has gathered a rather large force just to protect a city. What's he protecting it from?"

"From itself," the spy replied. "The City is harbouring Migrants who elude the police because they are cared for by packs calling themselves Citizens Brigades. These Brigades have sprung up everywhere like fleas and talk of Revolution." At the word *revolution*, the grizzled veteran turned pale as a true soldier does when military affairs are confused with politics. He had no more to say.

\* \* \*

"Well, what do you think?" he asked Sleekfoot after the spy had been led away and fed.

"I think you need to give direction to all these volunteers." Sleekfoot gestured towards the camps stretched along the beach in front of Creek Town. "Also, you should send a spy to the City to keep an eye on things over there. Maybe the spy could spread the rumour that there's nothing stirring at the Creek. That our forces are negligible. That this hero is just a figment of idle gossip that fills the air when a leader is away. That will buy you time."

"To do what? Prepare our defenses? Meatbreath can crush us with one paw tied to his tail." Clutch gestured at the reunited families stretched along the beach. They were singing camp songs.

"Courage, brother. You seem to have a spirit of luck on your side. You'll snatch victory from the carrion jaws of defeat."

"I'm not afraid of what will happen if we lose," Clutch said. "I'm afraid of what will happen if we win."

# 35

THE YOUTHS AND MAIDENS who made up the Honour Guard were well-fed, beautifully groomed raccoons. Bunched in their company, Bandit decided that maybe he might be attractive too. In fact, a girl with a honey-tinged fur, who turned out to be the Judge's grand-daughter, touched noses freely with him, and it was only the second time they'd bumped together. Inhaling the lightness and purity of her scent and feeling the ever-so-soft nudge of her body against his flank, he concentrated on the sound of the early morning traffic passing over the river bridge at the top of the park.

From his place at the back of the stage, Bandit could see everything he needed to without turning his muzzle. At the right of the stage was a High Guard squadron. Disturbing and unnatural how they stood still in straight rows waiting to be told what to do. The City Elders, all male raccoons, milled about at the left. Below the open side of the stage to his front was where tonight's spectators would gather, and where now a few curious citizens, mainly parents of cadets in the Honour Guard, watched the rehearsal in the early dawn light. The shifting, vague moods of people waiting for something to happen. That something was the promised entry of the official party, with Sensibel among them. Would the Protector put in an appearance?

Someone coughed. City Elders whispered their concerns to each other in hushed voices. From the bridge came the whir of cars taking their Primates to work.

Nothing to do but look around for things to notice. The two High Guard cavaliers Sensibel had rebuffed whispered side-of-mouth exchanges. Well, they'd be in for a surprise, watching her enter beside their leader. The Judge was at the front of the stage in the space reserved for the special party. And sure enough, Lockjaw, the escort service owner, and Drooplip, his ladies' manager, hovered in the wings. If they wanted to this pair could blackmail half the Elders on the platform.

Two quick-moving assistants come onto the stage and wait near where the special party will assemble. The rehearsal for tonight's Proclamation is about to begin.

Suddenly, the soldiers stiffen; City Elders assume their public demeanors; the crowd presses closer. A party is climbing the steps onto the raised rectangle from the back of the stage. An intake of breath. Sensibella has glided onto the stage out of a dream. Another female follows. She's middle-aged and lean. Undersized body. Lifeless, calculating eyes. Prominent nose. Disregard her – all eyes and ears are on his Sensibel. Then a sound one hears at Raccoon, not Primate, occasions. The sniffing of dozens of noses.

*I know her!* he wants to shout. She's my speech-friend and companion.

Instead, he bites his lips as the two guests of the city are shown their places on the stage. Immediately, the assistants spring to life. One quickly brushes Sensibel's tail. The other touches up the older woman's fur. Is this all there is to the official party?

Then, a hush of curiosity and suspense. The Protector has entered the space. He is confident, bursting with virile energy. Not like him to miss his own rehearsal. He'd take centre stage at his own funeral. How massive he is! What an enormous ruff! He touches noses with the Judge who yields the centre of the stage. Spares a wave to the few spectators. He moves briskly with excitement, looking left and right as if responding to adulation, giving the impression of having too many fans to greet all at once. Except there are no fans, only an uncertain staring. The Protector looks around for someone to recognize.

What if he recognizes me? I have his black mask, his body smell.

The mystery female now standing behind Sensibel whispers something into No Name's ear. It brings a frown. A weight of silence falls upon the square. Overhead, an air machine leaves a white scratch across the sky.

The Judge wheezes forward. Apparently, he is to give a welcoming address. The Protector falls into an attitude of unwilling attentiveness, tilting his head meaningfully to the left.

*"Honoured Guest, Associates and Escorts of the Guest, City Elders, Citizens. On behalf of the City, I am most pleased to open this Occasion and introduce ..."*

Bandit's mind drifts to the pillar of beauty called Sensibella. She has suddenly grown up and become a woman. She never looked this mature before. When Meatbreath appeared, it seemed as if her heart leaped. She broke into a smile, and for an instant she shared a laugh with him. She has found a place in the world of grown-ups. Pomp and circumstance. But also the intimacies exchanged between a couple, secrets he'd never know. She hadn't even remembered to look for him among the Honour Guard when she came onto the platform. She didn't give a whisker toss about him.

"... *and I am honoured to introduce his Guest, Sensibel of the River Clan Family at the Pond ...*"

Scattered applause from several spectators signified by the rubbing together of paws. A High Guard soldier gives a wolf whistle: jocular unanimity in the audience. Sensibel curtseys and appears to blush.

"*And now a third person, who is not a guest because she is a leading Administrator of our city ...*" the Judge paused to find the right words to say next, then finished abruptly. "*... about whom I have nothing more to say. At this time.*"

The Protector nods his head with approval. The Judge has said the right things. The Judge is obviously Meatbreath's personal wimp.

The High Guard snapped to attention. They stood like a row of saplings while the official party left the platform. Then everyone relaxed. Conversation broke out. The Honour Guard, sons and daughters of the leading City Families, rushed over to talk to their parents. The two cavaliers in the High Guard unit recognized him and winked.

He had no one to talk to. Except Sensibel. But she was being led away by Meatbreath. Where was he taking her? His *father*! Would she ever again confide in him? He could keep a secret forever.

*Attention!* The powerful small Administrator takes centre stage. Two High Guard officers stand behind her and they are high level territorial heads commanding several family hunting grounds. The sons and daughters leave their parents and quickly re-group their line. He hopes the Honour Guard for City Ceremonies and Occasions, as it is formally titled, isn't going to be ordered to take a side in the city's political struggle, because he quite likes his fellow cadets. They are spontaneous, free-spirited, and actually quite ordinary youth, without the social superiority that makes Aunt Pawsense a pain in the tail. Athletes, not fighters. The mystery woman clears her throat.

"Alright, you lot. Stand easy and listen. The City's about to undergo a transition of leadership, and your role is to ease that transition. You know what I'm talking about. We don't want fighting, do we?"

He kept his eyes straight ahead.

"No, we don't. Accordingly, you need to be very clear about where you stand in the transition. Right now, you serve the City Fathers. After the Declaration of the Protectorship, you will serve The Protector. He wants to work with the City's youth to build a better world. Got it?"

His neighbour's body is no longer pushing against his flank.

"As you know, I serve the City Elders. After tonight, I will serve The Protector as his Director of Security. So think of me as a wire between the two authorities, a *very thin wire*."

Got it! Tread carefully. No messing with her.

"Consider me the one reliable principle in the change of power. I *am* the Transition. You will serve me and no one else. Questions ...?"

Funny. No one had a question. Yet he sensed uncertainty and discomfort among his comrades.

"Surely someone has a question."

She is as taut as a hydro pole cable. If someone doesn't come up with a question soon, she'll ...

"*I have a question.*"

Bandit looked left and right for the simpleton idiot who had a question. Then he realized it was himself.

"Yes. You in front." The Security Director seemed relieved that someone had broken the tension.

"My question is ... are you telling us that we're serving you right now?"

Titters throughout the ranks. The two senior High Guard officers look at each other and make loopy gestures around their heads.

"What's your name, cadet?"

"Bandit, ma'am."

"You're not City, are you? Where you from, Bandit?"

"East Bank, ma'am."

She was looking him in the eyes now. It felt like she was looking through his eyes into whatever grey matter had somehow accidentally lodged in his skull. And through that feeble excuse for a brain to the top of his spine where a lizard was curled up and its name was Cunning. And she was sniffing him imperceptibly. She reached out and fondled his ear.

"How did you get into the Honour Guard?"

The two High Guard commanders moved in, sensing a traitor. Their eyes squinted like the headlights of the Primate automobile that pasted Uncle Wily.

"Ma'am. I was personal bodyguard to The Protector's designated escort, until he ... took her over. They had nothing for me to do, so she asked him to put me in the Honour Guard."

"Okay. Honour Guard dismissed. Assemble here at nightfall. You. Remain here."

"Me, ma'am?"

"Yes, you." Her voice seemed relaxed now. Even gentle. He kept his eyes looking over her shoulder.

"Can I trust you with a mission?"

"Yes, ma'am. But begging your pardon, if it concerns the business of the City, maybe you should give it to one of the cadets."

"I am the City."

"Whatever you say, ma'am."

"There is a small gap right now between the City Elders and the Protector. You're going to squeeze through it. The others can't be asked to. Instead, they'll be assigned to lead units of the Peoples Corps."

"Thank you, ma'am."

"These so-called Citizens Brigades did not spring up spontaneously like mushrooms. They're being organized by a Resistance cell. They know how to exploit the media. Your mission is to find out where that cell is and report it to me. Clear?"

"Very clear, ma'am."

"You know how to talk to people who live in chimneys. Honour Guard brats can't do this. You know how to talk to drunkards and burnouts. They have a nose for criminal behaviour; they'll tell you where the cell is. Then you go there undercover and penetrate it and obtain the names of the leaders."

"You'd like me to identify the leaders. What if they think I'm a spy?"

The Director looked at him sweetly. It was as if she loved him for his innocence. "The one thing we know about them is that they are the authors of all the statuettes of The Protector. They call themselves the Makers."

"Makers," Bandit said. He hoped he really did sound as if he didn't know what the word meant. He was a raccoon without guile. "Can I ask something, ma'am?"

"Of course."

"I understand that I'm acting under your authority. Is that because The Protector will be out of town?"

"He may be temporarily … indisposed. As City Director of Security I'm assuming his authority until the Protectorship is declared official."

"When should I complete the mission?"

"Before the sun is down. Off you go." The Director wheeled around with a surprising agility and walked stiff-legged to join the two officers. He watched them disappear around the restaurant.

Deep breath. Smells like an autumn day. Now, where to get started? The traffic bridge, of course.

*"Here you are!"*

Bandit jumped. He knew that voice. It was …

Friskywits looking up at him with her kid sister eyes.

"I knew I'd find you. But I never thought you'd turn up in an Honour Guard. Isn't the city glorious? I told you you'd find freedom here. Nobody cares where you're from or how you look …"

"Sssh, Frisk. Not now."

"Well, maybe they don't care deeply. They aren't sensitive to kinship relations. But they are marvellously open to strangers. I've made five friends already. That's how I found out about the rehearsal. How did you get to be a cadet?"

"Can we talk somewhere else? I'm working undercover."

"Oooh! That's a slack wire to be out on. Are you guarding Bells?"

"Sssh! Walk with me."

They ambled north through the park towards the traffic bridge. Beside them came the hum of the refrigerated trucks – food for to-night's feast.

"Bandy – you mustn't worry about Bells. She's is a professional romantic, but that doesn't mean she's dumb."

"I don't want to talk about her – okay?"

"Sure. We'll talk about someone else. Do you want to know why I'm here?"

"Sorry, Frisk. I'm having a bad day."

"I came to warn you that Father sent out scouting parties from the Heights to search for you. Well, not you exactly, but Sensibel. They mean to drag her home."

"Good luck."

"My sentiments exactly. Still, both of you should hide. Maybe swim over to Aunt Slypaws's home."

"If Mom finds out Sensibel's with Meatbreath, she'll take this city and shake it until Sensibella drops out. Then she'll take her to her chimney and home school her till she can recite the gender positions of every tree in the forest."

"She already knows that stuff. Never underestimate the sexual imagination of four sisters."

"Where are they keeping her?"

"In an unknown place. Everyone can tell it's unknown because it's guarded by loads of soldiers. Up on the hill beyond the Strip. She's in the steeple of an empty building where Primates go to sing to their Ancestor. Oh, please Bandy, not under this smelly bridge. It's where Ne'er-do-wells hang out. There's so many fleas here that your fleas will leave you to join their mates and party. Take me to the Strip – this is my first time in the city."

"There's nothing doing in the Strip now. It's almost morning. Don't you ever sleep?"

"No."

"The bridge is the only place Sensibel knows where to find me. But she probably can't go out without an escort."

"Well, we'll just go to where she is? I'll tell the guards I'm her sister and I have an important message to give her personally."

"What will I do?"

"You come too. You're a cadet in the Honour Guard. I thought you looked handsome up there on the stage. I'll say you're my escort. They'll let us in to see her. Besides you look like one of Meatbreath's sons."

## 36

"I'M SORRY, BUT I need to wake you up."
Touchwit heard his voice as if it was calling down to her from the top of a chimney. She was stuck in a crazy dream involving her mother floating by the island in the night, talking. Immediately, smells drifted in. Leafy decay. Dank water. Endless forests of pine. Pollen from goldenrod. Then came the sounds. Early morning traffic on the automobile bridge. A seagull calling overhead. Sights: Mindwalker, wide awake, concerned and wet. After the crisis meeting, they'd swum over here to Halfway Island and spent what was left of the day sleeping. Long ago, a homeless Primate had cleared a space in the saplings for a tent and a campfire. That was where she collapsed from fatigue. She must have gone on sleeping right through the night. "It looks like I'm caught in a diurnal sleep cycle," she said. "Where'd you go?"

"I swam across to get the morning news."

"What's happening?"

"Serious scat! First, there's gossip that No Name is going to make a Declaration tonight. Then there's a news release from the City Elders saying the Occasion has been delayed: watch for it the night after tomorrow. But immediately counter-messaging starts up and says it'll to be tonight. Of course. That counter-messaging is ours."

She sneezed the pollen out of her nose. Her fingers hurt. For most of yesterday morning in the Root Cellar with other Makers, she'd fashioned identical images of Meatbreath until her fingers started to cramp. She ought to invent a technique for replicating likenesses so that a Raccoon doesn't have to strain her paws. Multiplying the same image in countless Makings felt wrong. She got the idea from Meatbreath, so it must be wrong. There was something mindless about repeating the same Making. The activity was obsessive. But this was a crisis. She was taking the Protector's thinking and using it back on him.

"No Name was sighted for the first time in the city. An hour ago. It's uncanny how someone who likes to be in your face all the time can be so invisible."

*I saw him.*

"He was at a dress rehearsal for the Declaration. So now we know the shape of the event, we just don't know when it's going to happen."

"I'm awake. Let's swim over and check the networks."

"Funny, No Name's two-sided like you. He's diurnal-nocturnal. They say he never sleeps."

*I slept.*

"We'll have to move around quickly. Apparently, there's a spy trying to track us."

\* \* \*

They made their way south from the café boat dock picking up news. *Help Make History – Join a Brigade. It's Illegal to Join. Who sez? Don't know. But it's Against Custom. The Protractor's Left Town. Untrue, Untrue. The City's Unprotected? Bollocks! Have you seen the Peoples Corps? Bunch of Losers. Lost outside Uptown Tavern: Tail Ring with Elegant Stitches. P.C.s = Protecting City. Wrong! P.C.s = Politically Correct. Who's the Protector's Playmate? Don't know. I'd follow her anywhere!!! Muster to Destroy Tonight's Declaration. Watch for Time and Place. Moist-touch, please find me – I'm at our Favourite Tree. Alert! P.C.'s trying to shut down the Harbour Area. Moist got arrested, Sister – Very Sorry. Whoever's destroying Protector statues, Please Stop. I've got your Tail Ring. Look for me at the Declaration, near the water.*

"I don't know if I like the sound of this Peoples Corps," Touchwit said.

"The well-fed find a way to protect their place at the top of the food chain. They create a disgruntled, hungry population, then exploit their anger by recruiting them to fight imaginary threats from the sides, not the top."

"Let's go down to the harbour and see for ourselves."

"I wouldn't risk it. Anyway, what we need to find out isn't there."

"Which is …?"

"What No Name's plans really are. Why are his High Guard slipping out of the city in ones and twos? Is there trouble over at the Creek? On the Southern Frontier?"

"That would explain why there's a delay with the Declaration."

"It smells like war," Mindwalker said. "It's the kind of confusion you get before conflict: unexplained delays, sudden reversals of intention, waiting and not knowing. It makes it hard to plan a resistance. I wish we could find out what's going on."

"But we can!" Touchwit said. "Excuse me for a minute." She left the pathway with its double row of young trees. Those long-stemmed weeds by the riverbank would do. Quickly, she wove a handful of them into a wreath. Then she waded out into the river and waved until the Seagull sighted her.

## 37

CLUTCH'S RAGTAG MILITIA didn't look very formidable frolicking in the lake, laughing and splashing water on each other in the early morning light. They'd never killed anything bigger than a vole. How could they defend Creek Town from the Protector's alpha males? Yet they possessed two advantages: numerical superiority and the power of the Clan Mothers. The second factor was not to be taken lightly. Led by the Mothers, his war bands had mastered the art of taunting during last night's practices. They could make a pack of Droolers turn tail. Raccoons, like most mammals with the notable exception of humans, rarely fight to the death. Territorial skirmishes are won by displays of aggression: hackles raised, teeth bared, ears flat against the skull, and blood-curdling guttural growls and hissing spits. To picture them in battle is to imagine an aggression that is everything short of actual physical conflict – a display combining elements of a Chinese riot, a Climate Strike, and the Maori *haka* performed at the beginning of New Zealand All Blacks rugger games. Irish oral tradition remembers that prior to a battle the contesting armies sent out their satirists. On one occasion, the verses of a satirist were so virulent that the opposing king's face broke out in blotches, causing his army to desert him. I am told that a legend in the *Burmese Glass Palace Chronicles* says that in early Buddhist times, when two armies met, they would build rival *stupas*, the shrines in the shape of domes that contain religious relics and statues of the Buddha. When the erections were complete, the armies would compare them and the army that saw the other's was more beautiful would run away. This is what I mean by raccoon conflict. At the sound of a Clan Mother protecting her territory, an alpha male would have a bowel movement on the spot. Bandit was right: the politics of combat was decided early on by who could break the other's spirit, who would fight and who would flee.

What was that Seagull doing? It was strutting back and forth holding a doughnut in its beak, trying to get his attention. A third guide presuming to give him advice? First, there had been a mouse, then a fox, now this gull. Curious how these councillors appeared at dawn.

The seagull dropped the object at his feet. It wasn't a doughnut; it was a circular Making woven out of ironweed and loosestrife. The gull indicated he was supposed to sniff it. He didn't need to.

"Is Touchwit safe?"

"Greetings, colleague. You are standing alone in thought like a Gull, so I take you to be a wise leader."

"A wise leader follows the people."

"A Raccoon Saying, doubtless."

"From the lips of Procyonides the Sage."

"Was Procyonides born in a chimney?"

"No. He was born in a distant land where Seagulls aren't rude."

"Perhaps it is such a wise place that the Raccoons there don't eat the eggs of Gulls. Show me that paradise and I'll fly there and live happily ever after. In these uncertain times, Raccoons and Seagulls should live in harmony. We both prize clams and live off the avails of Primates. Most of all, we are survivors. You are having a territorial dispute."

"Tell me your message and begone."

"Of course. Your sister sends her compliments. She asks: would you create a diversion to draw off Meatbreath and a portion of his forces? She wants you to pin them down for one night, tonight to be precise, so that her colleagues will have time to organize to defend the city."

"Where? Did she say where to make a feint attack?"

"Personally, I find organized masses of bodies brawling in space rather tedious. You should try living on a sea cliff packed together with countless individualists, each caring only that they have enough space to roost."

"I would lose my wits in an instant."

"Your colleague sister didn't mention it, but I can add this to her news, for you to take as you wish: some of Meatbreath's fighters are leaving the city by stealth, as if intending to return to these hallowed shores."

"Very interesting. A reconnaissance in force."

"They are spending the day sleeping in trees proximate to the Sanctuary for the Dead."

"The place where the Primates hide their bodies when they are finished living in them."

"Precisely. But I did not say *in* the Sanctuary. Raccoons are afraid to go there. I said *proximate to* the Sanctuary. To be exact, on its city side."

The seagull pulled up one of his legs and stood casually on the other while Clutch assessed the information.

"How many warriors?" he asked the bird.

"Ah, Raccoons can count. How interesting. I should have guessed a fellow scavenger can count. I count as many warriors as you have toes on your four feet, together with two other raccoons with all their toes."

"Not so many as to take back the Creek. But as few as can be recalled quickly to the City in a crisis. Or reinforced to repossess their homeland, if required."

"It is beneath my beak to speculate about matters of mechanical physics," the seagull said.

"Would you take this message back to my sister Touchwit? Tell her that tonight I will hold Meatbreath's forces at the Dead Zone."

"You will hold his forces tonight at the Sanctuary. Astonishing."

"Don't lose touch. That's a joke," Clutch said.

"Raccoon humour. I understand. It's based on a play of double senses. Cheers."

The seagull was gone in the twinkling of an eye.

# 38

"YOU SHOULDN'T HAVE COME HERE. They do frightful things to spies."

Sensibel had either abandoned her life of peril, or she'd promoted herself to the role of double-agent. Seeing her lounging in the slats of sunlight coming through the window of the bell tower, Bandit decided she'd somehow done both. Her methods were subtle compared to the raw equation that had taken possession of his gut. Fight or Flee. This stark choice had reached its end-point. It was now Win or Die. For Bella. He would accomplish both.

"They practically saluted Bandit," Frisk said. "He looks just like the Protector."

"You do," Sensibel said to Bandit who had made a face. "It's to your credit. Your father is treating me with courtesy."

"Meatbreath's a thug and a bully. If he doesn't treat you with respect, I'm going to tear off his ruff."

Sensibel considered her reply before answering. "Your impulse is quite noble, Bandy, but I can handle him easily. In any case, I find him generally agreeable. I prize the frank, eager character. Warmth and enthusiasm in a gentleman captivate me. And his name isn't Meatbreath. It's The Protector."

"You're sounding like your mother."

"In the assessment of character she has no equal."

"She didn't have a high assessment of my character."

"That was because she was afraid I would find you intriguing, you being an ineligible mate and therefore an object of fascination."

"She thought *I* was vulgar! Now look who you're with! Lord Vulgaroso himself."

"He's not as coarse as I feared. It's just a manner he adopts to set himself apart in people's minds from the earnest and solemn Problem Solvers."

"Apart from being a self-aggrandizing slob, he's your aunt's mate, which makes him your uncle. Did you let him sniff your anal glands?"

"Bandy – I do believe you're jealous."

"I'm not jealous. I'm trying to protect you."

"Protect me? I have two alpha males to court me, both seeking to be my Protector. Lo! I am a maiden in a tizzy."

"Get serious, Bel. It's not all about you."

"But I am having fun. Aren't double agents allowed to have fun?"

"What did you do together?"

"Well, dear cousin, if you really have to know, we ate dinner. Pizza. He ate two whole pizzas, dripping with mozzarella and simply loaded with mushrooms and pepperoni. I believe the reason he wants to protect the city is so he can come across the lake and eat pizza."

"Did you eat pizza too?"

"I don't like cheese. It gets in my whiskers. He let me have some of his mushrooms."

"Did he say how he was going to take over the city?"

"No. He's not interested in politics. He's just interested in his own potency."

"What about the Declaration? Did you find out what he's going to declare?"

"Oh, yes. The Declaration." Sensibel began to sound excited. "It's to happen tomorrow night. We're going to arrive just after the Primates have gone home. There'll be hosts of raccoons there – he's invited the whole city."

"Yes. It's all over the network."

"First, he's going to inspect the Honour Guard. I assume you'll be among them. Then he's going to say a speech about something."

"What's he going to say?"

"I don't know. I forgot. Something about Uniting the Ancestral Lands of the River Clan. Anyway, he's going to give this major speech, with all his favourite sons arrayed behind him."

"Where does he get that idea from?"

"From the Security Director. The Pro doesn't have any ideas."

"And you're supposed to look like the ideal mother of all these sons."

Sensibel seemed surprised by his characterization. She was examining him keenly to see the spirit in which the remark was meant.

Plainly, she hadn't thought of herself before as a mother – still less as a poster child for motherhood in general. He quickly intervened before she thought about it further … "What are you meant to do at the Declaration?"

"I'm supposed to stand behind him, a little to his left so people can see my tail." Sensibella flounced out her magnificent golden tail.

"It's a fake."

"Oh relax, Bandy. Bell's enjoying her fifteen minutes of Pomp and Circumstance."

"Don't forget, I'll be there tomorrow night. Right behind you in the High Guard. As soon as there's trouble, come to me."

"Bandy. You'll always be my number one Protector."

She suddenly gave him a mischievous lick on his muzzle. "Oh, I just remembered. I heard him say he can't get messages in or out of Creek Town. But someone came here from the Creek just after the storm. A woman. She reported that the community has been taken over by one of his sons: a mysterious, unknown son. The Creekers adore him."

"Who is he?"

"She didn't know his name. She said that he was an outsider. A maverick. The only thing the Protector said was that he can't keep track of his sons anymore, but it doesn't really matter because he won't ever sire anyone who is smarter than him."

"You're the Queen of Double Agents," Frisk said.

He thought he could hear Sensibel purr.

"One thing I'm sure of," he told her, "is that everybody in the city is confused about when the Declaration is happening."

"Yes, the Protector says it's because people are putting out fake news. He's as cross as two sticks about it."

"Maybe the best thing we can do to keep our mouths shut and watch Meatbreath make an idiot of himself."

His suggestion brought a frown to her broad forehead. Unnatural for her to frown. Her face wasn't constructed to register doubt. A ray of sunshine made her tail glow.

"I don't know," she said eventually. "He enjoys going out on a limb. He might go across the lake and check out this rival, then double back in time to make his Declaration. Then I don't know what …?"

"Then what? We hightail it out of here, that's what."

"Bandy, it's not about the Protector. It's about the City. I've been here three nights, and I've seen the highs and lows of it: I've seen a City Elder who is a Judge and I've seen Miscreants and Ne'er-do-wells. The City is freedom. I breathe deeply here. It would be a cage trap if it were to be run like a dysfunctional family headed by a missing dad who visits whenever he wants to eat pizza. The city's a place where I can be myself. What if every raccoon could be herself? Or himself? Or theirself? Imagine!"

"But Meatbreath …?"

"There's a would-be Protector under every bush," Sensibel replied. "I've met four already. An escort service manager, a judge, a politician, and (forgive me for putting you in their category) you. Where do all these protectors come from? They come from people's imaginations. They exist in make-believe because raccoons think they need an alpha personality to ensure their security. They're ready to give up their freedom in exchange for a Protector."

"I have to stop believing that Meatbreath exists?"

"No, you must start believing that *you* exist."

He didn't quite understand this. What he understood was that Sensibel was flirting with imbalance. Like going out to the end of a limb just to prove you could do it.

"Mother's making dramatic speeches and blaming herself for what she calls your *undoing*. Father's sent out family squads to hunt you down."

"I shall be quite safe in this tower." Sensibel moved out of the sunlight; it was too bright for her nocturnal eyes.

"When are you saying goodbye to it?"

Sensibel looked at Bandit affectionately. "When I've found out all I need to know."

"Such as …?"

"The Protector's caught off-balance. He needs to take over the city by tomorrow night or he will look like a fake, but the main part of his army is far off on the Southern Frontier holding back Migrants. Is he going to go and get it personally? He might, because there's some sort of trouble at Creek Town. He'll take the risk of leaving just for a night so long as there's no threat to his Declaration."

Bandit thought furiously to himself. He knew some things about balance too. It was a principle of wrestling. Exert a force against your opponent that he isn't braced against and the balance is lost. Your adversary topples over and you can pin him to the bulrushes. He saw The Protector's point of weakness. Now, what was the unanticipated force?

"We need to go," he told Frisk suddenly.

"Why? What's happening?"

"My father's going to hear that one of his dumb sons is in the tower with his consort. He'll storm up here and throw me out the window."

"Yes, it's probably a good idea that you leave. You too, Frisk."

Quick goodbyes. He left, carrying Bella's scent in his nose.

\* \* \*

Bandit didn't talk until he was in the Crosstown Creek thoroughfare.

"What are you thinking?" Frisk asked.

"I'm thinking that Sensibella is going to become the wife of her uncle if she isn't careful. That will be a tangle."

Frisk thought for an instant. "You're a subtle thinker, Bandy."

"I need to know something. Tell me, who is the Maker your sister was infatuated with?"

"I don't know. Just someone she saw at a distance on the Heights. An *artiste*. He's long and tall. Why? Are you jealous?"

Bandit tried not to show a reaction. "I am going to do an errand for the Security Director. Will I see you at the Declaration?"

"Of course, you will! After I do an errand too."

# 39

S LY AND TWITCH, two ex-moms loose on the city, are wearing red
citizen's hats tied under their chins at a rakish angle by a patriot
nymph who said she was a Daughter of the Commonwealth. It is one
of those languorous autumn-like nights with a magical golden haze
in the air. Raccoons are filling the streets, stopping each other to find
out about the political situation and where the fun is happening.

"I have no idea what these silly hats mean, but they'll help us
blend in with the carnival," Twitch said gaily.

"Nothing will help us blend in," Slypaws replied. She hadn't had
a good day's sleep in the tenement tree with its party going on until
all hours in the upper branches. Besides, she had picked up fleas.

"Ears up and nose to the wind, Sly. This is our chance to have fun."

"Define fun."

"It's being hot alpha babes on the prowl, released from motherhood, cubs, menfolk, and every other mind-numbing obligation.
We're starting from scratch and doing it right this time, freely on our
own terms."

"Free love for all. Away dull care!" Slypaws said. She couldn't
imagine a single night when she wouldn't be thinking about her cubs.
Moreover, tomorrow night was their Birthday.

"You ladies lookin' to party?"

Twitchwhisker stopped to survey the ruffian. One ear drooped at
a wicked angle and a gap between his incisors when he leered. "Not
with you, you scabrous lecher. Go mate with a beer bottle."

"I don't want to subtract anything from your defiance, which
is most worthy, but I think you may have been a bit harsh to that
solicitous unfortunate," Slypaws said afterward.

"The nerve of him thinking we're party ladies," Twitch replied.

They shuffled shoulder to shoulder down the Crosstown Thoroughfare, climbing out of the ravine made by the creekbed onto the
patio of a café. From there, they crossed the street and plunged into
a labyrinth of back lanes and alleyways known as The Strip. Young

raccoons gave way to them respectfully because of their age, the only sign of anyone making a social distinction in this city. Slypaws wished they wouldn't do that. But she wouldn't admit to Twitch that she wanted to be young again. She wouldn't admit it to Twitch because she wouldn't admit it to herself.

"Did you hear the news?" It was one of the street leaders who were popping up everywhere. His Citizen's hat held a sprig of orange rowan berries.

"No. Tell us."

"His Impotence has left town. Tonight's Declaration has been postponed."

"What are we to do with this gladsome news?"

"Be ready to mobilize. Have you joined a Citizens Brigade?"

"I think we won't just yet, if that's alright. My revolution, when it comes, is going to be individual, personal, and highly sensual."

But the boyish leader had already turned his attention to another stroller.

"Whatever did you mean by that?" Slypaws asked.

"I mean, I am going to turn the regime of patriarchy upside-down. I shall have as many lovers as Meatbreath has wives."

"Somewhere in a revolution there must be a middle ground between collective action and individual acts of suicide," Slypaws said.

They turned into a narrow space between buildings. This time, the young raccoons coming in the opposite direction wouldn't yield to their seniority. They were two male soldiers, barely out of their teens.

"Give us a lick and we'll let you pass."

Slypaws immediately began to growl.

"You don't want to mess with her," Twitch explained. "She's seriously out of season."

"You're wearing Resistance hats. We could arrest you for treason. We're High Guard."

"This is a free city. You have no power here."

"We do now. The law courts have been turned over to the Director of Security. She's been personally appointed by The Protector."

"I'm not aware of his official endorsement by the City Fathers." Slypaws had ceased to growl. Instead, she had acquired an icy calm.

"It was to occur tonight, but now it's been postponed, hasn't it? Or don't you know?"

Twitch added her bit: "You're Creekers, aren't you? Go home to your mama and learn some manners."

The cavalier officers made mock bows as the two Citizen ladies passed. The ladies continued along the alleyway to emerge shortly after onto a route running down to the river. Dizzying scents of pork, beer, and corn filled their noses.

"Are we going down there?" Sly asked.

"Let's go and take a look. What's this?"

It was a small Protector statuette – an exact duplicate of his mammoth girth and overwhelming tail, but hollow spaces where his eyes were supposed to be.

Slypaws tore its face off in one swipe.

"Wow!" Twitch said. "What was that you said about a desperate individual act?"

"Blessed Hapticia, that felt good!"

Now what? A barricade had been put across the raccoon track. It was made of packing crates, recycling boxes, shopping carts, and an old sofa.

"Stand and identify yourselves," a voice shouted from behind the barrier.

"Slypaws and Twitchwhisker, tourists, but sympathetic to the cause." They approached so the resistance fighter could see their hats.

"Pass, Citizens!"

"Why the barricade?" Slypaws asked the squad leader.

"We're occupying the City before the Pro returns with his army" was the answer.

"But the High Guard is still here. We just bumped into two officers."

"There aren't as many of them around as it appears. We've heard he's taken the High Guard to Creek Town to recruit more warriors."

"Good luck to the struggle," Twitchwhisker said.

"¡No passarán!"

Slypaws liked the young female commander in her cockade hat. So determined to do the will of history.

They resumed their stroll along the darkened avenues toward the river in a mood of mounting excitement. They watched more street barricades go up, more of the City's restless young joining the struggle. A constant tribal drumming and shouting of Primates from the direction of the water. When they got close to the park with its smell of food, they met a fog coming off the water. The wind had gently shifted to the north, spreading cold air. Soldiers called at them through the mist – rough city voices, but led by officers who sounded distinctly like Creekers.

"We'd better get back to our tree, Citizen Sister," Twitch said.

"I believe I'm alive in the Historical Moment," Slypaws declared.

“ *T*HE WILDEST AND MOST BEAUTIFUL *of forest streams.*" This is how a nineteenth-century settler described the river where these stories take place. Its name is Otonabee. We pronounce it *O-tón-a-bee*, a mispronunciation probably originated by Irish settlers who stressed the second syllable of names beginning with O. Its name in the language of the Indigenous Anishinaabe people is *Odoonabii-ziibi*. It is a river (*ibi*) and a racing heart (*ode*) turbulent like boiling water (*odemgat*). A rapidly beating heart. You might think this agitation belongs to the river because it once pulsed through continuous sets of rapids. Or maybe it is the excited heart of a paddler shooting those rapids. But it is probably the heart of Mother Earth. In Anishinaabec belief, the streams and rivers are her veins and arteries.

With the coming of modernity, hydroelectric power dams were put above each set of rapids, pooling the river into a series of reservoirs. Yet the wilderness found a use for these holding ponds and they are now full of geese and ducks and turtles and muskrats who value a reedy shoreline. The European settlers found a home on the river too, and on the biggest of the abeyances, named Little Lake after an early farmer, they founded a city. Here where the water partially surrounded a hill they built a cemetery in the style of the Victorian burial parks in London, with artistically placed trees, circular roadways for horses and carriages, and on three sides a view of the lake.

Today, the tombstones tilt and nod solemnly with pious inscriptions about the brevity of mortal life in relation to human aspiration. A Daniel Macdonald (1838-1871), famous in his time as a weightlifter, paid the price for his vanity:

> *Ye weak beware, here lies the strong,*
> *a victim of his strength.*
> *He lifted sixteen hundred pounds,*
> *and here he lies at length.*

Point taken. But the person I have learned much from has a simpler inscription carved on a tall Celtic Cross:

*Isabella Valancy Crawford*
*Poet*
*By the Gift of God*

Not much is known about her early life – tragedy fell on her family like a shroud. But one thing for sure, she was a firecracker. She was the only woman in Canada to make a living from her writing during a time when the literary world was the preserve of gentlemen. And she did it while being outspoken about the social pieties of her day: patriarchy, racism, war, social class, inhibited sexuality. For this last concern, see "The Lily Bed." It begins:

*His cedar paddle, scented, red,*
*He thrust down through the lily bed;*

*Cloaked in a golden pause he lay,*
*Locked in the arms of the placid bay.*

*Trembled alone his bark canoe*
*As shocks of bursting lilies flew*

*Thro' the still crystal of the tide,*
*And smote the frail boat's birchen side.*

Somehow Isabella's poetry manages to be genuinely awful and full of awe at the same time. This is often the case with mythic people writing for a conventional society. Outwardly, she is "an intelligent and industrious female songbird of the kind that fills so many anthologies in the nineteenth century." The words of a literary critic – but a great critic, Northrop Frye. He sees that deep inside herself Isabella faces the world with a soul torn open by Romanticism. Her visionary images turn reality inside-out. At the bottom of her writing is an insight that the interior of nature is a wild culture in which trees, animals, and the spirits of the forest are equals. For glimpses of this unborn commonwealth, I prefer her lyrics, but I take note of her long poem, a domestic idyll set in myth.

Isabella Valancy Crawford, 1846 to 1887.

Little Lake Cemetery has other memories in its soil. Some of my partner's family are buried here, and as a young girl she stole in at night with two of her girlfriends to hold a séance. It was the site of a battle between Mississauga and Mohawk warriors. It is the site of a battle in the scene to come, a contest between visions best understood in Isabella Valency Crawford's terms.

# 41

SOON AFTER NIGHTFALL, a host of raccoons swam the narrows between Creek Town and the Sanctuary of the Dead. Clutch watched with satisfaction as the First Wave crossed and vanished among the trees and standing stones. Hearing no calls of distress from them, he sent his Second Wave. Then he took to the water himself with Sleekfoot and Lightfinger, and the female friend whose name he forgot but who insisted on being his bodyguard since the day she had nursed his wounds. She always stood behind him silently, and after a while it became easier to accept her presence instead of asking her to go away.

It wasn't fun in the water. He'd never swum far in his life and he felt exposed under the limitless sky. And there was a noticeable current where the lake funnelled into a river drawn by the plunge at a dam. A light westerly would put his army downwind of the Protector's forces, giving him an advantage. But where was the Protector? And how many warriors would he bring with him? The anxiety went away once he reached the far bank and felt ground under his paws.

A runner from the First Wave waited while he shook water out of his fur.

"Compliments from Floppy Ear. She wishes you to know that her hunting groups are deployed wide open across the western side of the Dead Zone. No sound or scent of the enemy."

The forager groups, led by clan mothers and operating like families, had the advantage of speed and agility. In contrast, the High Guard was said to move slowly together in a line, bunching and loosening like a caterpillar.

"Very good. Has she captured any scouts?"

The runner's face went blank.

"*Why don't I know this?*" Clutch barked so loud that his bodyguard jumped. Sleekfoot and Lightfinger frowned. It wasn't their fault. It wasn't the runner's fault either, though he looked like he wanted to sink into the soil of this morbid place.

"I'll go back with him and find out," Lightfinger said.

"Very good. I'll be at that building on the top of the rise. It appears to be a place of Ancestor worship. Sleek, would you go to the southern fenceline and send a runner to me when the Second Wave has deployed?"

Sleek nodded his head and became a shadow flitting through the stones.

The rhythmic percussion from upriver began to hurt his ears. He sniffed. Yes, the breeze had shifted. It brought an autumn chill. How cold was it going to get? He listened to the counter-rhythms that rose all around him since he had arrived in this abidance of trees and stones. The soft *treet, treet, treet* of crickets. Near and far, they called, making a single thrilling symphony. How cold was it? Ask them. He cocked his ears toward a nearby call and counted on his paws the number of *treets* in the time it took him to breathe deeply three times. Then he counted the fingers and thumb on his left paw and added their total to the data supplied by the cricket as measured by his breathing. It might get quite cold. Better for scents and noises. Better for ambushers. The soothing enchantment of the Snowy Tree Crickets reminded him that the life-world went on all around the forthcoming battle.

The building was fanciful and beside it stood an equally fanciful tree that invited climbing, but for now he stayed on the ground where he could be seen by runners. Soon, one arrived from the Second Wave, reporting that its forager groups were in place to catch enemy fighters trying to sneak along the south fence of the Sanctuary to the railway bridge across the Narrows. The rusting disused bridge had a span left permanently open to allow boats through, but an especially brave raccoon could make the water crossing to Creek Town. Or several scouts. He didn't expect more than his hunting groups could handle either at the south or west gate of the Sanctuary. The Gull had said that only scattered units had been assigned to reconnoitre the Creek. But again, the dreadful question – where was The Protector? What if he brought the High Guard from the city?

Clutch lay belly to the grass looking down a little hill toward the western gate of the cemetery. In the neighbourhood beyond, enemy scouts would soon be waking up and leaving their trees. Because the gate had been left open (he hadn't counted on this), they would enter the Sanctuary here, rather than squeeze through the spike metal fence. They'd huddle into one force and wait until the Protector arrived. Then they'd cross the Dead Zone quickly, swim across the Narrows, and put down the insurrection at Creek Town. This was the Pro's intention. He guessed the strategy on the assumption that enemy scouts didn't want to spend the night sleeping in this landfill site for used bodies.

On his flank to the south and in front of him to the west, his own Creek Town raccoons crouched behind bushes and stones in the dank, fertile rot. They had conquered their terror of the Dead Zone. Having learned several times in quick succession to face his fears, he taught them by example to face theirs. The only uncertainty that remained to him was how big a force The Protector would bring.

The rhythmic pounding upriver had stopped.

What was that? A light dancing over one of the standing stones. It disappeared. But another light ascended slowly in the air to his right. He blinked to clear his vision, but the point of light didn't vanish. Then it suddenly went out. What could it be? Then more of these lights, hovering over the standing stones. They would flash briefly and disappear. Were they the souls of the people buried beneath the stones? Had he disturbed their spirits? It seemed they were trying to tell him something. And now another ...!

"Ladyfriend," he said without taking his eye off the lights, "what are those?"

"They are called *Fireflies*. They are so named because they have the power to turn their bodies into light. It is said they do this to attract mates. There are many of them. The heavy rains this spring allowed for slugs and snails for their larvae to eat."

"Thank you. I have never seen them before."

"They are a wonder." His silent companion concluded the exchange.

Bustling at the west gate. Then snarling and spitting. Not outright shrieking and war cries. Prisoners being taken by the family foraging packs, to be led back to the Creek.

And now Lightfinger climbing the hill to report. "We think we got most of them. But at least two slipped away."

"That's good. We want them to tell the Protector we're here in force. We need him to pull his High Guard units out of the city long enough for the Resistance to take over."

"What if he comes here with a whole army?"

Good question. "I'm counting on him coming here in person to find out how big the problem is before he moves major forces around. His scouts are disappearing. And what is this rumoured Creeker army? Why has it crossed the Narrows? Is it to advance on the city? He'll come with part of the High Guard, but no more. He's perilously off-balance."

"How do you know he'll do that?"

"Because he's cautious. He listens to his fears. He's afraid to put his warriors in the Dead Zone in case they have the trembles. He'll have a Reserve of the High Guard within reach, in case it turns out he has a fight on his hands."

This seemed to satisfy Light, who was only being curious. She returned to the front line of skirmishers.

He lay in the grass and counted Fireflies. The activity separated the bright part of his mind that made decisions from his dark under-mind that was gathering anxiety about what he would do if he found himself nose to nose with The Protector. It amused him to think that he used his adversary's preferred name. Was it out of respect for a fellow commander or in deference to his begetter who gave him the gift of military acumen? In fact, a son was challenging the rule of a father. His anonymous companion curled up around him. She smelled like sunlight on dry moss. "He'll come at dawn and then we'll see how many soldiers he has," he told her. "He's diurnal. That's what allows him to wear out his opponents. He never sleeps."

"Umm."

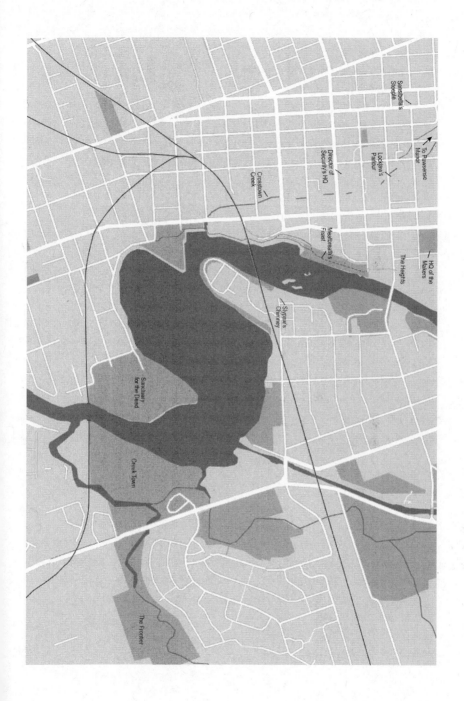

Sensibella's Steeple

To Pawsense Manor

Lockjaw's Parlour

Director of Security's HQ

Crosstown Creek

Meatmouth's Feast

HQ of the Makers

The Heights

Slypaw's Chimney

Sanctuary for the Dead

Creek Town

The Frontier

## 42

THE PLACE WHERE RACCOONS founded a city in the wilderness has seven hills, like Rome. Indigenous humans knew it as a resting stop between sets of rapids on a major canoe route. Sometime later, settlers came and raised a limestone church and a court house on the hill closest to the river. They repeated these symbols of Church and State in a huddle of similar edifices at the bottom of the hillside: two places of worship, a municipal office, and an armoury for the militia. To the west of this civic centre is the entertainment district and beyond it is a second hill surmounted by several churches, and it was in the steeple of a disused church that The Protector made his headquarters. The Primate use of geography to magnify civil and religious authority set the stage for the future struggle between Tyranny and Democracy in raccoon civilization. For while Meatbreath organized his occupation from the western hill, the leaders of the democrats – Mindwalker and Touchwit – planned the resistance across the plain on the eastern hill. This was where they were standing on the morning when fog enveloped the city.

"*Clutch*! I don't believe it. My anxiety-prone brother Clutch scarfed Creek Town right out from under Meatbreath's paws. Help, this is dizzying."

The seagull took her words at face value and hopped out of the way.

"Clutch is my older brother," she explained excitedly to Mindwalker. "I know he's got an obsession with his father, but stealing his power isn't exactly a subtle way to get over the obsession."

"I'm sure your brother will handle power evenly," Mindwalker said.

"You spoke to him. What do you think?" she asked the gull.

"I had insufficient evidence to venture a determination. He seems like a trustworthy colleague. But power shows its quality in how an individual behaves in relation to someone of a different gender. I didn't see such a person within a clam's toss of him."

"I've never seen two Seagulls together as a couple," Touchwit responded, defending her brother's lack of intimacy.

"Seagulls all look the same, don't we? It goes with the superstition that gulls don't have names. That's acceptable to us – it affirms our sense of equality."

"You have a name?"

"I have several, depending on which gull dialect I'm speaking. But as to the intimacy of genders, you'll be surprised to know that Seagull males share child care equally with females. I've done my share of egg-sitting. What is that you've made?" The gull referred to a woven artifact leaning against a tree in front of the court house. It was Mindwalker's latest composition of bulrushes, loosestrife, and grape vines.

"Oh. That's my story of the Island." Mindwalker seemed reticent about his Making. "For me, a Making is the personality of a Place made apparent to the eye, nose, and touch. Helping a Place become apparent in a Making is an act of resistance."

The seagull tilted his head and examined the work critically. "It has the calling of the forlorn in it. The transcendental homelessness of a Raccoon without a place in the world or an Ancestor in the sky. Yet its patterns speak even down to its tiniest particulars."

"I'm glad you like it," Mindwalker said. "I gave up my home, wealth, social rank, and reputation to make it."

"I believe I can hear it singing inside itself," the seagull said. "That means you have released some animated pattern."

Mindwalker raised an eyebrow.

"Animated pattern is pattern that thinks and feels. It is the vibrant density we live in."

"How is that different from patterned animation?"

"Patterned animation is merely the surface of a thing decorated so as to appear alive."

Touchwit saw her Stranger and her Seagull dissolving into collegiality. They looked ready to go off together and have a wonderful talk about the philosophy of Making over clams and black beer. She hated to break it up, but she needed to bring the two of them down-to-earth. First, to the gull: "Did you tell Clutch to lure Meatbreath out of the City tonight?"

"I did."

"Does Clutch have enough forces to pin down the High Guard?"

"I have never seen Raccoons fight. But if they were Primates I would say yes. Provided they aren't outmanoeuvred. But we don't know where the High Guard is. All Gulls are grounded because of the fog."

"It'll burn off in mid-morning, then we'll find out," Mindwalker said.

"If it's not too late," Touchwit said.

A shape moving low to the ground stirring the fog. A raccoon in a hurry.

"Bandit!"

Brother and sister touched noses and licked muzzles. But most of all they inhaled their common scent, familiar since cubhood.

"Who's this?" Mindwalker asked. "Another brother?"

"Meet my brother, Bandit."

"You're in the Honour Guard," Mindwalker said warily.

"Strictly undercover. Glad to touch noses."

Brotherly touch. Scent of mussels and dark beer.

Brusque touch. Scent of sandwich scraps, construction lot rubble, and automobile oil beneath a bridge.

"You can call me Mindwalker."

"What's that?" Bandit flattened his ears at the Making as if it was a threat.

"That's the combined contents of Mindwalker's unconscious," Touchwit said affectionately.

"It's leaning against a tree," Bandit said. It was the only observation he could make. This Mindwalker was long and tall. Just Sensibella's type.

"It wants to be outdoors," Mindwalker explained. Who was this upstart?

"That Seagull seems to be listening to us," Bandit said.

"It's okay. He's a colleague."

"Can he understand Raccoon?"

"Ask him."

"Excuse me, Mr. Gull, or Ms. Gull, or some other appellation of your own choosing. Do you wish to say something?"

The gull stared blankly at the new arrival.

"I guess he can't speak Raccoon."

"I can't believe you're up to your snout in espionage," Touchwit said, changing the subject.

Bandit couldn't tell if she was surprised to discover he could be subtle. She'd grown up too. Just like her to find a mate who was a Maker. Wait till she saw him and his Sensibella for a display of maturity.

"Maybe working undercover has given you something you can share with us." Mindwalker wasn't going to relax until this ambiguous brother showed his colours.

"You're the leader of the Resistance, aren't you?" Bandit asked.

Mindwalker said nothing.

"I need to report the location of your cell to the Director of Security. It's around here, isn't it?"

Mindwalker looked up towards the sky.

"I have to identify an actual place for her to raid. You don't have to be in it. Just your scents need to be."

"Why do it? Why not defect?" Mindwalker asked.

"I can't. I need to be in the Honour Guard tonight. To protect ... someone. To stay in the Guard, I have to give the Security Director the information she wants."

All froze.

A new shape moving up the hill to the Court House. A lithe, quick-moving female like Touchwit. In fact, she looked just like her up close.

"Hiya, Bandy! I knew I'd find you here."

"How on earth did ...?"

"I snooped around until I found a Brigade Commander. Then I back-tracked his scent trail. I expected it would lead me to the Makers' headquarters. Where you would be." Friskywits going on in her enthusiastic way. "How do you like my espionage work? Oh, you're cousin Touchwit, aren't you? Let's hug. I remember you from your visit to Mum's pond. Isn't Bandit marvellous? He's managed to burrow right into Uncle Protector's headquarters. He's going to ..."

"Shut up, Frisk!"

"... rescue Sensibella."

"I should have guessed," Touchwit said, looking at him. This time with astonished pride. He gritted his teeth to erase his smile.

"Better tell us your plans before I give away our headquarters." Mindwalker looked at Bandit with an air of strained authority.

"I can't. I don't have any."

"He never has a plan," Frisk explained. "The plan sort of makes itself up on the spot."

Mindwalker looked east to see if the fog was lifting. It was dense here because they were near the river. And under trees. Trees like fog. It moistens them. They pull it around them like cloaks.

"News, top to bottom," Bandit said in his best military manner. "Two High Guard commanders are trying to raise a mob to defend the City from the Migrants. They're calling it the Peoples Corps. It's meant to counter your Citizens Brigades."

"We know this," Mindwalker said.

"They're being promised a bottle of beer to join, plus cheap jobs."

"That's what lies beneath the regimes of Meatbreath and his ilk," Touchwit said. "Poverty-level wage work without job competition from migrants. In return, the people labour in food centralization and distribution so everyone can make a basic living. Those left over get to join a huge useless army."

"No adequate homes. No secure future for cubs. Is there something we could compose to put on the oral net?" Mindwalker asked.

Touchwit shut here eyes and recited:

> A *household debt to please the bankers;*
> *Piss-free beer for lazy wankers.*

"That's good, Touch. Did you compose that yourself?" Since composing his courtship poem for Sensibel, Bandit had acquired a grasp of poetry.

"You said *two* High Guard officers. Why did you say *two*?" Mindwalker asked.

"Because there aren't any others around. The entire High Guard left the City."

"What! The High Guard's left the city?" Touchwit turned to Mindwalker. "We didn't know this."

"No, we didn't. But it's good to know. It means the Protector-designate has no forces at the moment to protect the City except a secret police and an untrained pop-up army led by … by what? Honour Guard cadets, I expect." Mindwalker examined Bandit with the contempt of a drill sergeant confronting a new recruit.

The gull loosened its wings and shook off the moisture.

"Confirmed," Mindwalker said. "Now, what will we do about the question of revealing the whereabouts of our headquarters?"

"It's over there in a root cellar," Frisk said.

Mindwalker gave her a withering stare.

"I'd better go back now and report it," Bandit said. "Sorry you have to give up your headquarters, sir, but reporting it will allow me to rescue Sensibel from right under Meatbreath's nose. You'll see I'm contributing to the Resistance."

"I don't see how you're contributing to anything at all."

"You *are*, Bandy. I'm proud of you," Touchwit said. How was she going to keep the Resistance leaders together?

"See you tonight."

"I'll be there tonight too," Frisk said. "But first I have to do a subtle errand."

## 43

"GOOD MORNING LADIES! MY name's Flaxentip. I'm canvassing for the City Fathers. Is it alright if I ask you a few questions?"

Slypaws groaned and rolled over. Twitchwhisker stuck her head out of the hole.

"Oh, I hope I didn't wake you up, ma'am. I listened first to make sure you were awake."

"What's she want?"

"She's in the Honour Guard. She wants to ask us a few questions."

"Let me deal with it." Slypaws stretched, dusted her whiskers, and joined Twitch at the mouth of the hole.

"Hi, my name's Flax and I'm ..."

"It's okay. I got the message. What time of day is it?"

"It's certainly hard to tell, isn't it? The fog just won't lift. But I'd estimate it would be late morning if we could see the sun."

"How can we help you?" Slypaws felt like turning pleasant. The canvasser was a well-mannered if innocent sounding girl. She was just doing her job, whatever it was.

"Are you citizens of the City?"

"I don't know – are we, Twitch?"

"I'm sure I've been here long enough to qualify. I don't know about you."

"I'll put you both down as Citizens. It's obvious you aren't Migrants."

"Oh!"

"Second question (this won't take long): Are you aware of the Declaration tonight? It's happening at the riverside park, as soon as the Primates leave. The Protector is going to be officially named."

"Yes, we're aware of that."

"Would you be going by any chance?"

Slypaws looked blankly at Twitch. "We honestly don't know."

"That's okay. You don't have to be there. But can the Protector count on your support?"

"*NO!*"

"No?"

"I'm not a tree branch for him to walk over."

The nice young girl looked puzzled.

"You asked 'Can the Protector *count* on my support'. So I'm answering your question as you worded it. No one but my children can *count* on my support."

"That's right," Twitch said. "We don't want to be taken for granted."

"I quite understand, ma'am. I'll put you down as *undecided*. You're still considering your options."

"Don't put us down as anything, sweetie. We just want to live in a city where freedom to choose our leaders matters. That means a society where words have meanings."

"I have to put you down as something," the girl said.

"No, you don't. Just pretend you never saw us."

"She can't do that, Twitch. She has to report she canvassed us, otherwise she's being derelict in the performance of her duty. She's a soldier."

"I understand where you ladies are coming from. I don't want to have to choose sides myself. I'm losing buddies left, right, and centre. Leave it to me – I'll think of something on your behalf."

"What if instead of supporting one leader against another, we forced our leaders to collaborate on policy solutions?" Slypaws asked.

"That's a great idea! I'll pass it on to my supervisor. Thanks for giving me your time. Have a nice day!"

"Such a sweet girl," Twitch said when she was gone.

"Let's get some sleep," Sly said.

\* \* \*

"*Shut your muzzles and descend the tree in an orderly fashion. You're under arrest.*"

*"Frig off! We're Citizens, not Migrants."*

*"What's the charge?"*

*"You'll find out at the station."* Then in a lower voice to a subordinate, *"Anyone else in this tree?"*

*"Two ladies in the lower cavity. Said they were tourists. Couldn't explain themselves."*

"What's happening now, Twitch? Celestial Mother, a person can't get a decent day's sleep in this city!"

"What's going on is I think we're about to be arrested." Twitch pulled her head in from the hole opening. "You shouldn't have told the nice canvasser that we're undecided."

"You shouldn't have told her not to report us."

"You shouldn't have told her we were Citizens."

A grizzled alpha face at the hole. Clearly a police sergeant. "Alright, ladies. Break it up! You're going downtown."

"My dear sergeant – Good morning! Do we look like criminals? We're decent, law-abiding tourists doing our very best to respect the customs of your fine City."

"I don't care who you are. I only care that you exit your cavity forthwith. Otherwise, you'll get a bite on the nape."

"We'd better do what the dear sergeant says," Twitch said.

They descended the tree nose first, followed by the two officers. It felt like mid-day, but the fog was still thick. Slypaws sensed aggression all around her – not just from the arresting sergeant and his deputy but also from a surrounding squad of Peoples Corps. Snitches and Ne'er-do-wells, they'd been given an important role in society for the first time in their lives. They were working directly with the police. She joined the end of a line of youthful neighbours who'd done nothing but party all night and were now suspected criminals. This was unjust. She wanted to say something.

"Sly, this might be a good time not to argue. We need to behave like confused tourists who were scooped up accidentally."

Alright. That sounded reasonable.

\* \* \*

"Alright then. These three are going to be tormented. The rest are going to the School for Re-education. Now, what about the two ladies?"

"Failure to explain themselves, ma'am."

"I see. Well, let's sniff them out."

Slypaws felt Twitch stiffen beside her. Twitch wouldn't be able to handle interrogation. Already, at the sight of eight of the City's young being led away to the back of a forbidding building, she was beginning to shake. And the Interrogator looked like she could split a walnut with her eyes.

"What's your business in the City?"

"We're tourists, if you please." Slypaws looked the Interrogator in the eye and met a force like steel. An elongated nose to sniff out a traitor. Eyes pinced together to fasten on a goal. An eye wrestle. Defeated. Sly stared at her accuser's toes. So evenly spaced. The Security Director was a Rodent who waited for an opportunity, then pounced.

"We haven't been doing anything questionable." Twitch's shaky, pleading voice. "We're just keeping our noses clean, not getting in involved in anything."

The Interrogator broke her stare long enough to glance at poor Twitch. "Explain why you have two Revolution hats in your tree hole."

That finished off Twitch. She began to blubber.

\* \* \*

The dark place had screams baked into the walls. Smell of old tires, crankcase oil, gasoline, dust, derelict automobiles, cobwebs, stale coffee. It must be a place where Primate automobiles are sent to die. Unwanted cars that once drank bog oil put here and forgotten. She was splayed on an old wooden wall like an animal skin that Primate farmers nail to their barn doors as trophies. Twitch tied to another. There was no reason to torture Twitch – she'd tell the truth as an act of apology even without being terrorized. The Interrogator wants to use her to force me to confirm her account. The Rodent applies cruelty to obtain quick results.

"*You will provide full and accurate answers to the questions. You will not hold anything back. You* will *talk in the end.*"

"We're ready to talk right now. We can tell you anything you need to know, can't we Sly? Just ask us. Anything. Just ask us ..."

The Interrogator turned her back on Twitch. The aim of the torment was to extinguish a raccoon's nature. With raccoon nature out of the picture, there was no basis for hope. With hope gone, there was no reason to endure. Slypaws resolved that if she got through this, she'd be impossible to deal with for the rest of her life. Whatever doesn't break you makes you stronger.

"*You. Slypaws. Describe your relationship to the cell called the Makers.*"

"I have no idea what the f— you're talking about."

A noise of someone climbing on metal. What was this? A motor vehicle facing her about three bounds away. She hadn't distinguished it from the other vehicles which filled the dark space like ghosts. A security squad member had climbed the grill of the car and was squeezing through a shattered front window. Dear Hapticia, Mother of Heaven – what is going to happen?

No, not this! *Headlights!* They'd turned its headlights on. And the car as close as three bounds away. Twitch screamed. The blinding light seared into her skull – it would be inside her brain for the rest of her life. But worse was the fear of ...

The lights went off.

"*Now. Describe your relationship to the Makers.*"

Defiance. White, blinding rage. She blinked trying to find a focus. The fear would go on and on and on. You can't reason with it. You can't give it sympathy. It would be unrelenting. Focus on that old licence plate nailed to the wall. She would endure this experience one more time, then ... what? Would she be a chittering idiot like Twitch or would she just curl up and shake? It was too late; the assault had already done its damage. The fear knew her name. The worst fear a raccoon has – being run over by a Primate car. Twitch wouldn't survive a second session. I have to give the Interrogator something.

"I have a daughter who fancies herself as a Maker. She ..."

"*Name, please.*"

*Please.* The Interrogator had said *please.* "Her name is Touchwit ..."

"*Of the Island, River Clan – right?*"

They had her number. No. They didn't. She'd given her clan-family identity to the Interrogator earlier.

"*Do you know the whereabouts of your daughter?*"

"No. I honestly don't."

"*You're over here in the City to find her, is that it?*"

"No. I have no reason to believe she's even here in the city. I do not know where she is. I swam over with Twitchwhisker just to see the City."

The Interrogator shifted her gaze to Twitch. "*Is that correct?*"

"That's right. She came over with me to help me find a lodging. We've been exploring the City. And I wasn't doing ..."

"*What about the Revolution hats?*"

"They're tourist souvenirs. We didn't realize they meant something offensive. We're sorry we caused you this trouble. We'll do whatever you want."

The Interrogator considered this information. Twitch can really sound naïve, Slypaws thought. She might be believed. But the raccoon witch isn't finished with me.

A door opened to her right. A swirl of mist. Another Security officer. These people weren't High Guard, they weren't Peoples Corps, they weren't City Police – they weren't anything and they were responsible to no one except the Witch. Her personal army.

A whispered huddle beside the car. With eyes unable to see, her hearing made acute by pain, she strained to listen.

"*Your agent just reported, ma'am. The Makers' headquarters is in a root cellar of a house on the Heights just above the factory.*"

"*I know it.*"

"*He wasn't able to obtain names.*"

"*I see. Where is he? I want to talk with him.*"

"*He said he had to go off and find the names, as you commanded.*"

Silent, seething anger. She could smell the Security Director's anger.

"*Okay, take these two down from the wall and put them in the Bin.*"

Two shadowy creeps materialize at the periphery of her vision field – was she going to be permanently blinded around her focal point? And what about poor Twitch whimpering gently beside her? At least they probably wouldn't be tortured again. The pace of events was overtaking the Interrogator's merciless efficiency.

# 44

THE DANCING POINTS OF LIGHT left an idea behind his eyes. The way the Fireflies appeared, then disappeared, then reappeared unexpectedly somewhere else should be copied by his foraging packs. They would be vulnerable if spread out in a line. The Protector's professional warriors would cut through them, then swarm the huddled survivors. But not if the foraging groups operated independently and harassed the enemy formation from unexpected angles. The fog rolling off the lake would make the High Guard stay within sight of each other in unknown terrain. But there was no reason for his own units to be visible. They could dash out of the fog, vanish, then appear somewhere else. Like Fireflies.

However, the Protector had gained one advantage from the fog. He could keep the size of his forces secret until the moment they engaged. And also their location and point of attack. They would be rested and fresh from a night's sleep while the Creekers would be exhausted from spending a sleepless night in this place where the main biological activity was the decomposition of corpses.

No. That was wrong to say. For as the fog brightened behind him and creatures woke up, Clutch discovered he had other powers on his side. The Dead Zone was full of life: chipmunks, squirrels, rabbits, and groundhogs. And somewhere in the distance, a flock of geese honking nervously in the fog. The Protector couldn't take him by surprise.

* * *

Spitting growls from the cemetery gate. The screams of raccoons. His bodyguard became taut, sniffing the moist air. More shrieking. Then the war cry of the High Guard. Where were the runners? Last time he'd seen them, they were curled up on the horizontal rock slabs, taking in the warmth left in the stone from yesterday's sun. The attack had started. The High Guard was in action. *Where were his runners?*

A runner came, but she wasn't from the First Wave. She was from Sleekfoot's Second Wave watching the abandoned railway tracks just outside the cemetery's southern fenceline.

"My compliments, sir. Sleekfoot sent me up for news."

"Go and find out for yourself, then come back and tell me before you return to him. But be careful."

The runner was swallowed by the fog. Surely his own runners would return from the cemetery gate ...

His bodyguard began licking his hackles, trying to make him relax.

A raccoon popped out of the fog. The Second Wave runner. "Compliments from Lightfinger, sir. She's facing a full-on frontal assault from a big High Guard unit. Company-strength. She can harass them but she says she can't hold. She's falling back."

Why didn't he order the runner to bring another runner with her? "Very good. My compliments to Sleekfoot, and would he prepare to move a company to reinforce the main gate? But not until I give the command."

"Sir!" The runner loped off south down the roadway. She was using even ground; the soil around the tombstones was too bumpy.

"Ladyfriend?"

"Yes, you want me to be a runner. I'll go to the gate and tell Lightfinger that reinforcements are ready when she requires them. And I'll try to find the missing runners."

He noticed the silver fur on her heels just as she entered the fog.

Now he was alone at the base of the ancient tree beside the Primate place of Ancestor worship. Funny, he hadn't thought of the Great Raccoon Ancestor lately. Not since he'd met the fox. What side of the coming battle would the Ancestor favour? Would the god side with him or would he support the imposter? Or did he care at all about the skirmishing of mere creatures? Maybe he had larger matters to attend to, such as the migration of species and the change in habitats around the world. For a dreadful second Clutch thought the Ancestor didn't care about even that.

A runner emerged on the path from the main gate. "Lightfoot's compliments, sir. She is outnumbered. Reinforcements are required. Most immediate."

The runner lay on the grass, panting.

"Can you go to the Second Wave? Along that path. Go at your own pace. You'll likely meet a runner coming in the opposite direction. Give the runner the information, then find an upright stone to rest behind within hearing distance of me."

"Aye!" The runner picked her body up from the grass and headed south.

It was frustrating being at the mercy of runners. But he had divided his army in order to cover two possible vectors of attack, and he could lose control of the show at any moment. Worse, a High Guard scout could slip away and follow the scent-trails of the runners to where they met at this central command point. He felt terribly exposed. And without his bodyguard. He'd better climb this old tree beside the worship place. Its broad lower limb was horizontal with the ground for as far as he could stretch, then it made a right-angled curve and shot straight up to the heavens.

Clutch climbed the trunk and lay on the branch. It allowed him to look in three directions without being seen. But the security of the limb didn't relax him. His mind kept returning to the suspicion that what he had done, the splitting of his forces and their linking by runners, had been anticipated.

A leaf dropped from higher up on the tree.

Then a voice. A voice that was not unkind, for it held the power of the Ancestor.

*"So, little one. How do you like being the Protector?"*

## 45

"**D**ID YOU MAKE YOUR report?" Frisk asked.
"Not all of it. I only gave them the location of the resistance
headquarters. And I only gave it to the Security Director's assistant.
She'll have to torture the scat out of me before she gets the names."

"We'd better lie low."

"Where? There are P.C. security squads roaming the city, sweeping up young people who can't explain themselves. The first place
they'll look is under the bridge."

"I heard of a tree that's popular with the fun crowd. It's just west
of the entertainment district, beside the Crosstown Creek."

"Let's go."

Raccoon shapes slipping between buildings in the late morning
mist. No one wore a revolutionary hat because of the arrest squads.
It was impossible to tell friend from foe. The shapes bumped against
Bandit and Frisk without stopping to apologize, not even exchange
sniffs. It seemed everyone had something on their mind.

"This is getting heavy," Frisk said. "I love it! In fact, I haven't
had so much fun since I got into an argument with the Etiquette and
Deportment teacher and she sent me off to continue my argument
with the Vice-Principal. It was ..."

"Sssh!"

They had come to an entry place to the tunnel holding the Crosstown Creek.

"Frisk, if this is the only time in your life you'll ever be silent, it
is now. Those are P.C. thugs."

"Mnff."

Three Peoples Corps Volunteers and a young commanding offi-
cer-cadet controlled the pathway to the underground stream. They
were letting individuals through after checking their intentions. Bandit walked right up to the Honour Guard cadet.

"Oh, greetings mate. I didn't know it was you," the lieutenant said.

Frisk was beginning to believe that her cousin owned the town.

"I'm on Detached Special Duty. Okay if we go through? This is my cousin, Frisk."

"Hiya!"

"Sure, you can go through. Long as you're not a rebel or a migrant."

"Anything to watch out for up there?" Bandit indicated the hole in the culvert.

"No, it's clear up to the western hill and beyond. If you see a skirmish, keep your heads down. We've got orders to stir up conflict. Create an excuse for the High Guard to take over the city and keep the peace. Our parents are getting nervous about their tree houses."

"Weird! An alliance between the very rich and the very poor," Frisk said when they were safely in the tunnel.

The passage up the tunnel was uneventful. The only raccoons in the Crosstown Thoroughfare were the elderly going about their business. The young were away staffing street barricades. Beyond the Entertainment Zone, the creek came out into the open and proceeded through a strip of parkland which had once been a railway bed. The ground sloped up to the west, one of those elongated hills called a drumlin, where the Protector had his headquarters. Sensibel was there. Bandit put Sensibella out of his mind. Times were too edgy to think of soft things. Beside the creek was the tree. Impossible to miss. An ancient stooping Sugar Maple that served as a tenement for young raccoons. Beer cans and pizza boxes littered the ground around its trunk. But the tree was eerily silent.

"They must all be sleeping it off," Frisk said. "Let's see if there's an unoccupied cavity. Why are you sniffing?"

"It doesn't smell right. The scents are old."

The first cavity they came to just where a huge lower bough branched out was empty, except for two Revolution hats.

"What is it, Bandy? You froze."

"Mom's been here. I smell her. And another raccoon. Female. But there's no one in this tree. Everyone's gone."

# 46

THE BIN TURNED OUT to be a tool shed across a dirt parking area from the garage where they'd been tormented. It had a window, and through its cobwebs and grime Slypaws watched for changes in the activity of her captor. The fog had lifted, revealing a wrecking yard for old gasoline automobiles. No guard dog, fortunately. This was the headquarters for the secret police who were now enforcing the City's security.

"Uh-oh!" she said.

"Let me have a look." Twitch shoved her whiskers against Sly's face. The other prisoners crowded in behind her.

A new raccoon stood blinking in the late morning sun. A senior male yet without the manner of belonging to a hierarchy. A loner.

"I wouldn't let that one within a sniff of me," one of the prisoners said. It was the newly pregnant Creeker woman who kept her misfortune to herself.

"Is he the one who made you this way?" Twitch asked.

"No. But he may as well have. He sells woman prisoners as entertainment escorts to the City Elders. The jailer is his accomplice."

The jailer was a middle-aged female who had been born in a sewer. Her lip drooped on one side, suggesting she'd lost one fight too many, and her eyes peered through a greyish-white film of disease. Sure enough, she appeared from underneath a truck and with the ruinous memory of a sexual swagger sidled up to the male.

"Handsome couple," Twitch said dryly.

"May I be sympathetic and ask why you are in the Bin?" Since the sufferer had volunteered to speak about her tribulations, Slypaws thought it wasn't untoward to offer her friendship. How could she not with the broken-spirited Creeker pressed close to her behind the window?

"It is not presumptuous of you to ask under these circumstances. All of us in here are charged with Undesirable Activity in one form or other. In my case, all I did was pass on information as I should as a citizen of Creek Town. This is where citizenship gets you."

"You have my sympathy and, if you desire, my friendship."

"Thank you. My name is Lickfoot."

The jailer received her orders, nodded, and slinked toward the shed.

"Get ready to run," Slypaws whispered over her shoulder.

"Sly – we can't take this power couple. I can give the doxy a second drooping lip so she at least acquires the virtue of symmetry, but I can't go up against her Big Guy. He fights dirty."

"We have no other choice. Everyone has to squeeze through the hole one by one to get out of here, and we can't go through at all if that hideous couple is right outside."

"I'd rather die beside you than watch you sacrifice yourself in vain."

"That's very noble, Twitch. But let's see what she wants."

They listened to the car wheel being rolled away from the hole. Daylight showed between the dirt floor and the bottom of the shed wall. The jailer stuck her nose in.

"We want fresh water," Twitchwhisker demanded.

"Shut up, dearie, else I'll give 'ee a slap across thy snout."

"You touch her, you scabrous heap of filth, and your entrails will be draped over the rafters."

Drooplip squinted at Slypaws, then decided not to push it further. "We're moving you'se all."

"Where?"

"It 'tain't none o' yer business, issit? But I'll tells ye: you'se already know there's a threat to the City. The Protector's son is coming 'ere wid his throng o' followers – why are ye prickin' up yer ears?" She directed the question at Slypaws.

"No reason. I didn't think any of Meatbreath's sons were old enough to attract followers."

"Well, this one is. Not that it matters to me. One Protector's as good as t'other – that's what oi say. They's all the same to a Businesswoman such as meself."

"A Businesswoman! Give me a break!"

"Protectors need chattels. Which is what you'se lot are."

"I'm not anyone's property. I'm a free Raccoon Citizen," Twitch declared.

"Sure you are, sweet'eart. You can say that to your designated lover. It'll increase his ardour."

"Maybe it'll be the Mini-Pro."

"Twitch, be careful," Sly whispered.

"Roight, then. First couple. You'se are comin' out by twos, get it? No funny business. No, not you two."

"We're content to go last," Slypaws said.

The first pair went out – two yearling women brashly wearing their Revolution hats. A shadow fell over the entranceway. Twitch sniffed and made a face. The male loner. "Go and reason with him," she whispered in Slypaw's ear.

"No, it's useless."

"I'll try then."

"Be careful what you say."

Twitch put her nuzzle to the hole and called. "Yoo-hoo! I want to propose a bargain."

"Sure. Speculate away, so long as you keep it under the table."

"That's very clever. With whom do I have the honour of making a transaction?"

"Trusty Lockjaw is the name. And sellin' ladies is my game. Let's hear your proposal."

"I propose – just speculatively speaking, of course – that you re-lease me and my friend. In return, we'll promise that the Protector's Son takes you as his Business Manager. For *all* the affairs of the City."

"You know this guy?"

*Shut up, Twitch!*

"No. Never met the dude. But we believe we can ... work out a deal with him. He'll be happy that you guaranteed our safety."

"You don't know him, but you're going to deal with him! Nice try, ladies." The shadow withdrew from the entranceway. Light flooded back in.

"Wait! I've got more ..."

The listening shadow returned.

"The Mini-Pro is from the Creek, isn't he? I'm a leading Clan Mom there."

"So? Lots of Creeker Moms here in the City. If you told me the Protector's Son is your direct kin, we'd be having a different conversation."

"She knows him because his mother is standing right here. Behind her," the abused Creeker shouted.

"I don't believe you, Lickfoot. You're a turncoat spy," Lockjaw said.

"I smelled her up close. That's his mom, or my nose is an oil can."

"Your nose is going to be slimed forever when I'm through with you," Twitch growled.

"Sssh! Let's see how this turns out," Sly whispered.

Lockjaw thrust his head into the hole. "Which one's the mother?"

"I am that," Slypaws said in her proudest voice. "And sometime companion to his father too."

"Fascinating. I want you out here in the sun. And your bargaining agent as well."

"I'll proceed first." The pregnant Creeker pushed between Slypaws and Twitch.

"Not you, you idiot. He means Slypaws."

Slypaws exited first. Then Twitchwhisker. The Creeker informant began to wail. The automobile wheel slid back into place like the gate of hell.

"Thus perishes a coward bitten by her own timidity," was Twitch's comment.

"Don't be hard on her," Sly said. "It's so easy for a person in a servile position to mistake power for security."

"Her mistake was thinking Lockjaw would find her profitable because she held the proof of your identity. She never thought you'd actually verify who you were. But you did. And now we're profitable."

"We're worth our weight in beer," Sly said.

" SO, LITTLE ONE. *How do you like being the Protector?*"
The voice was patient but weary around the edges – the voice of one who has endured much, the voice of an Ancestor. It had spoken out of the mist in the upper foliage at the top of the tree. How do you address a god? Do you say "Your Infinity" or "Your Omniscience"? There was no account in oral scripture of anyone talking face-to-face with the Great Raccoon. Not even Procyonides the Sage had spoken with him. The only thing to do was to be forthright and try not to tremble.

"I am not the Protector. I am but the servant of my Clan. Possessing some few qualities of leadership, I presume to direct my Clan in the defense of its homeland."

Silence. Did the tones given off by his heart sound right? Was he really a humble servant or did he secretly aspire to be a Protector? He used the Other's thoughtful silence as an opportunity to swivel his ears toward the west gate. That chanting in unison was the High Guard. They sounded unnerving. The cries of the Clan Mothers were sporadic and scattered. Not a good sound.

A shuffle in the branches. The Ancestor has altered his position.

"*If you are only a servant, why do you adopt the Protector's instruments of power? The summoning of an army. The control of feeding and breeding?*"

Just a flick of mockery. The Ancestor was objecting to his assuming the Protector's role, but he didn't sound all that positive either about the subjugation of the Clan Mothers and the portioning out of sustenance. The god was calling upon him to justify his violations of Custom.

"A disease has possessed the thoughts and feelings of Creek Town. I am the fever necessary for a cure."

He flinched when he gave this answer back to the mist. It sounded vain. And something was agitated? Was he shuddering – no, it was the leaves of the tree. The tree was afraid. Was it afraid for him?

Everything now depended on his measured reasoning. If he argued awkwardly, he would lose his balance.

"*The cure is the disease made worse.*"

The simple statement had the force of a paw-swipe. Yes, he was in fact using the Protector's methods in order to end the Protector's regime. And he could easily be corrupted by those methods and merely reproduce the Protector's state of unfreedom. The worthy Creekers had willingly loaned their freedom to him because he was a good Raccoon and would give them back their freedom when the crisis was over. But power reached for more power to be effective. Power rarely wanted less power. That was what concerned the Ancestor.

"*You may relax. Your behaviour is in accord with the sacred rhythms. I have something to tell you if you are going to do the work of a Protector.*"

"I heed any wisdom I may receive in so vexatious a matter."

"*Heed this then: Consider this Oak tree you are balanced on. For season after season she decides to withhold her fertility. She produces no acorns. The scarcity of acorns is a message intended for the eyes of squirrels and jays. It tells them they are going to starve and their own fertility will be diminished if they continue to expect this temperamental tree to supply them with nuts. Accordingly, they depart for a better locale where they will be better nourished. But then after a season, behold! the Oak suddenly produces an abundance of acorns – she releases her fertility by the mouthful. The few squirrels and jays who have remained in the vicinity of her beneficence feast gloriously. And the Oak prospers because the greater part of her acorns have fallen to the ground uneaten, and some of them will give rise to stout Oak children.*"

A sound teaching! Rooted beings could be tricksters. And the Ancestor had supported his wise counsel by referencing the holy rhythms, specifically the Principle of the Inverse Alternation of Scarcity and Abundance in a Relationship of Hosts and Guests. Destiny had called upon him, Clutch, a senior brother and major son, to restore a balance. This validated his leadership of Creek Town.

There came a hum rather like that of a power transformer atop a telephone pole. Doubtless, the god had again turned his mind inward into its infinite depths. Probably he was taking instantaneous stock of all the rhythms of plenitude and poverty in creation, making sure they were all running smoothly. Clutch took the opportunity to return for an instant to his own immediate worry. Where were his runners? There was a sound of skirmishing down at the southern fenceline where Sleekfoot's Second Wave was watching the railroad tracks. He couldn't do anything about it. He was cut off from his forces; cut off from his sister Touchwit's effort in the City; cut off from the whole world of outlines and distinctions because the fog had turned existence into a deathly sameness. The inscriptions were coming off the stones. He was alone with his god. A cough clearing the fog out of a throat. The Ancestor had come to give him courage.

"*Consider the Primates, for it is said 'As Primates evolve, so Raccoons evolve'.*" The Ancestor waited the appropriate interval for the saying to achieve its silencing power of assent. "*The Primates, too, engage in this rhythm of withholding and releasing in order to obtain a future for their young. They deny themselves the small immediate comfort in order to obtain the larger future security. Do the Primates not behave like the Oak tree?*"

A Dialogue! He used to engage in Dialogues with Uncle Wily, who taught by means of the Procyonic Method. He suddenly realized how much he had missed dialoguing.

"I would say the Primates behave in the same manner as the Oak tree," Clutch answered. "Yet they perform their behaviour at the end of a very slender limb."

"*Yea!*" the Voice from the mist intoned. "*They have played with taking risks for so long that their risks have come to be impressed on the sacred rhythms of things. Is it any surprise, therefore, that the sacred rhythms broadcast back those selfsame risks in exaggerated oscillations? This ultimate risk-taking is Earth trying to recover her lost balance. It is dangerous – very dangerous to herself. May we hope that she is magnifying Scarcity in order to exhaust risk-taking behaviour altogether, thereby achieving for the few survivors of her desperate experiment an outlook conducive to a harmonious plenitude!*"

"Yes, that is exactly what the sacred rhythms appear to be doing," Clutch replied, practically swaying with the eloquence of the Ancestor's prose. "They are denying fertility almost to the point of no return in the hope of averting extinction." The Ancestor is his wisdom had adopted his fever necessary for a cure argument, and extended it to the behaviour of Earth. So far, the Dialogue was sound. How powerfully the Ancestor reasoned. But where was it going?

"*Having so educated the rhythms of things in this habit of risk-taking, it falls to Primates – if they wish to survive themselves – to take their paradoxical logic to the end. They must use their very risk-taking to correct the consequences of their risk-taking.*"

"I agree. There is no other option."

"*This they must do,*" the Voice went on, "*by planting the seeds of future life in new habitats that have been especially fashioned to receive them. Is this recourse not in accord with the Principle of Scarcity and Abundance?*"

"It is," Clutch said warily. "Yet the Principle itself has become bent in practice. It is so badly warped that it may no longer be of service to us as a guide to the various ways things flourish. For by applying the Principle directly to the Principle itself, the risk-taking behaviour seeks an outcome that can't ever be predicted. It can be likened to a Raccoon holding a broken branch under his feet and trying to walk on it."

Had he performed one balancing feat too many? he wondered. First, he had taken an awful risk by raising a militia to challenge the Protector. Second, he had taken an even more breathtaking risk by moving his force to the Dead Zone, hoping to tie up the Protector's forces, which were unknown. Was the exposure to mischance succeeding? He could make out confused sounds from the southern boundary. From the west gate came the bitter defiance of the First Wave. They sounded like they were being forced back up the hill. It wasn't working out. The fog would lift, revealing a landscape of raccoons panting and licking their wounded spirits. Striding among them, scornful victors. The Ancestor had come to draw out the moral lesson of his defeat and thereby make him a better Raccoon.

"*We have agreed, have we not, that as Primates evolve, so Raccoons evolve. Are Raccoons in a time of crisis not justified in copying Primate behaviour?*"

Clutch began to feel a massive headache. It felt like a Drooler had caught him out in the open and put its jaws around his head and was closing them slowly, tighter and tighter. Everything the Ancestor had said had confirmed that he had done the right thing in assuming the role of Protector. At the same time, the Great Raccoon was warning him that his improvised leadership required him to take dangerous risks. A single risk was easy to justify; a decision to adopt risk-taking as a general behaviour was another thing entirely. The fever necessary for a cure was like fire-sugar in a bottle found in a recycling bin. Deadly intoxicating. The fever could be more harmful than the disease itself. A raccoon could go around in a fever solving crises that didn't exist. Then to prolong the excitement of the fever, he'd start making up crises in order to solve them. Why hadn't the Ancestor mentioned this? Presumably like a good teacher he was enabling his servant Clutch to discover it for himself.

The defeat lament. His Clan Mothers were singing the dirge of defeat to keep their broken spirits together. *Where were his runners?* Could he ask the Ancestor to allow him to briefly leave his solemn presence and find out what was happening to his Clan?

"*Your runners were ambushed one-by-one in the fog,*" the Voice said, reading his mind. "*And one paw of your army no longer knows what the other paw is doing.*"

Clutch felt his spirits turn to the cold slush you find on a street in March when you're foolish enough to go outdoors before winter is over. The hope of Creek Town was lost. Its people would paddle back in ones and twos to the beloved shore, preparing themselves for a lifetime of bondage and sorrow. Some would flee, as they had done before, to the distant tributaries and headwaters of the creeks. His colleagues, Sleekfoot and Lightfinger, whom he had let down, would walk away from him without a word. His ladyfriend would be taken away to be the servant to some scarred warrior back in the City.

"*I can get you out of this,*" the Ancestor said. Soft, firm, a kindly whisper.

"What must I do?"

"*First, since you are a reasoning Raccoon and make a point of never proceeding without knowing what you are doing and why,*

*I will tell you a story about the philosopher Procyonides and draw out the lesson therefrom."*

"The thinking of Procyonides is always timely, especially at the collapse of hope," Clutch said. The Great Ancestor seemed fond of the Classics.

*"One soft night, it happened that Procyonides was walking in the woods. And the soil was damp on account of a recent rain. The Sage looked behind him and saw that he was leaving footprints. And it occurred to him that each print made by a paw was identical with the last print that the aforementioned paw had made. 'Eureka!' exclaimed the Sage. 'My markings have told me something significant and worthy to be applied to memory. It is that there are two of me. There is the Raccoon who is walking and there is the replica of me walking'."*

The Ancestor paused in the manner of a teacher in a Dialogue. *"Would you say this replica is real?"*

"No, the replica is not real. There can be only one real maker of the footprint." He was following the exchange as it was given in the ancient Dialogue. He knew it well. It had been one of Uncle Wily's favourites.

*" 'Yet,' said the Sage to himself, 'the footprint is as real as the foot that made it. If you were a blind Raccoon, and you did not know of the footprint, and you sniffed the footprint with your eyes closed, your senses would conjure a real Raccoon for your mind to consider. Your hackles would rise. Your ears would flatten. Your tail would tuck in ...'"*

"I suppose ..."

*"That is what Procyonides thought that night. He thought another raccoon, coming along, would sniff the print and imagine that he, Procyonides, a real Raccoon, was present. 'How then?' said the Sage, 'can we say that only one entity is real?'"*

"Both are real but not equally so," Clutch said quickly. Then to himself: Let's get this over with. I'm losing a battle.

*"I shall continue. It came to pass that Procyonides died and alas was no more. But the tracks he had made remained, and became a permanency to his disciples. They coveted the paw prints and they went frequently and sniffed thereof, because they were all that was*

*left behind by the wise and thoughtful Procyonides. For it is said: 'Who can recall a teacher's sayings? They are like the wind in the branches. But his prints endure forever.' But by summer's end there became no way of remembering the philosopher by his odour, because the rains had come and washed away his scent together with his footprints, and even the tracks of Procyonides were no more to his disciples."*

Clutch felt a tremendous sorrow at the loss of the traces left by the Sage. It was comparable to the sorrow he felt when he surveyed the smear left by Uncle Wily on the pavement on a similar wet night. "But it hapt that a Boy Cub was walking in the same forest one day," Clutch said, using the measured cadences of his late uncle. "And he saw that some mud had fallen into one remaining footprint that had been spared by the canopy of a tree. And over time the mud had hardened into clay. And he plucked out the hardened clay. And behold! He was holding a copy of the very paw that had made the footprint. Well, you can be sure he did washing motions as carefully as a good raccoon does with a clamshell …"

Here Clutch repeated the Hand Ritual.

"… and he took the model to his burrow, and set it up as a shrine, saying to his kinsfolk, 'Lo! Here is the eternal imprint of Procyonides the Philosopher. The mould is more important to us than any saying because when pressed against the soil it can re-produce the very paw print of the Sage, and it can repeat it accurately each and every time'.

"'No,' they replied. 'It is but a lump of clay. It is imperfect because it is only an impression, not linked to the Philosopher's real paw by a scent.'

"Accordingly," Clutch said, "the story teaches that there can be only one Real. The copy is but a mere sign that this reality existed and is not linked to it physically."

There came a wailing from the south. The shock and despair of a Clan Mother. She had lost more than a battle.

*"That is a quaint version of the story,"* the Voice said. *"It is outdated."*

"What other version is there?"

*"It goes like this: And so it came to be that the Artifact in the shrine became as real as Procyonides. Indeed, more real – because the sometime foolishness of the original Philosopher was forgotten, and instead his solemnity was praised."*

That wasn't right – it erased the mischievous Procyonides altogether so that it was as if he'd never existed in time. He existed only as an image held in the apparent timelessness of a shrine. Something was tangled in the Ancestor's reasoning. But there was nothing tangled about his power: the thoughtwaves coming out of the mist were making the leaves cringe.

*"And now your task,"* the Voice declared.

No! Not yet! The Ancestor's reasoning was tangled. It had to be corrected first – it had to be corrected because the right reasoning supported the rightness of his, Clutch's, claim to lead the Clan. If the reasoning was faulty, his claim was faulty. But how could the Ancestor's thinking contain an error? And such a simple error?

The crying of his kinsfolk travelled through the fog. The First Wave were still fighting as they retreated up the hill towards him – he could now see their contorted bodies through the mist. And there came continued shrieking from the Second Wave at the railway tracks. He sniffed the air of the bough. All he smelled was a variation of himself. Maybe the Ancestor …? What if …?

"Wait! I know another version of the story," Clutch shouted. "I must recite it."

*"Yet another version? There aren't any other versions. I do not know of it."*

"Why don't you know of it?" Clutch shouted. "You're omniscient!"

No sound came from the top of the bough. But in the thinning fog, a shape began to take form. It was titanic, divine, the shape of a god.

"Reveal yourself! I demand that you reveal yourself!"

No reply.

"Show yourself. Else I shall tell my version."

*"Do not speak it! Do not on any account speak it!"*

"I shall anyway. It goes like this. When the young Boy Cub released the clay pawprint from the cavity in the ground made by the

Sage, he held it up to his eye. And an idea came to him, and he reasoned thus. 'It would be dangerous if this image became generally known, because then it would teach Raccoons something harmful. And that harmful thing is that the original clay pawprint could be used to replicate itself in an exact copy. And that copy could make another copy and so on. This repetitious activity of making would persuade Raccoons that the person who possesses the mould or model of something Real wields great influence because that person can stamp endless identical copies of the Sage, each copy as true as another and each retaining the aura of the original.' So he took the moulding and smashed it against a rock. 'Cease to exist, thou dangerous and troubling Notion!' he said to it.

"End of story."

"*From whom did you hear this version?*" the Voice asked.

"I have never heard it," Clutch said. "I just made it up."

The shape of his father loomed out of the mist above him. He stepped delicately, stirring the fog which the tree had wrapped around itself. He planted his paws with care, along the bough. How could it support the size of him? The huge head with the darkest of masks outlined by a magnificent ruff. The powerful sinewy shoulders. Yet his father's arms tapered down to slender fingers, almost feminine in their delicacy. And the tail too, so bushy and luxurious, was a woman's tail.

"There is no genuine Original," his father said.

"There are no genuine copies," the son said.

"Let us put our differences aside. I will teach you what you need to know to govern a colony. Then you shall be the Protector of Creek Town and the streams running east into the interior. You have already taken command of the regime I've installed there. You may continue to govern in my name."

"And you, Father?" Clutch asked. He already knew the answer.

"I shall be Protector of the whole united River Clan. My den will be in the City."

Clutch turned the offer over in his mind. He'd been given a giant succulent clam and a set of rules for opening it. All he had to was follow his father's rules and there would be accord between Creek

Town and the City. Comings and goings between the two communities would be straightforward and untroubled; each would give wealth to the other and the supply chains would not be vulnerable to political whims. And instead of being punished as an upstart, tied upside-down to a tree until everyone recognized that he was unwanted, he'd be Chief Raccoon of the native home of the River Clan.

"We will require a common system of barter," his father said, "to assist in making food flow evenly across the lake. Clams and Bottles of Beer will signify the value of a commodity to the bartering parties. After a time, these equivalent objects of value will be simplified into symbols: the Shell and the Bottle Cap. Arrayed on strings, they will be worn by raccoons around their necks as signs of their wealth and their readiness to acquire more wealth. And on each clam and each cap will be the image of my paw to ensure that the symbols for bartering are trustworthy. The paw print will be made by means of a clay moulding created from my paw print on soft soil. You shall be the guardian of the Original Mould. No other Making of any sort will be tolerated."

He saw it instantly. The error of Procyonides: to revere the *moulding* as an imperishable Original, and value its stampings because they are identical copies bearing the imaginary scent of the Original. Thus, the Father present in his Cubs. The One in the Many. But this father was averting a threat to his power by offering a gift of leadership to the son. The faulty logic remained. Don't acquiesce yet. Tell him you need time. Think of a vexing detail.

"Father, what of the Migrants?"

"They will be held in check by the High Guard. The Migrants already in the City will be hunted down and expelled."

He'd never be able to look his mother in the eye. His sister Touchwit would destroy his spirit with remarks that stuck like burrs. Bandit would shrug and walk away. And he would despise himself because he had said the word *father* in order to placate him, and when he had said the word he couldn't help filling it with meaning. He'd uttered the word *father* with a son's obedience and respect.

"Nevertheless and for all that, I do defy you!" he blurted out. "I serve my Clan. I do not serve you."

The Protector froze. From the upright section of Clutch's bough, the huge head with its superior ears glared down at him. Had no one stood up to this bully before? Stand up to him is the right word. Because the contest would be fought on this tree limb, and he would lose his footing or submit just as his mother had done. The giant alpha male was descending nose first to shove him off the bough. Just his sheer mass would force him to fall to the ground. Then his High Guard soldiers would take form out of the fog where they'd been waiting. They would break his spirit with savage bites as a lesson to raccoons who disobeyed the Protector.

A shout from the ground. A raccoon's face staring up. "What is it now?" Meatbreath said wearily.

"It is the City. The Citizens Brigades have taken control of the City. The Peoples Corps are in disarray, and the Security Director has only the City Honour Guard left to protect your interests."

"Tell the High Guard units to pull out of this morbid place. And call in the main High Guard army from the Southern Frontier. We're going to retake the City and the whole West Bank. It's a weak, leaderless, decadent failed state. It needs a leader."

"Aye! What about these Creeker forces?"

"Leave them be. They don't look like they're going anywhere soon."

"And him?"

"You mean this broken mould? He's going to shatter into pieces."

Clutch couldn't counter the indifferent shove as his father went by casually on the branch. He hit a tombstone with his head, and that was all he knew.

# ACT V

## *To Make a World*

*Slypaws*, and her children:
*Clutch*, Governor of Creek Town and its militia
*Bandit*, secret agent of the Resistance
*Touchwit*, artist and leader with *Mindwalker* of the Resistance

*Twitchwhisker*, Slypaws's friend

*Pawsense*, and her daughters:
*Goodpaws*, a dutiful daughter
*Sensibella*, femme fatale and double agent
*Frisk*, comrade to cousin Bandit
and *Nimbletoes*, family messenger

*Smartwhisker*, community leader in the Heights

A superior Seagull

*Hala*, Princess and commander of the Southern forces
*Flaxentip*, Daughter of the City and admirer of Bandit
*Silverheels*, Clutch's ladyfriend

*Meatbreath*, Protector-Elect of the City
*The Security Director*, City bureaucrat and head of the Peoples Corps
*Lockjaw* and *Drooplip*, suppliers to the City

# 48

THE LANDMARKS defining their conflict stuck up above the fog – the western hill which served as Meatbreath's headquarters, and the eastern hill which had been Mindwalker's command centre. Down below in the mist lay the dim shape of an underwater city, the prize of their struggle. Yet the artist leaders couldn't be seen, high up on a patio surrounding the upper level of a building, with planters holding the trunks of vines that tumbled over the parapet to the ground far below. Here she was on top of that surprising wall of vegetation which she had relaxed under while guided by seagulls. Touchwit had never been above a city in her life nor for that matter a forest – for that was the sensation given by the cascade of foliage. She felt secure with the sunlight, the building shrouded in greenery, and the rustling and chirping of birds in the vines. Just below her was the site of Meatbreath's Feast.

A gull emerged from some envelope in the sky and joined its colleague on the parapet. The birds exchanged news in what sounded like bickering squawks, then Touchwit's friend spoke. "She says the entire united High Guard will be back in the City in ..." the gull canted his head to the sun, "... just a few degrees."

She knew what *degrees* meant. Gulls computed space and time according to the inclination of the sun. But how did the second gull know where the enemy was in the fog?

"She has a good sense of the unseen," her friend explained, reading her mind. "She uses her sense of smell to find direction."

"Can she smell Meatbreath?"

"No. The sense of smell is for navigating only. For finding land. She knows where the soldiers are by the sonic vibrations of their bodies."

Well, those were necessary skills for mariners. Often they had no visual landmarks in the indeterminate expanse of ocean. These gulls were mobile calculating devices.

Mindwalker frowned gloomily at the fog concealing the Lake. "We've been humbugged. Meatbreath stole a march, beat up the

Creeker militia, and is back in time to mop up the Citizens Brigades. Humbugged, I say!"

"Humbugged twice-over, if I may employ your military phrase," the gull said, "since the High Guard is now presumably at full strength, having been joined by its comrades previously deployed on the Southern Frontier."

"Three times humbugged if that's the case," Mindwalker said. "Because he would have caught Clutch in a classic pincer attack. The High Guard on the Southern Frontier would have come up his tail – I don't know how."

Touchwit decided that this curious word *humbugged* must be a euphemism for a vector of approach that was a surprise.

"The Frontier High Guard wouldn't have dared to swim the Narrows in a fog. Or use the bridges during the day. They likely got across the open span of the rusting railway bridge," the gull said.

"Bloody brilliant!"

"Where's Clutch? Is he alright?"

The seagull nodded to his colleague. She plunged off the ledge into the fog and reappeared seconds later flying toward the cemetery.

"We have to tell the Brigades to make themselves scarce. And I haven't a clue how we're going to seize the stage from the Protector tonight."

"I am by no stretch of the wing a military expert," the Gull replied, "but the Brigades shouldn't have been let loose in the first place. It was obvious the Protector was going to return to the city for his inauguration."

"The Brigades are excited. Think of the coming together of disparate flocks," Mindwalker explained.

"You mean to say it was impossible to contain their enthusiasm?"

"Exactly. The high spirits of the young won out against the commanding officers. Being young, they have a streak of anarchy."

"Perhaps Anarchists should not be led by Artists," the gull said.

## 49

"WELL, IF IT AIN'T *Signor Incognito*? Wot can oi do for you'se?"

"You can release into my custody two Clan Matriarchs who seem to have been imprisoned by mistake."

"Sorry, can't oblige. All miscreants are property of the City State."

"I have orders from the Security Director herself. Here is her scent on my ear for verification."

"Can't fool an ol' tart like me. Anyways, oi don't remembers no clan mums comin' in here."

Bandit grabbed Drooplip's ear and began to twist it.

"Oy! – don't do that. I already got one bad ear. I'll holler – the Guards are nearby."

"Wrong. They were summoned to re-possess the Downtown. The Brigades have taken it."

"Anyhow, I can't remember."

"Let's see if this will help you remember." Bandit twisted her ear hard.

"I remember now," Drooplip said. "Go and shout their names at the shed. Meantime, I have to go defend the City ... Who's this? You'se from the Pond?"

"None of your business," Frisk said.

"Hold her ear until I get this sorted out."

"With pleasure." Frisk gave the ear a meaningful twist.

*"Mom, it's me, Bandit. Are you in there?"*

Anxious faces pressed against the shed window. Young faces. But no answer.

"See, they ain't here. They never came here. *Ouch!*"

A voice spoke hesitantly from behind an opening blocked by an automobile wheel. "I know them. Let me out and I'll tell you where they went."

"I'll let all of you out if you tell me where they went."

"Oh, 'eaven preserve me! Oi'm doomed."

"No. Just let me out. They were taken away by that sicko's companion, Lockjaw. I don't know where."

"Droops will tell us where, won't she?"

"*Ouch!*"

Bandit put his shoulder to the wheel and rolled it away.

"Oi'm actually on the side of the Resistance. Workin' undercover loik. That's official."

"The only side you're on is the one you think is going to come out on top," Bandit said. "Anybody else in there know Slypaws and her friend?"

"Nice ladies."

"They were staying in our tree."

"They sounded like they were from across the pond."

"That's them!" Bandit said. "So now they're Lockjaw's bargaining chips – is that it?"

Drooplip looked up at the sky. "Maybe."

The raccoons, the City's young, started to teem out of the hole.

"Wot about me?"

"You're coming with us. You're our bargaining chip. That's official."

# 50

CLUTCH LAY ON A COLD DAMP SLAB, hearing voices he couldn't respond to. Any effort to talk, to even open his eyes, was resisted by a torpor that guarded him like a nurse. "*Not yet,*" it said. His hearing was diminished so that the only sounds he took in were close by, sounds that associated readily with scents, for his power to smell was unimpaired. He understood that the fog hadn't lifted, that most of the High Guard had departed, that his militia had been badly mauled, and that his ladyfriend was gone.

With this information scraped together provisionally in his consciousness, his inner nurse decided that he'd been allowed to know enough for the moment. He slept.

"*This is our commander.*"

A paw on his brow. A head pressed against his. Smelled female. Smelled of spice. Foreign. A mind probing into his depths. Because it was a caring mind, his nurse released him into this other's care.

"*His eyes are fluttering. Everyone please, I ask of you, stand back.*"

Clutch half opened his eyes and saw a woman leaning over him in the mist. Long slender forelegs and the most elegant claws. A mask of the darkest sable covered most of her face, giving an impression of modesty, except that by concealing her physical features – her mouth, her jaws, her nose and ears – the mask made her spirit the more visible. And her spirit was all in her large eyes that danced with every feeling and mood that passed behind them.

"I am Hala. I am commander of the forces of the South. And a King is my father."

"I regret … Princess … that I am not able at present to return your greeting with a matching dignity. You see, I …"

"It is okay. Everything has been explained to me. We shall talk later – yes? Your mind wants to be alone with you some more. So I will let you sleep. Much good thinking is done in sleep."

"I …"

"Sssh! God has time. Give yourself time. Take this into your comfort: your forces are hurt but they are intact; they are under no threat at present; and I have with me sufficient forces to protect them should the odious High Guard return."

With that news, Clutch went inward to be healed. It seemed the Pro had pulled his High Guard units out of the Dead Zone and gone back to the City. But he must have called up the main army of the High Guard on the Southern Frontier, because the Migrant forces there in the south, no longer held in check, had followed the retreating High Guard. But this was ominous, the High Guard on the frontier had joined the High Guard in the City. His father now had a complete united army under his command and he could control the West Bank.

Clutch began to count the mistakes he had made and the things he could have done better. "Ambushed," he heard his mind say. "I walked right into his outstretched paws."

## 51

THE CLAMOUR AND POUNDING of the Primates reached a frenzy then abruptly ceased. Now their young gathered up the waste, bellowing the last song that had been played by the band. As they left, their supervisor activated security cameras attached to lamp posts. The park fell into an eerie quiet, except for the hum of the refrigeration units of the meat trucks. Scents of ribs, chicken, fries, corn on the cob, and the dregs of beer glasses rose from the organic waste and recycling bins, with promise of more food in the trucks once their doors were popped. The air was clear and cool, with no breeze. All this was taken in by wet noses and beady eyes waiting in trees and bushes.

From the roof of a public washrooms hut in the park, the rebel leaders surveyed the scene with apprehension. Mindwalker summed up their mood best: "I'll be happy if we can just maul the Protector's speech and get away cleanly."

Touchwit agreed. "We can't prevent the handover of power. That's already happened. But we can knock Meatbreath's Occasion so out of shape that citizen raccoons will never again take him seriously."

"The Citizens Brigades will fight another day," Mindwalker said. He felt gloom. There is nothing worse than a lost revolution. The Brigade packs should have been better led. Starting the revolution prematurely just as the combined High Guard entered the city couldn't be blamed on the young. After all, it was in their high-spirited, pent-up natures to tell their officers to go climb a tree. "Where is the High Guard deployed? I need to know that."

Touchwit expressed their common fear. "If the Brigades go rogue again tonight, we won't get another chance in our lifetimes."

"We'll all be tied to trees by Meatbreath. Unable to scratch our fleas. Stinking in our own urine. Seagulls plucking out our ..."

"Stop it!" She enjoyed Mindwalker's feeling for imagery, but he really had a taste for the anatomically grotesque expression.

"Thank you," the gull said. "I'll go and remind them of their mission. It's a guerilla action, not a regime change."

She couldn't resist a rhyme:

*Hit hard,*
*Bite clean.*
*Slip away and*
*Never be seen.*

"The brawling of Mammals in two dimensions is too moronic to contemplate," was the gull's opinion.

"The rhyme is very apt, but guerilla action is not our ultimate mission," Mindwalker said, enlarging the perspective. "Our mission is to create a city in which every raccoon has a future. Nourishing food, spacious dens, free choice of partners, the opportunity to have children, unrestricted travel, and welcome migration."

"Perhaps if the mission had been clear, the Brigades would have been more certain about what they were fighting for," the seagull said.

\* \* \*

The last departing Primate checked to see that the restaurant café door was locked, turned off the lights, got onto his bike, and cycled off. Immediately, hunch-backed shapes glided out of bushes, stole up from the riverbank, walked down the trunks of trees. The lawn at the back of the restaurant became a carnival, literally a time to "put away" (*levare*) the "meat" (*carnem*). The masked shadows immediately began sorting themselves out. The greater part of them gathered on the picnic tables in front of the stage, becoming a patient audience: they were here for the feast marking the start of the fattening-up period before hibernation. Sure, there's going to be an announcement of some kind beforehand, but what event ever happens without a sponsor whose beneficence has to be acknowledged. Something about a change in the city's administration, with the leadership outsourced by the City Elders to a Protector they'd brought over from the Creek to manage the city's affairs for them. Of course, some of the spectators had opinions about this issue – you couldn't be deaf to the concerns that filled the oral web in the last few days – but politics was for the young, who doubtless would put on a demonstration that had to be tolerated along with the Protector's speech. Then … the drink would flow! And the food!

Ribs dry rubbed with unique blend of seasonings
smoked, slo' roasted and charcoal grilled
with Signature Sauce for the real BBQ taste

BBQ Chicken
dry rubbed, slo' roasted, charcoal grilled
brushed with bullet BBQ sauce

Texas Style Pulled Pork
sandwich smoked, slo' roasted overnight
hand-pulled, lightly sauced, simmered
and served on a bun

Bullet BBQ Beans and Cowboy Coleslaw

Look! They were repositioning the cameras so that they scanned the sides of the trucks. Peoples Corps Volunteers guarded the truck doors and the waste bins with steely eyes. Those P.C.s had teeth like broken bottles. Don't mess with them.

As for the City's young, they hung back from view at the edges of the crowd. They weren't here for food. They were here to turn an aristocratic gift of meat into an anarchist feeding frenzy. Raccoons would be free to hiss and spit over leftovers in the time-honoured way of individuals. And the idea of a city-state run by a Protector would be smashed.

A third group surveyed the scene where the idea of an orderly, well-fed state was about to be demonstrated. Called the High Guard, these silent, determined faces were veterans from the wars on the Southern Frontier. They were said to be ready to die for the Protector, and standing here and there in small formations they were never far from the stage. On the stage stood the fresh-faced daughters and sons of the Honour Guard as pretty as cheerleaders. Didn't they look sweet?

* * *

"You smell glad tonight."

"Thanks, Flaxentips." Late again, Bandit took his place in the line beside her. "But why does that surprise you? Do I usually smell miserable?"

"It surprises me because my whiskers tell me something absolutely crude is going to happen. Don't you sense it?"

"I do. But not in a bad way."

"You mean to say there's crude in a good way? Oh, I do hope you haven't become a rebel. I've lost all my friends to this stupid event. Half of them have been arrested. The other half won't speak to me."

"It's a change, Tips. Change is messy. I wonder who's going to lick up the mess?" He remembered Frisk licking his ear mischievously back at Pawsense Manor. Where was Frisk? She wasn't in the crowd. Had she been arrested?

"The one who comes out on top does the cleaning up."

"Right now it's her." Bandit pointed his nose at the Director of Security. She had found a place to stand at the back of the stage where she wouldn't be noticed.

"Don't look at her, Bandit."

He broke his gaze before the Director noticed. "If I don't get at that meat soon, I'm going to turn into a Drooler."

* * *

"Out of the way, ladies. Clear a path for the Official Party."

"Don't shove me, you bag of scat, or I'll report you to your superior."

"Go right ahead, you crazy bitch."

"Take his identity, Twitch."

Twitchfinger rubbed her ear along the soldier's coat.

The Peoples Corps Volunteer backed away politely. His scent had been recorded. Those two madwomen could make his life miserable. They smelled well-fed.

"You're a nice man underneath," Slypaws said. "And you'd be nice all over if it weren't for the deleterious effect of a command structure on your psyche."

252

"Don't look now, but there's the couple from hell." Twitch meant Lockjaw and his hussy, Drooplip, behind the corner of the stage, out of the way of the procession.

"Jaws is just waiting to repossess us, pending the outcome of the Occasion."

"Not this time, baby. He'll have to swim to catch me. He doesn't have the lungs." Twitchwhisker measured the run from the city side of the restaurant to the little harbour.

"I'd stay away from Droopy. She's got serious dental rot. One bite from her and you'll get Saint Hapticia's Dance."

*"Make way for the Protector Elect's party! Make way!"*

First were two Honour Guard cadets. Introducing the procession, they demonstrated that the feast to come was a City Function which meant that it belonged to every hardworking stiff who owned a den. Next came the Chief Magistrate looking as rotund as the speech he promised. He showed that, while the feast belonged to the citizenry, it wouldn't have been possible except for the adoration which the City Elders and their Leading Families had for the common folk. Then a squadron of High Guard; they acted as a symbol of the Protector's power, and Slypaws examined the commanding officers with interest because they were said to be his sons which meant, technically, that they were her stepsons – a ridiculous, brutal and contaminating thought which she banished instantly. Then ... well, who was this?

Twitchwhisker felt her friend quiver.

"That's Pawsy's child, Sensibella. My niece. What on earth is she doing here?"

"She's gorgeous."

"I don't want her to see me." Slypaws edged herself behind Twitchwhisker.

But Sensibella even while looking straight ahead was using her nose, and she smelled something familiar and paused to trace the scent. She saw Aunt Slypaws, Bandit's mom. She veered from the procession long enough to whisper something to her aunt in passing: "This isn't what it looks like."

"Does your mom know you're here?"

"It's too late to matter."

"Bandit's here. He's up on the podium."

"I know. Look, get out now before the event starts. It's going to be a total stain."

Sensibella slid back into her place without missing a step.

Now there came a gap in the procession and the sound of polite applause further behind.

"Should we?" Slypaws asked. The two of them intended to turn their backs on Meatbreath.

"I'm not going to let him see my face."

"I'm looking face forward. I'm going to look the Jerk in the eye. You can ignore him if you want to."

"I'll stand with you. He won't remember me anyway. But what about Bandit?"

"He's playing this double-agent thing, and he's not the type. He's only doing it for Sensibella. You want to know how I know that? He didn't mention her when he freed us."

"I'd say he's a cool double agent then. And he got us out of Lock-jaw's grip."

"Still, I've got to protect him if things turn sour."

* * *

A sigh travelled through the crowds below. Touchwit looked up with them. Lady Hapticia had appeared. The Clamshell she rides on has ascended over the river, and its light sparkled on the water. "Is that enough light for you?" she asked the seagull.

"Gulls simply don't fly at night, period. Whatever the conditions. It's a rule. It comes from flying over oceans. Think of what it feels like to lose all your reference points."

Mindwalker crowded the gull. "Reference points are precisely what we need right now. How is Clutch is doing? Is he a prisoner? Is he dead? Is he coming here with the Creekers?"

"You can assume that he's not coming here because otherwise he'd be here already."

Touchwit intervened quickly. "It's a comfort that you're staying up late with us."

"Thank you. It's past my bedtime."

"I've never seen a seagull at night before," Mindwalker said, straining to sound amiable. Normally, he was rather fond of the philosophical bird. "You don't roost in trees. Where do you lot go?"

"That's a secret known to gulls."

"Oh. Sorry I asked."

"But I'll tell you." The seagull lowered his voice to a whisper. He was going to reveal a special secret known only to gulls. Mindwalker leaned close to hear it.

"We pass through a tear in the sky into the Dream World."

\* \* \*

As soon as she saw that head again, her hackles shot up like thorns. Her tail tucked in for a brawl – she couldn't help it. That massive ruff, those lifeless eyes, that fixed smile. *Help me, Twitch. I'm going to take him out!*

Twitch felt her friend turn into a weapon, but she was tense too. "Do it with words."

Words crowded around her, offering themselves up for sacrifice. Self-absorbed scatbrain narcissistic callous impresario swallowed by your own ego.

The great head swayed from side to side. The Jerk was borne aloft on a tree trunk carried by six High Guard sons shuffling on their hind legs. When he came to where she was standing, his eyes swept over her, but the eyes were unfocussed, the nose wasn't engaged, and the ears heard nothing.

Slypaws shot barbed hateballs at him that stuck like thorns.

Then a High Guard parading past blocked her vision and the encounter was over. All that was left for her to see was the pointed end of the tree chewed by a beaver.

"I feel defeated," she told Twitchwhisker as the City Elders paraded through. "The indifference. He went by like a Primate automobile."

"There'll be another time."

"You're right. This evening hasn't even begun."

## 52

THE STATE IS AN ORDERLINESS made to further the joy of life of raccoons. Is this harmony not told us in the story of the mating of Hapticia and the Great Raccoon? She brought her keen eyes and fingerwork to the union; he, the gifts of mind and making. Together they fashioned the first City.

Such a public orderliness, as far as harmony is possible among members of an aggressive species crowded in one place, prevailed at least during the Protector's opening remarks.

The ordinary citizens maintained order by promptly forgetting every word that was spoken. They were here for the feast, something worth waiting for. Sons and daughters of the leading families who made up the City Honour Guard maintained order by standing still in one place. This reminded everybody that order had always existed in the city and was based on the concentration of wealth. If there was any doubt about this, the doubter need only glance at the units of the High Guard who affirmed the natural order by standing near the line of food trucks along the river side of the eating area. And to symbolize the orderly distribution of the plunder awaiting them, townsfolk could take note of the Peoples Corps ruffians guarding the organic waste bins. They could see how even the most disprivileged among us are elevated to a lofty station in life by their faith in public order. Meanwhile, the Citizens Brigades, concealed in the leafy foliage along the riverbank, contributed to the greater orderliness of things by imagining the new and better order they were about to make as soon as they heard the cue. For they took Procyonides's philosophy to heart – especially that oral text about the State being a Making just like an artifact you fashion with your paws. High overhead, tracing out the mouth of the cosmic den, which is the nest of the material world, Lady Hapticia gazed down on the sacred measures made visible by her light.

*"From the river to the western rise, from the lake up to the marshes, the citizenry and those working hard to join it have told me*

*that they want a City where no raccoon goes to bed hungry. That is
why I have placed before your City Elders a plan for public safety and
a guaranteed nightly sustenance that will give every citizen a secure
and well-fed future."*

The speech was grave, measured, passionately sincere. Each syllable was enunciated, and at the pause before the next point to be made,
there was an audible intake of breath that gave a thrill of excitement
to the message. The sense of an expectation being regularly fulfilled,
of a promise being inevitably delivered, was felt in the symmetries of
the phrasing and the vigour of the elocution. Who could doubt that
the speaker had the energy even if he lacked the will to do it?

*"And all across this City, from hill to hill to hill, citizens and those
seeking to become citizens have been telling me that they expect our
new Commonwealth to embrace the communities of the River Clan
on the far side of the river. Imagine! All the lands of the River Clan
once again united. That's what citizens want to see, and that's just
what they'll get."*

A raccoon went insane and had to be dragged out. The poor,
writhing noisemaker was disposed of face down in a wire mesh refuse
container with a lid on it.

Bandit, without moving his head, stole a glance at Sensibel. Her
face in the moonlight, serene as the goddess above, showed no sign of
noticing the disturbance. He looked at the Security Director. The One
Raccoon Empire was her idea, yet her face was without feeling. Why
there weren't more displays of irrationality vexed him, because he felt a
tension everywhere. The Honour Guard cadets were shifting from foot
to foot nervously. They knew Something Crude was about to happen.

*"And citizens, especially those living on the outskirts of the City,
have told me they want a policy restricting the influx of …"*

"Here it comes," Mindwalker said calmly.

*"Migrants. They are being welcomed by the decadent bottle-sniff-
ing artists who are trying to create a breakaway republic. But I have
listened to your stories, and so tonight I am announcing …"*

Someone shouted *"Free Pork!"* At the words *Free Pork*, Citizens
Brigade youths sprung out of the bushes and overpowered the Peoples Corps ruffians guarding the food bins.

*"Free pork! All you can eat. Come and get it!"*
*"Corn on the cob! Right over here!"*
*"Anyone want beer? First come, first served."*

The Protector stopped his speech and looked behind him to the City Elders for support. But their uselessness to the social order suddenly became obvious. On the lawn in front of the stage, a mammoth shift in the arrangedness of things was taking place as the populace became a mob charging towards the waste bins and food trucks. Soon the eating area was full of happy raccoons squatting on picnic tables, consuming the repast that was intended for them. From the sound of singing, it was clear that some had broken into the beer truck. Bandit looked out over the chaos, with Flaxentips clinging to him. From the corner of his eye, he glimpsed the Director of Security, impassive, self-contained, studying the breakdown of civil order with a detached self-interest.

For the chaos that ensued was epic in proportion. If you want an epic simile, you need only call to mind the legend of the violent wedding ceremony which Procyonides cites in his *Dialogue on State-craft*. It was the marriage of the Great Raccoon Ancestor, at that time in his terrestrial form, and Hapticia, the Moon Lady. They say the banquet was held in a shady cavern under a canopy of trees, and it rang with the noise of the feasters. For every raccoon clan in antiquity had sent representatives. Even the cloud-born Procyon-Aquilla, half coon, half eagle, came. Tucking their wings in tidily around their hind legs, they revelled as the scents of roasted flesh and sweet wine rose to the tree tops. But being creatures of the heavens, they could not handle spirit-sugar wisely, neither the beauty of mortal women. With wine dribbling down their beards, they carried away the bride whom they seized by the hair and dragged beyond the upset tables. And then did each Procyon-Aquilla grab a girl so that the whole scene looked like a city ravaged.

But then the Raccoon Ancestor pushed through the overturned tables and the shrieking women and rescued the bride Hapticia from the concupiscible passions of the sky dwellers. Crying "To arms, Citizens," he led the fierce raccoons of the River Clan against the winged marauders. Thus did he restore the rule of Concord over

Discord. Bringing all the wedding guests into the harmonious measures of Hapticia he established the foundations of the City as it is known to Raccoons.

But here on the banks of the great stream that gives its name to the River Clan, violence found no form that night, I can tell you. At the words *Tonight I will announce ... Free pork. All you can eat*, order forgot itself entirely.

\* \* \*

"Reserves, sir?"

"Commit them at once," Meatbreath said. Bandit heard the exchange across the stage, and felt the world become different. Seconds later, the High Guard army concealed in a parking lot to the west hit the rioters like a school bus.

\* \* \*

"Reserves? Have we any Reserves?" Mindwalker asked.

"Second Brigade is holding the railway bridge downriver," Touchwit said. "We can pitch them in, but we're feeding them to a meat-grinder."

"What's the plan of retreat?"

"Fall back and hold them at the bridge."

But already the High Guard was bunching the young people in the Brigades towards the patio of the restaurant. And to the north, another High Guard formation materialized out of the foliage covering the office building. There was no escape to the north. Nor to the south. No escape anywhere.

\* \* \*

Bandit caught Sensibella's eye. She was standing proudly aloof from the huddle of City Elders and their sons and daughters now joined by their mothers who had climbed up on the stage. He knew what they were thinking. If the long-dreaded Revolution had come, the Leading Families would become teaching exhibits about the imaginary nature of social order. Here they were, displayed on stage like the specimens of an extinct species, guarded by their useless, decorative cheerleaders. Moreover, the shifty and temperamental ne'er-do-wells who made up the Peoples Corps couldn't be trusted.

Sensibella's face brightened. She'd thought of an idea. What on earth was she about to do, striding to the front of the stage with her tail in the air?

* * *

"I'm going down," Touchwit said.

"If you choose. But why?" Mindwalker said.

"Mom's down there. Plus I have no idea what stupid thing Bandit's about to do on the stage."

"He's not stupid," Mindwalker said.

"He's besotted with Sensibella. Can you think of anything more stupid than that?"

"I can," the seagull said.

"Besides, it's not enough to sit back and lead. I have to get good and bloody."

* * *

The Citizens Brigades were trying to hold a perimeter. The zone they defended encompassed the patio at the side of the café, and down to the dock. But they couldn't hold their ground against the veterans of the Southern Frontier War. The High Guard soldiers were so efficient that the Peoples Corps Volunteers crunching French fries and pulled pork hung back and watched them do their work. Tricksters, skanks, and petty crime artists, they weren't all that much up to combat anyway, apart from a good street brawl. Besides, their boss, the Director of Security, had flown the scene.

"Citizens and kin. Friends of the Commonwealth," Sensibella called out to the crowded tables from the stage. Strutting back and forth with her glossy mane and her tail in the air.

"I don't believe this," Slypaws said. "She's twerking."

"She's absolutely gross," Twitch said.

Wolf whistles, mindless cheers, encouraging suggestions from the appreciative masses. Now this was worth coming for! The First Lady was offering them her wholesomeness as dinner entertainment. A reward for enduring the mind-numbing, hollow rhetoric of her spouse.

"Lift that tail, honey!"

"Let's see you shimmy!"

Bella did an off-hand pretense of a shimmy. Applause up and down the lawn. Meanwhile, the sound of guttural spitting and shrieking continued from the lake side of the restaurant.

"Hey, you guys in the Corps. Enjoying the ribs?"

Cheering.

"Glad to see y'all here. Now let's make this night a real party, right? Let's make it our own. There's loads of pork in the trucks. We just have to get those sticks out of the way. Tell them to piss off, eh?"

Everybody knew she meant the High Guard.

The Protector had watched long enough. The traitorous swamp bitch was trying to turn the ordinary folk against him. He strode to the front of the stage, knocking three Honour Guards out of his way.

"Where are you going, Big Guy?"

Who was this standing in his path? An alpha male. A yearling. Powerful and pumped. And he had a dark mask on his face. Could be one of his sons. "Do I know you?"

"You'll get to know me a lot better if you don't back off."

"She your girl? Sorry, buddy. I'm renting her for the night. Clear out of my way."

"*Honour Guard. To me!*" Bandit cried.

Flax was at his side instantly, and witnessing her spontaneous loyalty her Honour Guard comrades followed. Now they had a leader again. They formed a shell around the naïve outsider from across the river who was so sweet in his social awkwardness.

"See what we did? It's easy," Sensibel shouted.

The city folk put down their ribs and beer, and overwhelmed the High Guard soldiers still on the lawn. The Peoples Corps joined them without hesitation. And seeing the Protector immobilized, the soldiers didn't resist. But the main body of the High Guard didn't know what had happened. They were busy pushing the young people in the Brigades across the restaurant patio down toward the river and the dock below. The skirmish line swayed back and forth on the very edge of the riverbank. It could go either way. If the High Guard forced the city's youth into the water, the Peoples Corps would change sides again and take the side of the victors. If the action surged the other way and the High Guard surrendered, the P.C.s would join with the Citizens Brigades. But there was one constant in this equation. The High Guard never surrendered.

* * *

From the roof of the Primate urinal, it was easy to hear the disaster-in-the-making. The noise of shrieking warriors had diminished from the direction of the lawn, indicating that a victory had been won there by Sensibella's instant army, but on this river side of the café the Citizens Brigades were on the edge of defeat. And for raccoons defeat wasn't physical, it was spiritual. A loser could survive wounds and fight again another day. But to back down, to be pushed off a branch or into a river, was a loss of prowess that couldn't be survived. A broken spirit was forever.

"The Brigades are breaking. I'm going down there," Mindwalker told the gull.

"I shall catch a wink of sleep," the gull said, tucking his head under his wing.

* * *

The Protector, seeing his troops pushing the city's youth into the river, decided there was no reason why he should be obstructed further by these bucks and maidens fresh out of school dressed up as an honour guard. He simply lurched into them, shoving them aside like underbrush, and grabbed Sensibella by the scruff.

"Remove your paws from her, you beast." A blonde-tipped, snub-nosed maiden spitting venom.

"I paid for her. She's mine for the night," Meatbreath growled. His escort with the beautiful tail fell passive. But her mouth muscles were rippling. Oh god – she was going to speak. Please, not that! He could put up with her silent squirming rage, there was no way he could endure another word bath from the loquacious bitch. And now her vainglorious buck was coming at him with menace in his eyes.

"Paws off her, Meatbreath. Or you'll be upside-down in the river."

*Meatbreath!* The upstart stud had called him *Meatbreath*! He took his claws off the girl and went for the challenger. This wasn't a taunting contest to see which of them would back down. This was a fight to the finish. These things happen sometimes. They can be fatal. He had the force and weight. Let's see what the kid had.

Bandit, with the unyielding absoluteness of immaturity, put his head down and charged at his parent like a truck. The larger raccoon lost balance, turned the angle of force into a roll, and was back on his feet before the challenger found his throat. Bandit missed the jugular and ended up with a mouthful of ruff. And the adversary's ruff was enormous – he could chew into it for seconds and not get near the muscle. Meatbreath sat on his haunches, recovered his axis and re-arranged his mass – a whole planet, his girth like a sort of equator. He raised his head and began to shake his mane. He shook it back and forth, and Bandit flew this way and that in the air, still hanging on.

"Oh, you have come to rescue me from the sulphurous breath of that Vile Monster," Sensibella called out to him. Then in a softer voice, she explained to Flaxentips: "He's my paramour, and his loyalty is beyond question."

"So I see. But do you not think the Protector will kill him?"

"He is prepared to die for me," Sensibella said. "Who can kill such a fine spirit?"

"The Protector can. And afterwards he'll jump up and down on him until your Paramour resembles roadkill."

The other members of the Honour Guard thought the same. They had made a space for fighters, a circle of pitying eyes and sagging ears. In a fight to the finish, it is foolhardy to intervene.

Bandit, still clinging to the ruff behind the ear, changed his position so that he was riding Meatbreath's back. Meatbreath promptly rolled over and pinned the cub underneath him. He lay on him with his vast stomach in the air, hearing the cub's ribs crack and feeling him struggle for breath. It was then that Bandit, in a last act of defiance before he perished, reached up and tore his father's ear off.

Meatbreath jumped to his feet, spraying blood over Flax and Sensibel. His eyes were black holes of blind rage. A terrible darkness filled his brain. He began to salivate. His tail lashed like the worst kind of Drooler, those dogs with the black and tan muzzles who like to taste blood. Except they have *two* big ears. He only had one. The other was in his son's mouth.

"I'm done for," Bandit thought, seeing the giant raccoon measure his leap. Goodbye world. Goodbye Mom. Goodbye sibs. Goodbye Sensibella of the Pond with her breath like apples and her sighs like the breeze passing through willows. His short life flashed by in memory ... wrestling with his cousin in the bulrushes. Oh, how she could wrestle ...

In the instant before Meatbreath landed on him, Bandit performed the *osoto-gari* he'd learned from Sensibella. His adversary fell with a thud that made the stage shake. He hadn't prepared himself for the angle of the fall, and something else broke away beside his ear. What broke was his reputation. For the first time in his meteoric career, he'd been beaten. And in public view by a cub. He wasn't a fighter. He usually got his way by lying and bluffing, and aggressive force of personality. Like he'd done with that other trumped-up warrior chieftain who'd challenged him earlier in the Dead Zone.

Then he remembered. That one had called him *Meatbreath* too.

"Get up on your feet, Meatbreath," Slypaws said. "We have some unfinished business."

The woman in the crowd. The one who had drilled a capsule of pure fury into his skull as he'd passed.

"Bandit, will you give him back his ear? No, don't look around for it. It's in your mouth."

"Who in the hell are you?"

"I am just another one of your conquests. The ones without names."

"And you expect me to apologize? You know how the game is played. It's Custom."

"But you have given me a name, see? You made me a Clan Mother. I am Slypaws of the River Clan at the Islands."

Bandit spat the ear at his father's feet. "To the loser goes the ear."

"Congratulations! And this is your son. In point of fact, *my* son! He seems to be full of vigour. What are you complaining about?"

"What you do to maidens is what you do to everything. You manhandle us, then throw us in a dumpster."

"I don't know," Meatbreath said, "that this is the time for a lesson in etiquette. My High Guard is pushing your young people into the river. Pretty soon, they'll be crayfish snacks."

"This," Sensibella said, "is a perfect time for etiquette."

Meatbreath wiped away the blood flowing over his left eye. "I've got some etiquette for you, honey. Get a life. You're not a dumb coonette. You've got attitude in every hair in your tail."

"You are nothing without an army."

"Well, we'll see how it turns out. Right now, I'm hungry. Fighting gives a guy the munchies. As soon as this special military operation is done I'm going to hit the food."

"Why don't you eat your ear?" Touchwit said.

"Oh, god. Another one. Have you got any more cubs to inflict on me?"

"Indeed, I have. And I expect he'll be here shortly," Slypaws said.

"Oh yeah. The one who called me a bad name. He happens to be lying on a marble slab in the Dead Zone with his head broken. With his patsy army strewn all around him."

Lusty chanting from the direction of the river. It was the victory chant of the High Guard. The mean-minded, spirit-breaking bullying without even a gesture of respect for the opponents who had made the mistake of challenging them. They directed their chant at the line of defeated raccoons floating downriver with the current in the moonlight.

"That's the end of you lot," Meatbreath said, picking up his ear. "Now I'll go and eat some ribs with my *real* sons, unless you have more cubs."

A high-pitched, lyrical call to the south. The raccoons on the stage pricked up their ears. The defeated fighters in the river heard it too, and knew. There is no sound in the world like it. The ancient, thrilling war cry of the River Clan in battle.

"That would be Clutch now," Slypaws said calmly.

Meatbreath shrugged. It meant more mopping up than he'd anticipated. It might take until the moon passed overhead to subdue this lot. Then he'd eat some ribs. He'd eat them in front of these would-be leaders tied to trees, the juicy fat running down his muzzle.

But then there came the strange cry of some distant people. An alien, foreign cry. The long, brilliant keening of women in battle. He'd heard that cry before: it was the war cry of the Migrant warriors on the Southern Frontier, the cry they make when they are sure of victory.

Meatbreath, still clutching his ear, his tail dragging, lurched to the riverbank to gather his High Guard. He had a second option. He always had a second option. Proceed north to the traffic bridge beside the factory.

# 53

"Would you allow me, please, to make a humble suggestion, Brother Commander?"

"Certainly," Clutch said. But *humble* wasn't a word he could associate with the Princess commanding the Southerners. Her tall composure and casual competence suggested an immense inner pride. Lacking even a flicker of irony or sentiment, she was also, somehow, without the attitude one would expect to occupy the places of these vain emotions in her personality, namely sincerity. Hala was neither sincere nor insincere. She was critical, she was romantic, but she was not in the least sincere, at least not as far as he could discern. Perhaps the word *courteous* applied to her.

"Thank you, Brother. I am thinking – my fighters are fleet-footed and quick to pursue the racists. Perhaps they should run ahead and bring to quarter the hate-filled Oppressor."

"That is an excellent suggestion."

"Thank you, Brother. In this circumstance, it may not be clumsy of me to observe that your soldiery might enjoy what they are most suited to do – that is, re-possess the riverbank."

"Yes. Let's do that. But I think I should guard the railway bridge so that we have a means of escape, if needed." He felt a warmth rise up from his toes each time she spoke. He really was beginning to feel like her kin. "Tell me, Sister. What does the name *Hala* mean?"

"Ah! It is an ancient name among my people. It means *moonglow.*"

"How beautiful. To think that you move like a moonbeam over dark ground."

"No, I beg to correct you. Not *beam* like the Sun has a *ray*. Rather, the light that the Moon makes just for herself. Her ... radiance."

"Her *halo*," Clutch said.

"Yes, that is it. Her *halo*."

"So ... when our people say *hallelujah!* when they are glad, they are actually praising the moon."

Two raccoons from different parts of the Earth looked up at the same Moon.

"Yes, Brother. Peoples have more semblances than differences between them. But since we enjoy a further semblance ourselves in being commanders, may I ask, in return, what your name is?"

"It's Clutch."

"Clutch? Is that all?"

"Yes."

"But what does it mean?"

"Clutch means to grasp something solid and hang on."

# 54

"THE THING ABOUT CLUTCH is he's cautious," Touchwit explained. "I don't know about the Migrant commander."

Mindwalker shook the water out of his coat. He had been hauling defeated raccoons one by one out of the river. "She's said to think like a guerilla leader. She'll exploit weakness but not hold a position. And I think we'd better stop calling them *migrants*. They're here to stay."

Soon, sleek sable bodies could be seen dodging between trees and across parking lots towards the park.

"Where should we position them?" Touchwit asked.

"Wave them through to harass the enemy. They're good at that – they've been doing it all summer. They cover ground quite fast. Pray that they bring the High Guard to battle before it reaches the bridge at the factory. Then we can move the Brigades north to support her. If Meatbreath escapes across to the East Bank, he can re-take Creek Town. It's unguarded. Once he digs in there, he'll be an eternal nuisance."

## 55

B ANDIT REMAINED ON THE STAGE with his mother and her companion, watching the Southerners stream through the picnic tables towards the Heights. The sight was ludicrous. There was a battle going on for the soul of the City, and here were the city folk still roistering as if nothing eventful was happening.

"Not enough," he said professionally. He was a field commander now, having been promoted by Mindwalker, and was practicing the clipped, understated style that conveys clarity and control. His mission was to hold the eating area and keep his ears to the north.

"You're right. Not enough at all." Slypaws wondered at how her second son had risen in the world. He used to state the obvious. He still stated the obvious, but now that what he stated acquired a context he had suddenly become meaningful. If Meatbreath was able to keep the Migrant army in check on the Southern Frontier with part of his High Guard, think how easily he could ambush them here with all his warriors united.

"I must say the foreigners *are* impressive," Twitchwhisker said. "They don't talk; they don't even give orders. Do they read each other's minds?"

"They've been fighting together all their lives," Slypaws said.

Time to assert his new authority. The north end of the park didn't feel right: there should be sounds of contact with the High Guard; they couldn't have slipped away this quickly. If they had outpaced the Southern army, they'd be on their way across the river to the East Bank. "*Runner!*" he called.

A Brigade partisan hopped up on the stage to his right. "Citizen Field Commander."

"I want you to run north and obtain a report from Princess Hala."

A quick bow of the head. Command noted. The runner leaped off the stage. But he hadn't even crossed the eating area before he met one of Hala's runners coming south. They touched noses briefly, then came across the lawn together and looked up at the stage. "Field

Commander. Esteemed Sir, I am sent to convey the report of Hala the Glorious. We have met with an ambush beneath the traffic bridge. Most regrettable."

Of course, the perfect place to set a trap. He'd spent some nights there with homeless raccoons. A whole army could be concealed just behind the bridge. Why hadn't he thought of this earlier?

"Hala the Victorious respectfully asks for reinforcements, placed tactically south of her, to secure her retreat. She is going to fall back in stages."

The runner spoke evenly, but the concern flooding her dark eyes conveyed the fragility of the situation.

"Tell her to hang tough. Help is on the way."

Mindwalker and Touchwit on the patio, organizing the Citizens Brigade partisans who had been in the water. They'd seen the runner and were stalking briskly over. A liaison. At the highest level. Out of the corner of his eye, he realized that Flax, alone on a corner of the stage, was gazing at him with awe. "Don't go yet," he told the runners.

Mindwalker at his full height and military authority: "What seems to be the problem here, Bandit?"

"Our sister army ran into a trap. They need support to attempt a fall back."

"What's our exit plan?" Touchwit asked, raising the concern a whole new level.

"As before," Mindwalker said. "The railway bridge. Clutch is down there now. We can hold them at the west end of the bridge. It only has width for three or four of them to fight at a time."

"For how long? The enemy has all the food and we have none," Touchwit said.

"Meatbreath is going to force us right back into our chimney," Slypaws said.

"Listen." The clamour of combat. Full-throated shrieking and now and then a surprised howl of defeat. The northerly breeze carried scents of blood.

At the smell of blood, Mindwalker rose on his hind legs. "He's done it again. The fox has many tricks, the hedgehog one: one good one. I want all non-combatants down at the south end of the park beside the railway bridge. Non-combatants includes Peoples Corps Volunteers who want to take a chance with us. Can you manage them?" This last addressed to Slypaws. If anyone could inspire a collection of shifters and flip-flops, she could.

"Bandit. Do you think you could persuade your mates in the Honour Guard to join us and save their City? If you can, take them west to the street. We need to make sure Meatbreath doesn't outflank us."

"Now, you Runners! Yes, that's right. Both of you, in case one of you gets intercepted. Do you see what I've done? Good! Now, go and report it all to Lady Hala and tell her a Brigade is on their way. They're heavy from the water in their coats but they can fight."

The runners left, taking separate routes.

Now Mindwalker faced his field commander grimly. "We have to accept the possibility of defeat. Go and say your goodbye." He turned abruptly and strode back to the Primate latrine.

Bandit checked his sister's eyes. Yes, they held the same silent, bitter message. She gave him a lick and went to join her partner.

He didn't move. Who should he say goodbye to? Who did he *want* to say goodbye to? Sensibella, of course. She was the reason why he'd become a soldier. He fought totally for her. He felt proud he'd stood up man to man to his father, and defended her honour.

But then there was Flaxentips lingering at the side of the stage. He owed her a goodbye.

For some reason, he thought of little Friskywits. He'd gotten use to her company. She was always smart and happy. Well, she wasn't here to say goodbye to, so he started off to see Sensibel.

\* \* \*

The seagull was poised on one leg on top of the latrine.

"Are you going to stand there while we get pushed into the river again?"

The bird pulled its head out from under its wing and blinked. "Of course, I am. I find the panorama of bodies sorting themselves out in the material world luridly fascinating."

Mindwalker stood stock still and waited for his rage to subside. It surged up and bubbled like blood behind his eyes. It made him want to throttle the bird on the spot. Instead he said: "You don't care one way or the other who wins, do you?"

"You must allow that one who frequently stays aloft for long periods of time over a vast ocean conceives a perspective not indistinct from that of eternity."

"You're waiting for a feast, you rascal. You're just waiting so you can pick at carrion flesh. Carry away a dead raccoon's eyeballs, then come back to yank out his liver."

"I've already eaten a pork rib, French fries, and corn, thank you. If quadrupeds want to ease the pressures on the planet by depopulating themselves, let them do so. Once they deposit all their body-masks on the grass, doubtless carnivores of every sort will come to feed. That this park is already a historic feasting place has been noted by all and sundry."

"If you don't care, why are you here?" Touchwit asked.

"I am witnessing the making of an ideal Commonwealth. I don't suppose you thought to make a place in it for Seagulls."

"We'll do that later!" Touchwit said. "Right now I'm going to the heart of the problem."

"Which is what, exactly?" the gull asked.

"Which is that I'm never going to be a successful Maker until I get Meatbreath out of my system!"

\* \* \*

Bandit couldn't linger. He needed to position the Honour Guard at the city edge of the park where they'd ambush any flanking column sent by Meatbreath. He wanted to stay. Being with Sensibella gave him courage. He would give his life for her.

"Goodbye, Bella."

She gave him a sloppy lick on his muzzle. To die for.

## 56

Touchwit lay hidden under the wheels of a railway boxcar at the top of the park with a pack of Brigaders wearing their Citizen's hats. For the first time in her life she was going to be in a situation where she couldn't rely on her mind. Her intellect would be completely useless. When the High Guard came thundering down on her, she wouldn't even have an opportunity to analyse the situation. All she could do was get bloody. Revolutions are messy. You can't eat a crayfish without first ripping off its head.

A squad of Southerners retreating southward stopped at the boxcar and formed a rearguard. This defensive line had only one mission: buy time. Time for Mindwalker to arrange a defense of the bridge and get the City's young across the river to safety. The Southerners acknowledged the Brigades with a nod, and waited for their princess's main army to filter through. Soon they arrived, some limping, some with bloodied muzzles, one with a discharge dripping from the socket where her eye had been. Yet their spirits were indomitable. As they passed, they shouted a salute in their lyrical tongue, whereupon the rearguard abandoned its position and joined the retreat. It would now be up to the Citizens Brigade squadron to hold the enemy at the top of the park.

Then suddenly the High Guard was on top of them. The group of Citizens fell back, but they held. The snarling was feral – it was pure wildness. She'd never heard such language before. Whoever thought that veteran alpha males could be stopped in their tracks by a barrage of observations about their relative sexual prowess, the virtue of their mothers, the morals of their sisters, the loyalty of their wives, the trustworthiness of their cubs, if any? Not to mention, on top of this verbal bombardment, remarks about the comparative merits of their homeland, Creek Town, together with rumours about a hedonism that had recently possessed their kinsfolk there. Suddenly, under the duress of the taunts, an enemy fighter lost it completely and hurled himself at the line of Citizens. He was quickly herded into the river, still screaming abuse as the current carried him into the night. Yet the High Guard fought on impassively.

But look! Second Brigade had come and joined them. Her brilliant cautious Mindwalker had committed his forces to cover the general withdrawal to the East Bank. He meant to sacrifice the untested Second Brigade who had been guarding the railway bridge. This wasn't Fight or Flee anymore. This was Win or Die.

Then she found him. Her stalker. He was watching the moonlit battle from the shadow of a river willow. Alone, holding his ear. The great Number One who replicated himself in this mass of militarized cubs without moms. The One Who Cannot be Named who stripped the names off things. Animals and beings and places.

She ran behind the wavering battle line and popped out where it met the river, right in front of her father. She had no idea what she was doing.

"You're too young for me. And anyway I don't have time for you. Go back to your mammy."

"But I have brought you a new name to wear tomorrow."

"Oh, yeah? Well, I'll hear it tomorrow. Meanwhile, get lost. I have to win a battle."

"But I'm your daughter. And I'm smarter than you."

"The nasty one who told me to eat my ear. That's not very smart. No cub of mine is smarter than me."

"I am. And you're still holding your ear."

Meatbreath fondled his ear in his paw. His ear had become a talisman, a magic charm that reminded him that he was whole in spirit. As long as he held all his body parts, he was still in one piece. "If you're so smart, answer this riddle. If you win, you can have my ear. If you lose, I get your tail."

She analysed the wager for a split second. "Deal!"

Her father looked her in the eye. "How far is it from East to West?"

"I think that would be a day's journey. You see, I watch the Sun every day, and he starts his journey in the East and finishes at evening in the West."

"Not bad for an alpha maid."

"I'm diurnal."

"Okay then, Know-it-all. How far is it from Earth to Heaven?"

"Oh, that's easy. It is the width of an eye. Because the eye looks down and sees earth, and the eye looks up and sees heaven."

"How did you figure that out?"

"I figured it out because I'm smarter than you."

A cry from the battlefield. The terrible whimpering sound a raccoon makes when it submits. The crying of a broken spirit. A Citizen had fallen; the sound of defeat would spread among the Brigades and everybody would weaken. Soon their will would break.

"It seems I am about to win." Meatbreath paused. "And you are about to lose."

She braced her mind for the next riddle. Riddles came in threes, and this last one would decide her fate.

Again, her father looked down into her eyes. The force of his mental energy was like nothing she'd ever felt. It had forced her mom to submit. She wasn't going to submit though. Then, the riddle came:

"How far is it from truth to falsehood?"

Another riddle about the eye and distance. He was obsessed with his visual sense. The sense that controls space. That isolates objects against backgrounds. That alienates things from their processes. Her answer must come, therefore, from another sense. Touch – the haptic sense. The sense that the eye, in its singlemindedness, disregards because the eye is linked directly to the mind. Whatever the paw picks up is held under her nose for verification. And her nose is connected to her ears and her tongue by bodily channels that she can feel when she swallows. Touchwit looked her father Meatbreath in the eye. If she lost, she would have to roll over at his feet and submit.

"How far is it from truth to falsehood?" she repeated. What did the creep know about truth and falsehood? "That would be the width of my five fingers. The distance from my eye to my ear. Because, you see, the eye sees falsehood, but the ear hears truth."

"Truth!" she repeated. Her talisman.

He could not hold her gaze. His eyeballs began to quiver. It looked like they were going to rotate in his massive head. Spin away, eyeballs! Maybe you'll look inward and discover something about yourself. Then Meatbreath's gaze dropped to the ground. The High Guard warriors lay panting, waiting for the Protector to give them an order. They had won the battle. But she had won an ear.

Touchwit looked away from the strangely slim paw offering her an ear. Her citizen comrades were fleeing.

* * *

A high wavering sound. A battle cry of some sort. Two cousins, Bandit and Sensibella, still on the stage, pricked up their ears. The calling was in a foreign tongue, but it wasn't the flowing honey speech of Southerners. It had different pitches in it, like wind chimes. It came from the Heights beyond the top of the park. Again – the long, thrilling war cry. Sensibella knew the tongue. Her father spoke it to her when she was a cub and he visited the Pond. He was coming. He had raised an army among his kinfolk. A father rescuing his daughter.

A trilling ululation much closer, from the street where he was supposed to ambush a flanking column. The rescuing army had sent out a flanking column. The High Guard would be caught at the front and the rear. This general, thought like a pair of paws. Smartwhisker. Sensibel's father.

Then suddenly, the first warriors burst through the bushes into the park. And there was Friskywits at the front of them instead. Imagine – Frisk leading a wing of an army! She separated herself from her kinsfolk in the Heights and ran up to him on the patio and saluted smartly.

"I did my errand," Frisk reported.

* * *

Standing on the stage with Frisk, Bandit witnessed the last charge of the High Guard. They tore through the picnic tables like a pack of Droolers, aiming to re-take the battlefield, organize the Peoples Corps, and reinstate their leader. But the Peoples Corps volunteers who were still feasting didn't get up from their places and join the Guard. They had lost all interest in politics. But look at these Eastern citizens with their golden fur standing silently in perfect formation led by a warrior maiden? The Heights had come down to join the battle. The High Guard elite came to a halt. That was the moment when Bandit felt a strange kinship with the dozens of yearling males all bearing the dramatic face mask of their father. They looked left and right, but they had no father to give them direction.

A shape with one ear slinked along the bushes by the river and disappeared behind the outdoor restaurant.

"There's your leader," Bandit shouted. The yearling males looked to see who had spoken. A senior male stood on the stage in the blackest of masks, a look-alike of their progenitor. He could almost be their father.

\* \* \*

Clutch on the railway bridge with Hala, waiting for the High Guard to come down on them. The City's young are huddled on the railway tracks, ready to make their last stand, and it will be a brave battle with these Southerners fighting with them.

Instead of the High Guard there came the single face of their enemy, the tyrant Meatbreath. The bully stopped at the entry to the bridge, and saw that his way was blocked. He looked behind him to the west. There stood his son who had ripped off his ear. He looked to the north, back along the way he had come. There stood his daughter holding the ear. He looked south for an escape along the shore of the lake to the cemetery. There stood the mother of these brats. He looked back in front of him again to where he intended to cross the bridge to the East Bank and on to Creek Town. There stood the son who died on a tombstone. Amazing! His son had been reborn.

Meatbreath assumed the attitude of superior indifference that he relied on to shrug off a setback. He looked down into the dark river at his feet. "Well, we'll see how it turns out," he said. But first, he had some scores to settle.

"Don't look so smug," he said to the one who was a wrestler. "You used a trick. A foreign trick. It wasn't one of my tricks. You got it from a migrant."

"It was what you wanted – no holds barred," Bandit said.

"Anyway, you won unfairly. Now you. The nasty, clever one. You won the riddle contest, but that didn't do you any good. Because you walked into my charge south of the bridge, and you lost the battle. That's not very clever."

"Lost the battle? But you don't seem to have an army. Where's your lookalike army?"

"It doesn't matter where they are. They're a bunch of losers. Now, you ..."

"Me," Clutch said. "Your nemesis."

"You think you're so smart. But you lost because I blew you off the tree limb and you hit your head on a rock. I guess you're not so smart now."

"I won the dialogue. I argued cleanly. There was a flaw in your argument, and that flaw exposed the false premise of your sovereignty. In point of fact, the precise flaw was ..."

Meatbreath cut him off. "That's fake reasoning." He looked around for any further scores to settle. None. He took a deep breath and measured the distance to the surface of the water.

"What about me?" Slypaws said. "And all the others you violated."

"They don't exist."

"They exist in all your cubs. And your cubs have deserted you."

"Well, they are and ever will be a glory – the High Guard. They won the Battle of the Southern Frontier, the Battle of the Dead Zone, the Battle of the Park, and the Battle of the Ambush at the Bridge. Their conquests will always be remembered."

With that, the Protector threw himself into the river.

They rushed to the siderails of the bridge to see what would become of him. They saw only this great head floating away on the current, still talking.

"*You used a Migrant trick ... The riddles ... You cheated on the answers ... You lost your balance in the Dialogue and fell off the limb ... You rigged the outcome ... It's all fake news anyway ... I'll be back ...*" The voice ranted on into the distance ...

It was for Slypaws to make the final comment: "Exit: a colossal migraine."

## 57

CLUTCH KNEW that until his dying night he was never going to come down from the giddy peak of victory. It was a summit of all the little joys that make up being alive: climbing down from your first roof, standing up to an angry goose, vanquishing a drooler. This victory was like all those smaller triumphs bundled together by an adversary who had compelled him to prove his worth.

But surveying the rejoicing throngs – the Citizens Brigades, the Southerners of Princess Hala, the Creek squadrons, the new citizens from the Heights, and the older townsfolk who had joined with the City's young – he realized that this achievement wasn't individual. It was a unison of countless personal triumphs. For everybody here on the grass in front of the stage had in their own way experienced hope, setback, and triumph, just as he had. Opening his heart to their celebration, he felt the power of a moment, a feeling that time stood still. Wasn't this what Procyonides speaks of in his *Dialogue on Statecraft* when he tells of when the Great Raccoon God and the Goddess Hapticia founded the first city? They say the heavens moved so close to the Earth that night you could hear the stars singing.

He was at the right end of the stage with his mother and her new friend, Twitchwhisker. The jingling beside him was Hala: she had produced a headdress fringed with tiny silver bells that tinkled each time she tossed her ruff. Then Mindwalker, with a seagull riding on his shoulder, spoke with such an infectious enthusiasm that a group of Southerners on the lawn began dancing spontaneously in a circle. He'd never seen such a display before.

"It is the dance from the Masque of the Defeat of the Storm God by the Spirit of Spring," Hala explained with a jingle.

Next, his sister Touch, all grown up, waving Meatbreath's ear to the delight of the crowd and, beside her, Sensibella just as dramatic as when he first met her at the Pond. She had obviously learned good manners at her girls' school because she was keeping her eyes fixed on Mindwalker, the way a polite listener defers to the speaker who is the centre of attention. Beside Sensibel stood brother Bandit, raccoon of many parts, scowling at something. Well, he had good reason to scowl: one of his ribs was broken. Next to them stood Friskywits with her father Smartwhisker, who had saved the day with his army of Eastern people.

And as far as the eye could see, proud, exhausted raccoons. They had achieved the impossible – they had created a free City. And a diverse one. He remembered the end of the battle when the Southerners from the frontier mingled with the Easterners from the Heights. Though they had differing customs and tongues, they embraced each other as kin in a new Republic. Hala and Mindwalker had walked together, frowning at the bodies of insensate raccoons strewn under the picnic tables, still holding bottles of spirit-sugar.

The park fell silent. Sensibel had stepped forward. She took a deep, self-conscious breath and began.

"Hi, all you darling Citizens. And you up in the trees. And ..." she turned her head and looked up "... you up there on the roof. Yes, and you lovely Peoples Corps who have joined us. And you Makers – yes, I see you over there on top of the urinals, deliberating wisely. On behalf of the City, I want to thank each and every one of you, my dear people, for this victory. And for accepting me as your Chief Magistrate ..."

Cheering and applause from all the tables of the feasting area, the surrounding trees, the café roof. Clutch glanced at his mother in astonishment. Since when did Sensibel become Chief Magistrate? Slypaws raised her eyebrows and shrugged.

"Freely chosen, let it be said, by you all," Sensibel said. "Not secretly appointed on some west-end rooftop by the City Elders and Leading Families ..."

More applause. Suddenly, there weren't any Leading Families anymore. They still existed in their privacy, but without the capital L and capital F. The notion of an elite class bred in one locale had become uncustomary, refuted by this new Chief Magistrate who was the daughter of a Migrant and a Creeker.

"And in that spirit of free and open process, I will now share with you one of the new laws I intend to put before City Council. The law defining a wholesome and harmonious Commonwealth."

Did anyone really want to hear what the law was? For *harmonious*, they just had to look around; for *wholesome*, they only had to look at Sensibella, who was now striding back and forth across the stage. Clutch began to frown. There had been no choice of a new leader. No one had elected Sensibella.

"For instance, a law governing risky behaviour. The risk-takers have suddenly realized that the world has become an unsafe place for risk-taking. But since there's nowhere else to live, unless you want to live on the moon with the Goddess, the risk-takers have discovered that in order for their behaviour to prosper it has to ponder the consequences of what it does. It has to study the impact of a leap before it takes one. Our common task as Citizens is to help that thinking along. Those of you out there who are moms ... Where are you? Let's see those paws!"

All around the audience, mothers raise their paws.

"Bless you! And bless the even more of you than before who'll become mothers because of our new law giving you more dens and the power to select your mate. Now, don't you teach your cubs that acts have consequences, that cubs should take responsibility for the results of the risks they take?"

Heads nodding all around in agreement.

"The same thing now applies to risk-takers – it applies *especially* to risk-takers. They must take responsibility for what they do. They need to stop being cubs and grow up!"

Cheering. But Clutch didn't cheer. He knew that something in Sensibella would never grow up. Her argument didn't feel fully shaped and mature. There was a flaw somewhere.

Now Citizen Sensibella took another step forward. She stood at the front edge of the stage. Just her. Vulnerable. Alone. The crowd fell silent, expectant, for her summation.

"As a token of the new rule of self-responsibility, and of my service to you as your Chief Magistrate, I declare that I myself shall not mate with anybody." She dropped her voice to a whisper in a spirit of modesty and sacrifice. "You see, I do not need to."

Clutch glanced leftwards. Bandit's face had gone out of shape.

"Why not, you ask? Because I am *already mated to the City*. I am mated to each and every one of you. The Commonwealth is my partner and my own heart's love."

Delirious applause. Cries of support. Spontaneous dancing.

"Our world has become too hot," Sensibella said. "Let's make it cool!"

She'd make a good politician, Clutch conceded. Her proclamation did excellent things to the minds of the citizens. Raccoons who had never had an idea in their lives suddenly developed an interest in political theory.

\* \* \*

What kind of politician would *he* make? Clutch thought later that morning. He lay in the crook of a tree overlooking the scene of the victory, now empty of raccoons. Instead, seagulls were picking at the litter. The doors of the meat trucks swung lazily in the breeze off the river. It was that quiet day in the week. Soon the church up on the Heights would ring its carillon. The park would fill up with Primates out for family brunch on the café patio. The scents of fresh-baked croissants, scones, and muffins already drifted up. He wasn't a politician. In all his growing up he had never felt the instinct to lead. He didn't want to be Chief Magistrate for Creek Town. He wasn't a natural leader like the flamboyant Sensibel, or like Hala with her surprising pivots between a tender, sympathetic warmth and a hard, implacable grace. No, he would become a philosopher like Procyonides the sage. "In solitude, be to thyself a throng" – one of his Uncle Wily's sayings. He wanted to be left alone. He would mate with his studies.

"Ladyfriend?" he said to the form curled up behind him. "I'm afraid I've forgotten your name."

"That's okay," she said. "It's Silverheels."

# 58

T HE HEIGHTS SLOPE DOWN gently in the north to a widening in
the river overlooking an arched bridge in the French style. Here
on the riverbank is the tree house of Smartwhisker, leading citizen
in the migrant community that has settled this part of town. Three
mothers are enjoying his absence on city business to indulge in gossip.
Two of them are sisters, and the third may as well be a sister for the
intense time she has shared with Slypaws.

"Do ye wonder," Pawsense said, "that a raccoon so virtuous as
Smartwhisker should love to live in the City? I wish I could take him
to the ennobling bosom of Nature where his virtue would receive fit
nourishment."

Sly and Twitch glanced at each other and rolled their eyes.

"If I had a husband, I would lose him to the City," Slypaws said.
"I lost my three cubs to it."

"Mine too," Twitchwhisker said. "They're out there somewhere
dancing."

"It is the great boast of political philosophy to unite dispersed
people into societies, and build up cities to house them. Whereupon,
having brought them into cities, it becomes easy to cozen them into
armies to murder one another."

Slypaws raised her hand to object.

"'Tis true, they have done so," Pawsense said. "Philosophy first
arose when raccoons were hunters of wild creatures; those same
powers of intellect have now made them hunters of their brethren.
The city increases daily with their growth. The more people, the more
wicked the lot of them."

"I am sure there are cities where that is not true," Slypaws said.

"Nay, it is a natural law. When the population of a place becomes
too numerous, the Devourer must ever reach for his partner the Pro-
lific to balance things. Whereupon, war and wrack and ruin."

"I'm a bit winded by all these boom and bust cycles," Twitchwhisker said.

"I do so wish that philosophy could unravel what it has mis-woven, that we might live in innocence again, instead of a super-erogation of policies."

Slypaws took this statement to mark the end of her sister's effu-sions. "Many raccoons in far off places have never known wild in-nocence in a countryside, if there is such a thing. They must live four, five to a burrow in cities. Cities are natural to our species. Raccoons invented the first city."

"Procyonides cites a legend to that effect," Twitch said.

"Whatever the origin thereof, cities are our necessary ends," Paw-sense said. "'Twill be an uncomfortable life and ever in alarms. Our lodg-ings will be cramped and unpleasant and we will always need to keep an eye on our husbands lest they stray into the arms of rent-a-mates."

"Perhaps we will obtain both City and Nature together," Slypaws said. "Earth pushes back against her abuse by creating more foliage. And Primates, who are creatures of Earth, can be trusted to plant trees to swallow up the heat and the bad gasses. Imagine it! A Garden City. With trees everywhere for raccoons to climb."

At this moment, Goodpaws arrived on the bough. Sly thought that her eldest niece had become self-confident since she last saw her. Perhaps it was her new mate, Squire Hairball, who made her so.

"What is it, daughter?" Pawsense asked.

"I think you may be pleased to hear that Uncle Meatbreath is thor-oughly departed. He was last seen floating south beyond the Dead Zone."

"We should pray," Slypaws said, "that he was carried downriver by the current, to pass into the generating station, there to be trans-formed into billions of sparks to light our City."

"A just end for one so radiant," Twitch said.

Pawsense said nothing. Slypaws wondered if her sister secretly approved of the dictator.

"May I go, mother?"

"Yes, yes. Go about your life, as you see fit."

The daughter departed with a curtsey.

The three women paused to lick their mint-flavoured Sweet Tea and inhale the late afternoon breeze coming off the river. On this one day of the week when traffic was stilled, the river gathered a peace to herself. "Now, where was I?" Pawsense said.

Slypaws quickly took control of the discussion. "There is nothing that will stop raccoons crowding together in a city if it offers sufficient food."

"No, no sister. How easily you acquiesce to change! We ought in the choice of a dwelling to regard above all the healthfulness of a place in Nature. By that, I mean its capacity to regulate both nourishment and breeding so that we live within its means and allowances."

"I think the new Custom Sensibel has inaugurated giving the female the right to regulate her breeding will bring peace to the frenzy of mating," Twitch said. "It puts the would-be mother at the centre of the responsibility of populating a territory. No act even simulating procreation can occur without the female's consent. And raccoon women can now mate with whomever they desire. The other being willing."

"I do not know whether I should be pleased or no. I brought Sensibella up to marry a man, not a city."

Now it's Nimbletoes, the youngest of Pawsy's daughters. She too had grown up during the summer. Slypaws sensed the volatile temperament of a young adult.

"How was school today, darling?"

Nimble avoided the adoring gazes of three mothers by looking across the water at the bridge. "Okay."

"Just okay?" Pawsense said. "Didn't you experience joy today?"

A shrug.

"I asked if you felt any joy."

"Get off the limb, Pawsy! Just because you teach her the word, it doesn't mean she's going to feel it," Slypaws said.

"Of course, it does. If she knows the word *joy* exists, it's easier for her to recognize the emotion and embrace it. My children know all about joy. Prying open their first clam. Popping their first organic waste lid. Eating their first Delissio pizza. Joy! J–O–Y ... You know what joy is, don't you, honeytoes? Didn't I teach you all the things you can do in order to feel joy?"

"I guess ..."

"Think of something that happened to you today that gave you joy."

Nimble said nothing.

"She can't think of anything," Slypaws said.

"Try harder, sweetie."

"I … I helped an elderly Raccoon lady across the street."

"See! I told you she knows what joy is."

Nimble's eyes were still fixed on the bridge.

"What is it, child?"

"May I go to the City, Mama?"

"No, of course not. The place is full of flotsam and detritus of the sort that bobs in the wake of a revolution, and is unfit for one so tender in years."

Slypaws felt the growl begin in Nimble's tail. A strong, snorting, imprisoned noise breaking its way out of unfathomable dungeons through every possible outlet and organ. Travelling forward through her body gathering power from every sinew in her loins and upper musculature until it reached her heart, draining it of hopelessness, to emerge in a howl that could be heard as far away as the French bridge, the horizon of the girl's lost freedom. The deepest, the oldest, the most wholesome sense of the value of Nature – the value which comes from her immense babyishness.

"*WAAAAAH!!!*"

"Quick, honey. Remember what I told you to do when you're upset. Name the emotion."

"?"

"By naming it, you distance yourself from the unwanted feeling, thereby gaining control over it."

"*WAAAAA!!!*"

"Don't you think she ought to feel the emotion first, before she analyses it?"

"Thanks for the consult, Sly. But you know zot-all about anger management."

"She's not angry. She's miserable."

"No, rather she simply needs to regain her inner balance, don't you, love? Now, do what I told you and put a paw on the emotion so it won't push you off the limb."

The cub looked her mother in the eye. "I ... am ... feeling ... *miserable*."

"Indeed, we can all see that, darling. But what's the emotion that's making you so miserable. If you name it, the nasty feeling will go away."

"Do you really think cubs should psychoanalyse themselves, Pawsy?"

"Just say SCAT," Twitch said.

"*Know thyself.* It is the key to self-knowledge, something in which you, dear sister, are sadly lacking, having the worldliness of a clam." Then, to her daughter: "Try to attach words to your big bad feeling. Hint: if you can't name the emotion, name some object that feels like your feeling and can speak for it. That's what artists do. Cousin Touchwit deals with her emotions that way. She's one of those so-called Makers."

"I am feeling like the last High Liner Frozen Fish Stick left in the world, thrown up by a Drooler dying of rabies. I feel like Uncle Wily when he was run over by an electric car and became a smear with two eyes looking up to the sky and asking the question '*Why?*' I am feeling like I cannot endure one more moment of my miserable fucking life until I go to the City and make a world for myself ... There! That is how I feel!"

"See? It worked," Pawsense said. "The examined life *is* worth living after all."

Sister Goodpaws appeared again and curtseyed.

"What is it, child?"

"I intend to go to the City this evening, Mama?"

"If you must. You may take a message to Sensibella."

"I don't take messages, Mama. That is Nimble's task."

"Oh, alright Nimble. You can go to the City if you stick close to Goody and take my message."

"I don't take messages anymore."

Pawsense shrugged.

"What is it, Mistress Twitch?"

"I'm thinking about my two cubs. For the first time I've a mind to go out and find them. They need a mother. I beg leave of your company, Mistress Pawsense: I must go to the City with Nimble."

"I'll go too and help you find them," Slypaws said.

"I shall watch the sunset and take in the airs," Pawsense said.

# 59

WITH AN AFTERNOON SUN smiling down on her bell tower, Sensibel went over the new Consent Law with her chosen lover.

"New word: *Body*."

"C'mon. You think I don't know what a body is? It's what you hug and wrestle."

"That's not what the Law says."

"Yes, it is. If you cut through the verbiage."

Bella sighed. "Okay, I'll tell you what a *Body* is. Pursuant to the Law."

Both of them were touchy. The sunlight exaggerated Bandit's colouring so that he appeared to Sensibel to be a dark romantic stranger instead of her first cousin; as for him, the sun's radiance transfigured Sensibel into a huggable, furry angel.

"*Body*. It means that part of my spirit which is perceptible. The part you see," Sensibel said. "My body is actually a great big Spirit-Body, but you can't see it. You can only see a slice of it."

"What I can't see is why we have to go through this rigmarole."

"Because it says so in the Law." Sensibel straightened her back and quoted: "*All couples wishing to form a relationship, however urgent and timely, must apprise themselves of the concepts and terms set out in this, the Preamble.*"

Now it was Bandit's turn to sigh. But the exhalation didn't come out as stoical acceptance. It sounded like restraint approaching its snapping point. At last, after several nights of tense undercover work plus two strenuous battles, he was alone with her. His Sensibella. With her body as well as her great big spirit.

"The requirement is in the Preamble in order to educate Raccoons to the reality that they cannot go on living with beastly natures. They must understand that an offense against the Body leaves a sore on the Spirit."

"I'm not going to hurt your Spirit, Sensibel. It's so big it fills the universe, and anyway I can't see it."

"Of course, you can't, dear. But don't you think that's why it's appropriate in the New City Republic for prospective partners to know what they are doing and the consequences thereof?" She was quoting the Law. She couldn't help it. In fact, she was quoting herself.

"I know what I'm doing," Bandit growled under his breath.

Sensibel went on regardless. "You see, the *Concept of Consent* is basically good social ecology. It's basically an extension of the principle of *The Rights of the Party that is suffering Scarcity to be consulted by the Party that is enjoying Abundance prior to engaging in a non-exploitative Relationship.*"

"If that's the goal, it's never going to happen."

"It's aspirational. It helps you think of me as a Spirit. As part of the overall balance of life. Do you think of me as a Spirit, Bandy?"

Bandit tried to think of Sensibel as a Spirit. He tried hard. But it didn't work. Her body kept getting in the way. "Can we move on?"

"Alright. Let's see … Next we come to *Orifices*. Note the plural."

"You can skip that section too. I know what orifices are."

"You do?" Sensibel looked at Bandit with curiosity.

"Isn't there some kind of checklist we have to go through before we … ah, engage in the Bonding Act?"

"Oh, you've heard the new Law. Bandit, where did you hear the new Law?"

Bandit's mind went blank.

"Bandit, have you recited the Law before with anyone?"

"It's on the Net. Look, why don't we just go straight to the checklist like we're supposed to before we …"

"Before we what, Bandit?"

"You know. Tussle."

"Don't think that just because you have the desire that the aforesaid desire is necessarily right and proper in a given situation." Again, she sounded like she was quoting.

"That's not what the Law says."

"*It's exactly what it says. I know. I wrote the damn Law.*"

He backed away. The fur in her tail bristled. Sensibel was dangerously fragile.

"The whole point of having the Law is to teach raccoons that they need to anticipate the consequences of their acts."

"If we don't move on soon, there isn't going to be a consequence."

"Okay, I'll go quicker. Question One. *Ensure that your prospective partner isn't carrying a disease. (Hint: it's a good idea to check her/his/their/desired pronoun/gums.)* Are you carrying a disease, Bandit?" Sensibel tilted her head in a questioning manner.

"No."

"What happened to your fleas?"

"They all jumped with one accord onto Meatbreath when we were fighting."

"Okay. No diseases: check."

"Aren't I supposed to ask you the same question?"

"A Pond lady never has a disease. Next question. Oh, here is where we come to Specific Acts. *Parties contemplating a Conjunctive Relationship, however brief, must consent beforehand to each act of a conjoining nature that is contemplated or which might be reasonably be expected to occur during the Bonding Process.* Then there are a number of specified Acts, each requiring explicit consent. Are you ready? *May I have your consent to smell your anal glands?*" Sensibella paused. "I'm thinking maybe we should go through the entire list first and then check them off."

"Totally! Get it over with."

"*May I lick your muzzle all over?*"

"*May I roll on the soil you have lain on?*"

"*May I give you love bites on your ruff?*"

Where did she get this stuff from? Off the Net? No, probably from her sisters. What had she told him long ago in the willow tree? "Never underestimate the sexual imagination of four sisters." Then he remembered Frisk biting him mischievously on the ear that same day. Was that a love bite? Or was it simply Frisk being Frisk?

"*Will you consent to snuggle up in a cherry tree while it is blossoming?*"

"You can't use the Law to give people nice ideas."

"Why not? We use the Law to stop people from having bad ideas. I just thought I'd throw in something special for partners to try. The law is so boringly solemn."

"Sensibel?"

"Yes, love?"

"You said *partners*."

"So?"

"Define *partners*."

"I didn't put it in the Law because everybody knows what *partners* means. It takes two to tango."

"Partners *plural* means having more than one partner."

"Oh *shit!*"

"You should have thought of that when you put in the consent situation about having your tail lovingly braided by many nimble hands in a catalpa tree under a full moon."

"I have to revise the fucking Law."

"Maybe nobody will notice," Bandit said.

"I'll proceed to the end quickly. *Do you consent to play-fighting?* Check. *Do you consent to playing rough?* Check. Do you ..."

Bandit was beginning to grin.

"Bandit, good heavens, your tongue is hanging out obscenely. You look like a Drooler."

He pulled his tongue back in his mouth. It was wet. Yes, he'd been panting. The atmosphere in the tower was feeling urgent. "Skip to the end," he said. The mighty dust-covered bells were sweating. At any moment they were going to break out in desirous bongs.

The last clause. She recited it breathlessly. "*Do you consent that each situational agreement entered into heretofore will apply equally to repeated acts of the particular nature, (a) during the duration of the intended coupling? (b) during any and all subsequent couplings?*"

" Check! check! check! check! All done. Let's get started."

"Oh, I really do want to give it a try. You're a good raccoon, Bandy, and you're a safe person to explore the conjugal act with. But we have to go through the consent protocols properly, or else we'll be back to the days of Meatbreath dropping out of the sky on Aunt Slypaws."

"It had a consequence. The consequence was me."

"And I'm very glad it was. I'll just quickly run through my answers to the consent clauses. I'll probably consent to most of them, since I thought them up in the first place. Then, it'll be your turn. I'll repeat the questions to you and you decide whether you want to consent or not."

"Bel?"

"Yes, love."

"Bel, what if we just snuggle? Would that be okay? Maybe we can *Perform the Conjugal Act* another time."

"Oh! Is there something wrong, Bandy? Aren't you feeling well?"

"I'm okay. It's just that I'm ... a little tired."

"Oh."

"It's been a long day."

"Alright. If you say so."

"Goodnight cousin."

"Goodnight dear."

# 60

THE STRANGE, new atmosphere had given the grape vines a jump on low-lying growth on the Island. Grapes hung in curtains and where there weren't grapes there were cascades of hawthorn berries. But these hardy survivors flourished at the cost of the many various plants and saplings which they smothered. This seemed to be the way nowadays. The ocean far to the west was behaving like one of these opportunistic survivors. Like a hyperactive newcomer in the neighbourhood, it was sweating its heat into the air, and the air, muscling east, was pushing this long summer back so that the trees kept their leaves well into autumn, and autumn, in turn, was pushing winter out of its way. And winter, so vital to the dream-life of animals and trees, was becoming a short period of heavy rain. With this bullying taking over the age-old measures of Earth, was it any surprise that Raccoons chose bullies to be their leaders? Protectors who played to frightened notions of a secure clan hierarchy separate from the rest of raccoon society. At both levels – biological nature and raccoon nature – the world was collapsing into ugliness.

So unlike these Monarch Butterflies who were alighting on the Island in droves. They followed the Milkweed towards a home most of them would never know, laying their eggs on the underside of the thick leaves, then dying to make way for their hatchlings who immediately ate their protective covering. Because of this bequest, a child or even a grandchild would get to discover the original home of its species without ever seeing it before – a lost kingdom on a mountain to the south, near the winter den of the Raccoon Ancestor. Where was home for today's restlessly moving people? Somewhere in the future. Mindwalker seemed to be seeking it through his walk-abouts. The Island would do for her. For now.

The yellow and purple colours she remembered from her first Fall. Why did Autumn choose those colours for her flowers? Sturdy, forthright colours, they were often found together, for instance in these long-stemmed, daisy-like flowers with gold centres and purple petals.

Gold for glory, purple for grief. Autumn was vivid about the matters which concerned her – matters of permanence and passing away.

Touchwit reclined in the lap of the tamarack where she had spent her second night on the Island. Mindwalker lay stretched out facing her. There was himself and, just above him on the branch, the replica of himself he'd made to warn Meatbreath away. Well, the Image had worked, because her father was no more, his hole-shaped existence in her life having been filled by this gentleman-artist.

A balmy end-of-summer breeze brought a giant butterfly to the Island. A black and yellow one with a forked tail.

"I could fly with her wither she's bound."

"She's checking you out. She wonders if you're a flower."

"She's beautiful."

"If I told you her name, would she still be beautiful?"

"Try me."

"She's called a Swallowtail."

Suddenly the butterfly became an object. She had power over it. How vulgar! To be vulgar is to over-simplify.

"There's a saying by Procyonides. When the Great Raccoon Ancestor bestowed names on all of the creatures, he cancelled out their true existence as people."

A Swallowtail. Now she had the butterfly and now she had a name that was assigned to it. The creature wasn't any less – there she was still dancing in her own whimsical freedom. But she had become in part a creature she was not, namely a Swallow. Just because the Raccoon Ancestor had perceived a resemblance to the tail of one of his other creatures.

She answered Mindwalker: "Yes, she would still be beautiful. Except she's inside me. I can feel her behind my eyes. She wants to use me as a leaf to leave behind her self-image."

"No, she's outside you. You pushed her away by naming her."

"I'll bring her closer with a Making. Go where thou wilt, sweet unnameable Someone who flits like a Swallow – you need not linger. I will cherish your image for you, which you have laid in me."

Mindwalker laughed. "I wish Naming were that easy."

Which meant a turn in their conversation. The fun of their dialogues was the easy glide from topic to topic. "I named her without naming her by creating a Making. The Making did the naming."

"Exactly!" Mindwalker said, his enthusiasm rising. "According to Custom we don't ask for the name of a guest until we've made that stranger feel like kin, until they feel comfortable enough to tell a story about themself. A story telling where they're from, where they've travelled, what they're seeking. Those are all relationships. Relationships with people and places. Like the relationship you imagined that helped me think of a Swallowtail as a person. Someone seeming to stay but meaning to fly. She can't flit around: she has to be on her way. Do you know, *flit* means to *migrate*? Makers create relationships and those relationships do the naming."

Easy for him. He walked so discreetly among invisible relationships that they practically started naming each other. Then after a whole season of walking around, he produced one consummate Making that sang inside itself. Just one. This gave her an idea. "New topic," she said. "How did we make a City?"

Mindwalker furrowed his brow and reached for a daisy stem.

"It seems to me raccoon society is full of thousands of relationships it can't name, and only a few it can name, which then become Customs. Something you can talk about. Something you can measure your expectations against. Society is only capable of holding a few Customs in its mind at one time."

"How many?"

He put the daisy stem in his mouth and began sucking it. Weird.

"Five."

Why *five*?"

"I don't know why I said *five*. Maybe because raccoons have five claws."

Now it was her turn to be excited. "Society can only grasp the few Customs that it feels ensure its survival and prosperity. Those Customs are instructions for how to be a society. Like Sensibel's new laws. Everybody knows what they are; most agree that they govern the kind of society they want to live in. But they leave out thousands of situations; some of which haven't even happened yet. My question is: where are all the other relationships that aren't felt to belong to society's immediate self-interest?"

"They are like seeds no one has a use for," Mindwalker said. "Raccoons who are born different. The unmated. The poor. The sick. The migrant. The weird and frightening. All the unwanted among us. An uncaring society holds them in suspended animation in some dark place like bulbs in a root cellar. A caring society allows the diversity to flourish."

"Like seeds on this Island," she said. She thought of a rhyme:

> There is a Garden by a Lake
> That greener grows for Nature's sake,
> Than any garden ever planned
> By squinted eye or maker's hand.

"This little blessed Isle."

"Waiting ..." she said, prompting.

"Waiting. For the world to change and discover among those hibernating relationships a set of instructions for being a better society."

"Our City Republic was a dream in hibernation. We woke it up and made it blossom."

"You need more than a dream: you need changes in circumstance that favour the dream becoming real. The flood of migrants, the shortage of housing, the uncertainty about being able to raise cubs, the incapacity of the Leading Families to address these issues, the arrival of a catalyst like Meatbreath. Makers sensed the changes first. But it wasn't enough to sense them. They had to make an effort to fit a dream to the circumstances." Mindwalker took the daisy stem out of his mouth and examined it. He seemed surprised he had chewed the stem to pieces. He placed it carefully in the sunlight. "It's almost as if the dream of the democratic Commonwealth was already alive within the circumstances."

She put this next thought to him as a proposition. "The dream was thinking *I am becoming a nightmare.* It was thinking *I can't* breathe deeply. *The Customs are too stuffy, they only favour a few, they oversimplify, they feel uncomfortable.* Then it becomes time for Makers to dream up a different Custom. A Custom that will open up a tight society."

"Well, I didn't realize I was doing *that*," Mindwalker said – he was grinning. "I thought I was just hoping to find a place to be comfortable in myself. For the longest time, I felt most comfortable among the excluded people. Among the hopers and dreamers, but also the hopeless and the sufferers that the preferred Custom of being a society shuts out. Where people gather and carry on their silent, sympathetic conversations. But aren't we thinking too much of the dream on its own? A dream is already awake and aware within the circumstances."

"It is in the circumstances, then it overflows the circumstances," she said. "It was thinking openly, like this river. Normally, the river follows its timeless path, which is inscribed on the riverbed as its Custom. Its customary way of being a River. But what if the climate changes and there's a non-stop downpour? Big crisis! The river backs up on itself, consults its riverbed only to find out there are no instructions for how to be a river in this situation. Its only recourse is to send out a bunch of rivulets to explore a new landscape. Then negotiate with the new landscape about a new riverbed for the river to follow."

"I liked being a rivulet," Mindwalker said.

They basked in the silence of wondering. The noise of the city re-entered their senses. The smell of oats and honey coming downwind from the factory. The air vehicle droning overhead. In all these scents and noises, she sensed a greater sound. It was the music of a raccoon city singing in its sleep.

"I've got to go and meet Mom in the chimney. Clutch and Bandit are coming home. We're going to tell the stories of what happened to us on our adventures. She thinks the Idiot who lives behind our wall will still be listening to us. That he's going to fashion a replica of our stories."

"Tell him to put me in his Making."

"I will make a rhyme for him."

*Some night, fishing for the thousandth time,*
*you will find it.*
*The dream of the unborn City, the crowds at night singing,*
*the dancing, the laughter.*
*Oh, do not betray it. Hold onto it.*
*Keep it in your heart,*
*and it will blossom.*

# AFTERWORD

## By Margaret Atwood

IN THE SPRING OF 2019, Graeme Gibson received a story letter from Sean Kane. It was an account of a family of raccoons nesting in Sean's chimney: he'd been eavesdropping on them, he said, and was reporting on what had been going on in there. They were making quite a racket, with a lot of chittering, hissing, and screeching; anyone who's ever had raccoons in their attics or chimneys will agree that this part of the tale, at least, is accurate. They were also saying rude things about human beings in general, and Sean in particular. From the raccoon point of view, it seems we are a stupid, disagreeable, and uncooperative bunch.

This first letter was quickly followed by others. Installments of the saga arrived in brown envelopes. The raccoons were on the move. They were having philosophical discussions, they were arguing, they were scheming, they were indulging in power struggles, they were narrating. The story had taken on a life of its own.

Sean was writing this epic to amuse Graeme, who'd asked him to describe the wildlife he was witnessing in the woodlands and river-banks beside his home in Peterborough. At that time Graeme was in the seventh year since his diagnosis of dementia in 2012, a diagnosis he himself had sought. He'd suspected there was something wrong with him, and there was.

"What's the prognosis?" he had asked.

"Either it will go slowly, it will go quickly, it will stay the same, or we don't know," they had said. Not a lot of help, but accurate. For a while it stayed the same; then it went slowly. But by the spring of 2019 it was going quickly. Neither our family nor Graeme knew that Graeme would die of a cerebral hemorrhage before the year was over, though both Graeme and the family suspected this might be the case. We did not say as much to Sean, however, because you never know.

Going quickly meant that Graeme was losing the ability to use his computer or to read. He was still keenly interested in the natural world, however. I read the installments of Sean's story out loud to him because he couldn't read them himself. After a while, he couldn't follow the plot line or remember the cast of characters, so I had to stop reading. But Graeme still understood the intention: Sean's wonder tale about a bunch of fractious but savvy raccoons was a kindly gesture from an old and loving friend.

* * *

Sean and Graeme had known each other since the mid 1960s, through the Rosedale chapter of the New Democratic Party – they both campaigned for it in 1965. Sean was starting an M.A. in English. He was wondering if it was possible to be a serious academic and a novelist at the same time. Graeme was a failed M.A. who'd spent years struggling to write fiction. Out of desperation, he was teaching at what was then Ryerson College, where he was known as Bones; his course on modern European literature was dubbed, by the students, "Introduction to Despair." At the same time, he was toiling away at his first novel, *Five Legs*, which eventually came out in 1969, after a long and difficult gestation. This novel was an unlikely success – it's not exactly standard fare – and briefly outsold the hit pop writer Jacqueline Susann, at least in the bookstores of Toronto.

Both Sean and Graeme were part of a somewhat rackety group of characters in a pocket of South Rosedale that was not so posh then as it has become now. Decaying gentry, bohemian-minded semi-writers, various academics, several book publishers, a pessimistic early environmental writer, a forensic psychiatrist, a madcap housewife who later became a gardening guru – all this was before my time, but it seems to have been an eclectic and effervescent mix; sort of like the raccoons in the chimney. Touch football got played sporadically on Saturday mornings, I was later told. I get the impression that a certain amount of drinking went on.

Campaigning for the NDP must have seemed a logical outgrowth of the outsider position some of these folks felt they were experiencing. The likelihood of a social welfare party winning a seat in conservative Rosedale was nil, but low odds never stopped Graeme from trying something. Nor was he a socialist: he was more of a 19th century Conservative – a Red Tory, this lot used to be called in Canada before they went extinct – which meant that he couldn't bring himself to vote either for the Liberals or for the Conservatives as they define themselves today, nor even for the Conservatives as they were then constituted. Sean on the other hand was what might now be called a "progressive," a term I have caught him using, though Graeme would have repudiated this term for himself, since he was suspicious of things calling themselves "progress" – a word that had been used in his youth as a label from some dubious projects, such as eugenics and urban sprawl. "You can't stop progress" was the motto of many a rapacious business conglomerate from the thirties to the fifties. It was supposed to be a Final Word. (Just sayin'.)

Graeme was the sort of quasi-Tory who supported the arts and refused to wear a suit except to funerals, but kept the family silver and was good at fundraising among the establishment rich. Using the right fork at dinner was important to him – as was shortly to appear, when he founded the Writers' Union of Canada – solidarity among workers. Sean, on the other hand, was more cerebral, and was soon to morph into an academic specialist in "oral narrative, ecophenomonology, biosemiotics, and speculative materialism," to quote an online biography. (No wonder the raccoons in *Raccoon* make fun of him, although they themselves partake sporadically of all of these disciplines, if that is what they are.) So naturally both Graeme and Sean, being quixotic, went out ringing doorbells for the NDP. I'm guessing Graeme was the more persuasive.

From this tenuous association sprang a long friendship. The fact that both Sean Kane and Graeme Gibson were aspiring novelists made for companionship in misery, as the odds for a first novelist getting published in Canada were as low as the NDP's in Rosedale – especially if you wrote eccentric stuff, as both of them did. Both were interested in ancestral worlds, both also in natural worlds.

Sean eventually produced the now classic study, *Wisdom of the Mythtellers*, that explores ancient stories from four story-hoards

– Native North American, Australian Aboriginal, Celtic, and Ancient Greek – relating to times when the natural world was felt as powerful and numinous, not just a hoard of inert material to be exploited by humans. Graeme eventually wrote four novels, but his best-selling books were his "miscellanies" about nature, *The Bedside Book of Birds* and *The Bedside Book of Beasts* – collections of stories, anecdotes, myths, poems, paintings, carvings, masks – how people throughout time and across space have viewed birds and carnivorous animals. The first was more popular: we'd rather read about flying than about being eaten. Both Sean and Graeme were somewhat ahead of the zeitgeist. Nowadays their take on nature would be accepted wisdom, but back then – in the 1980s and 90s – it took them considerable time and effort to convince the publishers.

These overlaps may give you some idea of what cemented the friendship. More shared experiences followed, including adventures in small publishing and involvement with other young and youngish writers during the Wild West days of do-it-yourselfery in Canadian writing. All of this is the mulch – as it were – in which the comic epic, *Raccoon*, took root. (It's worth mentioning here that Sean Kane's campus novel, *Virtual Freedom*, was a finalist for the Leacock Humour Medal.)

I just called *Raccoon* a comic epic, but what literary form is it really? Is it a picaresque adventure story? Is it a sort of revenge drama, in which Mother Slypaws sets out to get her own back on the raccoon gent who done her wrong? Is it an animal fable? Is it a family saga? The raccoons talk and argue a lot, and discuss many things: perhaps *Raccoon* is the literary form called a symposium. However, nothing in nature exists in a sealed container, everything is part of a Bell-curved continuum, and *Raccoon* similarly refuses to be confined to a single category, like Andre Alexis's novel *Fifteen Dogs*, or Robert Lawson's *Rabbit Hill*.

Sean has given me to understand that *Raccoon* is also a roman à clef of sorts – that Mindwalker is a mask for Graeme – a pretty good name for him, I think, since he did spend a lot of time exploring roads less travelled, philosophically speaking – and that I myself am the precocious and devious (although bad) poet, Touchwit. One woman in her life plays many parts, so why not a smartmouth raccoon? There are worse things.

In our ends are our beginnings, to paraphrase Mary, Queen of Scots; and, I might add, vice versa. So, dear readers, here is the real beginning of *Raccoon* – the beginning that did not get into the actual book. And so I end.

\* \* \*

*12 March 2019*

Dear Graeme,

The wandering of the jet stream down into the American Midwest has given us the strange effect of waist-high snowbanks under skies full of spring light. Hibernating creatures are perplexed. The field mice are awake, and so there are snowy owls in the Kawarthas. One owl was photographed on a tree stump north of the city, waiting silently for a mouse to give away its location. A movement under the snow. Maybe a heedless singing in the spring air. (Mice, whales, dolphins, certain bats, and human beings are the species of mammals known to sing.)

Whatever the sensation of the mouse was, it was far off in a field. The photographer said it was *250 metres* away, under several inches of snow. I find this hard to believe. Can an owl with its acute hearing detect a mouse across that distance? It glided silently over and dropped on its prey.

Here is our bedroom window where I've let the cedar tree grow so birds can come. The squirrel couple who live in the apex of our roof are prying peanuts out of the bark of trees where the chickadees have jammed them. The chickadee family itself – a male and (I guess) two wives – are coming to the window ledge.

And the raccoons living in the wall of my study are in a ferocious quandary. As I sit at this desk, they are three feet away, at ear level, in a disused chimney. I hear a rapid thumping. Someone is scratching fleas. Silence.

I imagine they are bunched together where the brickwork forms a ledge. At the suggestion of milder weather, the whole family of them wakes up, and breaks immediately into hissing and snarls. Only one kind of animal is so full of anxiety and quarrel. It would be nicer if they could sing.

I put the stethoscope to the wall ...

# ACKNOWLEDGMENTS

Concept development: Eugene Benson, Owen Kane, Kelly Liberty, Ian McLachlan, Julian Samuel

Literary editing: Stan Dragland, Hilary McMahon

Tree science: Drew Monkman

Young Adult market assessment: Eleanor Chapman, Madeline Chapman

Adult market assessment: Sarah Berti, Michael Cain, Avrah Pernica, Carolyn Tate

Educational market assessment: Kate Taylor, Don LePan

Maps: Anna Narday

Production editing: Gary Clairman

Cover design and typesetting: Rafael Chimicatti

Copyediting: Kelly Liberty

Promotion: Anna van Valkenburg

Sales and Marketing: Nour Abi-Nakhoul

Editor-in-Chief: Michael Mirolla

Publisher: Connie McParland

# ABOUT THE AUTHOR

Sean Kane became a storyteller through the efforts of his aunt Alice, who babysat him by reciting wondertales – those longish stories about adventures with the intelligences and feelings of nature told around the world. Alice Kane D. Litt. (hon.) went on to enjoy an international reputation as a performing artist of this genre and author of a collection of her favourite wondertales, *The Dreamer Awakes*. He in turn wrote *Wisdom of the Mythtellers*, which established the ecological politics of myth as the popular alternative to twentieth-century approaches to myth through psychology. Sean Kane lives on the Otonabee River northeast of Toronto, downstream from Trent University where he is emeritus professor of English Literature.

Printed in February 2023
by Gauvin Press,
Gatineau, Québec